D0257820

Please return / renew by date shown.
You can renew it at:
norlink.norfolk.gov.uk
or by telephone: 0344 800 8006
Please have your library card & PIN ready

NORFOLK LIBRARY
AND INFORMATION SERVICE

Edgar Allan Poe
and the
London Monster

KAREN LEE STREET

POINT
BLANK

A Point Blank Book

First published in Great Britain and the Commonwealth by Point Blank, an imprint of
Oneworld Publications, 2016

ISBN 978-1-78074-930-3
ISBN 978-1-78074-931-0 (ebook)

Typeset in Dante by Hewer Text UK Ltd, Edinburgh
Printed and bound in Great Britain by Clays Ltd, St Ives plc

Visit our website for a reading guide
and exclusive content on THE EDGAR ALLAN POE SERIES
www.oneworld-publications.com

Oneworld Publications
10 Bloomsbury Street
London WC1B 3SR
England

Stay up to date with the latest books,
special offers, and exclusive content from
Oneworld with our monthly newsletter

Sign up on our website
www.oneworld-publications.com

The boundaries which divide Life from Death are
at best shadowy and vague. Who shall say where
the one ends, and where the other begins?

(Edgar Allan Poe. "The Premature Burial")

ACKNOWLEDGEMENTS

I am incredibly grateful to my superb agent, Oli Munson, and also to Becky Brown, Hélène Ferey and Jennifer Custer at A. M. Heath for their invaluable efforts on my behalf. Enormous thanks to my editor, the wonderful Jenny Parrott, Paul Nash, Sophie Wilson, Margot Weale, Cailin Neal, and all at Oneworld Publications who have been a delight to work with. I'm appreciative for the insightful feedback from writer/reader friends Shauna Gilligan and Sally Griffiths, who critiqued early drafts, and to readers from my time at the University of South Wales, especially Rob Middlehurst, Chris Meredith, Sarah Broughton and most particularly Philip Gross, who encouraged me to write the novel when my embryonic summary "set his whiskers twitching." His ongoing enthusiasm for the story and constructive feedback kept me working on what seemed at times a daunting project. Thanks also to Alain Noslier, Kate Brown for her encouragement while sharing parallel writing-life experiences and, especially, to Darren Hill, without whom . . .

* * *

It is of a Monster I mean for to write,
Who in stabbing of ladies took great delight;
If he caught them alone in the street after dark,
In their hips or their thighs, he'd be sure cut a mark.

(*The Monster Represented*, a collection
of verse published July 1790)

The frightened Ladies tremble, run and shriek,
But Ah! in vain they fly! in vain protection seek!
For He can run so swift, such diff'rent forms assume;
In vain to take him, must the Men presume.
This Monster then, who treats you so uncivil,
This Cutting Monster, Ladies, is the Devil!

(*The Monster Detected*, a satirical print, 29 May 1790)

* * *

AUTHOR'S NOTE

Edgar Allan Poe and the London Monster is based in part on true events. "The Monster" did indeed terrorize the ladies of London from 1788–1790, slicing the derrières of over fifty victims, many of whom were quick to make public the indignities they suffered as the villain had a reputation for targeting attractive, well-dressed females. When the Monster's attacks escalated in 1790, Londoners were gripped by mass sexual hysteria. Men formed "No Monster" vigilantes to patrol the streets at night; rhymes and plays were written about the Monster; and caricaturists produced saucy prints of women using copper pots to protect their bottoms from a fearsome half-human creature. Descriptions of the Monster varied so much that some journalists of the time conjectured that more than one culprit was responsible and an actor with a gift for disguise might be involved. The one hundred pound reward offered by John Julius Angerstein for the capture and conviction of the Monster resulted in the arrest of an unemployed Welshman. The accused was initially tried on 8 July 1790 for the felony of assaulting "any person in the public streets with intent to tear, spoil, cut, burn, or deface the garments or clothes of such person," a crime punishable by death or transportation. He was convicted but secured a second trial, and although he was convicted again on 13 December 1790, it was for the lesser crime of "brutal and wanton assault" for which he was imprisoned in Newgate for six years rather than hanged. This was almost certainly a miscarriage of justice, given there was little or no hard evidence to prove that the accused had committed any of the attacks.

I first came across an account of the Monster in John Ashton's *Old Times: A Picture of Social Life at the End of the Eighteenth Century* (1885), while researching an idea that will now form the core of the sequel to this novel. I cannot recall what inspired me to connect Edgar Allan Poe and the Monster— perhaps it was the peculiar nature of the crimes along with the memory that Poe's maternal grandparents had been actors on the London stage during the late eighteenth century. As little information is available regarding Poe's grandparents, it seemed at least plausible that they might have played the clandestine role of the Monster. I settled on revenge as the motive for these unusual crimes and from that evolved the stormy (imagined) relationship of Poe's grandparents, with each fictitious letter exchanged between them referencing an actual crime committed by the Monster.

When writing a mystery in which Edgar Allan Poe is the main character, it is difficult to ignore C. Auguste Dupin, the "ur-detective" created by Poe. I decided to make Dupin an old friend of Poe's, suggesting that Poe is the anonymous narrator in his Dupin detective stories, and that the tales are based on "true crimes." Further, I've alluded to over thirty Poe stories, poems and essays in the novel, thus creating another puzzle for the reader to solve.

PROLOGUE

PHILADELPHIA, DECEMBER 1840

The jittering candlelight brought it back from the dead with a flutter and a blink. It was violet in color, luminous, and might have been a thing of beauty if its stare were not so very persistent. *I will keep you and those you love safe. I am your amulet, your charm against the past, your talisman for the future.* Its promises were as hypnotic as its gaze.

I levered up one plank, then two, and worked feverishly to dislodge a third, thus fashioning a crypt beneath the floor. There it would not haunt me so, the mahogany box that held the antique letters and that glowing orb of amethyst. *I will keep you safe. Listen closely and do what I bid.*

Its relentless whispers set me on edge, sharpened my senses to an unnatural degree, but truly madness had not overtaken me. I was lucid, utterly so. And yet, my fingers crept toward the box like a spider, as dread pattered over me. One final time! Then I would close the lid, turn the lock, hide away my legacy. *I will keep you and those you love safe.*

And there it was upon my palm, its gaze conquering mine, my amulet, my talisman—that malevolent, all-seeing eye of violet, *her* eye. If it could speak of all the things it had witnessed, all those very cruel things, how calmly it would tell the whole story.

Dear Husband,

Have you had news of the extraordinary performance near the Royalty Theatre today involving your dear friend Miss Cole? The tattlers and wags are consumed with it, and I feel compelled to put pen to paper while the delicious escapade is still fresh within my mind.

It was noon and our morning rehearsals at the Royalty were not long finished, when Miss Cole was making her way down Knock Fergus, which was lively with beggars, gin-soaked trollops and washer-women occupied with more honest work. Your Miss Cole, who was born to the Rope Walk and its surrounds, looked uncharacteristically out of place there, for she was wearing a green-and-white striped taffeta caraco and a dress of olive-green silk adorned with two rows of flounces at the hem. The dress was not enviably fashionable, but was adapted by a deft hand to seem so. There were stains upon the fabric that could not be removed, and the age of the garment was apparent upon close inspection. (Indeed, one might say the same for Miss Cole.) But the rogues on the street were well enough impressed with the effect and loudly admired her costume, failing to recognise that it had been worn by Miss Kate Hardcastle in our recent performance of *She Stoops to Conquer*. How amusing of Miss Cole to reverse the role and elevate herself to the semblance of a lady with a borrowed dress from the theatre.

But let me not digress from my tale. As Miss Cole turned from Knock Fergus onto Cannon Street, she took note of a cocky young gentleman striding several paces behind her. He was an elegant fellow, handsomely suited with a pale-blue coat, neckcloth, striped waistcoat, neatly fitted breeches and white silk stockings. He wore a black surtout that added bulk to his frame and buckled shoes with heels that greatly increased his height. His lightly powdered hair was frizzed at the sides and plaited at the back in a fashionable manner. What a fine manly specimen he was. And yet—the brim of his beaver round hat was tilted down low to obscure his features. This observation alone might have sent a shiver of unease through a more astute female, but alas, that was not the case with your friend. She seemed gratified by the gentleman's presumed interest and obligingly slowed her pace as she neared her shabby boarding house. It was only when he was at her side that she noticed the vicious blade clutched in his hand.

The fiend flew at her, dagger held aloft. Once, twice! He slashed across her flank and back again. The knife slit through the green silk like a thorn tearing through flower petals, and the flesh underneath gave way like a peach. Her attacker was gripped with fascination as crimson stained the verdant fabric until his victim's yelps of fear broke the spell, and the young man took to his heels as Miss Cole collapsed gracelessly to the road.

What an extraordinary performance from the scoundrel! She was fortunate to escape with her life, if not her dignity. Her assailant's intentions must remain a mystery, but I confess to feeling gratified by his actions—indeed, one might say <u>avenged</u>—for Miss Cole insulted me unpardonably when she directed her intentions towards you so keenly after the curtain fell on last night's performance. She compounded her insults this morning when she arrived for morning rehearsals very late and made a point of asking me, in front of all assembled, whether you were recovered. I was forced to explain your absence with an improvised account of the ill-advised meat pie that had confined you to bed since last night, the deleterious effects of which had completely incapacitated both your mind and body. (A masterly allusion I think we might both agree.) How your friend smirked, knowing full well that you had failed to spend the night at home, but Mr. Lewis seemed satisfied with my necessary fabrication and your position at the theatre is secure.

Now let us see if the intrepid Miss Cole struggles to Goodman's Fields with her damaged buttock for tonight's performance, or if today's trauma makes her sacrifice her one unforgettable line to her understudy, as she likes to call my dresser. If she does undertake the hazardous journey to the Royalty, no doubt she will tell you of the crazed monster who attacked her, and will show you her damaged wares as proof. In what shadowy corner will she manage this, I wonder? Women of virtue can only hope that the slashing of Miss Cole's hindquarters will put that ambitious harlot back in her place.

But enough of these matters—I hear our daughter crying, and Lord knows she sees more of Mrs. Bartlett than she does her own mother. After I attend to her, I shall make my way to the theatre and trust that you will be there, fully sober, with another fine tale to explain where you spent the long hours of last night.

Your ever-devoted wife,
Elizabeth

27 Bury Street, London
Eight o'clock, 6 March 1788

My dearest Wife,

I cannot deny that the letter I discovered in my nightgown pocket this morning astonished me, but you looked so content in sleep—well-deserved after your triumph on the stage last night—that I did not wish to wake you. I thought it better to leave this response upon my pillow to greet you when you rise as I have an appointment with Charles Dibden about his new opera at the Lyceum. This could present an improvement in circumstances for us, and I am certain you will not begrudge me leaving you before discussing the matters detailed in your missive.

First, I must defend myself. You misunderstand me most completely! My friendship with Miss Cole is nothing more than that. Why do you presume that I would find another woman more appealing than you? The London masses applaud your capacity on the stage—your voice, your ability to make any role come to life. Why would your husband think less of you than your public? You continue to doubt me, but as Mr. Belleville said to Captain Belleville, "The man who wishes to become virtuous is already become so." It is true that Miss Cole calls upon my experience at times. She has ambitions to make her name on the stage and believes I can assist her. I do, after all, know by rote the most performed plays and have been admired well enough for my voice. It is no great sacrifice to teach her a song or two, and there is nothing more to it than that.

But I am curious to know how you learned of the assault on the lady—you transcribed it so accurately! Of course, as you are aware, Miss Cole did get herself to the theatre for last night's performance for she greatly feared reprisals for borrowing the dress. She had stitched up the tear and removed the bloodstain from the fabric, but could not remove the stain of her ordeal from her heart. The scoundrel was at least six foot tall, with the frame of a navvy—"his dagger was fearsome" were her precise words, and she thought herself ruined when she saw his blade. It was only to clear up any misunderstanding about her meaning that she revealed the wound upon her flank. Her attacker had been ferocious! The cut is at least eight inches long, and Miss Cole was so inflamed that a judicious application of apothecary's balm was insufficient as a calming agent. She is perpetually reminded of the fiend whenever she seeks repose.

And when you arise from yours, I shall be home and we can discuss these matters more fully. I hope to have good news about our future.

> Your admiring husband,
> Henry

ON BOARD THE *ARIEL*, PHILADELPHIA
TO LONDON, JUNE 1840

Thin, greenish light trickled over my face, coaxing me from insentience. An unpleasant odor permeated the atmosphere— the scent of brimstone or the perfume of decay. I tried to rouse myself, but could not move for I was twisted up in a shroud, my limbs bound to my sides by the dank fabric. Fear struck like a ravenous seabird delving into flesh—dead! Dead and laid out in a sepulcher by the sea. As darkness pulled my reluctant soul toward the abyss, a terrible thrumming rose up around me— louder, louder, *louder*. And when the shadows had near dragged me under, it came to me that the noise echoing in my ears was the palpitations of my own heart, and I had not yet succumbed to the conqueror worm.

But the terror did not recede, for surely I had been entombed alive by some monstrous error. The scream that formed in my throat could find no release as I struggled against the cataleptic trance that held me prisoner and as the very air turned to dust, a macabre thought took seed within my mind. What if no error had been made? What if this were *murder*? Driven by some superhuman energy, I struggled upright and gasped as the semblance of life settled over me. My eyes slowly adjusted to the shadows, and I saw that I was entangled in bedsheets soaked through with the brine from my own body. The room around me was in disarray, and bottles were clustered on the night table. Gradually I recognized it as the stateroom I occupied on board the ship bound for London. Fever, natural or self-induced, had subjugated me, and I had no sense of how long I had been confined to my chamber. Unfurling my body, I stretched my legs toward the floor, and as I stood up, my vision fizzled away like oil on a hot skillet.

* * *

When I awoke again, my face lay against cool wood and sheets of paper surrounded me. At once fear had me in its grip again—the letters from the mahogany box! Had my room been ransacked? I dragged the nearest page toward my eyes and as my vision cleared, my heart calmed. It did not belong to the peculiar correspondence that had occasioned my voyage to London, for the paper was new, the script frenzied, the ink smudged and blotted by a careless hand. I staggered to the jug on the washstand, praying it contained water no matter how stale or I would surely perish. Thankfully it held a clear elixir I immediately gulped down—it mattered not if the liquid was laced with poison or was from the sea itself, for my thirst was as feverish as my mind When the jug was fully drained, I sank back onto the bed and looked more carefully around me. It was the den of a madman, my possessions thrown about the room, my clothes trampled and dirty. I turned my gaze to the mob of bottles—surely the cause of all that I saw—and in urgent need of comfort, reached for the closest with quaking hand. It was a large flask of rum, a type favored by the most hardened sailor, and there was but a solitary finger of drink remaining. Beside it stood its vanquished twin, a depleted bottle of laudanum, and an empty apothecary bottle that had no label. As I held the rum to my lips, its thick smell made my stomach heave like the waves that tortured me, and I cursed the demon that had drawn me under its tutelage yet again.

I am not certain how much time passed as I sat huddled in my room, trying to muster the energy to tidy my garments and the courage to leave my crypt. How could I brave the company of my fellow passengers when I had no recollection of what I might have said or done during my spree? After a night at the Crooked Billet, Wasp and Frolic, or Man Full of Trouble drinking establishments, a friend was sure to steer me from catastrophe and guide me back home. I had no such friend upon the ship.

A gentle tapping broke through my morbid thoughts and the door swung open to reveal an angel framed in light.

"You are with us at last. We were worried, Mr. Poe."

The empyrean creature approached and I shrank into myself—was I awaiting the mercy of God after all? As she came nearer, I saw that she was carrying a tray holding a jug and dish of bread. When she placed her burden upon the table, her eyes slid to the empty bottles, and I was filled with shame.

"You have had quite a time, but my husband and I are determined to remedy that." She held her hand over the jug and several glistening drops fell into the vessel like celestial rain. "Drink as much water as you are able and try to partake of some bread. I have had your shirt and suit cleaned and will have the same done with those if you will kindly put on fresh attire. My husband will come by presently to check on you." With those words, my guardian angel dissolved into the light that flooded through the door.

I felt no hunger but managed to consume the bread after dipping bite after bite into a cup of the water. As I ate, I tried to remember the events that took place before my quarantine, but beyond boarding the ship and a nightmarish memory of seasickness, my mind was blank. When I finished the bread and a goodly amount of water, I peered into the looking glass to assess the damage and recoiled as a wraith with sunken cheeks and feverish eyes greeted me, its hair unkempt, lips parched, skin sallow. The clothing it wore was a disgrace—rumpled trousers and a loosened shirt tinged gray, with a split along one seam. My aggravated breath accelerated with a greater fear when I remembered my locket and my fingers crawled like a horde of spiders through my shirt until at last I found the jewel secreted in its folds and opened it to gaze at the portrait within. My mother's gentle smile greeted me, but I drew no consolation from it, only admonishment.

For modesty's sake, I locked my stateroom door and proceeded to remove the soiled attire. Shame overwhelmed me—how my appearance must have repelled my seraph visitor! I washed with the remainder of the water and retrieved the last clean set of clothes from my trunk. When I was as presentable as I could make myself, I straightened up the soured bedclothes, collected the scattered papers and arranged my personal effects.

"Mr. Poe! Are you there?" a hearty voice sounded as the door handle rattled.

A woman's more gentle tones intervened. "Mr. Poe? I have your cleaned clothing here and fresh bedding." It was my guardian. I unbolted the door for her, but a heavily bearded, portly man forced his way inside.

"Poe! Good to see you up. Let's have a look at you." He pushed me into a chair. "Bring a candle, will you, dearest?"

The fair-haired angel lit a candle and held it up to my face. Even that small flame was like a dart shot into my skull. I tried to focus on her beauty, but my tormentor leaned in to study my eyes, then unceremoniously yanked down my jaw and peered into my mouth.

"Hmm." He pushed my jaw back into position. "There will be no more going to rum-addled sailors for medicine, sir. It will be the death of you next time." He punctuated this admonishment with a guffaw that was unsettling.

"You must listen to my husband, Mr. Poe. Loneliness cannot be conquered with the contents of a bottle."

"Indeed. If you are troubled with seasickness again, you must come to me."

I nodded, but was distracted by his wife, who busied herself with stripping the linen from my bed. My face reddened as I thought of the moist, fetid sheets in her dainty hands. "Please, do not go to such trouble," I implored in a small voice that was scarcely my own.

"It is no trouble." She shook out the fresh linen, which quivered like a sail in the gentlest of breezes and floated down onto the berth. "A boy will collect the old linen for the laundry." My nurse settled her eyes upon me. They were large and very striking, emphasized by the golden curls that framed her face. "We'll leave you for now, Mr. Poe, and hope to see you at supper. Six o'clock."

The doctor drew out his pocket watch and tapped it. "That is in one hour. And do listen to my wife. She is quite the capable nurse. Until later, sir." And they left me.

Alone once more, I went to my trunk and lifted out the mahogany box that was secreted there. My heart began to race again when I saw the key was in the lock, but upon lifting the lid, I was relieved to discover that the bundle of letters was still inside, knotted up with the green ribbon. I then turned my attention to the papers I had gathered from the floor. Amongst them was a solitary page written in a precise, relentless script:

No.33 rue Dunôt, Faubourg, St. Germain, Paris

6 April 1840

My dear Poe,

Your letter, so wilfully opaque, has succeeded in capturing my imagination. *Amicis semper fidelis*—as your friend, I will of course be honoured to assist you in your investigation. Indeed your request is most opportune as I have business to pursue in London.

I will meet you on the first of July at Brown's Genteel Inn, 23 Dover Street as you suggest and look forward to learning the details of the peculiar mystery to which you allude.

Your Obedient Servant,

C. Auguste Dupin

With unsteady hands I placed Dupin's letter to one side and gathered up the other ink-stained, crumpled sheets. This is what, with increasing consternation, I read:

The *Ariel*, 13 June 1840

Darling Sissy, my dearest wife,

I am writing to you from my stateroom on board a ship bound for hell. We are but a week out of port, and I fear I cannot stand the endless pitching of this vessel any longer. My health declines more every day, and it is impossible to maintain a grip on the earthly world when surrounded by nothing but water, day after endless day—water that won't lie still, but heaves and boils and threatens to swallow us entirely. With this fear of drowning constantly upon me, I worry all the more about losing you—my darling, my anchor. For I have lied to you. I have told you that I am visiting London on writerly business, when in fact I seek to uncover terrible secrets—secrets that may prove my blood tainted. If this mysterious box of letters is not an elaborate hoax and my inheritance is indeed a scandalous and sordid one, I fear your love and all its brightness will drop like a dying star into the dreaded brine that surrounds me. And if that love, that brightest truest love is lost to me, then surely I too will be extinguished.

A storm rages outside, my emotions made manifest. It tears at the ship's sails and at the very fabric of my being, so rash was I to leave my family in search of answers about a past that claims to be mine by blood if not by action. I must prove it wrong! For surely words upon the page tell lies if the writer wishes to deceive.

But know, dear Sissy, that my sentiments are true. I will entomb them inside a bottle and cast it into those tormenting waves so they might carry it across the miles, to the place where the sea transforms into the Schuylkill River, and that bottle will ride the currents all the way into Philadelphia until it finds you walking along the river bank, as we do of an evening. And when you capture this bottle and claim its contents, then you will know, Sissy, my love, that Eddy thinks of you still from the very bottom of the sea.

I remain with devotion,
Your dear lost boy

The letter clutched in my trembling fingers stunned me. Only *I* could have written it, and yet I had no recollection of having done so. Once again my sinister twin, the shadowy figure who possesses me on occasion, was taunting me. I had promised full temperance to Sissy and although I had no memory of breaking my pledge, there was more than enough evidence to prove my failing. No eyes but mine must ever see that letter. I gathered up the pages, stuffed them in my pocket, and left my stateroom, determined to deliver the evidence to the bottom of the sea.

The saloon was empty, and I managed to escape onto the deck without notice. The ship bucked and charged like an untamed horse and vertigo assailed me as I staggered aft. I grabbed for the side of the ship as my legs buckled under me, but too late. I collapsed onto the deck and all was darkness.

"Mr. Poe!"

I heard a voice above me. Strong hands gripped the undersides of my arms and lifted me back to my feet.

"Still no sea legs. Let me help you to the saloon."

The robust doctor hauled me along beside him, his arm locked around my back. While not happy that my mission had been interrupted, I was relieved to be rescued from further embarrassment—fellow passengers would inevitably think me the victim of drink if I were found lying senseless on the deck.

"Ah, Mr. Poe." I heard the mellifluous tones of the doctor's lovely wife. "We are so pleased that you will be joining us for supper, but you must take care on such a treacherous night." She linked her arm through mine, and the two Samaritans guided me back to the dining area.

The saloon was now awash with candlelight and three strangers stared up at me as I entered the room. Their countenances ranged from mildly welcoming to hostile, or so it appeared to me.

"Mr. Poe is back with us," the doctor said.

"So we observe, Dr. Wallis." A thin, sallow-faced man, bald but for two parallel hanks of hair draped over his pate, scrutinized me with pale eyes. He was dressed in somber clothes not unlike my own and his demeanor was self-righteous. "Have you quite recovered, Mr. Poe?" His query had the tone of an accusation.

"He is rather delicate still, Mr. Asquith," the doctor's wife interrupted. "We must all assist Mr. Poe along the road to recovery."

Mr. Asquith's eyes narrowed as he exhaled audibly through his nostrils. "The man who resists the agents of Satan will follow life's path to Heaven's door."

"And it is our duty to assist our fellow travelers along that path," she responded.

"It is our duty indeed. And forgiveness is a gift from God," declared a woman of middle age with hair that matched her pewter-colored dress. "We are pleased you are able to break bread with us again, Mr. Poe."

"Madam, thank you. I am appreciative of your kind support."

I presented a nervous smile to my fellow diners and noted that one person had yet to comment on my appearance. He was a short man of athletic build—thirty years old, perhaps—with auburn hair and mustache, dressed in an alarming green frock coat, yellow neckcloth and dandyish trousers with a wide green stripe down the leg. He might be considered handsome if one overlooked his arrogant expression and garish clothing. The fellow shifted his insolent green eyes from the doctor's wife and focused on me like a cat stalking a wounded bird.

"Ah, Poe. We are indeed delighted to see you on your feet again. Much more befitting for a man of your position." His theatrical voice boomed through the small room, and I recognized an accent from my childhood—Virginia or further south.

"Mr. Poe, do sit. The food will be here shortly, or so we all hope. They are devilishly slow with supper most nights." The doctor indicated the bench in front of me and once I had seated myself, he took the position to my right. His wife gracefully arranged herself on my left.

"You were privileged to have Mrs. Wallis as a nurse. I was almost envious of your compromised health." The man in the vulgar frock coat inflected the last two words with just enough sarcasm to avoid straying from the bounds of polite conversation. Mrs. Wallis flushed. I awaited a remonstrance from her husband, but he was focused on lighting a cigar and appeared oblivious to the scoundrel's words. "And please know that I have taken no offense at your critique of my pathetic scribblings. It was educational to have the opinion of a professional editor."

I could feel a wave of heat rush up from my neck to my face, but was saved the embarrassment of making an immediate reply by the arrival of two young men carrying in soup, meat and bread.

"Mr. Mackie, please," the doctor's wife intervened in a soft voice. "The food is here. Now is the time for pleasant conversation."

Mr. Mackie nodded his acquiescence to her and smiled, but his eyes were chill when he gazed back at me. Pathetic scribblings—his words or mine? I had no recollection of the man and certainly no memory of his writing. But making an enemy when imprisoned on a vessel in the middle of the sea was not a terribly prudent course of action. The smell of the food and Dr. Wallis's newly lit cigar had an unpleasant effect on my stomach. Anxiety added to my discomfort.

"Stick with the soup, Mr. Poe," Dr. Wallis said through a cloud of smoke. "Your stomach is unlikely to be ready for meat yet."

Mrs. Wallis filled my bowl with a dark broth and placed it in front of me. I managed a few spoonfuls, but as the pungent steam rose up and mixed with cigar smoke, cooked

meat and potatoes, the ship commenced a terrible dipping
and rising. The effect on my senses was immediate and
awful. I struggled to escape my position on the bench, and
when at last I was on my feet, rushed from the saloon before
I could disgrace myself further. The booming laughter of
the man in the terrible suit followed me as I emerged into
open air and staggered for the side of the ship, where I
expelled the contents of my stomach, thankfully without
witness. After the waves of dyspepsia passed, I gulped down
the night air. How could I rejoin my fellow travelers after
my uncouth exit? Then I remembered the letter. I retrieved
it from my pocket and hurled it toward the hungry sea
before my mission could be interrupted again. As the sheets
of paper disappeared into the night, I wished my humiliation would fly away with them.

When at last I turned from the water, fear tugged at me as a
shadow flitted across the deck and hid itself in the murk. Had
the antagonized scribbler come to defend his artistry in a
cowardly manner? I stood there, frozen, fear prickling up and
down my back with each creak and groan of the ship, knowing
that in my enervated condition, a confrontation would surely
not go my way.

"Wandering the vessel alone in darkness is foolhardy, Mr.
Poe," Dr. Wallis said, as he and his wife emerged from the
gloom to rescue me again. "The decks are treacherous when
slick with seawater. Come, let us lead the way." My new friends
linked their arms through mine, led me to my stateroom, and
bade me goodnight.

If I had hoped that solitude would provide succor from
my shame, I was wrong. The wan candlelight and creeping
shadows added unease to my self-reproach. Finally I put pen to
paper and wrote a letter to my beloved wife, describing the
camaraderie amongst the passengers, the benevolent weather,

the halcyon sea, the tales and poems I had completed to profitably pass the time. And then I sealed that wild fiction with wax and left it in my writing desk until it could be sent back to Philadelphia when the ship returned.

27 Bury Street, London
Wednesday morning, 19 March 1788

Henry, dearest,

I am relieved to find you at home this morning, seemingly well but for some over-indulgence in drink, judging by the heaviness of your slumbers. Our little company was concerned when you failed to arrive at the chophouse after the performance last night, and we awaited you in vain throughout supper.

Miss Cole was in a temper as she had witnessed you in lengthy conversation with a Mrs. Wright and her younger sister Miss Pierce, who has yet to snare a husband. The two sisters attend the theatre regularly, but Miss Cole swore that Mrs. Wright had designs on someone associated with the Royalty. Indeed, she was adamant that the lady was in pursuit of <u>your</u> attentions.

When I confessed that I really could not place Mrs. Wright at all, Miss Cole obliged me with a description: "Scrawnier than a drowned cat, but with feet as large as an elephant's and a pockmarked face shaped like that of a horse." This melange from the animal kingdom did little to focus the woman in my mind's eye, but when Annie added that the lady in question had been wearing a blue and yellow ensemble and a necklace of large blue stones set in what looked to be gold, I instantly knew of whom she was speaking. The dress was an unattractive combination of cerulean blue and canary yellow, made more vulgar with three flounces around the hem, lace ruffles on the sleeves and neckline, and an unfashionable red sash.

Mr. Blanchard confirmed your lengthy dalliance with Mrs. Wright. He had been obliged to make small talk with her spinster sister while Mrs. Wright regaled you with fascinating tales of her deceased husband's stationery shop on Watling Street, where she spends her afternoons assisting customers. How sorry I am to have missed such delightful conversation. Mr. Blanchard also rescued me from the intolerable embarrassment of confessing to all assembled that I did not have the price of my supper in my pocket. I have assured him that you will reimburse him in full tomorrow. I trust you will create a splendid story to explain your absence to Mr. Blanchard and will ensure that my dignity is not damaged further.

Your Wife,
Elizabeth

27 Bury Street, London
Friday, 21 March 1788

My dear Elizabeth,

Please forgive my delay in responding, but I have only just found your letter tucked under a flask of gin on the shelf. If my thirst had not got the better of me, I might not have discovered it at all!

First, I am sorry I failed to escort you to the chophouse on Tuesday night, but have no fear—your reputation is intact with Mr. Blanchard. He was most concerned when I informed him that a pickpocket accosted me outside the theatre and when I gave chase, the ruffian clouted me about the head. The blows left me disoriented, and I had no recourse but to proceed home for fear of ending up senseless in the street. Mr. Blanchard agreed to accept reimbursement for your supper after wages are distributed at the theatre.

As for Mrs. Wright, I am once more wounded by the envenomed tongue of slander. But unlike Lady Sneerwell, I take no pleasure in reducing others to the level of my own injured reputation. I really cannot say whose attentions Mrs. Wright was pursuing on Tuesday night, but yesterday evening she was courted in a most pointed manner. The tantalising theatrical unfolded thusly:

Mrs. Wright locked up her stationer's shop, walked down Watling Street and turned into Bow Lane. She had progressed a short distance when she felt someone brush against her and a sharp scratch upon her haunches. As she cried out, a man in red breeches, black surtout and a cocked hat with high brim and a cockade ran like the Devil down Bow Lane. Worse still, the culprit was laughing, and Mrs. Wright fell to the ground dizzy with fear and pain. She struggled back to the shop to collect herself and discovered to her distress that the backside of her dress had been slashed. That dress of cerulean blue and canary yellow you disliked so much is tattered, as is Mrs. Wright's posterior. She is quite unable to salve her nerves.

It is particularly disconcerting to note that details of Mrs. Wright's ordeal have a startling similarity to the assault upon Miss Cole—a slash across the hind-quarters, a ruined dress and the danger of a ruined reputation. And is it not peculiar that both women had been to the Royalty before they were attacked? This makes me fear for your safety, my dear, as these violent escapades occurred in broad daylight, were completely unprovoked, and, inexplicably, the ladies were not robbed. Please exercise utmost caution when going about your business.

With concern,

Henry

LIVERPOOL TO LONDON,
WEDNESDAY, 1 JULY 1840

More than three weeks at sea took me to the brink of madness, but I survived the remainder of the journey without further recourse to intemperance. Daily I wrote to Sissy and Muddy, my mother-in-law, a diary of my journey that was rather maudlin. I had promised my wife that I would use my time at sea productively to write a collection of stories and tried to draw inspiration from my monotonous surroundings, but after penning the beginnings of some sea adventures and pirate stories that sent yet another ship and its crew to the bottom of the ocean, I threw my half-hearted tales to a watery grave instead.

When the *Ariel* finally sailed into the port of Liverpool at dawn, my heart lifted. At last! I could put my sins behind me and become *Edgar Poe*—writer, critic and scholar. The man who inhabited my stateroom on the ship would be left behind. I pondered how arriving in another country gave a man the opportunity to begin again. It was possible to redefine one's character, adjust mistakes and start over if determined enough. This thought struck me as important, and I vowed to return to it when in a less anxious state of mind. First I had to find my way to the railway station and board a train bound for London without falling prey to the unsavory characters who frequented Liverpool's tippling dens and spent their days and nights wandering the vicinity's streets and alleys, looking for the chance to swindle an honest citizen. It was the same in every port, or so I presumed from the tales I had heard in the taverns down near the docks of Philadelphia.

It was still early morning when we were released at last from the *Ariel*; my fellow passengers and I made our way to Lime Street Station where we cordially said our goodbyes. Dr. and Mrs. Wallis were remaining in Liverpool where she had family. Mr. Asquith was going on to Manchester to give a lecture on the moral benefits of temperance, and Miss Nicholson was returning to Preston to visit with her aged mother. Mr. Mackie was traveling to London for a "rich theatrical engagement of his own devising." I wondered if a play he had penned was to be performed in some small theater, or if the dandified fellow had managed to persuade an innocent damsel of wealthy means to marry him, but I did not inquire further. We both boarded the London train, but made no plans to meet again, and seated ourselves in separate carriages.

My compartment was reasonably comfortable and once settled in, I began to contemplate my assignation at Brown's Genteel Inn with the Chevalier C. Auguste Dupin. I had first made Dupin's acquaintance in 1832, when staying in Paris. The location of our meeting was a library on the rue Montmartre where we were searching for the same rare volume of verse, *Tamerlane and Other Poems*, and this coincidence provoked a lengthy conversation about our interests, revealing a shared passion for enigmas, conundrums and hieroglyphics. After a time, Dupin offered me accommodation at his residence, which I gratefully accepted as I was running low on funds. Dupin, it seemed, was also in straitened circumstances, but the neglected state of his house did not reflect that of his mind; he

was a great scholar and ratiocinator who never failed to find the
solution to any puzzle. Rarely have I enjoyed a more intellec-
tually stimulating evening than those spent with Dupin,
discussing the contents of his extensive library or exploring the
city by night. This shared sympathy made me confident that
together we would answer all the questions that had tormented
me since the day my Pa's new wife had sent me the mahogany
box of letters and told me it was my legacy.

My restless mind was eventually lulled by the hypnotic view
through the carriage window: endless green fields, tenebrous
woodlands and cloud-speckled sky, until that vision faded, and
I fell into unquiet slumber. I know not how much time passed,
but my eyes opened to utter darkness and the sense that someone was in my compartment. And then, in the blackness, I
perceived the glint of two wild, violet-colored eyes. My body
was chilled to stone as a pale-skinned woman with long curling
ebony hair emerged from the shadows and moved toward me,
gliding noiselessly as if she were a part of the night itself. She
held a goblet in her hand and as she loomed above me, three or
four drops of ruby-colored fluid fell into the goblet, like drops
of brilliant blood, and she pressed the malevolent vessel to my
lips, forcing me to drink the contents. As she pressed in closer
still, her hair—blacker than raven wings—enveloped me, dragging me deeper, ever deeper, into the suffocating darkness.

* * *

The train's whistle and my own ghastly yowl juddered me
awake just as we pulled into Euston Station. I emerged into
an eerie gas-lit world and quickly made my way to a hackney
coach, bidding the driver to take me to Brown's Genteel Inn.
We moved at an uncanny pace through the streets of London,
the horse's hooves clattering like the Devil's on the

pavements. There were times when I wondered if the coach would fit through the narrow passageways, and if we would stay upright as we careered around a corner. I perceived very little of the city due to the soot-stained windows and my attempts to retain my dignity upon the slippery seat. When the coach stopped, I felt quite without breath, as if I had just finished a foot race.

The fatigue from my long journey and my unsteady sea legs gave me the unfortunate appearance of a man on a spree, but the atmosphere of Brown's Genteel Inn greatly improved my temper. The English reign supreme in the art of internal decoration and the hotel foyer proved this through example. There were none of the costly appurtenances so commonly found in American decor, which is fashioned on an aristocracy of dollars. In England, the true nobility of blood does not indulge in vulgar displays of wealth.

The desk clerk, a mustachioed, balding fellow who was probably no more than five and thirty but looked a decade older, attended to me efficiently and courteously, despite the discomfort I tried to hide when he revealed the first week's bill for my room and Dupin's. As the agent who booked my sea passage had also secured rooms for us at Brown's, I was ill-prepared for the cost, and if I had not invited my illustrious friend to aid me in my investigation, I would have searched for less expensive accommodation. I could not, of course, embarrass either of us by suggesting we move to shabbier lodgings, and vowed to enjoy the elegance denied to me since I was half-driven from the home of my adoptive parents.

"We trust your suite will fully satisfy all your needs, but do not hesitate to ask if you require anything further," the desk clerk said, handing me the key for room eight.

"Cigars would be a pleasure."

"We have taken the liberty to supply those, sir."

"And I should like to leave a message for Chevalier Dupin who is also a guest here."

"He has left a message for you." The desk clerk handed me a note, and I immediately broke the seal and opened it.

> Dear Sir,
>   Shall we meet for a late supper tonight? Ten o'clock.
> Room twelve.
>   Yours respectfully,
>   C. Auguste Dupin

He had anticipated my arrival perfectly. I retired to my chambers to refresh myself before supper, and when the door opened, my rooms were revealed to be gratifyingly genteel. An Argand lamp with a ground-glass shade emitted a tranquil radiance and the carpet was of Saxony material half an inch thick. Two windows offering a view of Dover Street were framed with draperies of rich crimson silk fringed with gold, their deep recesses curtained by thick silver tissue. An attractive landscape painting was hung above the fireplace; the sofa and two conversation chairs were of rosewood and covered with crimson silk patterned with gold flowers. Next to these was an octagonal marble table with a tall candelabrum upon it. If I had the means to house my family in a manner more compatible with my taste, these pleasant furnishings would compose the environment of my reading room, a place for contemplation, study and composition.

As I unpacked my trunk and readied myself for supper, the pleasing environment raised my spirits. At ten o'clock I made my way to room twelve, carrying the mahogany box under my arm, and rapped on the door.

"Enter."

When I pushed the door open, Dupin rose from a large armchair to greet me, and I was momentarily taken aback—it

was as if I were unexpectedly confronted by my own i
a looking glass. We were the same age, thirty-one, and c
same build and height. Even our clothing was similar, for
Dupin habitually dressed entirely in black, like an entity of the
night, as was my own predilection.

"Poe, it is my great pleasure to see you again."

"And I am very pleased to see you, Dupin." I stepped
forward, prepared to shake his hand, but he dipped his head
and shoulders into a formal bow; wrong-footed, I awkwardly
reciprocated. My happiness at seeing my friend after such a
lengthy interlude had made me forget his disinclination for
displays of amity.

"Please, sit." He nodded to the armchair opposite his and
made his way to a side table where a decanter of wine stood
breathing. I did as he bid and placed the mahogany box next to
my chair as the octagonal marble table was full with covered
serving dishes, which could not contain the delicious aroma of
our supper. Dupin handed me a glass of wine and retreated
into his seat, where he gazed at me intently, waiting for me to
speak. We might have been back in his library, debating some
intellectual puzzle or a perplexing mystery delivered to him by
the Paris Prefect of Police; it was as if eight years had not
passed since we had last seen each other.

"To your health." I raised my glass and he reciprocated. As
we sipped and contemplated the wine, I scrutinized my
companion. Dupin had a noble bearing inherited from his illustrious family and a high forehead that added to his aura of
intellect, but he had not been gifted with a robust constitution.
I was gratified to note that the usual drawn pallor of his face
was improved, and his large gray eyes were clear and alert. I
knew the same could not be said of my own appearance.

"I hope your journey was bearable," he offered, as if reading
my thoughts.

"Bearable enough."

"The hotel is most agreeable. I must—"

"I am delighted you find the accommodation agreeable," I said, halting his words of thanks so they might not embarrass us both. Dupin's financial circumstances had improved little since our last meeting, and I had, of course, offered to finance our investigation. The poverty into which my Pa's unkindness had thrown me had been auspiciously, if temporarily, alleviated by the handsome sum I had received from a wealthy English woman named Helena Loddiges for editing an amateur ornithologist's study of rare Central and South American birds. The fact that my benefactress lived in London allowed me to provide my wife with a reason for my journey, and as I had every intention of calling on Miss Loddiges, my conscience was not burdened by a falsehood. "You do me a great favor, Dupin, and I am relieved that Brown's Genteel Inn honors its name with such pleasing rooms." Happily, his suite was of the same quality as mine, with the harmonious addition of several large Sèvres vases filled with vivid flowers that curiously had no scent. "It may surprise you that I cannot find any fault with the decorations," I added.

Dupin smiled, knowing full well my philosophy of furniture. "Most surprised. But I am curious if there was a reason—beyond the exemplary décor—for choosing this particular inn."

"I confess that I knew nothing of the place beyond the handbill I sent to you with my letter."

He drew the elegant handbill from his coat pocket and passed it to me. I remembered it well, but inspected it again as Dupin seemed to expect me to. The paper was thick and of good quality, with an ink sketch of the establishment on the front and the descriptive details inside the folded paper, written in a hand so meticulous it might have been typeface:

Brown's Genteel Inn
23 Dover Street,
Mayfair, London
Located in close proximity to Green Park,
London's theatres and historical locations,
and shops patronised by the
fashionable Ladies of London.
This inn for Gentlefolk is furnished
to the highest standard,
with the strictest attention given to the comfort of those
who may favour it with their patronage.
All servants are charged for in the bill. Meals provided.
Proprietor: Mr. James Brown, former valet of Lord Byron.

"An unusual advertisement," Dupin said. "How did you obtain it?"

"It arrived with my ticket for the *Ariel*. The agent took the liberty of booking me accommodation, and organized an additional room at my request."

Dupin retrieved the handbill and returned it to his pocket. "Let us now see whether the establishment's cooking is as commendable as its decoration." He lifted the silver lids from our dishes to reveal a supper of roast chicken, carrots and potatoes. My stomach rumbled and Dupin quickly served us both. We spoke nary a word after picking up our cutlery. Once our appetites were sated and the dishes cleared onto the kitchen's trolley, Dupin poured us each a cognac and clipped two cigars.

"I believe you will find this more than satisfactory." Dupin lit his own cigar with a friction match, then held the flame toward mine. As it caught, I savored the smoke.

"Excellent."

"The New World produces some goods of very high quality." His words seemed to transform into smoke, then back into words again. We enjoyed the cigars for several minutes, but

Dupin's silent curiosity brought a sense of disquiet to the room—the cerebral always took precedent over corporeal pleasures with Dupin. I placed the mahogany box on the marble table.

"I must thank you for coming to my aid when I gave you so little information about what brought me to London."

"I am honored that you presumed I would," Dupin responded. "And I am most curious to learn more about your historical puzzle."

I nodded at the mahogany box. "Of course this relates to my mystery, as you will have gathered."

"Of course."

"I am afraid the route to the heart of my problem will be circuitous if I am to make sure you are in possession of all the facts."

Dupin gave a hint of a smile. "You know me well. Better to presume that all details are important rather than the reverse, or we may overlook what is hidden in plain sight."

I took a goodly sip of cognac before commencing my tale. "I cannot recall if I ever mentioned that my mother was born here in London. While still a child, she emigrated to Boston with her mother who was an actress and made her own theater debut not long after arriving in her new homeland. My dear mother proved to be a fine actress and eventually met my father, who had ambitions to perform in the theater. He had little of her talent and perhaps envy was the cause of his abandonment, for he left her alone and penniless with three young children. She did her best to provide for us, but ill-health reduced her to ever more desperate straits, and she died in Richmond, Virginia, when I was not yet three years old." I paused to inhale the rich smoke of my cigar as an all too familiar melancholia welled up within me. Dupin did the same, but his eyes remained intently focused upon me.

"Happily, my mother had a great many friends who did their best to help, and we three children were distributed amongst as many families. I considered myself the most fortunate of my siblings as my adoptive parents, John and Frances Allan, took me into their Richmond home and treated me as if I were their son by birth, insisting that I call them 'Ma' and 'Pa'. I had a privileged life, an idyll that was only disrupted when we moved to London when I was six years old. We stayed in London for five years, but my Pa's business venture proved unsuccessful and my Ma's health began to decline. Even our return to my Ma's beloved Richmond could not save her, and she left this world prematurely, which cut a deep wound into my heart. Her husband did not suffer as much, for he remarried with unseemly haste, which caused a terrible quarrel between us."

Dupin acknowledged the summary of my past with a single nod as he puffed on his cigar. My relations with my adoptive father had been acrimonious during my time in Paris, but Dupin knew little more than that.

"When my Pa's health suddenly declined, his new wife failed to inform me that he was ailing, and the opportunity was lost to reconcile with him. I made my way to Richmond for the funeral, but was treated as a person of no consequence. I am not ashamed to say that I had expected to be heir to a large fortune."

"It is a reasonable assumption, given the strength of the bond between you and your adoptive mother—and indeed for many years with your adoptive father."

I nodded vigorously, gratified that Dupin understood my position.

"But of course the new Mrs. Allan would take a contrary position to Mr. Allan's deceased wife," Dupin continued, "and would wish that only her children would benefit from Mr. Allan's fortune."

"Which is most dishonorable." I felt my face flush with anger and gulped some cognac to cool myself.

Dupin raised his brows. "Of course. But rarely is honor employed when it comes to property. The child may expect to inherit from his parents as is his right by blood, but even so, his legacy may be stolen by the cuckoo waiting by the nest."

"And certainly I was raised as if I were my Ma and Pa's only son. It was cruel to cast me aside after Ma's death—she would not have allowed my exclusion from my Pa's will. I endeavored to make this point to my Pa's widow after his funeral, but the discourteous woman utterly disregarded my presence in Richmond."

Dupin expelled a plume of smoke, which gave him rather a ferocious air, but his voice was typically measured. "It is natural to become embittered when one's legacy is stolen by a rival with the scruples of a common thief, yet it is important to plan one's retaliation most carefully. *La vengeance se mange très-bien froide.* Rarely do we prevail over our adversaries when hot with fury—it is he with the coolest head that is the eventual victor."

"Fear not. I have no plan to journey back to Richmond and take my revenge on the new Mrs. Allan, for I cherish my liberty too much. There is something far more pressing that I need your assistance with."

"Something that links your adoptive father's widow, your legacy, London and this." He nodded at the mahogany box.

"Correct. Imagine my astonishment when in late February of this year, I received a large parcel from Mrs. Allan accompanied by a letter that stated she was turning over to me certain artifacts that were my birthright. Her words gave me some hope that she might at last behave honorably toward me, but these expectations were dashed when I opened the parcel and found this inside." I indicated the box in question. The flat lid was mounted with a squared brass handle and a heart-shaped brass escutcheon adorned its front, which held a key decorated with a red tassel. I reached over and opened the box, revealing an interior lined with crimson leather and the bundle of letters knotted together with a green ribbon. I placed them on the marble table.

"Seven missives written over half a century ago, in two distinct hands, and documenting a scandalous series of events." I lowered my voice although there was no one else present to hear. "It appears that I have inherited evidence pertaining to several villainous attacks committed in London in the year 1788."

Dupin continued to puff on his cigar, his expression unchanged. "In two distinct hands, you say?"

I nodded. "Those of an Elizabeth and Henry Arnold."

Dupin scrutinized the bundle of letters, the smoke from his cigar curling around him like an unearthly mist.

"And what do you know of Elizabeth and Henry Arnold?" he asked, fixing his eyes upon me like a baleful cat.

"Very little," I said cautiously. "Only what I find in this correspondence. That they were husband and wife, and actors on the London stage."

Dupin's eyes narrowed slightly. "It is peculiar that the box and the letters within it were released to you in such an inexplicably tardy manner if truly a legacy from your adoptive father. Was there any note from him?"

"No. Just a letter from Mrs. Allan."

"Do you still have her letter?"

"Yes, but I did not think to bring it with me this evening."

"I should like to see it." Dupin ran his finger along the edge of the mahogany box, then leaned to peer inside it. "Quite a large vessel for its cargo," he murmured before settling back to sip his cognac. I wished I had not drained my glass quite so quickly, but did not wish to play the glutton and ask for another.

"Let me be direct, Dupin," I said. "I think these letters must be forgeries, designed by the pernicious Mrs. Allen to distress me by suggesting that I have some connection to the scandal contained therein." A sigh escaped me. "It is one thing to disinherit the child one has raised, it is quite another to burden him with such a peculiar legacy, and while my adoptive father was certainly aware of my passion for conundrums, he never sought to encourage such intellectual proclivities within me. I cannot believe that he wished the box to be sent to me."

"And so you think that John Allan's widow desires to cause you pain by sending you a box of forged letters?"

He tapped ash from his cigar and then drew on it until it flared crimson like a demon's eye, hypnotic and cruel. It *was* what I believed, but when Dupin expressed my thoughts, he made them sound ridiculous.

"Read the letters. You will see what I mean." The cigar smoke and heavily perfumed tapers in the candelabrum began to overwhelm my senses and an intolerable weariness swept over me. "Thank you for dinner, but I am terribly tired. Shall we take up this conversation tomorrow? At eleven perhaps?"

Dupin's eyes were fixed upon mine. "Of course. Leave the letters with me. I would like to read them."

* * *

Once back in my room, I thought to calm myself by writing a letter to Sissy, but found I had nothing to tell her that would not make her anxious. The windows began to rattle with a hard driving rain and a chill came upon me. Feeling utterly enervated, I fell into my bed, but sleep eluded me. An iciness pervaded the atmosphere and with a sickening of my heart, I sensed a presence in the room, a presence that emitted a pestilent and mystic vapor, which grew stronger and brighter, like a flash of lightning captured by storm clouds and frozen. Then a glowing red eye pierced through the blue haze—a solitary eye of fire, mesmerizing me, completely overwhelming me. The bedclothes clasped my body like some supernatural entity and as I struggled to breathe, I wondered if I would ever see my darling wife again. Just as I drifted toward nothingness, the veil was lifted and my eyes fluttered open.

I was at once confused and relieved to discover that it was morning.

27 Bury Street, London
8 May 1788

Henry,

I had expected that we would meet yesterday
evening at the Westminster School of Eloquence as
planned, but my hopes were in vain. I wonder if you
have managed to secure us a tour for the summer
season as you promised? I am increasingly concerned
for the well-being of our daughter if our finances
remain so precarious. Surely you understand that I
cannot request aid from my father again. The fact that
he has a new wife does little to aid my attempts to
placate him.

The disagreeable state of our personal affairs made
the topic of the last night's debate all the more
pertinent: "Is the common saying true, that there is no
medium in the marriage state, but that it must always
be extremely happy or very miserable?" I was curious
to hear your opinion on this subject. The audience
was divided on the issue. Many argued that a medium
between happiness and misery is the norm in marriage,
that one cannot expect perfect happiness in a union, as
man and woman are fallible creatures more often
driven by emotion than reason. And one must not
accept perfect misery, despite the ignominy of divorce.
This last statement caused much controversy. Some in
the audience declared that it was the duty of husband
and wife to sustain the marriage state as they had
forged a bond under the eyes of God; it was of little

consequence if their characters were of conflicting humours and there was no joy in their union.

The heated argument that ensued reminded me of the April debate at the Coachmakers' Hall. The subject, if you remember, was whether jealousy in a husband or inconstancy in a wife is more destructive to matrimonial happiness. A woman who had written a novel entitled *The Fair Inconstant* had suggested the topic and the eventual consensus of the audience was that inconstancy in a wife is the more destructive. I suggested that the debate should be extended to inconstant husbands and jealous wives. You might remember that Mrs. Maria Smyth, an acquaintance from my youth who is now profitably married to Dr. William Smyth, claimed it was the jealousy of wives that caused inconstancy in husbands and, therefore, the subject was not worthy of debate.

Mrs. Smyth was also present at last night's debate, and it was quite clear from her limited contributions that her intellect has failed to improve at all. She made a point of humiliating me in front of her witless companions and dullard husband by commenting on your absence and then stating with mock commiseration that a stable marriage was requisite if a couple were to discuss the evening's topic in public.

I am still smarting from her slight and your broken promise. I trust I shall see you at the theatre tonight.

Your Wife,

Elizabeth

Dear Elizabeth,

It is hardly ideal for a husband and wife to be forced to spend so much time apart, and I am truly repentant for missing our assignation at the School of Eloquence, for I know how greatly you relish the opportunity to display your superior education. But my absence from home these last few days has been unavoidable as I have been working unrelentingly to secure us employment over the summer season and, thankfully, have succeeded. I cannot divulge the full details yet, but it is likely that we will spend the next few months, and perhaps longer, at the Theatre Royal in Margate. I hope this makes you feel a little more kindly towards me. And perhaps a smile will be brought to your face when I tell you of the indignity that befell Mrs. Smyth the evening following the debate at the School of Eloquence.

She was walking in Fleet Street, on the way to an informal soirée at a friend's house and claims that a thin, vulgar-looking man wearing a blue greatcoat and cocked hat began to follow her—a man of middle size, with a villainous, narrow face and very ugly legs and feet. His voice was peculiar—rather high and tremulous—and he made shocking comments to her. Mrs. Smyth attempted to ignore him and quickened her pace, but the ruffian stalked her all the way to the house in Johnson's Court, which was her destination. As she banged desperately upon the door, the man leapt onto the step beside her, struck her a blow beneath her left breast and slashed at her left thigh. This violence was committed with perfect composure and the rascal gloated as Mrs. Smyth began to swoon. He took to his heels only when the door to the house finally opened and her friends helped her inside.

The wound on her thigh was slight and the blood was stopped with balsam. Mrs. Smyth's stays protected her breast, but her clothing was quite ruined by the weapon, which she believed was a lancet or penknife. The damage to her dress especially aggrieved Mrs. Smyth as it was, she claimed, a very expensive Polonaise gown made of imported, hand-painted cotton. She demanded that her attacker be pursued and arrested for destroying her dress and her derrière (in that order, I believe), but Mrs. Smyth's friends begged her to keep the incident quiet for the sake of her reputation. Oddly, they have little hesitation in discussing the matter quite openly themselves. The good Dr. Smyth is concerned about his wife's fragile nerves and, being a cautious man, wishes to gather more information before accusing any specific person of the attack. I will follow his enquiries with interest.

You wonder what my opinion is on the subject of marriage and whether it must always be extremely happy or extremely miserable. It seems that I am not a man of the crowd for I do not see the misery in extremes, but rather the excitement. We creatures of the theatre must thrive on the variances of emotion, or how would we perform the roles required of us? It seems to me, my dear, that you understand this very well.

    Yours,
    Henry

27 Bury Street, London
26 May 1788

Dearest Henry,

Have you heard? Not one, but two females were assaulted yesterday. This is terribly disconcerting as both ladies were attacked at approximately the same time, which would indicate two ruffians at work. It would seem that one scoundrel is imitating the other. I wonder if his motives spring from admiration for the original performance or some peculiar titillation of his own?

The victim I am most familiar with is Mrs. Chippingdale, who is the lady's maid of Viscountess Malden. She is also the sister of vocalist Mrs. Davenett, who introduced me to her at the theatre. Mrs. Chippingdale has a haughty nature as she believes that her employer's status somehow reflects brightly onto her own reputation, and while one of her position should have a mastery of the finer points of etiquette, Mrs. Chippingdale requires some further lessons in good manners.

Mrs. Davenett and Mrs. Chippingdale make a habit of visiting their aged mother on Sunday afternoons, but dispense with their show of sisterly affection after the meeting and go their separate ways. Mrs. Chippingdale was soon confronted by a rascal who declared that her over-festive dress gave her the appearance of a lady of ill-repute. The garish costume was of rose-coloured silk with pink stripes and a rosebud pattern. Pink roses were embroidered around the décolletage and a cascade of frills adorned the ends of her sleeves. It was the perfect Spring ensemble for a young girl meeting her beau for an afternoon stroll, but far less appropriate for a woman of her years alone after dusk. The predatory rogue attacked her on St. James's Place, first making filthy proposals. (I have some doubts as to the veracity of this.) He then produced a knife and quickly attacked her garments. The pink silk tore open under the sharp blade, exposing her cotton petticoats. Her attacker slashed the costly silk again, splitting the fabric across her derrière and quite destroying the dress and her hindquarters. As her costume is no longer in a condition to wear in high society (even in the position of lady's maid), perhaps Mrs. Chippingdale will display some generosity and donate it to her sister for use in the theatre?

Of the second attack, I have far less to tell you. It seems that a very pretty maidservant was accosted on Jermyn Street at approximately the same time that Mrs. Chippingdale met her nemesis. She described her attacker as a tall, stout officer dressed in his uniform and one would hardly think anything more of her story except for her claim that the rogue declared, "Submit to Captain Belleville" and "I demand my rights to your affection!" As you and I and any other folk familiar with Mrs. Brooke's play *Rosina* know, the correct lines are: "Allow me to retire, brother, and learn at a distance from you to correct those errors into which the fire of youth, and bad example, have hurried me. When I am worthy of your esteem, I will return, and demand my rights in your affection."

How very appropriate those words are, would you not agree? I will be relieved to adjourn to Margate and leave such horseplay behind us.

Your Wife,
Elizabeth

Despite the torments of the night, my first morning in London began most satisfactorily. A large breakfast was brought to my room at nine o'clock as requested, along with a copy of *The Morning Chronicle*. I scanned the newspaper while drinking very good English breakfast tea and eating sausage, toast and egg, which had a positive effect upon my constitution.

There were some accounts of local crimes in the *Chronicle*'s pages that might inspire a tale or two. I was intrigued by the story of Edward Oxford, who was to be tried for high treason at the Old Bailey on the sixth of July. The eighteen-year-old public house waiter had discharged two pistols at Queen Victoria as she rode with Prince Albert in an open carriage on the tenth of June—the boy objected to the country being ruled by a woman. The uncanny tale of a criminal transported to New South Wales a decade ago for the theft of three linen handkerchiefs appealed to my imagination. He had recently returned to England a wealthy man and bought a mansion near his birthplace, much to the displeasure of certain persons of distinction. No explanation was given for the man's surprising reversal of fortunes or his return to his childhood home. Had he committed a more profitable crime? Had luck become his friend and allowed him the discovery of gold or opals or some other precious commodity? Or did he make a pact with the Devil or whatever other accursed creature wanders the deserts of that far-flung colony? I resolved to keep this story for further contemplation.

I flicked through the other pages of the newspaper and found nothing else of interest until the "Announcements" on the back page.

Arrived in Liverpool on the first of July from Philadelphia, the packet-ship Ariel, *having on board Mr. Edgar A. Poe, highly regarded American author and critic. Mr. Poe proceeded immediately to London by train to take up residence at Brown's Genteel Inn. He will be available during his stay for public recitations of his newest tales and a lecture on the Art of the Literary Critic. We will confirm in these pages the date and venue of this much-anticipated literary evening.*

I was filled with gratitude. Solving the mystery of the box of letters was the primary reason for my journey, but I had two additional aspirations for my visit to London, my childhood home. I had written to an author whose work I had greatly admired when I reviewed it for the *Southern Literary Messenger* and more recently for *Burton's Gentleman's Magazine*, a man whose newest effort, *Nicholas Nickleby*, was his best—superlative praise indeed. From his tales I felt him to be a kindred spirit and expressed my hope that Mr. Charles Dickens's schedule would allow for a meeting. I enclosed a copy of my *Tales of the Grotesque and Arabesque* with my letter and put my position to him honestly: I wished to find a publisher in England and his assistance in this would put me forever in his debt. If the opportunity to read some of my own tales to a London audience arose, or perhaps to give a lecture on the art of composition or literary criticism, I would be highly gratified to do so. It seemed from the newspaper announcement, which Mr. Dickens had surely placed, that the honorable man was advancing my cause in a careful and delicate manner. I could now look forward to receiving some communication from Mr. Dickens with details of this lecture.

I finished my tea and rose to my feet feeling invigorated. I would write my daily letter to Sissy, have a perambulation in Green Park, and return well before eleven so I might collect myself before meeting Dupin. Perhaps correspondence from Mr. Dickens would be awaiting me at that time.

* * *

My walk in Green Park did much to revive me, but my hopes of hearing from Mr. Dickens were dashed when I re-entered Brown's. I retrieved Mrs. Allan's letter from my room, then made my way to Dupin's chambers. The welcome smell of coffee greeted me as my friend opened the door.

"I hope you are feeling rested, Poe. The coffee is very good here—a fine restorative. Shall I pour you some?"

"Please. And here is the letter from Mrs. Allan that you requested."

"Excellent."

Dupin placed it on top of the other letters, which were stacked neatly on the octagonal table next to the mahogany box. We settled ourselves into the armchairs and sipped at the coffee for several minutes before Dupin spoke. Many would find his lengthy pondering silences unnerving, but I was familiar with his eccentric manners and took no offense.

"The first question you would like answered is whether the letters are a hoax," he said, while staring into his coffee cup, as if some vision there had mesmerized him.

"Yes, that would seem the correct place to begin."

"To elaborate, you wonder if the crimes referred to are fabricated and if the signatures on the letters are forgeries."

"Indeed. Everything about the letters is a mystery to me. I undertook some research in Philadelphia, but discovered nothing relevant. Perhaps the truth is to be found only in London, where the crimes allegedly took place."

Dupin nodded. "As you know from our time together in Paris, I have conducted an extensive study of the science of autography, building on the early research of Camillo Baldo, which indisputably demonstrates that no one person writes like another and that character is revealed through his chirology."

"Your research is of great interest to me, and I confess that I have dabbled in the subject myself."

"Very good. I would like to conduct an experiment if you are willing."

"Of course, I am perfectly willing," I replied.

Dupin retreated to another room and returned moments later carrying a portable writing desk, which he placed on the table in front of me. It was a fine piece made of ebony, inlaid with tortoise shell and brass. He lifted the upper lid and exposed a mahogany compartment complete with stationery, two inkwells, pounce holder, pens and other writing utensils. The front panel opened to reveal a leather writing surface, upon which Dupin placed a sheet of excellent paper—stout yet soft, with gilt edges.

"If you would oblige me with the following—please write your usual signature and today's date." After I had finished he said, "Now please write out the names Elizabeth Arnold and Henry Arnold and the year 1788."

When I had completed my task, Dupin placed two of the antique letters and the missive from Mrs. Allan that had accompanied my legacy next to the signatures I had just penned. He studied the four pieces of paper carefully.

"Interesting, a most interesting case. Look here at the 'E' and the 'A' in your signature. Now consider the 'E' and 'A' of Elizabeth Arnold's signature." Dupin held the two names side by side. "Quite a similarity between the construction of your characters and Elizabeth Arnold's."

I felt my face flush. "Sir, you are not suggesting that I am the true author of Elizabeth Arnold's letters?"

Dupin looked amused at my discomfiture. "Do not jump to conclusions. I am merely indicating a certain likeness of style." He indicated my attempts to write the Arnolds' names. "We can see here that your efforts are very different to the genuine signatures. Further, it is obvious to even the untrained eye that the paper of these letters is far older than that of your letter to me."

"But the age of the paper does not guarantee the letters' authenticity," I suggested.

"No, it does not, but let us examine the letters more precisely. Through the science of autography, we are able to learn much about an author's character as revealed through his or her hand-writing." Dupin indicated my letter to him. "The paper on which you wrote to me is excellent, the seal red. This indicates the refined taste of the author. The penmanship is highly legible and the punctuation is faultless. The lines are at proper intervals and perfectly straight. There are no superfluous flourishes and there is an air of deliberate precision to the writing, a mingled solidity and grace that speaks of the scholar."

I felt obliged to protest Dupin's flattery, but he waved his hand to silence me.

"Consider Elizabeth Arnold's letter. The paper is good, the seal small—of green wax—and without impression. This penmanship is quite different. The characters are well-sized, distinct and elegantly but not ostentatiously formed. The paper has a clean appearance, and she is scrupulously attentive to the margin. The t's are crossed with a sweeping scratch of the pen. While the letter is written with a very good running hand, the lines are not straight. One would suppose it written in a violent hurry. The whole air of the letter is dictatorial, but still sufficiently feminine. There is a good deal of spirit and some force."

"And Henry Arnold's letter?"

"Quite a different character. The writing has an air of swagger about it and would seem to indicate a mind without settled aims, restless and full of activity. The characters are bold, large, sprawling and frequently impaired by an undue straining after effect, but by no means illegible. There are too many dashes and the tails of the long letters are too long. Few of the characters are written twice in the same manner, and their direction varies continually. Sometimes the words lie perpendicularly on the page, then slope to the right, then fly off in an opposite way. The thickness of the characters is also changeable—sometimes very light and fine, sometimes excessively heavy. It would require no great stretch of fancy to imagine the writer to be a man of unbounded ambition, greatly interfered with by frequent moods of doubt and depression, and by unsettled ideas of the beautiful."

This interpretation did not surprise me when I remembered the content of the letters.

"And now we must consider the letter written by Mrs. Allan." Dupin picked up the folded paper and laid it flat before us. As he studied it, a frown settled between his brows. "You say this note accompanied the box of letters?"

"Yes, most assuredly."

"You are certain that Mrs. Allan composed it or you presume so?"

"Well, of course I must presume so." Dupin's frown deep-
ened, so I elaborated. "I have never exchanged letters with my
Pa's wife as she did not deign to respond to anything I sent her.
Her lawyer communicated with me about my disinheritance."

Dupin nodded, a satisfied expression on his face.

"Why do you ask? Do you suspect that the letter is not from
Mrs. Allan?"

"Do you?" Dupin puffed on his cigar and studied me, which
lent the uncomfortable sensation of being on trial.

"No, why would I? Does the handwriting indicate that someone else penned it? What does the handwriting suggest of Mrs.
Allan's character?" I hastily added before Dupin could counter
my question with one of his own.

He scanned the page again. "The author seems to take pains
with her handwriting—the letters are well-formed, every 't' is
crossed, every 'i' dotted, the punctuation is very precise and
there is a sense of uniformity throughout. This suggests a
methodical, determined character with a steadiness of purpose.
An autocratic air pervades the whole, however, and the sharp-
ness of the upstrokes and the downstrokes indicates a vengeful
nature. The flourishes, which are not many, seem deliberately
planned and firmly executed, as if the author is consciously
presenting a cultured façade to the world. The paper is very
good and the seal is gold, which adds to this illusion of cultiva-
tion. And while the handwriting has a pleasing overall
appearance, it differs from that of her sex in general by an air
of great force and its lack of feminine delicacy."

"I must say that this description of Mrs. Allan is more than
accurate. I am astonished how much of her character you are
able to fathom with the aid of such a short text."

Dupin narrowed his eyes slightly, but said nothing as he
looked carefully at each letter again before setting them down
upon the table. "Of course we must also reflect on the

similarities between elements of your handwriting and that of Elizabeth Arnold's. What secrets might this hold?" Dupin scrutinized my face as if it were handwriting on the page.

My desire to escape Dupin's questions overwhelmed me. "I am sorry, but I suddenly feel most unwell. I must either retire to my bed or seek air to refresh me."

Dupin gently placed his fingertips upon the letters before him and adjusted them into a perfect line. "I would advise fresh air," he said. "Perhaps you should visit the haunts of your youth, those associated with happier times. It is all too common to be held captive by one's own darker thoughts, and too much solitary contemplation leads one down the path toward madness." I felt my hackles rise at Dupin's unflattering words, but he continued before I could speak. "Your company in Paris saved me from myself, Poe. I did not like to admit it then, but I see it now. I trust you will allow me to return the favor. You were truthful with me then, and I hope you will always do me the honor of such candor."

No suitable response came to me, so I simply nodded.

"I have research I can pursue for the remainder of the day," Dupin continued. "Might we meet again this evening with refreshed minds? At eight o'clock at the Smyrna Coffee House in St. James's?"

"Very good. Thank you, Dupin."

He shrugged away my thanks. "May I keep the letters for now? I would like to study the details of the crimes."

"Of course." I left Dupin's rooms, already knowing what my destination would be that afternoon. I would walk to Bloomsbury parish where my Pa had rented apartments for our family more than twenty years previously. I had long been curious to see the place again.

* * *

The desk clerk that morning was a middle-aged man who was immaculately dressed but of dour demeanor. While I had the fanciful notion that my feet would guide me to my childhood home, I asked him for guidance in finding my destination and also some shops where I might purchase some charming fripperies for my wife and mother-in-law. The fellow was left-handed and held his pen at an awkward angle to avoid dragging his hand through the ink, but the map was elegantly drawn and noted several purveyors of ladies' finery.

I left Brown's Genteel Inn, map in hand, using my umbrella as a walking stick, and made my way down Dover Street to Piccadilly and on through Burlington Arcade, which had an array of wonderful shops. I was particularly captivated by window displays that ingeniously promoted the virtues of the products sold within. The hatters, for example, had a pair of scales in the window to prove the lightness of a hat and a glass globe filled with water in which a hat was placed to demonstrate its superior waterproofing. But it was on Oxford Street that I saw a window display that stilled my breath. A company of varying ages—three gentlemen, four ladies and three children—dressed in elegant mourning costumes, stood solemnly before an ornate casket decorated with a large immortelle wreath of porcelain lilies. This *tableau vivant* proved to be an illusion when a window dresser stepped amongst the wax figures to make adjustments to their funereal accouterments— black kidskin gloves, sober hats, necklaces of jet. I hurried away, determined to shake off the gloom that had descended upon me. I would look for gifts on the way back to Brown's.

My mood lightened again as I neared High Holborn, which was lively with a variety of pedestrians: coal-men delivering small barrows of coal to houses; girls carrying baskets upon their heads containing fresh vegetables and herbs for sale; men hurrying toward their places of employment; and women attending to the purchase of household necessities in the shops. A milkmaid wearing a yoke to carry her wares shouted "Milk!" at each person she wandered past, with little strategy and even less success in terms of selling her load. The distinctive sound of horse hooves on cobbles mixed with the rattle of the coaches, and the shouted commands of their drivers added to the bustle of this busy thoroughfare. Two men armed with shovels roved the area, collecting the manure deposited in copious amounts by the carriage horses. Straw was scattered on the walkways and in front of shops to aid the absorption of the previous night's rain, the mud and other less pleasant effluvia, but it did little to alleviate the stink, which was pungent as old meat and amplified to a terrible degree. I soon wished that I had doused my handkerchief with cologne.

After turning into Southampton Row, I quickly located number forty-seven. It was our first home in London, quite a cozy place where I spent a few pleasant months with Ma and her sister Nancy before being sent away to boarding school in Chelsea. The exterior was tidy enough but not exceptional—a plain brick façade similar to its companions along the row. I had remembered the architecture as far more imposing, but youth's perspective tends to exaggerate the scale of things. I felt an urge to knock on the door and ask to see inside, but decided against this foolish whim. Instead, I walked the short distance back down to number thirty-nine, a rather larger apartment my Pa had rented during our final year in London. While the lodgings were more commodious, they had held little joy for me during my brief time spent within their walls due to my dear Ma's unhappiness. As if in sympathy with this memory, a light rain began to fall, and I unfurled my umbrella. Tempted as I was to return to the comfort of Brown's Genteel Inn, first I wished to go to Russell Square, a park I had visited often with my Aunt Nancy. She was charged with my care when I returned home from boarding school for holidays or a special weekend, and was typically as eager as I was to escape the confines of our Bloomsbury home when the weather was fine.

When I turned into Russell Square, I entered the park at the entrance near a curious statue that had fascinated me as a child. Francis Russell, fifth Duke of Bedford, had one hand upon a plough and ears of corn clutched in the other. Beneath his pedestal, there was a sheep and four cherubs representing the seasons, all quite unclothed with the exception of a heavily bundled up "Winter." I had remembered the statue as poetic, imbued with the very spirit of agriculture, but with maturity found it over-stated and somewhat repellent. Keen to further my exploration, I made my way along the horseshoe-shaped pathway under the lime trees, and was pleased to discover that Russell Square was quite as I had remembered it: neatly laid out and well-planted with attractive flowers and shrubbery, not quite the English garden my Ma had so admired, but dignified and pleasing to the eye. Due to the inclement weather, the square was empty of the attractive, well-dressed ladies who had strolled through the pathways when I was a child, which made the place rather less picturesque.

I thought to rest a bit on one of the seats in the trellis-covered shelter, but found a bedraggled woman sitting there, a small child tucked up under her shawl. As I stared at this apparition, an inexplicable sense of dread came over me. Shaking off my nervousness, I set down my umbrella and fumbled inside my frock coat for the purse that hung from my belt, determined to give the woman some coins for her child. Suddenly, my head was blasted with pain, the ground tilted, and I fell to a place of perfect stillness.

* * *

How much later was it that I came back to myself? I could not fathom this with any accuracy. As the world emerged from shadow, I found blue eyes staring into my own and felt damp earth against my cheek. My head throbbed, and there was a tugging at my frock coat and then a hand wormed its way into my trousers pocket. What insult was this? I thrashed out and heard a yelp. When I struggled to a sitting position, a small urchin was squatting next to me. His mother was busily scrambling backward down the footpath, fear imprinted upon her features. Then I heard the sound of running footsteps and turned to see her accomplice dashing in the opposite direction. Another woman! Slight of build and fleet of foot, the treacherous pickpocket vanished. I patted at my chest and discovered with much relief that my locket was still in place. Only my purse was gone, the contents of which I had been willing to give to the woman with the child in charity, but now I had a sore head for my efforts and felt most aggrieved.

"Go to your mother," I said to the small creature. "Leave me quickly or I will thrash you with this umbrella." As I shook it feebly, the child scuttled away as fast as its broken shoes would allow.

I got to my feet. The unpleasant sensation of my wet clothing and the additional discomfort of my throbbing head brought me back to full cognizance. As I tidied myself as best I could with my handkerchief, I discovered the most extraordinary thing. In my buttonhole was a small boutonnière of violets—artificial flowers of purple and green velvet so precisely crafted they appeared to be genuine upon first glance. I had most assuredly not been wearing them earlier and the only explanation for their mysterious appearance upon my person was that my attackers had attached them to my frock coat. The thought repelled me so utterly I threw the thing away from me as if it harbored some creeping disease. A deep foreboding settled upon me, and as much as I tried to divert my thoughts away from those feral mendicants, they haunted me as I made my way back toward Brown's. There was something terribly *familiar* about them. I revisited the attack again and again as I hurried through the London streets—the mind is like a box with many locked compartments and the secrets therein are recovered when the correct key is found. I was determined to find that key. The violet boutonnière tickled at my memory until I remembered where I had first come across those seemingly innocent velvet flowers.

* * *

"You will receive a fine education, my boy. That I promise you. And you will make us proud, won't you, Eddy?"

"I will do my best, Pa."

It was the day of my interview at the Dubourg boarding school in Chelsea. The school was run by two sisters—the Misses Dubourg—whose brother was a bookkeeper at my father's company. The interview with the two ladies went very well. They declared me a "delightful boy," so Pa decided to take Ma, Aunt Nancy and me for a celebratory luncheon nearby. We had walked just a short distance from the school when we came across a peculiar character, a gaunt ragbag of a man who wore several hats upon his head and, it seemed, all of his clothing at once, with an old military jacket over the top. He had but one arm and wore a long beard that was yellowed from the sulfurous fumes of hell, or so I imagined. A wonderful wooden ship and an old cap sat in front of him; Aunt Nancy hastily dropped some small coins into the cap as we passed him.

"Have you bought me the ship?" I cried delightedly.

She flushed quite crimson. "Hush," she whispered as she grabbed my arm and marched me smartly away.

one's parent nation. You must hope ⟨...⟩ with it."

I nodded, but hoped no such thing. War seemed a great adventure to me, especially battles at sea with flying cannon balls, the pirates' sails ablaze and treasure sinking to the bottom of the sea. Then an extraordinary sight was revealed to me. On the street outside a somber building we came upon a crowd of men in uniforms—both sailors and soldiers—and their uniforms were in a condition as tattered as the men themselves, most of whom had lost an arm or a leg. As I gaze⟨d⟩ a fearful notion sprang into my head.

"Is there to be another war, Pa? Will they come to fight with us again?" I had no true memory of the War of 1812, but had overheard my adoptive father speak with much fervor of its repercussions on his business.

Pa laughed heartily. "Should those men come to fight us it would be a very short battle."

I nodded, trying to pretend that I understood, but noted that my Ma frowned at her husband. "Hush, now, John." She grasped my hand and said, "That is the Royal Military Hospital and those poor men were grievously injured in the war. Th⟨...⟩ sacrificed much for their coun⟨...⟩ pension f⟨...⟩

"War is an evil thing, Eddy, most particularly war against..st hope you never are faced

his living, or he must plead for charity."

much use in the navy, and so he must find other ways to make

as does the empty sleeve of it. A one-armed sailor is not of

and the ragged jacket he wears suggests that he has seen battle,

explained. "His wooden ship informs us that he was a sailor,

"We did not need to speak to the man to know his story," Pa

smiled up at both of them.

"But you will tell me." I took her hand and my mother's and

It is enough to drive one quite mad."

Aunt Nancy sighed with exasperation. "So many questions!

did not speak to the man."

I was mightily confused. "But how do you know that? We

fighting against us."

"And so he deserved to," said my Pa, "for indeed he was

anxiously at my Pa as she spoke and was terribly flustered.

who suffer. He lost his arm fighting for his country." She looked

It is called charity," my Ma said. "We must be kind to those

..e him money? He is a grown man."

..y. I gave him money for

..ezed at the military men,

I eventually managed to wriggle out of her grasp and planted myself in front of her. "Why did you pay him for the ship and leave it behind?" I demanded.

"I did not pay him for the ship, Eddy. I gave him money for food."

"Why give him money? He is a grown man."

"It is called charity," my Ma said. "We must be kind to those who suffer. He lost his arm fighting for his country." She looked anxiously at my Pa as she spoke and was terribly flustered.

"And so he deserved to," said my Pa, "for indeed he was fighting against us."

I was mightily confused. "But how do you know that? We did not speak to the man."

Aunt Nancy sighed with exasperation. "So many questions! It is enough to drive one quite mad."

"But you will tell me." I took her hand and my mother's and smiled up at both of them.

"We did not need to speak to the man to know his story," Pa explained. "His wooden ship informs us that he was a sailor, and the ragged jacket he wears suggests that he has seen battle, as does the empty sleeve of it. A one-armed sailor is not of much use in the navy, and so he must find other ways to make his living, or he must plead for charity."

"War is an evil thing, Eddy, most particularly war against one's parent nation. You must hope you never are faced with it."

I nodded, but hoped no such thing. War seemed a great adventure to me, especially battles at sea with flying cannon balls, the pirates' sails ablaze and treasure sinking to the bottom of the sea. Then an extraordinary sight was revealed to me. On the street outside a somber building we came upon a crowd of men in uniforms—both sailors and soldiers—and their uniforms were in a condition as tattered as the men themselves, most of whom had lost an arm or a leg. As I gazed at the military men, a fearful notion sprang into my head.

"Is there to be another war, Pa? Will they come to fight with us again?" I had no true memory of the War of 1812, but had overheard my adoptive father speak with much fervor of its repercussions on his business.

Pa laughed heartily. "Should those men come to fight us it would be a very short battle."

I nodded, trying to pretend that I understood, but noted that my Ma frowned at her husband. "Hush, now, John." She grasped my hand and said, "That is the Royal Military Hospital and those poor men were grievously injured in the war. They sacrificed much for their country and are here to collect a pension for their services."

This I did not understand. "But surely we are not paid for our sacrifices. A sacrifice is given quite freely."

My Ma frowned more deeply and my Pa roared with laughter, throwing me into a state of confusion as I had hoped to please both of them with my precocious learning.

"The boy will make a very fine businessman, that is certain! Education will indeed be the making of him." He slapped his thigh and laughed again.

I was pleased to make my father proud and stared at the bedraggled men, unaware of their precarious position in life. Once I took up residence at the Dubourg School, I became accustomed to seeing beggars—male and female—on the streets of Chelsea and began to recognize several who sat in the same spot every day, their tales written out on cards and placed in front of them or scratched in chalk onto the pavement. I noticed one in particular, a woman who sat daily quite near our school, with her hand outstretched for alms, a basket of artificial nosegays next to her. Sometimes she had an infant wrapped up in her shawl and on other occasions there was a small child in her lap. I noticed her particularly as I could not fathom how a lady could be a soldier turned beggar, and did not understand at all what the flowers symbolized except perhaps the fallen on the battlefield. It is with shame that I recall my scorn for those poor souls, thinking them indolent wretches just as my entrepreneurial Pa did.

Fate eventually saw to punish me for this haughty contempt. It was the Christmas season, and I was in an excitable mood, very glad to be back home. To give my Ma some respite, Aunt Nancy was charged with taking me to Noah's Ark toy shop in High Holborn. We had a glorious time there, and it was quite dark when we returned to our dwellings on Southampton Row. As we approached closer, I noticed a figure huddled near the entrance, a basket of artificial flowers next to her—it was the beggar woman who sat so often outside my school. She held out a nosegay of dainty violets.

"Here, darling. Come over here. Take one for your mother. It's close on Christmas."

I looked to my Auntie, but saw that she was engaged in conversation with a man who seemed to be asking for directions. The woman smiled kindly at me. She was a good deal older than my Ma, closer in years to my Pa's mother.

"She can pin it on her dress or in her hair and will look very fine indeed."

I thought the nosegay would make a good present for my Ma—it was pretty and would look very well on her. "What must I pay you?" I asked.

"What's your name, son?" she asked in return.

"Eddy."

She nodded. "I've been told your mother was a great actress, Eddy."

This compliment had the desired effect upon me. "Yes, she was. But she died when I was very young."

She smiled kindly. "Ah, but you're alive and your new family must be very wealthy."

I nodded, for so it seemed. "But I do not get much pocket money," I added, "so I hope the nosegay is not so very dear."

The beggar lady laughed. "No, indeed it's not, for I will give it to you." She handed me the bunch of purple velvet violets just as Aunt Nancy joined me.

"It is for Ma," I said proudly. "A Christmas present."

She frowned, but my excitement must have persuaded her against making me return the nosegay. "How much?" she asked the beggar lady.

"A penny," the beggar woman interjected before I could speak. "You won't find a better nosegay made anywhere in London."

Nancy sighed and fished a coin from her purse before dragging me inside.

Later that same week, Aunt Nancy was charged with taking me to Russell Square, where I forced her to play catch with me until she was quite worn out. She went to fetch us some roasted chestnuts from a vendor not fifty yards away and as I carried on with my game, tossing the ball up into the air as high as I could and running to catch it, I noticed a small child approach my Auntie and tug at her dress. This I found impertinent and was shocked when my Aunt gave the child a bag of chestnuts. But before I could voice my childish rage, the very ground disappeared from under my feet, and I found myself being conveyed at speed through the park, clutched by some stranger whose face I could not see. A dirty rag was stuffed into my mouth, cutting short my yells of anger and terror. I could see little but the ground bouncing beneath my abductor's feet, which were encased in broken-down boots made from grubby, brown leather—men's boots, but worn by a woman with legs like a plough-horse. The reek of her much-patched dress was similarly equine, months of sweat woven into the fabric and arising from its threads like fumes of manure on a hot day. She wheezed with the effort of carrying me, and as the shock began to subside, I struggled in her inordinately strong arms.

"Hold still, you brat," she commanded, but I kicked and thrashed like a caught fish until at last we both went tumbling to the ground. I scrambled to my feet and wrenched the filthy kerchief from my mouth as I ran back to Nancy, who threw her arms around me.

"Catch her!" Nancy shrieked as the beggar woman and the child ran for the gate. "Catch her!" But the beggar woman and the child eluded capture. I clung to Nancy, unnerved by my experience. She had lost all color, and I could feel her quivering. "You must not tell your parents of this," my Auntie said. "Your Ma will be dreadfully upset."

However, once home my fear dissipated, and I could not help but brag of my bold behavior in staving off my abductor. My tale did not have quite the effect I intended. My Ma fell into a faint and my Auntie immediately burst into tears.

"It was that beggar woman who has been sitting outside our doorway all the week," Nancy sobbed.

"And outside my school since before Christmas," I added.

Silence took hold of the three of them as they stared at me.

"Your school? Are you quite sure?" Pa asked sternly.

I nodded. "She is there most every day, selling flowers."

My Ma started her weeping again, and I was very quickly sorry that I had not listened to my Aunt.

"To your room, Eddy," my Pa commanded.

"But Pa, it is not my fault."

"Now," he answered.

After a day or two of much hushed discussion and tearful interludes, it was decided that I would go to a new boarding school in the countryside immediately after the holidays.

"You will be safe from the rabble there," my Ma whispered before kissing my forehead. "I could not bear for any harm to come to you, darling."

"Nor I you," I whispered.

And so I was sent away from my dear Ma to keep me safe from all the wretched flower sellers of London town.

The Cooper's Arms
Rose Street, Covent Garden
12 April 1784

My Rose, my Daisy, my Columbine,
Every flower makes me think of you. I would give
you scented violets and pansies to secure your thoughts.
I should send you rosemary for remembrance. Pray,
love! Have you forgotten me? I wear my heart upon my
sleeve for daws to peck at, but have had no word from
you since Thursday. Am I but a poor player that struts
and frets his hour upon the stage and then is heard no
more? Have your affections flitted elsewhere?
A pair of star cross'd lovers we may be when under
your father's hand. Saturday is the day to make our
own face. Come away with me—to liberty and not to
banishment. Your father will forgive you when you
return a wife. What father can ever refuse the truest
desires of his only daughter?
I await your letter and kisses,
Henry

20 Upper Brook Street, Mayfair
13 April 1784

Henry, my darling,
Do you think me so inconstant that I would forget
you? My heart is yours only, but think not of Juliet or

Desdemona or Ophelia when you think of me! And pray, be constant to one of the Bard's plays, one about love and with a happy resolution. Consider *A Midsummer Night's Dream*—it holds a mirror to some scenes from our story. It is indeed true that the course of true love never did run smooth.

These last few days I have tried to reason with my father, who thinks me a child at sixteen—a child he would marry off to a man twenty years my senior, with one wife already dead and buried. Marriage must be wed to love, but my father would invoke Athenian law given the opportunity. He cares not that I have no feelings for the banker, only for my security and status, both of which he threatens to withhold if I disobey him.

Could you still love me if you were all I had in the world? I await your answer.

Yours,
Elizabeth

The Cooper's Arms,
Rose Street, Covent Garden
14 April 1784

My Dearest Love,
One play is not enough to reveal my heart to you. If I must borrow every line of Shakespeare to persuade you to be mine, then borrow with abandon I will.

Doubt that the sun doth move, doubt truth to be a liar, but never doubt I love you and you alone. Your father could indeed find you a better match if marrying happily is wealthily. Who steals my purse steals trash, but he that filches from me my good name robs me of that which not enriches him and makes me poor indeed. I have little to offer of material riches, but all that glisters is not gold. Devotion is the jewel of my soul.

If your father must play the role of Egeus, then you must be Hermia and I, Lysander. My childless Aunt in the country is called Gretna Green. Let me take you to visit her. Your father will forgive us in time. No father can abandon his only daughter forever.

      Yours and yours alone,
      Henry

It was six o'clock by the time I arrived back at Brown's, where the desk clerk greeted me with a smile, despite my unfortunate appearance. He acquiesced politely when I requested that a hot bath be drawn for me and brought out a small packet from behind the desk.

"This arrived not long after you left, sir."

My heart leapt with expectation—a letter from Mr. Dickens! But when I looked more closely, I became doubtful, for surely the packet contained more than one letter. Perhaps Mr. Dickens had entrusted me with a tale—I had, after all, sent him a full collection. Or perhaps he was returning my tales with unfavorable news. It was with these conflicting emotions that I took the packet to my room.

I discovered that it was not from Mr. Dickens at all; in fact, the identity of the sender was a mystery, as no note was included, which made the packet's contents all the more chilling. Fourteen letters were inside, all antique, separated into two bundles, each tied with a length of green ribbon, which looked to be very new. I untied the first bundle of three letters and instantly recognized the handwriting as that of Elizabeth and Henry Arnold. The letters dated from 1784 and were older than the others in my possession; I read them with numbed stupefaction. I then untied the ribbon that secured the second bundle and glanced at the first few missives: one a peculiar Valentine and the next an account of yet another attack. Nausea overwhelmed me and my vision was so compromised I could barely see the third letter. I was finally released from my torpor by a knock upon my door and the voice of a servant informing me that my bath was ready. I thanked the girl for her timely arrival and scurried to the bathroom, relieved to escape whatever miserable tale the other letters held.

As I eased into the steaming water, confusion misted my mind. If Mrs. Allan—my adoptive father's widow—were the author of this dreadful hoax, how could she have known I was in London and staying at Brown's Genteel Inn? The bruises I had sustained in the attack began to throb, so I sank further into the bath, but felt the tip of a boot catch my ribs again. A shadow fell over me and with horror I saw the urchin's face leaning over mine and felt someone's hands pressing down upon my chest. My head began to sink and water seeped into my mouth—I thrashed and fought until finally I pulled myself into a sitting position. My gasps echoed through the tiled bathroom as I crouched in the tub, overcome by fear, until the water went cold and brought me back to myself. I realized that if I did not make haste, I would be late to meet Dupin, which would cause him to ask me questions I did not wish to answer.

* * *

Less than half an hour later, Dupin and I were seated by the front window of the Smyrna Coffee House, which looked out onto St. James's Street. Although my gaze was directed toward the outside world, my mind was distracted by all that had happened to me earlier that day. And yet I did not confide in

Dupin, I know not why. Instead I waited to hear what conclusions he had drawn from his further study of the letters. He was smoking a cigar, and it was unclear whether he was looking through the glass or if his gaze was lost within the smoke. He had not said a word since we had greeted each other, but this behavior was not unusual. When Dupin did not wish to speak, he was simply silent. He cared little for the niceties of polite company, but something was different on this occasion. His silence was neither companionable nor distant. There was an edge of hostility to it.

To distract myself from Dupin's mood and my own fears, I tried to focus on the people jostling along outside. There were women of all kinds: the beauty in her prime; the heavily painted and bejeweled woman of later years presenting a façade of youth; and the child dressed to exceed her age, coquettish and sly. There were men of privilege striding confidently and drunkards in battered clothing moving with an unsteady swagger. An assortment of professions was represented on the street, from artisan to laborer.

"If you observe carefully enough, you will discern various tribes within the crowd," Dupin said, breaking his silence at last. He pointed with his cigar at a small mob that had entered the coffee house. "Clerks," he said, "but of a junior order."

I studied the young gentlemen in tight coats with brightly polished boots and well-oiled hair. This was a kind of game we had often played in Paris—Dupin would make a cryptic observation, and I would try to fathom his deductive processes before he inevitably proved himself correct.

"And these here," Dupin continued, "upper clerks of established firms."

Those Dupin had labeled junior clerks had a supercilious manner and their clothing was the very height of fashion eighteen months previously. The upper clerks wore more somber clothes: brown or black pantaloons designed for comfort, coats, white cravats, waistcoats and solid shoes.

"I see the differences in the dress of these characters, those being rather too flash and the others far more somber and restrained, but I cannot guess why you presume them to be clerks?"

Dupin exhaled a fog of cigar smoke, adding to the patina on the windows, and waved a finger at the upper clerks. "Notice that these men all have somewhat balding heads. We have discussed their somber clothing. They all wear watches with short gold chains. The façade they strive for is respectability."

This was undeniable.

"See how their right ears are bent in a curious direction?" he continued.

"Yes?"

"The oddness of their right ears is from habitually holding a pen behind them."

Dupin's theory seemed as likely as any other to explain the clerks' odd ears.

"And this man here is of neither group. Indeed, he is accustomed to working alone." Dupin indicated a man of dashing appearance who had an expression of excessive frankness. "Notice his voluminous wristband."

"Pickpocket?"

"Indeed. He is a speedy judge of occupation and temperament. He knows at a glance which character is likely to provide him with the most sport."

At that moment, we were delivered two large bowls of meat stew with bread. Its fragrance made my belly ache with hunger, and I attacked my dinner with unseemly haste. Dupin extinguished his cigar and approached his food with what could only be described as caution. He prodded at the contents of his bowl for a time without partaking.

"I can assure you it is rather good, and I have not expired from the ingredients."

Dupin acknowledged my words with a nod. He dipped his spoon into the bowl, paused to inspect the stew more closely, then tasted it cautiously. His face was the picture of restrained disgust as he pushed the dish away. After a gulp of wine he returned his gaze to me.

"It seems the Arnolds are no mere figments of Mrs. Allan's imagination," he said, lighting another cigar. "They existed. Indeed I have found evidence of their elopement."

His words caused me to choke on my food. "But how did you come to know that?" I spluttered, when the coughing subsided. A strange brew of emotions flooded through me, with indignation chief amongst them. Had Dupin read the letters left for me? Had he been the one to leave the letters at the desk? I breathed deeply to calm myself and dispel my irrational thoughts.

Dupin retrieved a sheet of paper from his pocket and slid it toward me. "I located this announcement in *The Morning Post* when I was consulting the Burney Collection at the British Museum today and took the liberty of copying it."

I unfolded the paper to reveal Dupin's small, precise handwriting.

ANNOUNCEMENT

Miss Elizabeth Smith, the sixteen-year-old daughter of William Smith, eloped on Saturday the seventeenth of April 1784 from her father's house in Mayfair to Gretna Green with Mr. Henry Arnold, twenty-three years of age. The particulars are these: the Smith family had an evening of entertainment planned at Vauxhall Gardens, but Miss Smith suffered a dizzy spell and remained at home with her maid to attend to her. Miss Smith's indisposition proved to be a clever performance, however, and she and her maid spirited themselves away from the house and were met by Mr. Arnold in a post-chaise. They drove off into the night, and it was not discovered until morning that she had gone missing. Mr. Smith was highly angered to learn of his daughter's elopement. He had opposed the match as Mr. Arnold had been a footman and was lately "of the theatre", a profession Mr. Smith deemed unsuitable for the husband of his daughter. He had forbidden Miss Smith to have any contact with Mr. Arnold, but she is a young lady of stubborn and impulsive character. The two continued to meet in secret despite her father's wishes and the plan was concocted to defy him with an elopement to Gretna Green. It is said that Mr. Smith remains highly piqued with his daughter's actions and it is uncertain whether he will recognise her impetuous marriage.

I could feel my face warm with a rush of blood. "Are you quite certain this is genuine?"

"Most certain," Dupin said calmly. "I have no reason to deceive you."

"I was not suggesting that."

Dupin raised his eyebrows; it was clear he had discerned the hint of mistrust upon my face.

"I am sorry if I seem ill at ease, Dupin, but my nerves are dreadfully agitated. I was attacked when walking through Russell Square this afternoon, and harridans made off with the purse I was about to give them in charity."

"It grieves me to hear that. It is unfortunate that mendicants are often not content to beg for charity."

"There was more to it than that. Something rather peculiar."

I hesitated to mention the boutonnière, but Dupin stared at me expectantly. "It seems the thieves placed a boutonnière of artificial violets in my frock coat buttonhole. I must say it disturbed me rather more than the theft."

Dupin frowned. "May I see this boutonnière? It is singularly odd to leave such a token and certainly significant."

"I am afraid I threw the thing from me—I felt most repelled by it."

"Foolish, very foolish. It was evidence that might lead us to a larger crime," Dupin snapped, his face tense with an anger deeper than the situation merited. "Violets," he muttered as if to himself before turning his gaze back to me. "Do violets have any significance to you? Some meaning I should be aware of?"

"Perhaps. After the attack I remembered an incident from my childhood, an incident so disturbing I was forbidden to speak of it at home. I had all but put it from my mind until this morning."

"Go on."

As I recounted the details of the artificial-flower seller's attempt to kidnap me all those years ago, Dupin's frown deepened. "Extraordinary," he said when I had finished my tale. "I am surprised you did not immediately inform me of your attack," he added stiffly.

"There is more," I confessed, anxious to reveal everything at once. "When I returned to Brown's, these letters were at the desk. I have read these three," I said, handing him the smaller bundle, "which seem to have a bearing on what you have just told me."

His look of suppressed anger was replaced by intense concentration as he unfolded the first letter of the collection and quickly read it. "1784. How interesting."

"Interesting? Uncanny may be the better word."

Dupin tilted his head. "Made to seem so, perhaps."

"I am sorry, Dupin, but I am not following you."

He waved his hand dismissively as he scanned the next two letters. "And the others?" He nodded at the second bundle in my hand.

"I glanced at the first few, which are reminiscent of those delivered in the box. I am not certain that I wish to read the remainder." I placed the second bundle on the table before him.

"But you must."

I shook my head. "I would rather you read them first. I am confused by today's revelation and will not come to any sensible conclusion."

Dupin nodded, making it all too clear that he agreed with me. "I presume there was no note from Mrs. Allan with these letters."

I shook my head.

"Then of course we must deduce that she did not write the original note."

"Must we? It is possible she hired someone to leave the letters for me."

"Why would she do so? Why not simply deliver all the letters to you at once—the mahogany box is certainly capacious enough to hold all of them."

"To torment me."

Dupin frowned again. "Certainly someone wishes to torment you, but I do not believe it is Mrs. Allan. From your description of her, it is unlikely she has the strategic skills to engineer such a complex plan. As Mrs. Allan has secured all your adoptive father's property for herself, why go to the trouble of torturing you with letters?"

"To make me think I come from bad blood. To persuade me she was right to coerce my Pa into disowning me."

Dupin leaned back and relit his cigar. I realized from the expressions of the clerks assembled around us that I had been shouting.

"And may we now directly state that you know Elizabeth and Henry Arnold to be your maternal grandparents?" he said, exhaling a plume of smoke.

I could feel the flame of guilt ignite my face.

"You knew all along," he said, his eyes never leaving mine, "but you chose not to make the facts plain to me. I must wonder why."

I turned my gaze to the window. Evening had faded away, and lamplight illuminated the street with a garish luster. The crowd had altered as well, harsher characters predominating over more orderly folk. The effects of the light brought individual faces into focus if only for a moment and in that instant I felt that I grasped the history of each character caught in the shimmering glare, that I had assumed Dupin's uncanny ability to read a person's most private secrets.

"Poe?"

"You have studied the letters. Would you so easily admit that those who supposedly wrote them were the parents of your beloved mother?"

Dupin appraised me coolly. "You are right to say 'supposedly'. We have only just begun our investigation and still have not ascertained whether the letters were truly written by the Arnolds. But we will make no progress if we deceive each other. Truth must prevail between us or there is no reason to pursue this case together. You forget, my friend, how well I know you."

He was right, of course, but I could not bring myself to say so and simply nodded.

"We may then agree the following facts: Elizabeth and Henry Arnold genuinely existed and are not figments of a hoaxer's imagination, although their letters might be; they were your maternal grandparents; and they were married twice in 1784."

"Twice?"

"Yes. First they eloped on the seventeenth of April and then they were married at the Parish church of St. George, Hanover Square. I took the liberty of copying the announcement from *The Morning Post*. The marriage occurred on the eighteenth of May 1784."

I gave the paper a perfunctory glance for I had no doubt that Dupin had copied the notice precisely. "But why?" I muttered.

"You are missing the obvious hidden in plain sight. Elizabeth Smith and Henry Arnold eloped to Gretna Green. This caused a scandal. Mr. Smith was a man of substantial means and good social standing. It was less damaging to his status if the runaway couple were married in a church after the elopement. The marriage would appear sanctioned and the scandal quelled. Of course this would not prevent Mr. Smith from disowning his daughter."

Dupin's explanation was plausible. "And so, cut off from her father's support, my grandmother began her precarious life as an actress on the stage, a life repeated by my mother in America. I am doubly cursed with the affliction of penury if my grandmother was also denied a comfortable life that I might have inherited."

Dupin shrugged. "It would seem that your grandmother chose love over money. Whether an honorable or foolish choice is not yet clear, but you might perhaps take comfort in her idealism."

"But you believe my grandfather was less idealistic?" I said as the thought came to me.

Dupin shrugged again. "Certainly his handwriting gives no indication of idealism, and he had far more to gain financially from their marriage than she did. Indeed, he seemed to think Elizabeth's father would forgive her idealism and welcome her husband into the family fold, despite his lower social standing."

"Are you saying he duped her?"

"Duped? No. But her social position may have made her more attractive to him, which is not so different to her father hoping she would find the wealthy banker who was twenty years her senior attractive enough to marry. But the important issue is this: Elizabeth and Henry Arnold existed. Did they pen the letters in your possession and commit the crimes outlined within them? Perhaps."

"And perhaps not," I added quickly. "They were actors after all. Let us imagine they *did* write the letters. The contents might be an elaborate fantasy."

"It is possible," Dupin admitted. "We must ascertain the truth. And we must also discover who is sending Elizabeth and Henry Arnold's letters to you, and how they came to possess those letters."

I knew Dupin was trying to help, but his dispassionate words distressed me. The surety of my life in Philadelphia was a distant dream and nothing in my past was as certain as I had once thought. Were my grandparents common criminals? It pained me greatly to think it might be so. My attention drifted back to the window and the faces illuminated by pools of light, a dreamscape and yet somehow more truthful than reality. Suddenly, the face of an old man appeared in the window. He was perhaps seventy-five years of age, frail and disheveled. There was a curious blankness to his expression and yet he simultaneously exuded a mixture of detachment, malice and power.

"It is *him!*" I said the words before I understood their meaning. The old man was frozen in front of me, his face splashed with light and framed by the windowpane. The countenance, the shabby posture, the lurching walk—everything was familiar and yet I could not place the circumstance. And then he was gone. I seized my hat and cane, and ran from the coffee house to the street.

He was nowhere in sight and for a moment I felt the deepest despair. Then, I spied a shadow moving with uneven steps down a narrow lane and recklessly followed. The lane was very dark, and I moved forward slowly, not wishing to attract notice to myself. The fine mist that danced in the air transformed into steady rain. The cobbles were slick underfoot, the air thick with the scent of moldering vegetation. The alleyway turned sharply and opened up into a busier thoroughfare. I had lost all sense of direction, but was determined not to lose sight of my quarry and no longer cared if the old man understood that I was pursuing him. We approached a theater as its audience exited with much jollity, and then we arrived at a tavern crowded with unsavory characters. The old man seemed immune to either atmosphere. A maze of crooked lanes took us through a shabby area where only the most destitute lived. The old man's pace increased again—I chased him down a passageway and found that I was at the end of Dover Street, staring at the lights of Brown's Genteel Inn.

Incomprehensible rage filled me. How had he known my eventual destination? Was this a diabolical trick? Before the old man could commence his endless walking again, I placed myself in front of him, blocking his path. At last, we were face to face.

"Who are you, sir?" I demanded.

The old man quivered but said nothing. His eyes were closed, his lips trembled with gibberish.

"Tell me!" I grabbed the greasy folds of his coat and shook him. There was no weight to him and he flew up off the ground until the backs of his heels rattled against the brick wall. I squeezed his arms tighter and repeated my command, but the old man simply folded in on himself, eyes closed, twitching like a starved bird.

"Tell me!"

At last, he opened his eyes. They were of the palest blue, clouded with white—a vulture's eye. The old man looked into me and then right through me.

"I am nobody," he said in a voice frail as dead leaves skittering through air. "I am nobody at all."

14 February 1789

FOR MY VALENTINE

My heart, Valentine, and a key with this box,
Open it to find where our secrets are locked.
Night's curtain rises—what a bold masquerade!
Swashbuckling rogue armed with Cupid's blade
Tatters proud wenches (more thrilled than
    afraid).
Each cutting performance on London's stage,
Remembered with pleasure upon the page.

22 Jermyn Street, London
18 May 1789

My darling Husband,

    Who would imagine that abandoning our vagabond
life to return to London would bring me such sorrow?
How unlike Lady Teazle I am in that! Of course you
must pursue the opportunity for us in Bristol, but
understand that no wife is content to spend the fifth
anniversary of her church wedding apart from her
husband. I have been so miserable with loneliness and
idleness that I took up your challenge to continue our
private School for Scandal—with great success! As I
cannot whisper every delicious detail into your ear
tonight, I will put pen to paper for your delectation.

All of London will soon be lively with the tale of a most curious incident that occurred on Leicester Street. The lead player in the drama was Mrs. Sarah Godfrey—you may recall her as a frequent theatre-goer, despite her limited comprehension of the Art. She is the female (I hesitate to say lady) who was overheard making ill-considered comments about your interpretation of Sir Benjamin Backbite three nights ago. Her own performance unfolded in the following manner.

Mrs. Godfrey was walking unaccompanied along Bond Street. She was intrepidly attired in an indigo silk dress, its skirt boldly striped with white, its bodice decorated with lace ruffles that frothed over-merrily around her décolletage. The declamatory dress and her gaudy manner captured the attention of a young rogue who was dallying in the area. As she drew closer, he noted her identity and was infused with the desire to tutor the self-described lady of fashion in the art of etiquette. Mrs. Godfrey's would-be instructor followed her from Bond Street into Leicester Square and then into Piccadilly. He was a handsome, middle-sized man dressed in black and wearing a splendid cocked hat. Sometimes he walked before her, sometimes behind her, and occasionally he kept pace by her side. She pretended ignorance of his existence, but a smile revealed decided pleasure in the young man's attentions.

When Mrs. Godfrey reached her destination, her pursuer was overcome with delight. An upholsterer's shop! This made perfect sense of her costume. The lady had disguised herself as a piece of furniture! While the fabric of her skirts was unsuitable for a fashionable dress, it would look quite fine on a whimsical ottoman or an overwrought armchair.

Mrs. Godfrey took that moment to present the gallant with a half-curtsy. "Thank you, sir," she simpered, waiting for the young gentleman to open the shop door for her. As he complied, the rascal took the opportunity to bow deeply and declare, "You are indeed a fine sofa, madam."

The lady did not know what to make of the compliment and scurried into the shop. But the rogue was not finished with her. He waited until she re-emerged from the house of fabrics and shadowed her all the way back to Charlotte Street. She seemed to sense he was there, glancing over her shoulder from time to time, but did not call out. Before she could escape into her residence, the scoundrel attacked.

"Ho!" A dagger sliced through the air and the brash silk upholstery melted away like butter under a hot knife. "There, you!" The blade flashed again and he pinned the plump cushion of her upper thigh. Never has a piece of furniture shrieked so loudly. The poor little sofa overturned herself onto the ground, legs thrown in the air, her tatty undersides quite exposed. When she came back to herself, the monstrous fellow had disappeared into the darkness.

And so must end my intrepid tale. Alas, the written play is never as exciting as its enactment. When you are here again by my side, my darling, I promise a thrilling encore.

Send word soonest,
Elizabeth

The Theatre Royal, Bristol
21 May 1789

My Darling,

Rehearsals have at last finished and my fingers are worn to the bone from playing each song repeatedly as the silly girl cannot retain the lyric, despite the emptiness of her head. If only it were you in her place—how much happier we all would be! Of course I miss you and Eliza acutely, but it is work, though not <u>acting</u>, and I am made less miserable by the wages.

But your letter! I read it not once, but three times as soon as I opened it, as the account of your lively performance brought me such cheer. How admirably you met my challenge! And how like the conceited Mrs. Godfrey to presume a young man to be an admirer rather than an assailant—I pictured the scene completely and could not contain my mirth. My amusement was compounded when I read in *The World* of Mrs. Godfrey's complaint to the Bow Street magistrate. According to your aggrieved victim, the ruffian who approached her outside the upholstery shop made "a very indecent proposal" and "grossly insulted her". Again, how I laughed when I thought back to your letter. "You are indeed a fine sofa, madam"—such an unusual compliment! One would hesitate to call it insulting or indecent, but then I must wonder how the line was performed—that devilish rogue must have murmured it with exquisite lustiness. I am eager for the encore, to hear those indecent words fall from your lips, to see for myself how Mrs. Godfrey tumbled onto her back like a plump little sofa.

I shall be home tomorrow night, all being well, and will bring your letter so you might read it as a bedtime story for both of us.

With more than affection,

Your admiring Husband

I had not been in the mood for conversation after my peculiar turn at the tavern, and Dupin did not press matters; we simply agreed to meet in the foyer at eleven for a perambulation the next day. Dupin seemed to have a plan, but chose not to illuminate me. Sleep eluded me for what seemed like hours, my mind plagued by phantom thoughts and a terrible unease, but I did not wake until nine o'clock when my breakfast was delivered. The debilitating weeks at sea had taken their toll.

Just before the appointed hour, I made my way to the foyer. No one was in the reception area but the desk clerk. "Any messages for me?" The words came from my lips in half a whisper as I was filled with dread that more disturbing letters might await me.

"I am sorry, sir. Nothing today."

"Does that fill you with relief or consternation?"

I turned to see Dupin emerge from the shadows, a piece of paper in his hands. How had I not seen him just moments before?

"Dupin—apologies and good morning," I said, determined to hide my discomfort. "Is that an itinerary for our perambulation?"

Dupin stared, unblinking, like a mesmerist, silently demanding an answer to his question before he responded to mine.

"A certain amount of relief, I confess. I have yet to truly absorb the contents of those letters left here yesterday."

"Those you have read. We must discuss the others as well. As for the letter from Mr. Dickens that you are awaiting so anxiously, he will contact you tomorrow or, at latest, on Sunday morning."

I did not bother to question his pronouncement, in part because I had become accustomed to such declarations from my time in Paris, but primarily because I so hoped that he would be proved accurate yet again.

Dupin folded the paper in his hands into quarters and tucked it into his coat pocket, then extracted a meerschaum. "Shall we? The weather seems accommodating."

"Of course. What is on our itinerary?" I nodded at his coat pocket.

Dupin frowned. "It is not an itinerary, but merely a guide. It is often useful to see something by daylight and then again by night. Or vice versa," he said cryptically. He opened the door and gestured for me to precede him.

As we stepped outside, a sense of aggravation rose up in me. I had wished to keep my hopes of meeting Charles Dickens private, but Dupin had, with his usual acuity, deduced them. He flaunted that fact, and yet was secretive about his own intent for our excursion. To compound matters, he took a pair of green spectacles from his pocket and put them on.

"My eyes are further enervated by the sun's glare," he said, rather disingenuously. In Paris he had worn the green spectacles to ward off the sun's rays, but had also donned them indoors when questioning a person of suspicion. The green of the spectacle glass made it impossible to fathom where he was truly gazing, a disconcerting effect.

We walked down Dover Street in silence, toward a destination Dupin had yet to divulge, curling eddies of tobacco
smoke trailing after us. Slowly my antagonism abated in the
pleasant weather. The temperature was moderate for July,
when compared with what one would expect in Philadelphia.

"Whist. A very instructive game," Dupin said suddenly and
inexplicably.

"Yes?" I had played many games of whist in my youth, much
to my detriment. My luck had always been variable with cards,
particularly so when in my cups.

"Consider how the skills of an analyst make him the superior player of whist to one who merely adheres to the rules. The
analyst makes a host of observations and inferences regarding
his opponent by examining his countenance. He notes how the
face varies as the game progresses, the differences in the expression, be it certainty, surprise, triumph or chagrin. He can judge
a feint by how a card is thrown down. After two games are
played, the analyst can read the games as if the other players
had the faces of their cards turned outwards." We reached
Piccadilly, walked west briefly and crossed into Green Park.
"But remember," he continued, "that while the analyst is necessarily ingenious, the ingenious man is often remarkably
incapable of analysis." Dupin turned his face toward mine,
waiting for me to acknowledge his discourse. Light flared off
the green spectacles.

"Quite right," I muttered, despite my confusion as to his
point.

"Very good." He lapsed into silence again as we made our
way through the park. I amused myself by watching the
perambulators around us as Dupin worked upon some riddle
in his own mind. Three pretty, young ladies caught my attention—nursemaids by their uniforms. Each pushed a large
perambulator, and they were in lively conversation. Three

young children chased around them in circles, immersed in some incomprehensible childhood game.

"Have you had any further memories about the artificial-flower seller or thoughts as to why someone might wish you to remember the attempted kidnapping?"

His question took me by surprise as he no doubt had intended, which was compounded by his decision to veer to the left and stride across the parkland toward the boundary wall. I hurried after him, sorry to lose sight of the children frolicking with enjoyment. It occurred to me then that I too had been an innocent child at play, completely unaware that someone had been watching me—indeed *stalking* me.

"I have remembered nothing more about the flower-seller and cannot answer your question, but in truth I have keenly felt the presence of some *other* ever since I received my unwanted legacy."

Dupin nodded. "Your aggressor has been observing you for some time and knows a great deal about you. He sent the seven letters in the mahogany box to your home in Philadelphia and the fourteen additional letters to your accommodation in London. We must now determine what it is he wants from you."

At that moment we arrived at a gated passageway and I followed Dupin through it.

"Dupin, has our tour properly begun?"

"Indeed, sir."

"Will you illuminate me as to its purpose?"

"We are investigating all avenues, including your theory that the letters are forgeries."

"But how?" I asked.

"Would you agree that we each know far less of London than we do our home cities?"

"Yes, of course."

"And that the letters note a number of specific locations that may or may not exist?" Dupin continued.

I immediately saw Dupin's point. "Or if they do exist it might be that they are unlikely locations for the events described within the letters."

Dupin gave a thin smile. "Correct." He slowed to a halt and looked around him. "St. James's Place."

It was a quiet, elegant street of imposing houses. Dupin retreated into silence as if absorbing the very atmosphere. From our excursions in Paris, I knew better than to interrupt when he was in ardent contemplation. He then consulted his paper briefly and led us a short distance north on St. James's Street before turning left into Bennet Street, where he repeated his solitary contemplation of the area. Dupin retraced his steps then led us north on St. James's Street for a short distance before crossing over Jermyn Street and walking down Bury Street. When he halted, I saw that the address was number twenty-seven—the address noted on the letters delivered in the mahogany box! Such had been my shock at the content of the letters, I had thought little of the addresses written upon them, but Dupin missed nothing.

As he stood in front of what was once the Arnolds' home, he seemed to be scrutinizing every brick of the handsome, tall building. I looked from window to window, half-expecting to hear a rap upon the glass, to see a ghostly face peering out at me.

"Which floor do you think they lived on?" I asked, but Dupin did not favor me with an answer. Instead, he abruptly turned on his heel and headed back toward Jermyn Street, the fragrant smoke of his meerschaum trailing behind him. As we made our way past elegant men's clothing shops and the back of Fortnum and Mason, I imagined Elizabeth and Henry Arnold passing these very same establishments.

Our destination—ninety-three Jermyn Street—proved to be a bustling cheese shop.

"When you read the remaining letters, you will see that the Arnolds also lived at ninety-three and twenty-two Jermyn Street. I believe their lodgings were on the top floor at both addresses," Dupin said, and without further explanation he continued along Jermyn Street, leaving me to scurry after. I was beginning to profoundly regret my decision to give the letters to Dupin before I had properly read them. He now knew more about my grandparents than I did—indeed, he was privy to secrets that I had willingly relinquished to him. We paused at twenty-two Jermyn Street, an imposing white building that housed a cloth merchant's premises; there were four floors above the shop, each with paired windows that decreased in size as one ascended. I had no doubt that Elizabeth and Henry Arnold had lived for a time on the top floor with its less generous view out onto the world.

As Dupin led us across Haymarket and along Coventry Street, I tried to recall the precise details of the letters I had read without much success. We continued through Leicester Square with its rather grand equestrian statue of George I and turned into Leicester Street, which was lined with single-story shops. Again, Dupin slowed to a halt and silently studied the area.

"The site of another attack?" I asked.

Dupin merely nodded and would not be drawn. To ameliorate my annoyance, I watched two young acrobats for a time as they walked on their hands and helped each other somersault through the air. The raggedy children had probably never seen the inside of a schoolhouse, but had learned to earn their supper from the tricks they did on the street. Dupin ignored their antics and led the way to Charing Cross; we strolled north at a pace considerably slower than that adhered to earlier.

When we stopped again, he retrieved his watch, checked the time, then returned it to his waistcoat pocket.

"May I ask what you are trying to fathom?"

"The distance a lady would walk in the evening unaccompanied," he replied enigmatically. He turned to look at me, and the light flared off his green spectacles. "We have not yet discussed what happened last night," he added.

"No." I was not eager to change that situation.

"And of course we must. Why did you chase the old man? Had you met him before? Or had you been intemperate before our excursion to the tavern?"

I felt the urge to rigorously defend myself, but knew my actions had been peculiar. "I was quite sober. The man reminded me of someone. That is all I can honestly say."

"Someone you are angry with? Your grandfather perhaps?"

"I did not know my grandfather." I could feel Dupin scrutinizing me from behind the green spectacles, willing me to continue. "He did not sail to America with my grandmother. If he is alive, it is possible that he is still in London."

Dupin briefly contemplated this. "From the elopement announcement, we know that he would now be seventy-nine years of age. The vagrant you pursued looked as ancient as that, but moved with unlikely speed for one in his extreme dotage."

"True."

Dupin turned abruptly away from me and led us up Charing Cross Road without another word. As Charing Cross transitioned into Tottenham Court Road, it became busier with coaches and increasingly shabby, but this did not divert Dupin from his private reverie. He turned left onto Percy Street and then right on Charlotte Street. His pace slowed until he paused in front of a narrow house. He took out his pocket watch again, noted the time, then carefully refilled his meerschaum as he studied the building in front of him. At last, Dupin faced me.

"Very good. Shall we go back to Brown's for coffee?"

It was not truly a question. Frustrated and not a little annoyed, I nodded despite myself. We circled back to Brown's Genteel Inn.

* * *

The maid left a tray of coffee on the octagonal marble table and scurried from the room. Dupin seemed to frighten her, an effect he often had on the opposing sex. He poured the coffee then removed the green spectacles that gave him the advantage of scrutinizing his opponent unseen. My thoughts took me by surprise. Opponent? Truly I meant companion. As I sipped my coffee, Dupin carefully unrolled a paper and weighed it down with four small paperweights. It was a map of London, elegantly drawn in his meticulous hand.

"Here is the hotel." Dupin pointed at Dover Street where there was a tiny square drawn in black ink. "And here are the three locations the Arnolds resided at in London." He indicated small black squares at twenty-seven Bury Street, twenty-two Jermyn Street and ninety-three Jermyn Street. "And these initials mark where the attacks described by Elizabeth Arnold and Henry Arnold occurred." A minute "E" or "H" was inscribed in blue ink at Cannon Street, Bow Lane, Johnson's Court, St. James's Place and Jermyn Street.

"The attacks described in the letters that came with the mahogany box?"

"Yes. And these in green ink indicate the assaults described in the letters delivered to you at Brown's Genteel Inn, a number of which you have yet to read." He indicated Charlotte Street, Bennet Street, New Boswell Court and St. James's

Street. A small black square was labeled "Covent Garden Theatre."

I traced out our recent walk with my finger. "And so we visited the sites of five attacks today."

"Yes, of course. All very near your grandparents' lodgings, which makes it clear that the logistics of these attacks are credible."

I now understood Dupin's use of his pocket watch and careful surveillance of the areas we visited.

"They are also near enough to Brown's Genteel Inn, which is intriguing," he added.

"Surely a coincidence?"

Dupin raised his brows slightly, but ignored my comment. "I have also noted on the map where you lived as a child and the location of the attempted abduction and yesterday's assault, as I believe them relevant, given the location of the attacks, the mysterious boutonnière and the recently delivered letters." He indicated the red-inked P's drawn on Southampton Row and Russell Square, then settled back in his armchair, filled his meerschaum and lit the tobacco. "Now, let us analyze the situation, beginning with the earliest two letters. We understand that the Arnolds were actors, performing at the Royalty Theatre as noted in the letter dated the fifth of March 1788. Henry Arnold frequently neglected to go home of an evening, which did not please Elizabeth Arnold. As we ascertained from her handwriting, she was a passionate woman—dictatorial, but feminine, spirited and forceful. She decided to take revenge on her husband's mistress, but in a peculiar manner. Mrs. Arnold borrowed a costume from the theater, transformed herself into a man and slashed her rival's dress and hindquarters—a very pointed lesson indeed. She then informed her husband of her crime, albeit obliquely. She repeated this strategy on the twentieth of March 1788, slashing Mrs. Wright's gown and posterior."

"Or a hoaxer would like us to believe that Elizabeth Arnold slashed those dresses," I interjected.

"I agree that we must consider whether a hoaxer might wish to falsely accuse Elizabeth and Henry Arnold."

"Perhaps they had enemies."

Dupin exhaled impatiently and smoke whirled around him as if he were the Devil himself. "Perhaps. In any case, it is very obvious that you do."

His words unsettled me deeply, and truly I did not wish to believe them despite the compelling evidence. "We all make enemies when our ambitions collide with another's, but I do not fathom how my enemies might be connected to the letters."

"This is clearly our main task. And it will not be a simple mystery to solve." He puffed on his meerschaum for a time, in apparent contemplation. "We have agreed to discard the notion that your adoptive father's wife sent the letters—this was merely a ruse to persuade you to take a serious interest in the contents of the mahogany box. And while the note, purportedly from Mrs. Allan, is a forgery, the message itself contains truthful information and, therefore, is an important clue." He retrieved the missive from the box and read it aloud: "'Dear Mr. Poe, I am turning over to you certain artifacts that are your birthright. Most truly, Mrs. John Allan.' The letters and the box are your birthright as the grandson of Elizabeth and Henry Arnold. We can presume, I think, that the mahogany box is the one referred to in the rather poor acrostic Valentine written in your grandmother's hand and delivered with the latest set of letters."

Dupin's condemnation of the little poem, weak as it was, irritated me, but I shrugged to acknowledge the possibility of his words and nodded for him to continue.

"I would propose that with the use of the term 'birthright', the forger is insinuating that you have inherited responsibility for the actions of your forebears as described in the letters."

"What? Surely not. There is no logic to that."

"We need not consider something logical to discover that it is true, particularly in matters that contravene law or principles of honor."

I had to concede that this was correct.

"So let us return to the correspondence and your grandparents' relationship portrayed therein. The letters delivered anonymously to Brown's Genteel Inn include three missives dated April 1784, which refer to the elopement of Elizabeth Smith and Henry Arnold. It is clear, then, that the impressionable sixteen-year-old Miss Elizabeth Smith was infatuated with the bombastic Mr. Henry Arnold, who carefully seduced her. She risked disinheritance to elope with him."

"His manner may be florid, but my sense is that Henry Arnold truly pledged his heart to Elizabeth."

"As you wish," said Dupin, pausing again to puff on his meerschaum as he gently shuffled through the correspondence in question. "But we know from the letters sent to you in the mahogany box that his fidelity did not last—or so his wife believed—for her jealousy drove her to extreme measures. The letters between the Arnolds then cease until the clumsy acrostic Valentine dated the fourteenth of February 1789 and ten more letters dated from May to September 1789. We might observe from the letters that the disharmonious relationship of Elizabeth and Henry Arnold improved greatly by the spring of 1789." Here he paused and directed his glance from the pages in his hands to me.

"To confirm your surmise, I would have to read all the letters, but of course I presume you to be correct."

"One must also notice," he continued with a rather unnecessary sense of drama, "that the act of disguising themselves in order to accost women on the London streets and slash their garments and posteriors had such a beneficial effect on your grandparents' marital harmony that, by May 1789, the letters are positively amorous."

A smile seemed to tilt Dupin's lips, and I flushed to wonder what he might have read. Why had I given him those letters before reading them myself?

"All these uncontrolled emotions and peculiar actions make it difficult for me to believe that a hoaxer concocted the tale within the letters," he concluded. "Do you see, Poe?"

It was difficult to dispute Dupin's dry analysis, but I could not believe that my grandparents were base criminals. "I will clear their names, Dupin, I must!"

A look of contrition softened Dupin's face. He picked up the mahogany box and placed it on the marble table in front of me. "Read all the letters," he said. "It was not appropriate for me to study them before you I am sorry."

"Please do not apologize—I insisted upon it." But I was grateful for his words and Dupin nodded as if in acknowledgement of my unspoken sentiments.

"I strongly believe that delving more deeply into your past here in London will reveal useful information, but remember that a surfeit of emotion will seduce you into error or hurry you into miscalculation. We must employ the art of ratiocination above all else."

"Of course."

Dupin retreated into silence as he puffed on his meerschaum, then gently ran his finger from one mark on his extraordinary map to the next. "I do comprehend the need to defend one's family honor, Poe. Particularly when one is the last to remain outside the familial tomb. It is both a duty," he said softly, "and a curse."

22 Jermyn Street, London

3 June 1789

Dearest Wife,

How is the air at Margate? Is it true that half of London society has decamped to the seaside to enjoy its effects? As you so wisely recommended, I have spent my time educationally while denied the company of our Lady the Theatre, but I long for our reunion. Have you advanced our cause?

And now I must apologise for my tardiness in writing. I was determined to fulfil the delightful challenge you set me before putting pen to paper, but have met with unforeseen obstacles. The path to success is never without adversity! I had hoped to take to the London stage on the night of the Spanish Ambassador's gala to celebrate the renewed health of our King. There was to be a display of fireworks, which I felt would be a fitting backdrop for my performance. However, the damnable girl failed to arrive at our lodgings, and I had no mind to leave our little Eliza with that gin-soaked wretch downstairs again, so I postponed my performance and took a summer evening perambulation in Green Park with our daughter.

Our journey to the park was made jolly by the festive household illuminations—lighted candles glowed in windows and pretty lamps in a multitude of colours hung outside the houses, some with the most glorious transparent paintings. Eliza clapped her hands to witness those! She is very much the little lady and insisted on toddling a distance without the aid of her wooden walker, although she was happy enough to ride upon her horsey's shoulders when her little legs tired.

The park was lively with folk hoping to catch sight of the fireworks, and Eliza drew female strollers to her like bees to honey. The ladies were admiring of our daughter's sweet features and astonished that her dear Papa was playing her nursemaid. Eliza revelled in the attentions of her audience—how like her mother, even at the tender age of two. The sooner her education begins in the theatre itself, the quicker she shall achieve greatness. A worthy rival in time to Mrs. Siddons! Distinction is in her blood.

Yours,
Henry

The King's Head, High Street, Margate
4 June 1789

Dear Henry,

It makes me happy to hear that you and Eliza are doing so well in my absence, although I am quite certain that Eliza was not the only one revelling in the attentions of the female strollers. But it cannot be a bad thing for a father to play nursemaid on occasion, particularly when the daughter is such a delightful creature, the perfect combination of her parents with her ability to charm and her delight in independence. She will prove herself in the theatre before much longer as distinction is indeed in her blood.

Happily, my journey to Margate has not been a waste of time nor money. I have secured a role for myself in *A Bold Stroke for a Husband*, playing Carlos's mistress, Laura. An adventurous casting against type! It is not <u>Covent Garden</u>, but it is a good rehearsal for better things and to be paid for one's Art must only be good. Unfortunately, it was impossible for me to secure you a role, but please join me here with speed since you may then become your own petitioner.

I hope I do not need to remind you that you must take good care and attention when rehearsing upon the open stage. Teach a lesson, but do not tarry for the applause. Make your exit quickly—your audience will not always be kind.

With love,
Elizabeth

22 Jermyn Street, London
5 June 1789

Dear Elizabeth,

To be paid for one's Art is no bad thing, of course, but on occasion the Muse commands that we take to the boards without recompense and without the confines of a simple theatre. Let me tell you, dearest, of the most extraordinary, the most daring performance that has just taken place on the greatest stage of all—London itself!

The story begins yesterday evening. Eliza was in the care of a good lady friend, and I prepared my costume carefully, contriving curly hair in abundance and a very long nose, which looked convincing by evening light. I made my way to Vauxhall Gardens as it attracts self-important ladies in need of a sharp reprimand. I soon noticed a young woman quite alone in the gardens—uncommon for a lady of good character. Indeed, I recognised her from a tavern in St. James's Street I visit on occasion, a pretty enough girl known as Kitty for her sharp-clawed manner, daughter of old Parsloe the tavern owner. I prepared for my attack by way of some remarks designed to unsettle her, but the wretch was quite unfazed and shouted to a pack of philanderers who had also been observing her. They thought to teach me a lesson to impress her, and I thought it best to beat a hasty retreat.

But it is the man of fortitude who achieves success. This very afternoon I resumed my costume and took to the tavern in St. James's Street. My disguise proved a success. Some who know me well failed to recognise me, which reflected positively on my artistry, but Kitty the tavern owner's daughter was not serving ale that day. I was told she had gone to Green Park for a perambulation with her sister.

Undeterred, I made my way to the footpath near the edge of the park, certain I would spy the wench and her sister on their way home. My prediction was correct, and I followed them to Bennet Street, where I made my approach—*swish!* My blade cut through her skirts with one slash, and I ran off as they shrieked, "Monster! Fiend!"

It is indeed time to leave London. Eliza and I will make our way to Margate as soon as I have sold some old things unworthy of transport.

> With anticipation of seeing you,
> Henry

The King's Head, High Street, Margate

7 June 1789

Dear Henry,

While your tale is undoubtedly very well-told, I wonder if you have taken dramatic liberties with it to spare me worry? The attack upon Miss Kitty Wheeler was reported to the Bow Street magistrate and published in *The World*. The account claims that when a rogue insulted the girl, he was tackled by her father, Parsloe Wheeler, who shook him ferociously. The rogue shouted, "Murder!" as the two grappled, and a rough crowd gathered around them. Mr. Wheeler was deemed the villain and the crowd secured the release of the man in his clutches, who quickly ran away. It was also noted in the paper, in far less detail, that a pretty servant girl was accosted on New Boswell Court and had her thigh cut.

Dearest, I urge you to exercise caution and retreat to Margate immediately. The best disguise is one used at a good distance from your audience.

     With concern,
     Elizabeth

The journey to Stoke Newington was reasonably comfortable and our speed was good, the navigation steady. I felt quite confident we would reach our destination without mishap. Dupin seemed less certain as he muttered with each bump we hit and gripped the edge of the seat whenever the coach veered sharply. He had planned to spend much of the day engaged in research at the British Museum, but when at breakfast I confirmed that I had read all the newly delivered letters and intended to take an excursion to the school I had been sent to after leaving the Dubourg sisters, Dupin declared a wish to join me.

The desk clerk directed us to Bond Street for a coach and advised us to carefully inspect them at the stand to ensure a peaceful journey. I settled on a solid-looking green vehicle with yellow wheels that appeared to be all the same size. Both horses seemed well-conditioned fellows with calm dispositions and the interior of the coach was clean enough. Once under-way, we moved at a steady if slow pace through London, Dupin playing the role of Grand Tour guide, pointing out places of interest, including St. George's Church, where my grandparents had been married. Our speed increased when we reached Islington and continued on to Newington Green, where the noxious air of London began to recede. Eventually we came to Green Lanes, a long rather winding road leading to Enfield, which I remembered well from my youth.

"Any memories, Poe?" Dupin asked as if he had read my mind.

"Nothing significant. I absconded from school several times to come here with the older boys and watch trotting matches held by the trades-folk. On a few occasions we were taken for a swim in the New River, which I greatly enjoyed."

"I believe that is now forbidden as the river supplies the reservoirs."

"What a pity," I said.

"Not for the Londoners who now have clean water," Dupin observed.

I prickled with annoyance. Hadn't Dupin asked me to look to my past for answers? And yet when I confided my memories, Dupin dismissed them as little more than nonsense. It seemed that he had never had a childhood. Certainly he had never swum in a river for the sheer pleasure of it.

From Green Lanes we turned into a narrow road, Church Street, which was lined with attractive red-brick dwelling-houses fronted by decorative iron railings to screen them from the street. Stoke Newington, or "new town in the wood," had expanded considerably since I lived there twenty years previously. London was creeping ever closer, like a subterranean creature looking to feed on fresh flesh.

I had instructed the driver to stop about half-way down Church Street, but the coach rumbled past our destination despite my poundings on the coach wall. When at last we came to a stop and I exited, an unsettling scene met my eyes.

"What is this place?"

The jovial and, I suspect, somewhat intoxicated driver
squinted at the scene in front of us. "Looks like there's a burial
ground in there, sir."

It did indeed, but I had no recollection of such a place in
Stoke Newington. The air in my lungs fizzled away, and a sense
of foreboding settled upon me—what I had remembered as
genteel parkland was now a congregation of the dead.

"Are we in the wrong location?" Dupin asked.

"No, this is the correct street." I smoothed the perspiration
from my brow and breathed deeply. "It's just that this was not
here before." I indicated the burial ground.

"Well, it seems a good place to wait," Dupin said, gesturing
at the horses that had busied themselves with the grass verge.
"I doubt we will be more than an hour," he said to the driver.
"Shall we?" He indicated that I should lead the way and so I set
off walking west.

There were more houses than I remembered on Church
Street, but the place retained a village atmosphere. My
heart's beat accelerated as I caught sight of a large white
early eighteenth-century house with grand sash windows.
There was nothing particularly remarkable about the building, but Bransby's Manor House School had been my home
for two years and the place had made a deep impression
upon me.

I walked up to the school gates and peered inside the courtyard. My eyes immediately connected with those of a young
boy. He looked to be approximately the age I was when
I attended the school, and I was curious to hear the young
scholar's opinion of the place.

"You, there. Come here," I said in a low voice.

The boy stared at me and then at Dupin, his eyes widening
as he took a step backward.

"Closer." I beckoned the boy toward me.

Instead he took two more steps back, his face the very picture of fear, and ran. It was then that a memory began to coalesce.

"Something happened here, something terrible, I remember fragments."

"Something that made you run from it. Or someone," Dupin prompted.

"Yes." The faint picture in my mind became stronger, sharper.

"It was a bright day. Our studies were finished, and I was failing to find ways to amuse myself in the enclosed yard at the rear of the house. We were permitted excursions in the park on Saturday afternoons, in the company of two ushers, but were not permitted out on our own. The alluring weather made me increasingly enamored with the idea of exploring the twin lakes in Clissold Park, where there were a variety of water birds and, allegedly, a population of terrapins. I was determined to capture one, thinking it would make a fine pet. This yearning to escape the boundaries of our school walls would have remained just that, but some force—I cannot remember what—directed my attention to the front gate. It was moving very slightly, pushed by the breeze, unlatched and unlocked. I did not stop to consider any consequences for my actions, but slipped through the gate and scurried down Church Street, jubilant with my unexpected freedom."

And so I began to enact my childhood adventure, walking away from the school with Dupin following. In truth, I soon forgot he was there, so lost was I in my own reverie. The summer heat faded away—it was spring in Clissold Park and I was ten years old again. Couples promenaded around the perimeter, families sat on the grass with picnics, children threw scraps to the squabbling ducks. When we perambulated the area en masse on a Saturday, Reverend Bransby never missed the opportunity to educate us. The lakes were the last trace of

Hackney Brook, one of London's lost rivers. It had once flowed through Stoke Newington to merge with the River Lea, but had long since vanished beneath London. This tale fascinated me and made the lakes all the more alluring. How could a river simply disappear? What mysterious force had compelled it to sink beneath the earth's surface, into the foul, Plutonian waterways? I had written some childish verse on the subject, which rather impressed my teacher and my dear Ma.

But on the day in question, I was more determined to find myself a pet terrapin. I scoured the lakes' shores for the hiding spots to little avail and began to lose interest in my quest as a feeling of unease settled upon me. Something was not right, but I was determined to wear the bold mantle of an explorer and my terrapin hunt continued until I reached the far side of the lakes. There I came upon a collection of flat stones, the kind best suited for skimming across a lake's surface. Perhaps another boy had collected them and been called away from the pleasure of using his horde.

As I poised myself to hurl one of the stones, a flash of movement startled me. I stared hard at a copse of trees to my left, but could see nothing lurking there. Unwilling to give up my temporary freedom too soon, I continued to skip rocks until I reached four skips in one throw. But as the shadows lengthened, I perceived a *flitting*—something edging ever closer, as if it were tracking me.

Fear rose up in me when I remembered the butcher's lurcher, an evil dog that would appear suddenly and silently, baring its teeth like a wolf. It was no friend to the pupils of Bransby's Manor House School as the older boys had a habit of tormenting the creature. Without the security of the pack around me, I felt increasingly ill at ease, and when the church bells rang out half past five I thought it best to end my adventure.

When I reached Church Street, my sense of being followed became more intense. I listened hard for the sound of a dog's feet skittering on gravel and turned frequently to look behind me, trying to catch a glimpse of my pursuer, but saw nothing. Still, my sense of dread grew.

When I reached the school gates, I discovered to my horror they were locked. I would have to find a way to scramble over the wall or pull the bell and face certain punishment from Reverend Bransby.

Then something caught at my coat and as I turned to free myself, I saw gnarled fingers plucking at the fabric. A thin man with lank gray hair and shabby clothes had my coat in his grip. He was probably in his middle years but looked older, haggard and unhealthy, in the same condition as the beggars I had seen in London. I tried to tug myself from his grasp, but he held on tight.

"I know who you are, boy. I know who you are," the gray man whispered, his stale breath buffeting my nostrils.

"What?" I tried to answer. "Who are you?" But no words escaped my lips. I wrenched against his grasp but he held tight and tighter still. I reached for the bell pull and yanked at it with all my might.

The gray man reached into his pocket, then silently raised his arm. There was a flash of silver and a knife swept through the air. The gray man hissed, "Tell your mother I know where you are." His eyes held mine captive. "I *know* where you are." And he disappeared like the Devil himself. I stood frozen until the sound of feet on gravel turned my fear into words.

"Help! Let me in!" I shouted. "Murder!"

The startled face of the young housemaid Bess peered through the gate. "What in Heaven's name! Get in here right now, young fellow."

I shook the bars pathetically.

"Locked out after sneaking out, are you? You'll be in a world of trouble." She pulled a bundle of keys from her apron and unlocked the gate.

I was one of Bess's favorite boys and confess that the comforting sight of her brought tears to my eyes.

"Oh, stop that now." She pulled me inside and tousled my hair.

"But that man . . ." My words were interspersed by little gasps for air.

"What man? I didn't see any man."

"He ran away after he tried to murder me. See." I patted my back and put my hands in front of me, expecting them to be covered with blood.

"And very grubby hands they are too. Let's get you inside and wash those." As she pushed me through the door, she discovered a long rent down the back of my jacket. "You little scamp! And that a new jacket just last month."

"It isn't my fault! The man—he tried to stick me with a knife and then ran away!"

"The tales you spin! Sneaking out of the school and ruining your new jacket in the bargain. I have half a mind to tell Reverend Bransby."

I know who you are, boy. My attacker's whisper slithered through my mind and the tears came again.

"Stop the play-acting now," Bess scolded. "I'll try to fix your jacket after supper. But don't you dare be doing anything like that again. Do you know how much trouble you could be in right now?"

I nodded, the tears flowing down my cheeks. Much more trouble than Bess realized. I had no doubt that the gray man would have sliced me to pieces if I hadn't rung the bell.

Bess finally clasped me in a hug and said, "Good boy. No more crying and no more lies." She held me away from her and dried my cheeks. "Promise me now."

"And so I did," I said to Dupin, whose face was the picture of concentration as I concluded my story. "But I could not understand why she made me promise not to lie and then told me to break that promise by hiding the truth of what happened to me on Church Street."

"Your attacker sliced your school jacket," he said. "Most interesting."

"In what way?" I was still shaken by the force with which my memories had come upon me.

"It cannot have escaped your attention that, in slashing your clothes, the old man was making reference to your grandparents' crimes."

I felt as if the wind had been knocked from me. "Surely not. It seems . . . *implausible*. Why would the attacker from my childhood think I would know anything about the crimes purportedly committed by my grandparents? What would he hope to achieve by terrorizing me at school?"

"That, as yet, is not clear. But we may certainly presume that whoever is stalking you now is somehow connected to this old man and the woman who attacked you as a child. Your nemesis—for that is what he surely is—seems to have a complex plan, and we must presume that he wishes to harm you."

"Harm?" I exclaimed. "But why?"

"At this point we cannot know. We must keep our wits about us and, of course, put a stop to his plan."

"I find this very difficult to take in, Dupin. If I have a nemesis with nefarious plans as you suggest, why has he surfaced now after all these years?"

Dupin paced in front of the school gate, taking in all details of the school and its surroundings. "That we shall have to ascertain," he finally said.

* * *

The journey back to London was slow and tiredness overwhelmed me. When the carriage hit a particularly large hole in the road, I was shaken awake and discovered that we were just nearing the coach stand on Bond Street.

"I am sorry, Dupin. Most impolite of me. I have not been sleeping well."

"It is understandable given the circumstances," he said.

We made our way to Brown's Genteel Inn and retrieved our room keys at the front desk. Dupin turned to me and gave a slight bow.

"It was a most instructive excursion. Shall we meet in my rooms for supper? Eight o'clock, perhaps?"

I was reluctant to prolong such a dreadful day, but Dupin's gimlet eye saw my weakness, and so I could not refuse.

"Of course. I will be there at eight."

"Very good." And Dupin took his leave, disappearing up the stairs without another word. Normally I would feel slighted by his hasty departure, but instead I felt relief. I longed to lose myself in the oblivion of sleep, if only for a few hours. I took a step toward the stairs, but the desk clerk's voice turned me to stone.

"Letters for you, Sir."

I should have been overjoyed at his words, for surely a letter from Mr. Dickens had finally arrived, but my neck prickled as if salt water were drying upon it and my hands were clammy as I accepted the two envelopes that bore my name in unfamiliar handwriting. I whispered my thanks to the clerk and adjourned to my room.

Such was my terror of what the letters might contain, I took my time preparing for the moment of opening them, first removing my soiled shirt and then washing the thin veil of dust from my face, neck and hair. Feeling somewhat calmed, I drew the curtains and lit the tapers to produce a more tranquil atmosphere. Finally I summoned all the courage I had, and opened the first envelope. It was from Mr. Dickens.

37 Albion Street, Broadstairs

28 June 1840

Dear Mr. Poe,

I am sorry not to welcome you on your arrival to London, but I have been kept busy in Broadstairs. I intend to return to London on the first of July and will leave a message at Brown's Genteel Inn suggesting a date and place to meet.

I was delighted to receive your collection of stories, *Tales of the Grotesque and Arabesque*. It is a consuming work, and I am full of admiration for your imagination and literary style. I will do my best to help you find a publisher in London.

In the interim, I have been making enquiries about a suitable venue for a lecture and recitation. The Literary and Scientific Institute in Islington has been secured for the eighth of July, which I do hope is convenient. Please advise me soonest if it is not. Once I have your approval, an announcement regarding the date and venue of your presentation will be placed in our best newspaper, *The Morning Chronicle*. I will, of course, attend, but hope very much to meet you before then.

Your Obedient Servant,

Charles Dickens

My relief to find the letter to be from a benefactor rather than malefactor was great, though I was disappointed that the first of July had passed without the promised message from Mr.

Dickens. Still, his efforts to organize a public lecture were noble, and if his pledge to assist me in finding a London publisher also succeeded, I would be forever in his debt.

I was anxious to inform Dupin of the correspondence from Mr. Dickens and tore open the second envelope with haste. As I extracted the letter, a smell of briny water and rotting sea creatures tainted the atmosphere. The paper was stiff with salt. When I unfolded it, I discovered to my horror the pages I had thrown into the sea when on board the *Ariel*. The ink was smeared and faded, the paper sea-water stained, but it was undeniably my letter to Sissy, re-emerged from the depths, retrieved by some unholy means. Words leapt from the smudged page—

> Darling Sissy, my dearest wife,
>   a ship bound for hell
> impossible to maintain a grip on the earthly world
>   I have lied to you
>   terrible secrets—secrets that may prove
>   my blood tainted.
>   my inheritance is indeed a
>   scandalous and sordid one
>   your love and all its brightness
>   is lost to me
>   a past that claims to be mine by
>   blood if not by action.
>
>   Your dear lost boy

—words spoken to me from a distance, yet echoing in my mind like the fragments of a nightmare. As I held the paper, I heard the hush of time trickling through an hourglass, then a gentle rustling, the sound of minuscule crustaceans scrabbling on sand, their hard shells dragging across the softness of damp flesh. I felt the malignant creatures emerge from the envelope in my hands and creep across my wrists, up my arms, pincers digging into flesh, burrowing underneath, until I could feel a thousand or more of them crawling furiously beneath my skin.

The Old Crown Inn, Birmingham
18 September 1789

Most daring, dainty Libertine,

Our fortuitous encounter in St. James last night and your subsequent <u>mannish</u> performance made for a memorable evening of which I have much more to say. I truly regret the necessity of two weeks in Birmingham.

Should you in my absence make the bold move of taking refuge in the nunnery again, pray acquaint yourself with a particular shop in Covent Garden with which all good men (or those aspiring to manhood) should be familiar, for as the sensible proprietress advises:

> To guard yourself from shame or fear,
> Votaries of Venus, hasten here;
> None in wares e'er found a flaw,
> Self preservation's nature's law.

Herewith find one of her unsurpassed engines and remember that armour is the very best disguise for we gentlemen of intrigue!

With unfailing respect,
Your most devoted Partner

93 Jermyn Street, London
20 September 1789

Wicked rogue of a Brother!

Let me express my deepest appreciation for your useful gift after our timely "family reunion" at the St. James's Street establishment. When jousting with nuns of an unsanctified order, armour is indeed best worn to protect the errant knight—and to safeguard those most dear to him. One hopes that <u>all</u> men of good standing make use of such "unsurpassed engines" when recumbent.

Although I took great comfort at my brief sequestration in the St. James's Street nunnery, which offered a welcome refuge from Miss Forster's would-be avengers, I have no plans to commune with the ladies again. In truth, I found their company rather tiresome, and if I were to play the critic, their performance ill-rehearsed. The Abbess sorely underestimated the critical faculties of her audience. To cajole the spectators into a state of good humour, she was obliged to copiously dose them with wine of dubious quality. After a time, this did have the desired effect of putting the assembled fellows in a carousing mood, and so the Abbess and her quaking nuns were vindicated.

Let us be clear—when viewed through unglazed eyes, the pageant was a shabby affair. The costumes were threadbare, and while one might argue that they were discarded with alacrity, thus rendering their quality of no importance, the slow, deliberate abandonment of finer attire would contribute to a more entrancing ambience. It is not the mere revelation of hidden treasures that is stimulating, but rather the *anticipation* of those treasures. And must I point out that it is not merely lust that impels the clever man, but rather ideals of a higher nature—artistic truth, justice and, dare I say, the finely honed blade of <u>righteousness</u>.

In fraternity,

E.

The Old Crown Inn, Birmingham
23 September 1789

Censorious Sibling!

May I remind you that it is far simpler to play the critic than to be the player. The Abbess and her devout charges have a singular reputation here in London and much further afield as the reliable Jack Harris, a critic far more knowledgeable of these spectacles than your good self, critiques the Abbess and her little troupe most favourably.

Furthermore, I regret to say that your own performance was far from your best. Few can compare with your skills on the stage when playing Polly Peachum, Mrs. Candour or Kate Hardcastle, but when in the guise of my dear brother—a fellow actor and young man in search of entertainment—you were far less convincing. The Abbess is shrewd, and if it were not for my efforts at diversion, your disguise would have been penetrated.

Let me impart a few lessons in how to bring more veracity to your performance, for if you allow your mask to drop in our current production, the consequences will be far greater than a barrage of vegetables. Your walk is improbably dainty for a man of enterprise—your steps small, your arms overly still. A young man must swagger with confidence, head held high, arms vigorously propelling him forward. Lead from the hips like a lusty gentleman— do not swish them from side to side like a milkmaid. When a nun divests herself of her habit, direct your gaze at her display and express your appreciation. You made the unpardonable error of avoiding the full glory put on view and fixing your eyes on me, which left the Abbess with quite the wrong impression. My brother, you must study the gestures of the stronger sex and make them your own if you wish to freely roam London at night.

    With concern,

    Your devoted Kinsman

93 Jermyn Street, London

25 September 1789

Oh, scoundrel of a Brother!

It is no hardship to apologise for my uncertain performance, and I freely admit that being pulled— quite literally—into such an unexpected situation had an adverse effect on my delivery, but I cannot say I am sorry that the Abbess had the wrong impression of our relationship if in future you will hesitate before visiting her nunnery. It was <u>most</u> transparent (and displeasing) that your acquaintance with the premises and all therein was very well-made.

Let us not forget that the object of our little game is not for me to persuade the nuns through a convincing performance, but rather to teach a hard lesson to the haughty ladies of London who believe that money and fine dresses make them better human beings. Consider the odious Miss Forster. Am I not her equal? Are we folk "of the theatre" or of reduced income inferior to a woman of feeble intelligence and insipid character trussed up in a pretty dress? I was born to the same class as our victims. Surely, the quality of my blood has not been diluted through my straitened circumstances!

Care must indeed be taken as we make our mark. Transportation or death is not our aim. We have many more to educate with our performances.

> With respect,
> Your forthright Collaborator

Splinters of light pierced my eyelids, and I discovered myself collapsed across the small sofa, still dressed. My shirtsleeves were unfastened and there were long, livid trails across my arms. The room had a peculiar smell. I breathed more deeply—seaweed, flotsam, fish trapped in ghost nets. My legs were unsteady, but this was from an empty belly rather than an excess of drink. I checked my pocket watch: five o'clock. I undressed and tried to sleep in my bed, but spent a restless two hours drifting in and out of dreams that had me back at sea on a cursed ship that could never dock.

At seven o'clock I washed and put on fresh clothing, but felt utterly depleted in spirit. It was not ennui, but rather a feeling of acute anxiousness. Something was stalking me, biding its time, its breath tickling up and down my spine as it waited for opportunity. It was unwise to remain alone in such a state, so I picked up the sea-stained letter and went directly to Dupin's room. I rapped but once upon the door, and he instructed me to enter. Dupin was seated at the table, a hearty breakfast spread before him. The smell of fish assaulted me.

"Herring. Would you care to join me?"

I was transfixed as he quickly sliced the length of his herring, teased back the flesh and extracted the skeleton intact, which he set onto a side plate. Revulsion washed over me as he severed a piece of the flesh and delivered it to his mouth.

"Quite acceptable," Dupin remarked after contemplating the flavor. "Please, have some."

"Just coffee, thank you."

Dupin shrugged. "Sit. And please help yourself." It was then that I noticed there were two place settings. Dupin anticipated my question.

"I tried to summon you for dinner, but you would not be roused. I presumed that you preferred to dine alone, but hoped you would wish to breakfast with me."

"I was, in fact, ill. I had some peculiar news." I placed the ghost letter on the table in front of me. Dupin continued dissecting his fish as he waited for me to say more. I poured some coffee, drank it quickly to ease the dryness of my mouth and helped myself to another cup. "This is a missive I threw over the side of the *Ariel*. The desk clerk gave it to me yesterday. Note how it is water-stained and smells of the sea. Someone collected the pages from the very wind itself and put them back together. It was folded and sealed in an envelope with my name upon it. There was no note with it, no return address."

Dupin consumed the last of his breakfast, dabbed at his mouth and folded his napkin neatly. He pushed his plate to one side and reached for the letter.

"Do you mind?"

"No. It is no longer private."

Dupin scanned the missive quickly, then shifted his eyes back to mine. "You were anxious to destroy a letter written in the throes of inebriation lest the contents worry your wife."

I nodded, misery embracing me again.

"And it has come back to haunt you, most mysteriously."

"Like a curse."

"Not unlike your inheritance."

"Indeed."

"I am confident the perpetrator has more physical substance than a phantom, despite his efforts to persuade you otherwise."

I was less sure than Dupin, but felt momentarily comforted by his words.

"We can be certain now that your opponent was on the *Ariel* with you. Have you any thoughts as to who it might be? I suspect he would have taken advantage of the journey to study you and your habits very closely."

I tried to quell my horror at the thought of being imprisoned on a ship in the middle of the Atlantic—much of the time barely cognizant—with a man who wished me ill. My mind flicked through the passengers on the *Ariel* I had met: my saviors, Dr. and Mrs. Wallis, the prim Miss Nicholson, temperance lecturer Mr. Asquith and the bombastic Mr. Mackie.

"Of course there were other passengers in steerage and the sailors themselves, but there was one passenger who shared our dining area who seemed to wish me ill. Mr. Mackie, who dressed in a most vulgar fashion—checks, a bright green frock coat—appeared angry that I had criticized some prose he had written. I have no recollection of the piece or the conversation we had about it, but his manner toward me was most aggressive."

"Was he from Philadelphia?"

"From his accent, I would presume Virginia originally, but perhaps he spent time in Philadelphia. I cannot remember if we discussed it at all."

Dupin raised his brows slightly and nodded. "And he traveled to London?"

"Yes. We took the same train, but did not sit together."

"Have you seen him since?"

I shook my head. "Mr. Mackie so enjoyed being the center of attention, it is difficult to imagine him fading into the background to spy upon me, but I can think of no other likely culprit."

Dupin nodded slightly. "Perhaps it is he." A gentle rapping on the door interrupted us. "Enter," Dupin called out.

A pink-faced girl opened the door and curtsied. She pulled a small table with wheels into the room and deftly shifted all the dishes from table to cart, her eyes nervously averted from Dupin. Within seconds she was gone. Dupin stood up and indicated the armchairs next to the marble table where his map was spread.

"Shall we?" As we took out seats, he continued. "Was Mr. Mackie left-handed?"

"Left-handed? I truly have no idea. Why?"

"Autography suggests that the person who created the handbill for Brown's Genteel Inn was left-handed, and I believe your aggressor sent you the handbill."

"I am afraid that I am not following your logic."

"I showed the desk clerk the handbill when I arrived at the Inn. He had never seen it before and doubted its veracity. Apparently Mr. Brown does not feel the need to advertise his establishment."

"Perhaps Mr. Brown is not aware that an enterprising member of his staff has made an alliance with the booking agent so they might profit from any foreign custom secured by the advertisement."

Dupin shook his head, somewhat impatiently. "The person who delivered the letters surely sent you the handbill. The culprit wanted you to stay here for a reason." He indicated the position of Brown's Genteel Inn on the map in front of us. "As we discussed previously, most of the crimes occurred very near here and the Arnolds' various lodgings. This is clearly relevant. As for the attacks that occurred away from this vicinity, our perpetrators were stalking specific victims—Miss Cole, Mrs. Wright and Mrs. Smyth." He indicated Cannon Street, Bow Lane and Johnson's Court.

I noticed that Dupin had added small numerals to the map. "You have numbered the attacks in date order?"

"Indeed." He indicated a key in the lower left corner of the map with date and victim's name appended to the numerals. "Now that you have read all the letters written by your grandparents, have you had any thoughts regarding them?"

"Frankly, I believe that the contents of those from September 1789 strongly suggest that they are hoaxes. A nunnery in St. James's Street? Nonsensical, surely."

Dupin exhaled sharply, an expression of mirth. "Nonsensical? Not at all. A well-known nunnery was indeed situated there."

"Truly? I must confess, then, that the letters made little sense to me."

Dupin's amusement deepened. "I suppose it is a very English joke to call these particular ladies nuns and their place of work a nunnery when their occupation has little to do with celibacy. Or perhaps, more precisely, has everything to do with *vanquishing* celibacy."

Dupin was ridiculing me and irritation muddied my mind. "Elizabeth Arnold's letter refers to a theater production and the shabbiness of the performance and another one speaks of disguises. Is it a play?"

Dupin stared as if I were hoaxing him. "It seems to be a *very* English joke," he finally said. "If you remember, Henry Arnold mentions a gift he left for his wife. The gift is an engine— 'armour' for a gentleman's protection—gentlemen who are votaries of Venus, the goddess of love."

The allusions within the letters became horribly clear to me. I had missed the obvious hidden in plain sight as I had not wished to see it. Dupin, oblivious to my discomfort, carried on with his relentless explanation.

"We then learn that Elizabeth Arnold, disguised as a man, was pursued for attacking Miss Forster, and Henry rescued her by pulling her into a nunnery. Her husband found it a particularly amusing test of his wife's disguise—would ladies of little virtue fathom that the young man accompanying his older brother was actually a woman? A Shakespearian comedy of disguise played out on the streets of London."

"I would hardly describe it as a comedy. My grandfather was not just a philanderer with ladies of some breeding, but also with ladies of the lowest orders."

"You appear to be upset," Dupin said, eyebrows raised in what I took to be mock surprise.

I was more than upset, but certainly did not want Dupin to judge me as a man lacking urbanity.

"Merely disappointed," I lied. "I knew nothing of my grandparents until the arrival of these letters. I had hoped to discover that I descended from far nobler stock, but it transpires that my mother's father was an unaccomplished actor and a most accomplished whoremonger."

"The sins of the father are not necessarily visited upon the son—or the grandson. And objectivity is the key to unraveling this mystery, Poe."

"My disappointment will not compromise my objectivity."

Despite my efforts to keep a clear head, it began to spin with the smell of the herring that still haunted the room. Dupin noted my discomfort.

"Some air might do you good. May I suggest a walk through Hyde Park as we continue to review the letters. I have committed the important details to memory."

I gingerly rubbed the sleeves that covered my abraded arms. "I confess that I would prefer to remain indoors today. I am not feeling myself." My eyes drifted to the ghost letter, and Dupin's gaze followed.

"I understand your anxiety. The reappearance of your letter must seem mysterious, but I assure you that someone is trying to unsettle you. Hidden enemies are our greatest foes. The sooner we draw your aggressor out into the open, the sooner we will solve your mystery. Of that I am certain."

I was far less confident than Dupin, but reluctantly nodded my assent.

* * *

The London air seemed far more clean and pleasant amidst the trees and grass, but as we made our way west through Green Park to the southeast corner of Hyde Park, I could not shake my sense of foreboding. Every flitting shadow seemed to be tracking us, every unexpected noise made my heart race. If another person strayed too close to us, I immediately suspected nefarious intent and faltered in my pace.

"I am surprised that none of the attacks mentioned in the letters occurred here," Dupin said with unfortunate timing. He indicated the pathways around us, which were lively with perambulators. "This was where Londoners went to be seen, particularly ladies in search of a husband. It seems a place Henry Arnold would have enjoyed, even if it aroused a great deal of jealousy in his wife."

"Justified jealousy."

"Indeed. Disguising herself as a man and using her acting skills to secretly reprimand her husband's mistresses was an ingenious touch. Elizabeth Arnold's letters recorded the embarrassment of her rivals as well as her husband's frequent absences from home—another pointed reproach. The twist in this tale is that the attacks did not have quite the effect Mrs. Arnold was striving for: to cure her husband of his infidelity. Instead they inspired him to join in her game. As the two recorded and indeed exaggerated the details of their crimes for the other to read, an erotic tension grew and their marital bond was renewed. But Henry Arnold, motivated by lust, began to enjoy the game far more than his wife as the attacks began to lose *purpose*."

"Purpose? What purpose?"

Dupin shrugged. "Revenge of course." He paused to allow two ladies carrying parasols to cross the path in front of us. They smiled at his gallant gesture, but their coquettish demeanors dissolved away under Dupin's unresponsive gaze. He paid them no further notice, continuing his analysis. "And then we have the acrostic Valentine with its peculiar message: 'Monster.'" He shook his head. "Most unusual."

"What do you think it means? It is hardly an endearment."

Before Dupin could respond, a chorus of dogs erupted around us. Every canine in the vicinity seemed to be baying at once and our path was obstructed by the formation of a small crowd talking excitedly and pointing to the heavens. High above us was a magnificent blue balloon with gold embellishments that glinted in the sunlight; it floated like a celestial emissary with an angelic message for the gathering spectators and my sense of doom lifted with the glorious sight.

"How marvelous!" I cried. "This is not a sight seen often in Philadelphia."

"Nor Paris. The Montgolfier brothers may be the fathers of flight, but the architecture of Paris makes untethered ascents a foolhardy enterprise." The great balloon was descending slowly toward us, which caused the crowd to applaud and cheer. "The

English are determined to establish their supremacy in long distance flight," Dupin observed.

"Green, Monck Mason and Hollond?"

He nodded. "They were careless in their calculations of the winds and were fortunate not to be blown out into the Atlantic. While the sea offers few impediments that might endanger the balloon's fabric, its vastness would defeat the balloon's supply of gas."

As I watched the wonderful carriage of the air gliding overhead, I shivered to imagine it plunging into the cold depths of the Atlantic.

Dupin's cry broke my morbid reverie. "Extraordinary!" He pointed to one of the aeronauts, who seemed to perch right on the basket's edge. "I believe he is going to jump."

Some ladies near us gasped in terror upon overhearing Dupin's gloomy words. The reactions of other spectators were less sympathetic.

"Thinks he's a bird," quipped one young man.

"Watch your heads now!" yelled his friend.

Females tumbled to the ground, swooning, while others shrieked, throwing their arms over their heads. The man remained crouched at the basket's edge and each second passing felt infinitely longer as we watched, scarcely daring to breathe.

"What are you waiting for?" a rogue shouted. "Jump and be done with it!"

And he did, or so it seemed. The crowd roared in anticipation or fear as the man hurtled downward.

"And now," Dupin muttered. As he spoke, a silken canopy arose around the erstwhile balloonist. The onlookers gasped in astonishment as the silk captured the air, forming an inverted bowl, and the aeronaut floated toward earth like an autumn leaf.

"A parachute—no frame. Very interesting. Its top was attached to the balloon's equator by a cord, I believe, which broke when the aeronaut transferred his weight from the balloon's basket to that of the parachute."

I did not completely understand what Dupin meant, but that did not seem to matter as he was already hurrying to reach the aeronaut's landing point. I scurried after him, as did many of the other spectators. The balloon stayed aloft, the second aeronaut leaning over the basket to monitor the progress of the man in his parachute. We must have run close to half a mile, dodging perambulators, a pack of dogs at our heels that yapped and growled at the flying man. There was a great crackling noise as the parachute crashed through some shrubbery before the man landed, happily, in a grassy copse. Dupin, who had reached the parachutist with uncanny speed, leaned over him.

"Are you quite all right, sir? Can you move your extremities?"

The man gasped and struggled to breathe, his hand clutched to his heaving chest. Clearly the wind was knocked out of him. He gingerly shook his arms and legs, before struggling to a sitting position. "Yes, I think I am fine," he finally said in a strong French accent.

"*Vous êtes français? Bien sûr,*" Dupin nodded to himself. "A most extraordinary descent."

"And most dangerous," I added.

"But to fly, Poe! Would you not do the same to experience the sensation of flight?" Dupin's face was animated with an unusual energy. I had rarely seen him so excited.

"I fear that I would not. My natural element seems to be the earth rather than water, air or fire."

"The great men of science have long dreamed of flight. You must know that da Vinci designed a parachute, but it was Louis-Sebastien Lenormand—a Frenchman—who made the first parachute. He hoped it would allow people to escape from the top floors of burning buildings." Dupin gestured toward the sky. "Perhaps the natural element of the French inventor is air. *Qu'en pensez vous?*"

"*C'est possible,*" the French aeronaut said with a noncommittal shrug.

"*Comment vous appellez-vous, monsieur?*" Dupin asked his compatriot. Before the bruised Frenchman could answer, another roar came from the crowd, who had tired of the earthbound parachutist and were focused back on the balloon. It was considerably lower in the sky and heading toward us, which made a few anxious spectators gasp.

"I believe the balloon is descending, Dupin."

Despite a certain anxiousness regarding its proximity, I was glad to see the balloon more closely. It really was an extraordinary and beautiful structure—ellipsoid in shape, almost fourteen feet in length, its height was approximately six and a half feet. Beneath the center of the balloon was a wooden frame rigged onto the balloon itself with netting, and from the framework a wicker basket was suspended, which housed the intrepid aeronaut. Red and white banners festooned the basket and were in flamboyant contrast to the silken balloon. The top half was ageratum blue and the bottom featured cobalt sea waves that encircled the circumference of the balloon. A golden serpent's body wove through these tumultuous waves and its fierce head was reared up, jaws agape, fangs exposed. The object of the creature's ire was a blazing sun with a human face that had plunged half-way into the sea.

"Impossible," Dupin said in a low voice.

Elegant golden letters were above the fearsome picture. "'*Le Grand Serpent de la Mer,*'" I read out loud before adding in an attempt at levity, "This balloon's element seems to be water."

"Or metal in the shape of the guillotine. That is the face of Louis XVI imposed upon the sun, an image found upon some courtly decorations during his reign. The sun is obviously setting into the sea, powerless against the sea-serpent poised to devour it. A clumsy metaphor," Dupin said, all jocularity gone from his voice.

"And who does the sea-serpent represent? The king's enemies?"

"One particular enemy, I believe. A man responsible for much evil." Dupin wheeled to face the parachutist, who was now on his feet, watching the balloon descend with the rest of us. "Who owns this balloon?" Dupin demanded. At that moment a roar arose from the crowd, and we turned to see the hot-air balloon hovering just over our heads. Dupin turned from the hapless parachutist and pushed his way through the crowd toward the balloon, which provoked shouts of anger from fellow onlookers. "Who owns this hot-air balloon?" Dupin shouted at the pilot, attempting to grab the guide-rope as if he hoped to tether the balloon to the ground.

"Stand back, sir!" the aeronaut shouted at Dupin. "Back!"

"Answer me!"

"The man is quite mad," the aeronaut said to the crowd. "Do not let him scale the basket!"

Several burly men grabbed Dupin by the arms and dragged him away from the balloon. There was nothing I could do that would not get us both soundly beaten. I scanned the mob for the parachutist, thinking to interrogate him myself, but he had vanished into the sea of spectators.

The balloonist raised his arms and shouted, "My colleague and I hope you enjoyed our aeronautical display. I have flown from England to Germany and have made many other daring aerial expeditions. We have crossed the English Channel in this balloon and with the support of our kind patron, intend to cross the Atlantic in it. Until that glorious day, you may join us for a tethered balloon ascent at Vauxhall Pleasure Gardens." And with that, he threw a flurry of pamphlets to the ground while the onlookers applauded and whooped some more. "Farewell," the balloonist called out as the balloon began to ascend again. "Farewell! Remember, Vauxhall Pleasure Gardens!"

The balloon drifted ever higher, and I watched in bafflement as Dupin stood glowering at the aeronaut in his glorious flying machine until they were a mere speck in the sky.

"Dupin?" I stepped in front of him, attempting to break his gaze from the empty sky. "What the Devil is the matter?"

"The Devil is certainly involved," he growled. When he shifted his gaze to me, it was so fearsome I could not help but recoil. Dupin immediately closed his eyes and breathed in deeply, forcibly calming himself. When at last he opened his eyes, he seemed much more himself again. "There is someone I would like you to meet if you are willing. Someone I hold in the highest regard."

Never had I heard Dupin describe anyone in such an exalted manner. My surprise and curiosity were so strong I agreed without question.

"Then let us find a carriage," Dupin said.

* * *

Once on our way, Dupin lapsed back into silence, his eyes fixed on the scenery outside with the alert tension of a cat stalking some invisible creature. I awaited an explanation for his behavior in Hyde Park until I could bear it no longer.

"The aeronauts and the balloon disturbed you most profoundly. May I ask why?"

"Ah, I can see we have almost arrived," he said as if my question had never been voiced. "You are about to witness an astonishing display and will meet, I hope, the extraordinary personage responsible for its creation."

We alighted at the junction of Baker Street and Portman Square in front of a three-story building called The Bazaar. Dupin led the way inside. Horses and coaches were being sold on the ground floor of the building; Dupin continued to a hall, and we ascended a wide staircase to a salon embellished with a quantity of artificial flowers, arabesques and large mirrors. A long-faced man with lank gray hair and ill-fitting black clothes sat in front of the entrance to a larger hall. On a table next to him there was a metal cashbox and a large brass hand bell.

Dupin put some coins onto the table. "Entry for two, sir."

The guardian of the entrance picked up most of the coins and slid the rest back to Dupin. "Go and mingle with the mighty," he intoned.

I was surprised when a smile stirred on Dupin's lips. "We shall. Is Madame here today?"

The dour man silently nodded his assent.

Dupin removed a silver case from his coat pocket and took out a calling card. "Please give your dear mother this with my highest regards."

The gray-haired man glanced at the card, slid it into the cash-box and stared at Dupin with pale eyes. "Sir," he confirmed.

"Thank you. Shall we, Poe?"

"Of course."

We proceeded to the first room, which was roughly one hundred feet by fifty feet in size. It resembled a very grand salon with ottomans for contemplation and conversation. Plate glass embellished the walls, which were hung with draperies and gilt ornaments. Statues circled the room. A small balcony held an orchestra that played softly.

"What do you think?"

I could not help but grimace. "Very highly decorated. Louis XIV?"

Dupin smiled. "Indeed. The curator appreciates glitter and pomp. Or perhaps she is simply aware that most of her customers do."

This seemed to be the case. The sofas and ottomans were crowded with well-dressed people engaged in noisy conversation. At the room's periphery, silent observers contemplated the music. Dupin's interest in the gaudy salon puzzled me. He had never been a passionate connoisseur of the musical recital and his taste in interior design coincided with mine.

"The orchestra is very accomplished and the surroundings are certainly vivid, but I would not go so far as to describe it as an astonishing display."

Dupin appeared momentarily bemused, then said: "Look around you, sir, look around you. Once again your emotions are getting the better of your faculties of observation. Avoid the decorations. Look at the spectators."

I stifled my instinct to rebut his criticism and did his bidding. My eyes focused on the men and women who, despite the orchestra's best endeavors to retain their attention, were in voluble discussion. I could not perceive what it was that Dupin found worthy of observation. And then I looked to the quieter spectators and observed something highly peculiar. Unlike their garrulous counterparts, they were silent and utterly still. I strode over to the nearest figure—a dark-haired woman in a bold red dress. She had a regal bearing and imperious demeanor. To my consternation, I noted that her dramatic pose had been sustained for an impossible length of time.

"Maria Malibran, the opera singer. She was extremely popular here in London—and your New York."

A chill came upon me as I observed Maria Malibran's pallid complexion. It was as if she had been kissed by death, but had returned from the grave. Her forehead was high and very pale, her hair black as a raven's wing, her eyes strangely glassy. Her mouth was open as if in song, which tightened her lips and offered a glimpse of her teeth, which I found deeply disturbing. The veracity of her expression made it difficult for me to accept that this doppelgänger had never sung a note, had never drawn breath. Indeed, I thought I could detect her scent—a hint of lilies and spice—and could feel her breath upon me as her green eyes gazed into mine.

"Maria Malibran had the misfortune of dying in the bloom of youth. Or one might argue that her early demise was fortunate as she makes a very comely memento mori."

I thought of my mother, an actress known for her captivating voice, who faded from life at just twenty-three years of age. I thought of my maternal grandmother, also an actress and singer, who departed this world before I was born. And I thought of my wife with her beautiful voice and fragile constitution.

The woman before me seemed to draw breath as if preparing for song. I waited for her voice to align with the music, to captivate me. The lulling melody of the orchestra embraced me and words sprang from the music. I heard the voice of my Morella who, when the finger of Death was upon her bosom, declared, "I am dying, yet shall I live." I thought of the daughter who takes breath after the death of her mother and strangely takes on her countenance and character though the years. Morella! She was before me, perfectly preserved. And in her pale features I saw my mothers, both gone, my mysterious grandmother and my delicate, gentle wife. From her waxen lips I heard their voices entwined in song and my skin prickled with icy kisses.

"Poe!" Dupin's sharp voice brought me back to myself. I tore my eyes away from the dark-haired siren and turned to face him. By his side stood an ancient crone of four score years or more—I felt the blood seep from my face. Why had this witch, this creature of nightmares, cursed the songstress and turned her to stone? The crone's glinting eyes held mine tight. I watched in horror as her dry lips parted.

"Our opera singer is as feted in death as she was in life. Many people come here to see her." Her cracked voice dropped to a confiding tone. "And on nights when the moon is full, Madame Malibran's voice has been heard coming from these very halls, singing an aria."

Dupin intervened. "Allow me to introduce my friend and colleague Edgar Poe."

The crone lifted her palsied hand toward me. As I took it in mine, I wondered how her wizened flesh still pulsed with life, unlike the beauty next to us.

"This is the renowned Madame Tussaud," Dupin continued.

I bowed my head toward her chilly hand, but could not bring myself to touch my lips to the flesh.

"*Enchanté*, Madame."

"As you will know, she is the creator of this grand collection."

Dupin's gallantry overshadowed veracity, but politeness required that I draw a thick veil over the truth. I nodded in deference to her age and her mysterious collection of creatures of which I knew nothing.

"Of course. Madame Tussaud's extraordinary collection is very well known, even in Philadelphia."

Madame puffed with pride. "I am pleased to hear that, sir. Most pleased." Her words were carefully enunciated, her accent very French. She turned her gaze to my companion. "What brings you to this city? It is rare for you to leave Paris."

"A mystery, Madame, a mystery."

"There are many mysteries in London, my dear Chevalier. And many are depicted in my salon." Her eyes shifted to me and a shrewd smile creased her face.

"We look forward to investigating those," Dupin responded. "But first I must ask, for your ears are privy to much information, most particularly regarding any French citizen here in London. Have you heard anything of Monsieur Valdemar's presence in the country?"

Madame frowned slightly. "Ah, the elusive Monsieur Valdemar who seems able to vanish into the air itself."

Dupin grimaced. "Your allusion is more apt than you might have intended. I have certain information that indicates he may be in London very soon, but we had an encounter with a balloon aeronaut, which leads me to wonder if he has already arrived."

Madame shook her head. "I cannot say, Auguste. I am acquainted with the man only by reputation, but would certainly find a way to inform you of his whereabouts if I were aware of them."

"We are staying at Brown's Genteel Inn should you hear anything at all."

Madame nodded. "I am, of course, terribly offended that you failed to inform me in advance of your sojourn to this city, but I cannot help but forgive you." She smiled and continued before Dupin could protest. "There is a clandestine event in nine days' time that you may find informative. I can tell you no more than that as I have pledged my complete discretion. If you will be in London on that date, I will ensure that you gain access."

Dupin's face lit up with what might only be described as vengeful hope. "Thank you, Madame. I will indeed be here in London and of course would never compromise you." He bowed slightly and pressed her hand to his lips.

Madame smiled at his gallantry. "Monsieur Poe has waited so patiently while we have been exceedingly impolite. You must let me guide you around my exhibition. Few of my visitors have your capacity to truly understand the importance of my work."

"You flatter me—and us—with your kind offer," Dupin said. "It is time to introduce Mr. Poe to the true horrors of the Terror and only your instruction will do the tale justice."

Madame looked moved by Dupin's cryptic declaration. "I would be honored to bear witness. Let us go, good sirs, and mingle with the mighty."

"Indeed, Madame. With the mighty." Dupin offered his arm. They made their way toward a doorway to another chamber, her small, crooked frame in stark contrast to his tall, erect one. I followed them across the threshold into a world of pomp and pageantry, of kings and queens. Henry VIII, Mary Queen of Scots, Elizabeth I, Charles I, William IV, George IV and Victoria stood before me. The tableaux were impressive in their opulence. And there stood Cromwell, the cuckoo within the nest.

"The Golden Chamber," Madame said proudly. "A history of monarchy. I have worked to capture with precision the details of each monarch's attire. Physical details can give much insight into a subject's character. Look here. These are the original coronation robes of King George IV." She lowered her voice. "Eighteen thousand pounds to make, and I purchased them for three hundred pounds."

"Madame has an eye for detail and a head for business," Dupin observed.

"You would do well to learn from my example, Chevalier. As you will have noticed, I am not one to follow the vagaries of fashion. My clothing is practical, well-made and will see me to the grave." She indicated her plain brown skirt, white high-necked blouse, woolen wrap and bonnet. "But you will forgive me for observing that while you are meticulously groomed, your clothing is of a style favored in Paris more than a decade ago. This of course causes me to make assumptions."

I flushed to wonder what conclusions the gimlet-eyed creature had drawn based on my own lack of dandified attire.

Surprisingly, Dupin seemed to take no offense. "Your eyes miss nothing. Suffice to say that your observations are correct, but I fear it is too late for me to acquire your business acumen and so my wardrobe must suffer and, no doubt, see me to the grave also."

Madame nodded benignly. "I am most fortunate. These figures are like my children to me—precious. You may not prosper from your Art as I have, but that does not tarnish the value of your skills. Remember that, dear Auguste. Now come, follow me. You and Mr. Poe will find the Adjoining Room of particular interest, I am certain."

Madame moved with more speed than I had assumed her capable of. I followed Dupin like his shadow, and fear followed me. Each tableau in the next chamber was constructed by the hand of Death, whether through the foul deed of murder, the justice of execution, or the two in terrifying combination.

"The public calls this Bluebeard's Chamber," Madame said. She indicated the first tableau, which resembled the interior of a barn and featured a young woman who had been fatally shot by a young man. "The murder of Maria Martin by William Corder. A terrible story. Corder promised to marry Mademoiselle Martin after he got her with child, but she disappeared. Her stepmother repeatedly dreamed that the girl had been shot and buried under the barn. The premonitions were accurate. Corder was arrested, half-insane with guilt, as he believed he could hear the beating of his victim's heart beneath the floorboards."

The grisly story made my own heart pound uncontrollably. Madame looked to me for comment. "The agony of guilt can drive a man to the edge of madness and beyond," I offered.

Dupin nodded his head in agreement. "And lead to a confession when the dead come back to haunt their murderers." He indicated Corder's face, which was terrifyingly realistic in its depiction of murderous fury. "Madame had the privilege of constructing Corder's death mask after his hanging. Imagine how much her hands have learned about human character through these reconstructions. Consider how her work might advance the science of phrenology."

Somehow, I could not see this as a privilege. The thought of caressing the hanged man's features into a mask of death was repugnant to me, despite the secrets that might be unlocked with phrenology.

Madame indicated another tableau that featured two men of clear ill-repute. "William Burke and William Hare. Very famous."

"They made a habit of killing impoverished men living on the streets and selling their bodies to Edinburgh Hospital," Dupin added. He indicated the craniums of the murderers before us. "Note the over-development of the fourth, fifth and seventh brain sub-organs. It seems certain that a combative character mixed with a destructive nature might tend toward violent murder. And if the subject is also inclined toward covetousness, we may deduce through simple ratiocination that the motive for murder is money."

"We might also venture that the twenty-fourth and thirty-first sub-organs are under-developed or faulty, resulting in a lack of compassion for their fellow man and little reverence for God," I suggested.

A bitter look came over Dupin's face. "Yes, in my experience that would seem accurate. Most astute, Poe."

"I know little of phrenology," Madame said. "But your words ring with truth as surely this must reveal." She indicated the chamber's main display—a guillotine surrounded by severed heads. "This is a working model of the guillotine used in Paris with the actual blade and lunette. It was a terrible time," Madame murmured. "Crowds baying for blood. Innocents forced to kneel beneath her blade."

The display had an unfortunate effect upon my constitution, and I found it difficult to physically contain my horror. I expected Dupin to be unaffected by the gruesome tableau, but once again he surprised me. He was focused on a basket of severed heads that were arranged—most ghoulishly—like cabbages at market. Two heads at the apex of the heap secured his clearest attention: a man of perhaps thirty-five, solemn of expression, with dark hair, an aquiline nose and a determined chin; and a woman, very attractive, with ebony curls, porcelain skin, a small well-formed mouth and clear gray eyes that shone with intelligence—or so one might think if the eerie craniums had truly been fashioned by Nature herself. Their features were frozen at the moment of death, or perhaps at the soul's abdication, and yet fear was entirely absent on either countenance. Dupin wore an odd expression as he gazed upon these peculiar memento mori—brooding, or indeed one might almost say *pensive*. This was not an emotion I had ever discerned upon Dupin's face before. Objective, dismissive, impatient, arrogant, perhaps, but never one of the weaker emotions.

"*Que Dieu apaise leurs âmes,*" Madame whispered and crossed herself. "*Je n'ai pas pu les sauver, et il était de mon devoir de préserver leurs corps sinon leurs vies.*"

"*Ils en auraient autant de reconnaissance que je n'en ai moi-même,*" Dupin murmured.

"*Si cela vous réconforte, je suis satisfaite, Chevalier.*"

Dupin nodded and presented Madame with a faint smile. "What is your opinion of the display, Poe?"

"Most macabre," I could not help but mutter.

"Macabre? Perhaps. But it is history, my dear sir. This was the fate of French nobility during the Terror and almost the fate of Madame Tussaud. She was arrested on suspicion of royalist sympathies and imprisoned to await execution."

Madame nodded. I felt ashamed by my squeamishness when the display had such personal resonance for my companions.

"Please, tell me more."

"I was admired as a waxworks artist in Paris and was invited to Versailles to give Louis XVI's sister, Madame Elizabeth, lessons in the art of wax modeling. I lived there for a time, but returned to Paris after the storming of the Bastille. Then I was imprisoned. Thankfully, my talent saved me from execution." Madame held up her gnarled hands. "I was commanded to make death masks of those they executed. Many of the victims were my friends." She indicated the basket of severed heads.

"It took much courage to deal with such a terrible situation," I said.

Madame Tussaud fixed her sharp eyes on mine. "It was a privilege, dear sir. A privilege to make my friends immortal." She stared at the execution victims before her, a wistful look upon her face.

"Madame, there is much to learn from your example. Some day, I hope, you will instruct me in the art of replicating the human form, which is far more complex than reconstructing human motive."

"Perhaps, dear Chevalier. If the Fates allow. But now I must leave you. Take your time and enjoy the manifestation of history. Come find me at my station before you leave."

"Thank you, Madame. The experience has been all the more vivid through your guardianship," I said.

She nodded like a queen and silence descended fell us when she left the room. Dupin's eyes remained fixed upon the guillotine, his expression enigmatic. I had no doubt that my own face revealed my horror at the gruesome tableau. I could think of nothing to say and as the silence grew increasingly uncomfortable, Dupin indicated the door and said, "Shall we?" We made our way from the exhibition chambers to the hall where Madame Tussaud now presided, taking money from more visitors to her macabre waxworks.

"Gentlemen! You are leaving so soon?"

"I am afraid so. It was an informative experience and now we must use what we have learned." He smiled warmly at Madame, who beamed in return.

"I am glad my menagerie has helped your investigation in some small way." She looked to me for comment or, more accurately, for praise.

I bowed and said, "Madame, I hope you won't mind me saying that your collection is both disturbing and spectacular. The artistry is undeniable, but your chamber of horrors would make the bravest of hearts accelerate with fear."

Madame Tussaud's face creased with a broad smile. "Chamber of horrors? Monsieur Poe, you have a gift for description. It will be the making of you, mark my words." She turned to Dupin. "I hope to see you in nine days' time, but if that proves impossible, please visit me again before I find my place in Heaven."

"Madame, Heaven will be impatient to receive you for many more years."

"Et lorsque le paradis m'accueillera, je raconterai à vos chers grand-parents quel homme exceptionnel vous êtes devenu."

"Et je leurs dirai avec quel grand art vous avez honoré leur mémoire." Dupin leaned to kiss her wizened hand.

For the briefest of moments, the rose of youth settled on her features, and I caught sight of the woman as she was in an early incarnation, but her rusted voice erased the illusion. *"Ce fût un honneur pour moi."*

My facility with the French language had diminished with limited use, but I grasped Madame Tussaud's reference to Dupin's grandparents. He rarely spoke of his forebears, and while I was, of course, aware that he descended from noble stock, only in that moment did I fathom that his grandparents had been victims of the Terror and were now immortalized in Madame Tussaud's collection. Icy fingers gripped my chest as a vivid image of the basket of severed heads materialized before me. The solemn gentleman with noble expression, aquiline nose, dark hair, lofty forehead and the handsome, porcelain-skinned woman with delicate mouth and large gray eyes so full of clarity—combine their features and one would have the very double of Dupin. How could I have missed the ghastly truth behind the tableau? Madame Tussaud had indeed preserved the mortal images of her two dear friends, when their souls had not long been separated from their still warm bodies. I was ashamed to have missed the obvious hidden in plain sight, blinded by my emotions regarding my own family.

"Au revoir, Monsieur Poe. Perhaps some day you and your brother Dupin will join my grand menagerie."

Her words brought a deep chill to my heart. "Thank you, Madame. I hope I prove worthy of such a compliment." I bowed politely and hurried with undue haste to the doorway, leaving Dupin to make a more gracious farewell. As I stepped into the afternoon sunlght, I could not shake off a lingering sense of fear, as if the eyes of the ancient crone's subjects were still upon me. When Dupin joined me at last, we searched for a coach stand but had little luck until a whistle pierced through the noise of the busy street and, fortuitously, a coach stood before us. We asked the driver to take us to Brown's Genteel Inn and climbed inside.

"I am sorry, Dupin. It must be distressing to see such a grue-some homage to your grandparents."

"Not at all. Indeed I draw strength from it."

"Will you tell me more about Monsieur Valdemar and why you are so anxious to find him?"

"All will become plain in due course. Let us focus on your mystery first."

Just then the coach shuddered and bounced; something slid across the floor and hit my feet. I looked down and saw a parcel—some unfortunate lady had forgotten her shopping. But when I picked up the package, I saw it had an address on it, and a pall enveloped me that rendered my flesh as cold as those entities that inhabited Madame Tussaud's kingdom of the dead. *Mr. Edgar Allan Poe, Brown's Genteel Inn* was written in elegant, flowing script across the brown paper of the package I held in my trembling hands.

AN INVITATION

Mr. François Benjamin Courvoisier,
convicted of the crime of murder,
will be publicly hanged by the neck at Newgate until he is dead.
The performance begins promptly at Eight o'clock,
Monday morning, the sixth of July 1840.
It is recommended to take a position at the
barriers nearest to the scaffold
no later than seven o'clock.

Darkness, utter darkness. As I lay upon my bed in the pitch blackness, I *felt* the bedroom door creep open, little by little, pushed steadily by an unseen hand, yet I could see nothing, could say nothing, my fear was so acute. Slowly, my hearing sharpened as my nervousness increased—was it minutes or hours as the door inched inexorably inwards and the ominous presence filled the doorframe?

"Who is there?" a voice cried out, vibrating with terror. "Who!" I realized the voice was my own.

Three wavering flames appeared in the darkness. A form slowly materialized—a hand holding a candelabrum, and then a spectral face—Hermes come to lead me to Hell's gate. "It is time. Are you ready?"

My heart pounded like a drum, and fear held my throat shut. The candle-glare flickered, mesmerizing me.

"Poe, it is time." The specter proceeded to light the candles in my bedchamber, one by one, and as the room glowed with sinister light, sleep released me from its grasp.

"Dupin, it is you," I muttered with relief.

He was swathed in black as if with the night itself and, like the moon, his pale face hovered in the gloom.

"Were you expecting another?" he asked with saturnine amusement.

"Given yesterday's events, perhaps."

"I am sorry if I frightened you. I thought the din would have awakened you."

It was only then that I heard the sound of people in the corridors and out on the street. I picked up my pocket watch. Half past three in the morning and the entire city seemed awake. Dupin had proposed that we rise at this ungodly hour and set off for our destination well before dawn—a destination that filled me with horror.

"Come, Poe. I have had coffee sent to my room. We should commence our journey in twenty minutes if we are to find your aggressor at the assigned location." Dupin retreated, candelabrum in hand.

I arose from bed, shivering despite the warm summer night, and peered out the window. Small gangs of people walked north along Dover Street, lighting their way with gaily colored lanterns and passing flasks amongst themselves, which no doubt contributed to their celebratory mood. This made me tremble all the more, but I dressed quickly, extinguished the tapers and hurried to Dupin's room. When I entered his chambers, the aroma of coffee brought me closer to full cognizance.

"Have you had any further thoughts about your aggressor's invitation—as it were—to Courvoisier's hanging?" Dupin asked as we gulped down our drinks. "Occasionally sleep may prompt a memory."

The macabre invitation had been included in the packet left for me in the carriage and was accompanied by further letters written by my grandparents.

"It infected my dreams, but the little sleep I managed brought no useful recollections. I cannot think why Mr. Mackie would wish to meet me at such a gruesome location."

"It is far safer for him to reveal himself in a crowd, which the hanging will provide. And he wishes to unsettle you, of course."

"I have terrible reservations about this assignation. Surely it is safer to wait for Mackie to make himself known to us here at Brown's?"

"He certainly will not do that for he will fear arrest." Dupin placed his pocket watch and purse upon the table and added: "I strongly suggest that you leave behind your watch, money, any jewels, your handkerchief. Pickpockets, cutpurses—all of London's villains will be in high attendance."

"Your evaluation of the audience we will encounter does little to make me feel safe." I knotted my pocket watch and purse inside my handkerchief, but left my locket around my neck. Dupin noticed my refusal to relinquish it.

"It would be wise to leave the jewel here," he said, nodding toward its location. "I will wear these for protection." Dupin drew on a pair of black kidskin gloves that obscured his gold and lapis lazuli *chevalière*.

"I made a pledge to Sissy to wear my locket always. It will be quite safe."

Dupin shrugged, entirely unconvinced. "It is your choice. You must obscure the jewel completely with your stock and refrain from touching your fingers anxiously to its location or it will be gone." He reached into his waistcoat pocket and pulled out what appeared to be a snuffbox. "A necessary precaution, I fear." He opened the box, dipped in his fingertip, then daubed a goodly layer of clear balm under each nostril. Dupin handed the container to me. "The scent of London streets is rarely agreeable, but this morning we will experience the malodorous vapor of the mob itself. This is but a partial remedy."

I applied the unguent in the manner Dupin had demonstrated and was overwhelmed by the scent of Christmas.

Dupin was amused at my reaction. "Oil of Neroli, clove, calamus and benzoin Sumatra. I have found it very effective for masking unpleasant aromas while simultaneously clearing the channels to the brain."

"Extraordinary. I have never encountered such a remedy before."

"It is said to be a discovery of the Comte de Saint-Germain. Perhaps vanquishing the city's vapors was his secret to immortality," Dupin said with a thin smile. His attempt at levity did little to calm me. "Shall we commence?" he asked.

I inhaled deeply, drawing in that joyous smell of Christmas, hoping to repel the fog of dread that clung to me. "If we must."

* * *

The streets of London were as bustling at half past four in the morning as they had been in the afternoon and our progress was slow. House windows were lit up with candles and the gin shops were open for custom. Coaches careered past, drivers swearing ferociously at each other. Pedestrians tramped all around us in a mob, which seemed a living entity in itself. Our mad carnival had no need for the grotesquery of masks or costumes, for reality was sufficiently monstrous. The overblown sense of revelry was riddled with unease and the cold whiff of fear. When we reached Snow Hill at last, St. Sepulchre's bells rang out six o'clock, and Newgate Prison came into view. There, hideously before us, was the gallows, pressed up against a small door in the prison wall. I came over quite numb, and Dupin reached out to steady me on my feet.

Our fellow onlookers were far less affected by the props on the stage before us. Men and women wove their way through the unending crowd, selling snacks and drinks and execution broadsides with "his last true confession" and promising details of the execution, which had yet to take place. Every shop window with a view of the gallows was hired out to spectators. Houses overlooking the scene had faces peering from each window or voyeurs gathered up on the roof. My heart was pounding and my breath was near squeezed from my body as we surged forward, ever closer to the scaffold, pushed by the crowd. Truly I wanted to fight my way out of this sea of people and Dupin seemed to sense this as he steered me forward by the elbow.

"There is nothing to fear," he said. "Trust that it is better to confront your enemy than to have him tracking you like a hunter."

"It is difficult to imagine Mr. Mackie playing the hunter when his gaudy attire makes him so highly visible."

"Perhaps he was incognito while on the *Ariel* and his garb is normally sober."

"Whatever he is wearing, I will certainly recognize him from his insolent demeanor."

"Auburn hair and mustache, approximately five foot six, stocky, pale skin, green eyes and perhaps thirty years of age," Dupin recited. "A theatrical voice, surfeit of confidence and lack of objectivity."

"That is precisely how I remember him."

"And so we must try to fathom how your grandparents' letters came into his possession and what within them provoked his ire. And of course why he believes this is the appropriate location for your assignation."

"Yes," I said, looking for Mackie while Dupin pushed his way through the crowd so that we might secure our place near the barriers directly in front of the scaffold.

When at last we achieved our position, we simply waited, as did all the others. The atmosphere was far quieter than I would have imagined, considering the general caliber of the voyeurs. Both sexes were present, men often circling around the women to offer protection against the inebriated and the general crush of the thousands that thronged to witness the hanging of Courvoisier.

"Would Philadelphians behave in such a manner?" Dupin asked.

I observed my fellow bystanders chattering, drinking and singing to pass the time, thus creating an odd atmosphere of gaiety.

"Perhaps once, but no longer. Philadelphia is a city of Quakers with a great affection for peace. Only murder in the first degree is punishable by death and hangings are conducted privately, without the mob in attendance."

"And what of the other cities in America—are they equally squeamish of public executions?"

"Not at all. In Richmond and Baltimore public executions continue and one might find that the public is as eager for the spectacle as here."

"But you have never previously attended such an event."

"I have until now been quite able to contain my enthusiasm for a good public hanging."

Dupin smiled. "It may surprise you that the only public execution I have attended until now was molded in wax."

I thought with horror of the execution scene at Madame Tussaud's and wondered what effect this terrible event must be having on Dupin. Had Mackie planned it this way? Had he more dastardly intelligence than I had presumed?

"But look at our fellow voyeurs," Dupin said with utter calmness. "For them it is a spectacle to relish—high theater with no need to purchase admission."

This was undoubtedly true. A well-dressed group near us was telling jokes and laughing boisterously. Three pretty sisters dressed in rag-shop clothes and greasy bonnets were taunted by sallow, raggedy lads and responded in an equally uncouth manner. Young dandies wearing gaudy shepherd's plaid trousers and kidskin gloves dyed bilious colors—mint, turquoise, butter yellow—lounged nearby, smoking cigars and arguing about nothing of importance. Further away, a group of honest workers and their wives were gazing calmly upon the scaffold as they sipped cups of tea. There was something terrifying about their gleeful attitude toward the impending execution.

"Are you aware that Mr. Dickens and Mr. Thackeray are also in attendance? Courvoisier's situation has caused quite a stir with the London literati."

Dupin succeeded in capturing my full attention as he had no doubt intended. "I have been so caught up in our investigation, I confess I have read nothing about Courvoisier."

"The London police acquitted themselves very well during their investigation. The case is a fine example of applied ratiocination. I shall outline the circumstances, for surely they must have some bearing on your assignation." Just then the workmen began to ready the scaffold for its victim—an unpleasant accompaniment to Dupin's words.

"François Benjamin Courvoisier is from Switzerland and was engaged as Lord William Russell's valet. He was a resident at his employer's home at fourteen Norfolk Street, Park Lane, along with two other servants: a housemaid and a cook. Lord Russell was found murdered in his bed on the sixth of May this year. Courvoisier raised the alarm and claimed that a thief had forced his way into the premises and had killed Lord Russell. The police examined the house carefully and realized that the scene of the crime was constructed to suggest a ransacking, but they correctly noted that the perpetrator made several fundamental errors in his attempt to place blame elsewhere."

"Such as?"

"A parcel was left behind for effect, but it contained items any thief might have hidden in his pockets. Nothing was stolen from the parlor or drawing-room, but objects of value were missing from his lordship's bedroom that had been locked away in drawers or his trunk, for which Courvoisier had keys. An opportunistic thief would not be aware of where Lord Russell kept these valuables, but the Swiss valet would. Further, Courvoisier claimed that the perpetrator had forced open the pantry door to gain admission to the house, but when the police inspected the door, it was clear it had been forced from the inside."

"And this added to the suspicions regarding Courvoisier."

"Yes," Dupin affirmed. "These suspicions were exacerbated by the discovery of the ten pound note, a Waterloo medal, a locket, five gold rings and five gold coins hidden behind the skirting board in the kitchen. Further, his lordship's pocket watch, which had been at his bedside on the night of his murder, was hidden behind a lead panel on the sink. Again, these are small items that any ordinary thief would have carried away on his person."

"Only someone who lived in the house would secrete stolen items on the premises," I conjectured.

"Correct again. Courvoisier, who had recently expressed a profound dislike for his employer and had stated his intention to return as soon as he could to his native Switzerland, was the most obvious suspect."

Our attention was momentarily distracted from the analysis of the case by the bells of St. Sepulchre ringing out half past seven o'clock. The horror of the impending event seeped into me like seawater into a drowning man. And where was Mackie? Was he truly here to confront me or had he merely sent me to this dreadful place to taunt me? My attention was caught by several neatly dressed policemen as they passed in front of us, patrolling the space between the prison and the timber barricades that kept the spectators and ghoulish souvenir hunters at bay. Their presence gave me some comfort, but did not deter the light-fingered. I watched a boy of no more than twelve dip his fingers into a man's coat pocket and extract a snow-white handkerchief. Dupin directed my attention toward an attractive young lady who apologized flirtatiously for jarring a corpulent man and walked away wearing a wicked smile and carrying his gold pocket watch.

"A public hanging clearly does little to dissuade the criminal element from theft," he said.

"I wonder if the same might be said for murder. Madmen presume they will never be caught."

"Quite right, Poe. The cold-blooded person who plots murder believes his superior intelligence will enable him to escape detection, whereas the hothead acts without applying reason and the murder is committed before he considers the consequences."

"Or she—I would presume the same applies to the murderess."

Dupin raised his eyebrows. "Is a woman capable of plotting murder with sufficient coolness of head and heart? Courvoisier's defense lawyer hoped to insinuate that the housekeeper or cook murdered Lord Russell and constructed the sham burglary, but this idea was dismissed as ridiculous."

"Surely it is an error to presume guilt or innocence without analyzing the evidence."

"Agreed." Dupin presented one of his saturnine smiles. "However, Lord Russell was found with his head nearly severed from his body. Would the frailer sex be physically capable of such a brutal act?"

"It seems unlikely."

"So thought the police. Courvoisier was brought to trial and he pleaded not guilty until the evening of the first day, when it was revealed that Madame Piolaine, the keeper of the Hotel Dieppe in Leicester Place, had in her possession some stolen plate that belonged to Lord Russell. The valet immediately admitted his guilt, but declared that he began his life of crime inspired by a book about a young profligate who lost all his possessions through gambling. He then claimed that he was driven to murder after attending a play based on William Ainsworth's novel about the criminal Jack Sheppard. I am certain you can conclude why London's literati are so interested in this case."

"Mr. Courvoisier is a devious man. He uses Newgate novels as his defense, playing on the misplaced morality of those who believe we may be driven to murder by Art itself."

Dupin nodded. "Mr. Dickens has been accused of writing Newgate novels as has Mr. Thackeray. These allegations raise a number of questions. If one writes truthfully of evil or diseased characters, does it valorize them? Must our perceptions of a person's character be formed by the subjects he chooses to write about?"

"And should a tale's merit be judged solely by the factual elements within it without considering its imaginative qualities, originality or overall effect?" I added.

Dupin turned his gaze to the scaffold before us. "But most importantly, is it possible for a person to pen a tale, whether truth or fiction, that drives its reader to murder? Clearly all the questions raised by Courvoisier's crimes are of special interest to any writer who examines characters motivated by the darker forces." Dupin frowned in contemplation. "We must wonder why your nemesis deems Courvoisier's fate important—why he invited you here. There must be a connection with the letters."

As Dupin uttered those words, St. Sepulchre's chimed eight o'clock. The time was upon us for Courvoisier's hanging! This provoked a horrible reaction—the vast melee around us began to murmur and hum like a swarm of terrible insects. As if in response to this hideous sound, women and children commenced shrieking and my blood turned to ice. All eyes focused on the stage before us. I scanned the faces around me one last time; if Mackie was nearby, he had concealed himself very well.

The crowd's noise increased and all turned to face the scaffold, as if hypnotized. A pale face emerged from the prison-door—a man in black appeared on the scaffold. The condemned murderer, accompanied by four men, walked to his destiny, arms tied in front of him, face contorted into a peculiar smile. He looked at the crowd, or so it seemed, before he placed himself under the beam and faced St. Sepulchre's, perhaps in prayer. The hangman abruptly turned Courvoisier around and put a nightcap over his head and face. I was filled with horror and yet could scarcely avert my eyes from the spectacle until Dupin, bafflingly, turned to face the mob behind us. His countenance was determined, yet calm. He scanned the faces that were focused on Courvoisier and his executioner.

The clergyman began to chant and my own gaze returned again to the scaffold, drawn by some infernal magic. "The Lord giveth and the Lord taketh away"—the rest merged with the strange mutterings of the mob, which increased in volume as the rope was put around Courvoisier's neck. And then—*crack!* The floor disappeared from beneath his feet and Courvoisier was dangling and jerking from the rope like a ghoulish marionette. A man emerged from the black hole beneath his feet and seized the kicking legs—pulling down until the very life oozed from Courvoisier and trickled into the darkness beneath him, into those gaping jaws that could only lead to Hell. The lifeless body of Courvoisier swayed gently, dead at last, and would continue to hang for a full hour, as was the law. The drama was over, but the crowd was in no hurry to leave the theater. Spectators expressed their satisfaction as they prepared for the journey home. "Kill a man and you must be killed in turn. An eye for an eye, a tooth for a tooth—blood demands blood."

"Cowards," Dupin muttered, still facing the crowd, his face contorted, his body held as stiffly as a military general on parade.

"But how can you bear to be here when your grandparents were executed on the public stage—when you have just witnessed their brutalized effigies!" And then a more unsettling thought occurred to me. "You chose to watch the hanging amongst this throng. Why immerse yourself in the basest of human reactions to a man's death?"

Dupin raised his shoulders and shook his head gently. "I did not watch the execution, I observed *the mob*. Now I have experienced firsthand how Paris reacted to my grandparents' execution." Dupin's eyes met mine with great solemnity. "And because I now have a sense of what they experienced when facing death, perhaps I know them better for it."

"They were brave, I am certain."

"Unlike the man who murdered them," Dupin said softly.

Before I could ask what he meant, our path was barred by a weasel-faced man with extraordinary whiskers and spectacles that magnified his eyes. He was wearing a battered rabbit-skin hat and an over-sized, patched coat with enormous pockets.

"Here, sir! The last lamentation of Courvoisier, his final words written in his cell at dawn, just hours before his hanging. Read on the page the poetic outpourings of his condemned soul!"

Dupin turned to face the ballad seller. "And how did you come by Mr. Courvoisier's final lament? Are you a friend of his?"

The little man scuffled closer and winked. "Not a friend of Courvoisier's, sir, but a friend of his jailer. Sat outside his cell all night and at dawn these words fairly spilled from his soul. It's often the case—a man faced with death wishes to relieve his burden." He held up a scroll of paper. "His final words in rhyming couplets."

"If only we all were so talented," Dupin said dryly.

"Common knowledge that imminent death brings out the muse in all of us. You will see that Courvoisier's lament is written down in a very fine hand. I was a scrivener in better days. See here. Eminently legible."

A disproportionate number of scribes I had encountered—in drinking establishments, it was true—drank to alleviate the boredom of their work and then lost the very work that had driven them to excess. The page before me was indeed in a very fine hand, but without the tell-tale wavering lines of the habitual drunk.

"And you may purchase the original and sole copy of his final lamentation for no more than a penny."

Dupin opened his mouth to answer, but I interjected first. "Here is your penny." I took the little scroll from his hands.

"Thank you, good sirs." The be-whiskered man backed away, smiling broadly, the morning light glinting off his spectacles. "Remember, sirs," he shouted merrily, "only our actions will tell if we'll dwell with the saints or are doomed to Hell." And the man was gone as quickly as he had appeared.

"A peculiar fellow," Dupin murmured.

"Most peculiar." An impatient urge to read Courvoisier's lament came over me, and I unfurled the scroll.

The Innocent's Lament
(Written by Himself)
Rhynwick Williams was held to shame,
Foul crimes besmirch his good Welsh name,
While, blade whetted for a lady's gown,
A Monster still roams London town.

Thus wrote the innocent, deceiv'd,
Condemn'd, thus he bequeathed
His last and only legacy,
Revenge for E— A—'s treachery
On her whole line, beyond her death,
Their heart's last beat, their final breath.

I stared at the paper shivering in my hands, then wildly into the crowd surrounding us.

"He is gone, Poe," Dupin said gently. "We shall never find him now."

I nodded, baffled by the wretched lament that was written down so prettily.

"It would appear that we have another mystery to solve," Dupin added.

"Who is Rhynwick Williams?" I wondered aloud.

"That should be simple enough to discover," Dupin said. "More importantly, who was the man with the false whiskers and how did he find us in this monstrous crowd?"

The Swann Inn, Tunbridge Wells
14 January 1790

My Dearest,

If I had your gift with rhyme, I would pen a poem to soothe your ruffled feathers and to damn that impertinent woman your father married, for surely it is not her invitation to withhold. Your new dress would render you the most delightful woman at the Queen's birthday ball and if you are absent, the event will surely suffer. But do not fear your gown wasted just yet. Do you recall Stubbs the footman? I saw him three days previously with my former employer, Mr. Richardson, who, whether he is deep in his cups or utterly dry at breakfast time, seems not to remember me at all. Stubbs has not changed a whit and takes great advantage of Mr. Richardson's weak memory. According to Stubbs, dear old Richardson is in receipt of several invitations to the Queen's birthday celebrations at St. James's Palace. I am working to secure us a pair, but with or without them, we shall attend the ball!

Your devoted husband,
Henry

93 Jermyn Street, London
16 January 1790

My Darling,

I cannot tell you how much your words mean to me—it matters not if they are expressed in rhyme when they are so full of reason and, dare I say, sympathy. As for my gown, it is hardly new, only made to seem so by its new decorations. I decided upon a royal theme in honour of Her Majesty—specifically, velvet violets in royal purple. Miniature bouquets of this dainty flower now embellish the décolletage and the new sash of pale lavender, which is quite striking against the silver muslin. But the details of my gown are unlikely to truly interest you; you may, however, find the following twist of fate intriguing.

When I went to Monsieur Amabel Mitchell's flower factory on Dover Street to have my gown refurbished, I was intrigued to discover that the flower makers are all women from France with the exception of a Welshman who looked terribly familiar. I could not recall who he was or how I knew him—he appeared to be about my age but from the state of his clothes, quite down on his luck. It was clear from the man's covert gazes that he recognised me also, but perhaps was too ashamed of his reduced circumstances to address me. I have an empathy for this condition and did not press matters.

However, when I had agreed the number of violets and silk ribbon required for my gown,

Monsieur Mitchell relayed my order to the man in question and the fellow's identity came to me. He was none other than the luckless Welsh ballet dancer who was apprenticed to Gallini! Do you remember? We were at the King's Theatre and had the misfortune of observing the wretch's attempts as a dancer— indeed all of Gallini's dancers were utterly without talent. Surely you must recall the debacle of a performance that Gallini refused to end, despite the abundant hisses, until the audience turned mob and charged the stage, threatening to murder all of us? The Welshman survived that terrible performance, but was finally dismissed when Gallini accused him of stealing his watch. The Welshman did not suffer the penalty of law for the alleged theft, but the accusation must surely have put him in his current dismal circumstances. I am happy to report that our heavy-footed friend seems quite dextrous at his new profession.

Eliza and I look forward to your return, dearest,
Your Wife

93 Jermyn Street, London
19 January 1790

Dear Father,

Thank you tremendously for securing our invitations to the Queen's birthday celebrations—what a thrill it was to attend incognito—our own secret masquerade! How amusing to play your son rather than your brother on this occasion—I am confident your lessons from the nunnery contributed to a most masculine performance.

In my guise as a wealthy gentleman bachelor, I found the assemblage a veritable garden, gaudy perhaps, but a delight to the hungry eye. Those bold posies vied to capture my attention—what colour and coquetry there was! As I swaggered through a bed of roses with colours ranging from the virginal ivory shades to the first blush of pink, moving through every rosy hue until the heated flush of lusty reds, I discovered that each dress was a reflection of its owner's experience. How I longed to slide my blade through the profusion of their petals, to feel it slip through the delicate silk, the sheen of organza, the soft-furred nape of velvet. But, as we agreed, I bided my time—it would not do to be caught pruning those showy blooms during the festivities themselves. I continued exploring this fine garden and discovered dramatic lilies in oranges and yellows, and stately delphiniums in rich blues and purples—though, dare I say, a fine display of violets would not have gone amiss. How I wished to supplant those insipid flowers that danced in your arms all night!

When the celebrations finished, I followed two unwary flowers—one in pale pink, the other wearing yellow—and a stout elderly woman who was their chaperone along St. James's Street. One lagged behind her companions, her feet seemingly injured from the dancing. As I approached, I recognised her as a plain girl who had flirted ferociously from the gallery, and when I said, "What ho, is that you?" she smiled with recognition. But as I advanced upon her, prepared to strike, she leaned unexpectedly to adjust her slipper, and I inadvertently clouted her on the head. The wretch shrieked and began to run, her sore feet utterly recovered. She passed her sister and chaperone and began to knock frantically upon the door of Pero's Bagnio. As her companions charged after her, I followed—a fearless Monster—and nipped the sister on the rump, slicing through the rosy silk of her ball gown, her petticoats and into the ample cushion of her flesh. And then, the door to Pero's flew open and the females pushed their way inside as a young man stared out at me. I gave an elegant bow, then turned heel and hurried away, the cries of the hysterical ladies echoing in the night.

But the Monster was not sated! I crossed over Piccadilly and hastened into Dover Street, where I discovered a lady walking quite alone, not far from the flower factory. I offered to escort her home, but when she hesitated, I gave her a sharp prod in the posterior to hurry her response. "Murder!" she shrieked, but I had already disappeared into the darkness. Two victims claimed in one evening—I hope your adventures were equally exciting, *mon père*!

Your respectful Son,
Mr. George Richardson

93 Jermyn Street, London
20 January 1790

My dear Son,
It was with great paternal satisfaction that I read of your enjoyment of the ball and all the flowers therein. Most surely the missing violets were a great loss, but

your presence at the event, dressed in your suit and astonishing whiskers were a fine thing to witness. And I very much enjoyed my performance as Mr. Richardson the elder. Age does not diminish one's attractiveness with the ladies when a wealthy man! My feet were sore with dancing by the evening's end, and it was a relief that the Queen decided to retire early or I would not have had the legs to chase my quarry.

When we parted on St. James's Street, I came upon a group of five ladies who had been in the gallery at the ball. What a challenge! I singled out the prettiest, and after a brief courtship of words, I directed my blade at the lady's posterior. It penetrated the silk and then the undergarments until tasting the fleshy peach beneath. I did not tarry to savour the sweetness, but went in search of further prey and quickly found a lady alone on the street. I tickled her rump with my blade, which brought forth quite a shriek. As she ran from my attentions, I dissolved into the shadows near Brook's Club and waited for another chance. A lady and gentleman strolled past my hiding place—another challenge! My blade flew through the air and slipped through the cloth of the lady's dress until it pierced the skin of her posterior—how soft it was! How fragile! But I did not tarry to watch the effect of my actions. I vanished into the night, satisfied with three victims in one evening.

> With greatest affection,
> Your daring Father

The dim light, the cool atmosphere and the heaviness of history erased the chaos of the outside world—it was a place designed to make a man forget for a time his daily cares and lose himself in intellectual contemplation. I studied the exhibitions around me as I made my way to my rendezvous point with Dupin in the British Museum library. The antiquities on display were absorbing, but it was not the jeweled artifacts from far-flung lands that captivated me, nor the mummified kings and queens of the Nile that fashionable ladies and gentlemen clamored to see. Rather, it was the wood and glass cases crammed full of oddities from some well-traveled old gentleman's collection, objects placed with little regard to logic or aesthetic order: sea shells from the Pacific, bird eggs, fossilized ocean creatures, pinned butterflies. There was an array of fauna frozen in time by a taxidermist's expertise: owls, stoats, an eagle, a fox, startled rabbits and mice, whose postures gave them the semblance of life, eternally preserved.

In stark contrast, one glass case contained the tiny corpses of gem-colored hummingbirds, huddled forlornly upon green paper; their feathers luminescent, but fragile, *vanquished*, the beauty of their flickering wings stilled forever. Miss Loddiges

had extinguished a goodly quantity of such beauteous creatures during her ornithological studies, and I could not help but
think of the lady when I gazed at the delicate hummingbirds
within the case. After the macabre execution, I had failed to
find sleep when we finally returned to Brown's Genteel Inn and
had traveled to Paradise Fields, Hackney, to meet my benefactress, who had extended an open invitation to visit and see her
collection of avian skeletons that had inspired the book I had
edited for her. My interest in the collection was limited, but I
was more than curious to meet the woman who had done me
a great service and with whom I hoped to work again. The visit
had not raised my spirits as I had hoped it would. While my
gratitude to Miss Loddiges was undiminished, the lady's Art
had repelled me, and seeing the tiny birds abandoned inside the
glass case at the British Museum filled me with a terrible
sadness. I left the dusty chamber with a shiver and went in
search of Dupin.

The library was predictably quiet with a quantity of scholars
at work. It did not take me long to locate my friend, and I drew
up a chair alongside him.

"I trust your visit with your benefactress was pleasant," he
said in a low voice.

"It was illuminating. She is an accomplished woman, but
taxidermy is a peculiar Art," I said. "And has your research here
revealed anything of value?"

Triumph gleamed in Dupin's eyes. "While I am afraid the
scrivener's intent remains a mystery, I have uncovered propi-
tious information about Rhynwick Williams."

"He truly existed?"

"Rhynwick Williams stood trial at the Old Bailey on the
eighth of July 1790, accused of the crimes committed by the
London Monster."

"The London Monster?"

Dupin nodded. "An infamous villain—presumed to be a man—who took to slashing the hindquarters of attractive females and thereby terrorized London for two years."

Dupin's pronouncement hit me forcibly. "Truly? And what was the verdict?"

"Guilty," Dupin said.

This pronouncement was more shocking than the first. "He was found guilty? And so my grandparents did not commit the crimes they write of in their letters?"

"I did not say that," Dupin answered. "I did not say that at all."

Confusion settled upon me as it often did when Dupin was gripped in the state of ratiocination. "Perhaps you could first explain how you discovered this information and proceed from there."

Dupin nodded. "Of course." The map he had drawn was on the table in front of him and he tapped at the key, which noted the dates and locations of the attacks referred to in the letters. "I carefully read through the London newspapers from that period, searching for any mention of these crimes. I found little of interest until April 1790 when all of London seemed suddenly alert to the activities of the villain called 'the Monster' who had been attacking the 'defenceless and generally handsome women' of London. The newspapers were full of salacious cartoons depicting a vile creature—half-man, half-demon—cutting the posteriors of attractive young ladies with a vicious dagger and further depictions of these same ladies affixing copper pots to their derrières to prevent the Monster from damaging their nether regions and dignity. Then John Julius Angerstein posted notice that he would award one hundred pounds to anyone who captured the Monster. I followed the trail, so to speak, and discovered that Rhynwick Williams was caught on the thirteenth of June and accused of being the Monster. Of course the man who lodged the accusation made claim to Angerstein's reward. Williams went to trial on the eighth of July for the crimes of the London Monster, and we must remember that to assault any person in the public streets, with intent to tear, spoil, cut, burn or deface the garments, was a felony punishable by death or, at best, transportation. Over fifty ladies claimed that they were attacked by the Monster between 1788 and 1790. As I said, Williams was found guilty on the eighth of July 1790, but he disputed his conviction. His case was taken up by a lawyer called Theophilus Swift, and Williams was given a second trial on the thirteenth of December 1790."

"And was found innocent?"

Dupin shook his head. "Guilty again, but for crimes deemed misdemeanors rather than felonies, with a far better outcome of six years' imprisonment rather than execution or transportation."

"But you believe the conviction to be faulty."

"Yes. The letters exchanged between Elizabeth and Henry Arnold perfectly reflect the events described in the newspapers, and some of those attacks, particularly on the eighteenth of January 1790, the Queen's birthday ball, were made simultaneously upon different victims at different locations—impossible for a solo perpetrator. The letters suggest that Elizabeth Arnold secured a role in a play about the Monster's exploits, but Henry Arnold did not, and *The Morning Herald* of the second of April 1790 confirms that a musical play entitled *The Monster* opened at Astley's Theatre on the first of April. And we must also remember that the lament tells us that Rhynwick Williams was Welsh. The letters do not mention him by name, but most certainly they refer to Rhynwick Williams."

"The flower factory," I said. "She recognized the Welshman employed there as a ballet dancer who had been booed off the stage at the King's Theatre."

"Yes, and the transcripts of the trial note that Williams had formerly been apprenticed to ballet master Gallini and, at the time of the crimes, was employed at Amabel Mitchell's flower factory in Dover Street."

"And so," I said slowly, expressing my thoughts as they came to me, "you believe my aggressor reserved rooms for me at Brown's Genteel Inn because it is in the same street where the flower factory once stood? The flower factory where my grandmother had a reunion—as it were—with Rhynwick Williams?"

Dupin nodded. "Autography suggests that Courvoisier's lament was penned by a left-handed person, as was the case with the handbill for Brown's Genteel Inn. It is revealed in the way the characters slant and the pressure upon the page. I have carefully studied the handwriting of both documents and am certain they were penned by the same person. Thus, if Mr. Mackie is left-handed, we will know that he is your aggressor. If the scrivener who sought us out at the hanging truly did pen the lament, he may be in league with Mr. Mackie, or he himself might be your aggressor. And let us not forget the artificial violet boutonnière put in your lapel when you were attacked in Russell Square."

That simple fact chilled me—it made allusion to both my grandmother's visit to the flower factory and the attack made upon me by the artificial-flower seller when I was a child. "'Thus wrote the innocent, deceiv'd/Condemn'd, thus he bequeathed/His last and only legacy,/Revenge for E—A—'s treachery,'" Dupin said softly. "It cannot be a coincidence. I suspect you will receive more letters that will reveal how Elizabeth Arnold deceived Rhynwick Williams and how that led to his imprisonment."

I knew he was right and shuddered as I remembered the last two lines of the lament: *On her whole line, beyond her death,/Their heart's last beat, their final breath.*

Dupin looked at his time-piece and stood up. "Do not dwell on the threat within the lament, Poe," he said as if he had heard my thoughts. "Only cowards make threats from the shadows. We will solve your mystery and vanquish your nemesis, have no fear."

"Thank you, Dupin. I shall do my best to heed your advice."

"The library is soon to close—let us abandon our reflections until our minds are refreshed with sleep." He ushered me before him through the corridors of the British Museum that echoed with the footsteps of other scholars leaving its hallowed confines.

When we reached the street, I began to make my way toward Brown's Genteel Inn, but Dupin hovered.

"Until morning, Poe," he said and bowed, dismissing me.

So curious was this I immediately retraced my steps. "Surely we will walk to Brown's together?"

A look that might only be described as evasive came over Dupin's countenance. "I am riven by exhaustion, but there is an event I am obliged to attend this evening. You must sleep, however. One of us must have a mind that is not dulled by fatigue."

I immediately knew that Dupin was being disingenuous—he went nights at a time without sleep. So piqued was my curiosity all thoughts of my nemesis lost their grip on me.

"What is this mysterious meeting, Dupin? Am I to think that you have an assignation with one of the fairer sex?"

I could not conceive of a more unlikely tête-à-tête as Dupin far preferred an evening spent in solitude with his books and rarely could be enjoined to attend a play or some other entertainment. My comment was designed to vex him, for when Dupin was vexed he was more apt to reveal the truth.

"I have no meeting planned," he said evenly. "It is an event, as I said, and in truth I do not particularly wish to attend, but it is my duty." He removed a pamphlet from his pocket and handed it to me. It was a Phillips Auctioneers catalogue for an auction to be held at seventy-three New Bond Street that very evening, following a reception at six o'clock. And then I remembered Dupin's cryptic comment in his letter accepting my request for help.

"The business in London you mentioned in your missive?"

Dupin nodded.

"May I?"

"Of course."

I opened the catalogue. The introduction stated that the items listed therein were part of an estate sale being conducted on behalf of a French aristocrat who wished to preserve his anonymity and that the unique and splendid effects were of the highest quality, produced by renowned artisans in France. I paged through the catalogue and noticed that a number of articles were notated—randomly it seemed—with numbers. "There are articles in the collection that interest you?"

Dupin raised his brows and nodded his assent, but gave no further explanation. I checked my own pocket-watch.

"Let us make our way there now, for the reception is about to begin."

Dupin was immediately and unusually flustered. "There is no need for you to accompany me. It is bound to be tedious."

Dupin's reluctance made me all the more determined. "Not at all. I should like to experience a London auction."

And so we made our way to seventy-three New Bond Street, me making observations about the streets of London and Dupin more than a little aggravated by my presence.

* * *

The auction rooms were far more crowded than I had anticipated, allowing little space to maneuver. All of London's aristocracy appeared to be there along with art dealers and, apparently, journalists, who scrutinized all assembled and scribbled into their notebooks. There was wine to drink and the crowd imbibed freely while gossiping and flirting. Dupin scanned the room carefully, but did not seem to find whatever he was looking for. He made his way to the back, where there was a doorway to another chamber with chairs set out before a rostrum and the items to be auctioned were available for viewing. There were *objets d'art* of both the European and Oriental schools: tapestries, some paintings, fine silverware, precious jewels, beautifully crafted time-pieces. Dupin opened his catalogue and began to compare the lots he had annotated with the items on display. He did not speak until he was finished.

"What do you think of the collection?" he asked.

"Most impressive. Very fine and wide-ranging, probably gathered over several generations as it is a family collection."

"Correct." Dupin walked closer to one of the glass cabinets that held a selection of exquisite jewelry, and as his walking stick clicked hard against the marble floor, the sinews of his right hand revealed how tightly he held it in his grasp. "A family collection indeed." He turned to face me, and I saw that his gray eyes burned with the icy fervor born from hatred. "But it is not the property of the person who is selling it."

It then occurred to me why Dupin—who had little interest in such events—had decided to attend this particular auction at seventy-three New Bond Street.

"These items belonged to your family?"

"Yes." Dupin's fierce grip upon his walking stick did not decrease, and I began to fear that he would swing the implement, shatter the glass case and sweep up the jewels that were exhibited inside, but he maintained his composure. "You wonder how our family possessions were lost to us?" he asked.

"Quite," I muttered.

"A liar and a thief betrayed my grandparents and, after they met with Madame Guillotine, he stole everything they had. My father was but a boy at the time and was sent to live with the de Bourdeille family—his mother's sister—who provided him with an excellent education but did not have the capacity to give him anything more than that." He raised his left hand and stared for a moment at the *chevalière* that bore the Dupin coat-of-arms. "Little remained of his legacy beyond this *chevalière*—and this." Dupin tossed his walking stick upward and caught it, revealing its top—the golden cobra with glaring eyes of Burmese rubies, its fangs exposed to strike. I knew from our previous discussions that the fearsome object had been in the Dupin family for generations and the beautiful yet deadly snake was a part of his family coat-of-arms. Indeed, I had seen a magnificent rendering of it displayed in his Paris apartment: against a field of azure, a golden human foot crushed a serpent that had its fangs embedded in its heel.

"You may wonder how I know these objects belonged to my family if they were stolen before my birth." Dupin again anticipated the question that preyed upon my mind. "My grandfather was a meticulous and prescient man. In his will, he noted in precise detail every family heirloom that his son—my father—was to inherit. The list is etched upon my memory."

"How did you know that the items were going to auction here?"

Dupin laughed bitterly. "I was sent the catalogue."

"But surely the thief would wish to keep any such sale a secret from you?"

"Not at all, Poe. He took great delight in taunting my father and now he enjoys mocking me."

"Forgive me for asking, but can you be truly certain these are the heirlooms described in your grandfather's will? The owner of the estate has not provided his name."

"I will show you. Here, beyond doubt, is my proof." Dupin indicated the glass case that contained an array of magnificent jewels and a large silver jewel box decorated with glittering stones. "Many of these were crafted by Henri Toutin in the seventeenth century." He pointed at a group of very fine enameled pieces decorated with hunting scenes, mythological figures and life-like flowers. "Notice the ring in particular. It too is of the Toutin school, but fashioned in the late eighteenth century. Look very closely."

It was a gold ring set with an exquisite painting of Cupid on enamel, which cleverly fronted a locket. As I peered more closely at the open locket, I saw there were two beautifully rendered miniature portraits inside it: a man and a woman.

"Do you recognize them?"

I was baffled by Dupin's question until I realized that I *did* recognize the images, for they were the likenesses of the decapitated man and woman in Madame Tussaud's chamber of horrors—of Chevalier and Madame Dupin.

"Do you need further evidence?" Dupin asked.

I shook my head. "But what shall we do now? Surely these are stolen items being sold under false pretenses. Will the authorities have them returned to you?"

Dupin's face tensed again. "That is a battle I am unlikely to win. Property stolen during the Terror is rarely returned to its rightful owner—indeed many do not consider *seized* property stolen at all. London auction houses have been very busy with such items for quite some time." Dupin stared at the magnificent display in front of us, as if committing the detail of each item to memory. Finally he spoke, very softly. "All I can do is take note of who purchases the objects in the hope that one day I shall be in the position to buy back the most personal items." Just then there was a hearty *rap-rap-rap* and the auctioneer's hammer brought the crowd much nearer to quiet.

"Ladies and gentleman, please take your seats so we may begin the auction of these most desirable objects." The auctioneer rapped his gavel yet again and the potential buyers made their way to seats near the front while the spectators stood at the back, curious to see what might be bid upon.

"One final question, Dupin. What is the name of the thief?"

He exhaled audibly then spoke as if the words pained him. "Monsieur Ernest Valdemar—the murderer of my grandparents and, I believe, my mother. He was my father's nemesis and therefore is mine. Ernest Valdemar is the man who did his utmost to destroy the Dupin family and very nearly succeeded."

The auctioneer rapped his gavel once again and announced, "Let us begin. Item one, a *bleu turquoise* Vincennes vase with a floral decoration, circa 1748."

The assistant auctioneer, a dapper fellow in a somber suit and white gloves, held up the vase for all to see. It proved a popular piece and the bidding was fierce, each potential buyer holding up their numbered paddle or simply nodding his or her head if they believed themselves sufficiently known to the auctioneer. When the vase was finally sold, Dupin noted down the buyer's number. Every vase and porcelain figurine sold with great rapidity, and he repeated the procedure of noting down the purchaser's number or name. There was something of a short intermission and the spectators gossiped amongst themselves as the assistant set up an easel and placed the first painting upon it. It was a worthy seascape and proved highly popular also. Indeed, all the scenic paintings on offer sold very quickly for impressive amounts. Object after elegant object went under the hammer and all the items sold, those going for the highest prices getting a round of applause from the spectators. Dupin's expression grew increasingly morose, but he continued his careful notations and said nothing. The jewelry was the last collection to go up for sale. The auctioneer gave a short introduction to the Toutin school to raise the crowd's interest and swiftly sold a number of pieces. Then the locket ring went under the hammer.

"A gold and enamel ring of the Toutin school. Notice the exquisite painted enamel front-piece—how life-like the flowers, how mischievous the Cupid!" The auctioneer gestured at the delicate image that no one in the audience could appreciate given the distance. "But there is much more to this ring. Ever so much more." The assistant opened the enamel front to reveal the two portraits.

Dupin leaned in closer as if hypnotized by the visages he knew so well through depiction, but had never met in the flesh.

"It should not be difficult to remove the portraits currently within the locket or replace them with gems, perhaps, if that is preferred."

Dupin's body tensed up and instinctively I held an arm in front of him, lest he leap from his seat and attack the auctioneer.

"Who will bid on this intriguing ring?"

I immediately raised my paddle, and felt Dupin's gaze burn into me.

"Thank you, sir. Do we have any others in our discerning audience who understand the quality of this piece and wish to add it to his or her collection?" the auctioneer asked, and he did. The cost of the locket ring rose ever higher thanks to my determination and that of my rival, who stood somewhere at the back. The crowd around us enjoyed our tussle immensely, the ladies gasping and fluttering fans with each incremental bid and the men murmuring amongst themselves like a hive of agitated bees. My excitement increased accordingly until I hardly heard the price announced by the auctioneer.

"Poe, you must stop. The gem is not worth half that and surely your pockets are not lined with gold."

"Sir?" the auctioneer questioned, his gaze back upon me.

My paddle went up. The auctioneer stared to the back of the crowd, as did all seated around me.

"Once," the auctioneer said loudly, gavel poised above his rostrum.

I turned to look at my competitor and saw an unprepossessing man of perhaps thirty years dressed in a somber suit that befitted a personal secretary.

"Twice!"

My opponent's eyes met mine and he put his hands together in silent applause, acknowledging his own defeat.

The rap of the gavel rang through the room. "The gold and enamel locket ring," the auctioneer said, as he scanned a paper on his rostrum, "goes to Mr. Poe." Thunderous applause met this announcement and all seemed to turn to look at me.

"Madness, Poe, utter madness," Dupin whispered.

"It would be madness to let someone destroy such an important memento. The ring, if nothing else, had to be saved."

When the auction ended, I made my way to the auctioneer with my number so that I might pay a deposit and collect my receipt for the ring. The rashness of my actions was setting in—I had been far too caught up in auction fever and had not thought clearly about how I would finance the purchase. Common sense begged me to put down the pen, embrace humiliation and return to Dupin with an apology, but instead I was determined to pay the deposit.

"Thank you, Poe. I am indebted to you," Dupin said, walking beside me.

"There is, of course, no debt between us. *Amicis semper fidelis.*"

Dupin nodded gravely. "I value your words as much as the gem itself and hope you understand that the pledge is reciprocated most completely."

"Of course."

But when we reached the clerk's desk an extraordinary thing happened. "Excuse me a moment," the auction clerk said. He carried the ledger and my receipt to the man at the desk behind him and whispered in an urgent manner. He, in turn, frowned and looked up at us.

"Is there a difficulty?" I asked.

The man in the elegant suit took the ledger and receipt and approached us. "Good evening. I am William Augustus Phillips, the owner of the auction house. Mr. Poe and—" He looked inquiringly at Dupin.

"Chevalier Dupin."

"Mr. Phillips," I interjected. "If there is a problem, inform us immediately."

The auction house owner directed his gaze to me. "I am afraid there is. A most unusual problem, Mr. Poe."

"The ring was stolen?" Dupin asked as if he had half-expected it.

"No, nothing like that. I am afraid the owner decided against selling the piece. Most unusual. He paid the auction house the commission it would have received for the sum you bid and withdrew it. Under the terms of the auction, there is little we can do."

Fury welled up within me. "This is most unethical, sir."

"It is unfortunate, but it is the owner's prerogative, I am afraid."

"And given the commission the auction house will receive for the ring and other items sold, you will not refuse Mr. Valdemar," Dupin said.

"I would not put it quite that way," Mr. Phillips protested.

"I will take action, you shall see. This must be a breach of contract," I countered.

"Come, Poe. The ring is gone, as is the culprit's agent. There is nothing to be done. It is, however, some small consolation that Mr. Phillips has confirmed what I suspected but could not prove: the French aristocrat who wished to preserve his anonymity is Monsieur Ernest Valdemar. Thank you kindly, sir." He gave the auctioneer a mocking bow and Mr. Phillips flushed crimson, doubly confirming what Dupin had fathomed through ratiocination.

93 Jermyn Street, London
20 April 1790

My Dear,

Fret not about the role of the Monster—Brinsley will never perform it as well as you. Our own play will be far superior to that silly musical, for ours draws on true experience not mere rumours. Indeed, your performance this evening exceeded that of yesterday, and I was so inspired by your dashing display that I went straight back to our lodgings ablaze. I have revised the closing verse and completed the chorus for the "wronged young maidens", both of which are enclosed. Perhaps you will find time to set the chorus to a simple tune if you find it good enough?

My mind is still dancing with ideas. What do you think of the title: *The Odious Monster at Large*? I believe now that our villain should escape from Newgate, not through a grand scheme or with assistance from a fellow villain, but he should simply vanish like a ghost into the night. And our narrator will inform the audience that the Monster was never heard of again in London town. But—and imagine the lights flickering as he speaks—one warm summer night, a pretty young girl is on her way home from the theatre. She is incautiously alone, thinking herself completely safe in the charming seaside town, amongst the crowds on the promenade. She is lost in contemplation of the marvellous play she has just attended, but as she reaches the sanctuary of her own doorstep, her reverie is shattered. A man—nay, a <u>monster</u>—materialises behind her and before she can call out for assistance a silvery blade tears through her silk skirts, her petticoats and then her flesh. The theatre plunges into darkness— and then . . . a piercing scream! Would that not be a most chilling effect?

    With deepest affection,
    Your Wife

                      93 Jermyn Street, London
                              27 April 1790

Dear Elizabeth,

    The audience that watched Brinsley when he took to the boards missed a far finer performance last night. The Monster leapt from the shadows and—*swish*! His blade slid across her breast, through her dress, her chemise and into her pink tender flesh. And then gone—back into the shadows the Monster went, merrily singing the tune I wrote for our play. Brinsley may get the applause tonight, but our Monster will be in the newspapers.

    Yours,
    Henry

93 Jermyn Street, London
30 April 1790

Dearest,

Our Monster has reached the pinnacle of notoriety! All the chatter about the need for copper skirts or pots and pans to preserve the rumps of London's ladies has inspired Mr. John Julius Angerstein, a man of wealth and little common sense, to offer a one hundred pound reward for the capture and conviction of the Monster. The posters have been pasted up all over town, and every man and woman of little means will accuse his or her neighbour in hopes of securing the bounty. Please let us be cautious. The streets are a-buzz with four attacks in the past few days—the Monster is far too busy when so many are seeking him!

Yours,
E.

LONDON, WEDNESDAY, 8 JULY 1840

The rain unfurled from the sky in long, twisting sheets and the
road was a muddy river—my mood made manifest. As I leaned
against the coach window, the cool of the glass against my
cheek, an odd thought came into my mind. I was *inside*,
always—a clear, perfect pane of glass between me and the
world; the room that I inhabited was airless, still and empty.
The thought filled me with melancholia made deeper by the
weeping skies. How I missed Sissy and Muddy and our quiet
summer days on the banks of the Schuylkill River.

"Poe? We have almost arrived."

"So soon?"

I should not have been surprised. The coach driver had
conveyed us through London at a speed that suggested Lucifer
himself was riding full pelt behind us. We reached Wellington
Street more than half an hour before the appointed reading
time and alighted at our destination with an unsteadiness of
foot that looked like intemperance, but truly was caused by
something akin to seasickness.

The Literary and Scientific Institute was quite new, built in a
stuccoed Grecian style, and was handsome enough. The
manager met us at the door. He was a small man both in

stature and bulk—he might have resembled a child of twelve
years or so if it weren't for the worry lines etched in his forehead, the bald pate and boisterous eyebrows. He looked from
Dupin to me and back again to Dupin.

"Delighted to meet you, Mr. Poe. I am Matthew Godwin.
Mr. Dickens has sung your praises vociferously." He grasped
Dupin's hand and shook it vigorously.

"Monsieur Godwin, I am afraid that you mistake me for my
esteemed colleague," Dupin said, his accent oddly emphasized.
"I am Chevalier Dupin and simply a champion of Mr. Poe's
works."

"Ah, of course." Godwin dropped Dupin's hand and grabbed
for mine. "Mr. Poe. It is obvious now that I look more closely.
You do indeed have the appearance of an author." He shook
my hand ever more energetically. "Come inside. Please do."
Mr. Godwin scurried through the door. Dupin and I struggled
to keep up with the nimble little man as he led us down a dimly
lit corridor.

"Right through here. I trust it will suit your purposes. Won't
know how many will come until they get here."

"Indeed," Dupin said with the hint of a smile.

The lecture theater proved larger than I had expected—quite
capable of seating several hundred people. While I was grateful
for Mr. Dickens's optimism, I hoped I would not be facing an
under-populated theater.

"I will ensure that the spectators sit at the front. It will undo
the effect of your work if you must shout to the back of the
theater."

"Thank you, Dupin. It is a relief to have you here." We both
turned to examine the room more closely. White walls—lamps
upon them lit the room. A lectern faced the spectators' chairs.
It was a good height and had adequate space for my papers, but
the room seemed more appropriate for discussions of science

than for a literary reading. I thought of the theater and how it influenced the audience—the costumes, the backdrop, the props, the lighting. "Perhaps a candelabrum on either side of the lectern for effect. Is that possible?"

Mr. Godwin looked confused but nodded. "Yes, if you like."

"Very good." I looked at my pocket watch—twenty minutes before my reading.

"Perhaps it is best to wait elsewhere and make more of an entrance when your audience is in place," Dupin suggested.

He was quite right. Waiting anxiously at the lectern was not good theater. Much better to enter the room once the audience was seated and quiet, carrying the candelabra for effect. I looked to Mr. Godwin. "Is there somewhere else I might wait?"

"Yes, yes. Of course. Come to my office. I will make some tea, or perhaps you would prefer a dash of Scotch courage?" He winked and grasped my elbow, propelling me toward a side door. Dupin watched us go but made no move to follow.

Mr. Godwin's office was a cluttered, windowless room. "Please, have a seat." He retrieved a flask and two dusty tumblers, which he filled. "I'll just go find the candelabra. The library, I think . . ." And he was gone.

I sipped the whisky and looked through my papers. I had read for Sissy and Muddy and at several Philadelphian taverns (of which I had little recollection), but never to an audience of such a size—presuming we would have an audience at all.

"Are these suitable?" It was Dupin with a candelabrum in each hand. They were terribly tarnished, but stately enough and fitted with fresh tapers.

"Thank you. Where is Mr. Godwin?"

"Ushering in your audience—punctual crowd. Shall I put a glass of water on the lectern for you?"

"You think of everything."

"It is a pleasure. If you make your entrance in five minutes, the crowd should be settled." Dupin left the room.

I helped myself to some more Scotch courage and drank it down in one.

* * *

I entered from the back of the room and walked toward the lectern, carrying two candelabra with tapers that burned eerily in the darkness. The theater was more full than I had dared to hope. Ladies in the crowd gasped, and I heard muted whispers. When I reached my position, I placed each candelabrum on a small table situated either side of the lectern. Dupin had judged the position of the tables perfectly—the candle flames flickered below my face, casting spectral shadows. I stood quietly for a moment, gazing at my audience, and noted that Dupin was seated near the door.

"Good evening, ladies and gentleman. My name is Edgar Allan Poe." Polite applause met this announcement. "Thank you for joining me this evening. I will be reading my new tale *William Wilson* and am happy to receive questions afterwards."

I scanned the audience, looking for Mr. Dickens. Dupin's eyes met with mine, and he nodded imperceptibly. I gathered myself and began, conscious to project my voice.

"'Let me call myself, for the present, William Wilson. The fair page now lying before me need not be sullied with my real appellation.'"

The candle glow shivered from an intangible draft in the room—all to good effect, as the capricious light threw mysterious shadows across my face and, perhaps, the shimmer of a halo round my head.

"'Men usually grow base by degrees. From me, in an instant, all virtue dropped bodily as a mantle . . .'"

As I continued with my performance, I scanned the crowd. *Was* Mr. Dickens in the room? My eyes searched the very back row, but I did not see a face that met the image I knew from his novel's front-piece. And then I caught sight of a countenance I did recognize and almost stumbled over my lines. Square jaw, thin lips, auburn hair—a man in a rambunctious checked suit popular with dandies who possess few critical faculties. Was he my nemesis, planning to humiliate me in public? My voice trembled and the text evaporated from my mind. I sought to control myself and adopted a faux-whispering voice for dramatic effect.

"'I have said before, or should have said, that Wilson was not, in the most remote degree, connected with my family. But assuredly if we had been brothers we must have been twins.'"

My mind went blank again. I looked down at my papers, pretending a dramatic pause. It was not the correct page. With a sense of panic, I turned one page and then another. Finally, I found my place and continued. But just as I had regained my concentration, using all my will not to look in Mackie's direction, a glint in the low light caught my gaze, and I noticed a man of about forty-five years of age with dark eyes and hair. He was utterly focused on my words and radiated tension like a venomous snake poised to strike.

"'The same name! The same contour of person! The same day of arrival at the academy! And then his dogged and meaningless imitation of my gait, my voice, my habits, and my manner!'"

I was transfixed now by the man with the snake-like eyes and glinting lapel. There was something familiar about him, but I could not place him. My anxiety grew and my memory failed me more than once, but I struggled through to the crescendo of the tale, scrabbling to find the correct page, throwing others onto the ground. Faster and faster I recited and read out the text; my anxiety must have added to the effect for my audience looked both frightened and absorbed.

"'Scoundrel! Impostor! Accursed villain! You shall not—you shall not dog me unto death! Follow me, or I stab you where you stand!'"

At that very moment, there was a slight commotion as Dupin sprang from his seat and ran through the door in pursuit of someone. My eyes scanned the audience—an empty seat where the glowering man had sat. My words dried up and, again, I feigned a pause for dramatic effect. I thought of my grandmother alone on the stage, singing to hundreds without fear, a mob that might shower her with applause or garbage from the streets. I was of her blood and now was the time to prove I had inherited some of her skill.

"'It was Wilson; but he spoke no longer in a whisper, and I could have fancied that I myself was speaking while he said: *You have conquered, and I yield. Yet, henceforward art thou also dead—dead to the World, to Heaven and to Hope! In me didst thou exist—and, in my death, see by this image, which is thine own, how utterly thou hast murdered thyself.'"*

With those words, I lowered my head. At first there was ominous silence, then like a throng of birds rising up in flight the applause began, hands pattering together like beating wings. But I had failed. The muse who inspired my grandmother and my mother on stage had declined to touch me. I waited where I stood, maintaining a solemn expression, when truly I wanted to bang my fists against the wooden lectern. Members of the audience slowly rose to their feet and those at the back filed out. Others hovered near their seats, chatting with their neighbors. Scanning the crowd for Mackie, I caught sight of a striking woman with raven hair who, despite the dearth of light, wore tinted spectacles, which only served to enhance her beauty. I wondered if she were blind, but she stood and undoubtedly smiled at me. And then my nemesis planted himself in front of me.

"Poe! Quite a story you gave to us. Highly unusual. Twins and tormentation and, finally, murder. Not a cheerful tale. *Dark*, one might say. And rather on the long side, perhaps. Do you find it difficult to edit your own work?" Mr. Mackie paused for breath, his green eyes staring into mine. My heart pounded so loudly I was certain my aggressor could hear it. Where was Dupin? Why had he vanished when I needed him? I did my utmost to exude complete calm and clasped my nervous hands behind my back.

"I am sorry my tale disappointed you, Mr. Mackie."

"Disappointed indeed. I had expected superlative things from you. What with your rigorous critiques of the great American writers and of their lesser cousins—my own poor scribblings for example. Yes, I had expected more." He took a step forward while I instinctively took one back.

"What a powerful story, Mr. Poe," I heard a mellifluous voice say. "I had no preconceived expectations, being unfamiliar with your work, but find myself deeply impressed." The raven-haired woman was next to my nemesis, the candlelight glinting off the olive green lenses of her spectacles. "It was chilling and compelling with elements of *the other*." She gestured gracefully at the invisible around us, then turned to Mr. Mackie. "It was such a pleasure, sir. I do hope we shall meet again at another literary evening." She gave a half-curtsy and, with a solemn nod of her head, elegantly dismissed him.

Mackie hesitated a moment, confusion upon his features, but such was her charm, he did not seem to realize that she had usurped his position. My nemesis merely dipped his head in return and said, "It is all my pleasure, madam. I, too, hope we meet again." He smiled at her as he backed away. "Farewell, Poe. I trust we shall have a deeper discussion in future." With those ominous words, Mr. Mackie strode away. I scanned the room for Dupin—where the Devil was he? He would miss his chance to interrogate Mackie.

"Fear not, Mr. Poe. You will not meet that self-opinionated gentleman again," the lady before me pronounced.

"While in many ways I hope you are correct, I suspect the gentleman and I shall convene again in less than friendly circumstances," I replied. While I more than loathed Mr. Mackie, I had to find out why he was tormenting me.

My delightful companion paused for a moment. I could see her eyes behind the green glass widen and then close. Her lips moved in a silent whisper until she shivered slightly and returned her gaze to mine. "You will find that I am indeed correct," she said softly. "I regret to say that Mr. Mackie will cross over far sooner than anyone might expect." Her expression was solemn, her voice filled with compassion. "A pity. A terrible pity, the ruffians who roam this city." My face must have reflected the sense of horror I felt at her words, for she reached out and touched my arm. "Fear not, Mr. Poe, fear not." She flicked her eyes toward the heavens and nodded gently as if in acknowledgement to some invisible creature hovering above us. "The future will be far kinder to you."

"Thank you," I said unable to think of a more appropriate response.

"Prescience is oft times a curse as well as a blessing," she murmured. "But our fate is unavoidable, as Mr. Mackie shall discover."

"As shall we all." The words came from me unbidden, but they seemed to please my companion, for she smiled and held her hand toward mine, palm facing downward.

"I am Mrs. Fontaine. Rowena Fontaine."

"An enchanting name. Most appropriate for its owner." I clasped her delicate hand in mine and wondered at the softness of her skin. An almost imperceptible scent of flowers—roses and perhaps honeysuckle—drifted through the air. She gently extracted her hand.

"You are too kind, Mr. Poe," she demurred. "It is true that I found your tale superbly crafted, but I was compelled to come and speak with you. I have a message." Mrs. Fontaine fixed her eyes on mine. "From your grandmother."

Her words made my muscles contract as if with cramp. "But I am afraid—"

"That she has passed," Mrs. Fontaine said, completing my thoughts. "Yes, of course. I have a connection with the other side. I am a conduit, one might say. It is a great responsibility."

I could think of no reply and merely nodded.

"My spirit guide normally connects me with those who have passed, but on occasion messages come to me unbidden and it is my duty to seek out the person for whom it is intended."

"And you have a message for me?" I asked in a whisper not unlike that of William Wilson.

"Your grandmother needs to speak with you—through me. You must come to our gathering tomorrow night."

"You are a medium?"

"I prefer the appellation *sensitive*."

Over her shoulder, I saw Dupin re-enter the room and somehow this threw me into a state of confusion. Consternation tautened his features as he approached.

"Promise me you will be there." Mrs. Fontaine touched my arm gently.

"Madame, I could not refuse you."

Her smile was captivating. "I will give you the address." As she reached into her beaded purse, her fine paisley shawl slipped back from her shoulder, and I glimpsed an extraordinary thing. Pinned to her dress was an fantastical brooch painted in the finest detail: a life-size vivid depiction of a human eye. That eye—brown, lustrous and piercing—glared alarmingly, turning me immobile with dread.

Mrs. Fontaine readjusted her shawl, breaking the eye's terrible gaze. She handed me a visiting card. "The address is here. We begin at eight o'clock. Goodnight, Mr. Poe." She inclined her head to Dupin, who suddenly was at my side. "Goodnight, Chevalier Dupin." She hurried away, her silk taffeta dress rustling like leaves before a storm.

I looked down at the card in my hand. In fine gilded script it announced:

Mrs. Rowena Fontaine
Sensitive, Spiritual Advisor and Guide.
16 Bayham Street, Camden Town.

"Of course you must not go," Dupin said.

"Indeed? And why is that?"

"Mrs. Fontaine is most assuredly a fraud."

Dupin's words irritated me, and I felt the need to defend the lady. "There are mysteries in this world that the most renowned Analyst cannot fathom. She knew your name—I did not introduce you."

Dupin puffed air through his lips. "That is not a difficult trick. I am not the ghost you imagine me to be. My presence in London has been observed, of that I am certain. Your presumptions regarding the limitation of Analysts may be correct, but I am not wrong regarding the limitations of your medium. And so I must try to dissuade you from attending her theatrical."

"I am afraid you cannot."

"Not if I tell you that your Mrs. Fontaine must be in league against you with Mr. Mackie and others of dubious character?"

"Your accusations sound rather desperate. Mrs. Fontaine

showed no acquaintance with Mr. Mackie and vice versa—and
I cannot think what 'others' you mean."

"The man I pursued from the Institute."

"Did you apprehend him?" I asked.

"No."

"Then I am confused, Dupin. Why do you suppose he was
with Mrs. Fontaine? They did not sit together or leave together.
What gentleman would allow a lady to make her own way
home?"

"I doubt very much that he is a gentleman, and while they
did not leave together, I am quite certain they arrived together.
I observed them enter the theater simultaneously, but after a
brief glance into each other's eyes, they chose seats in different
parts of the audience. There was an *understanding*."

"What kind of an understanding?"

"That I do not as yet know."

"Well then, surely we should attempt to ascertain more by
attending the séance," I said, pleased with my own show of
ratiocination. "If Mrs. Fontaine is in collusion with the dark-
haired man as you claim, then we have the opportunity to
discover their motives. Or perhaps Mrs. Fontaine's motives are
pure, and I will indeed receive a message from my grandmother. One thing is certain, Dupin. The lady has information
I need, be it gleaned from the dead or the living, and I intend to
find out what it is."

"I notice you say that 'we' should attend the séance," said
Dupin coldly.

"I would very much welcome your company," I said. "And
your protection."

Dupin was silent for a moment, most dissatisfied with my
pronouncement and not entirely persuaded by my flattery.
"Very well," he said at last. "You are quite right. We must on
occasion risk all we hold dear to discover the truth. Let us

attend tomorrow's séance, but let us also remain vigilant. Now shall we return to Brown's or would you like to speak further with your audience?"

A few clusters of people remained in the room chatting, but they seemed to have little interest in speaking with me. "I am more than ready to leave."

"Then let us." Dupin gestured toward the door, inviting me to precede him.

It did not take us long to find a coach, and we settled in for the journey back to Brown's Genteel Inn. Dupin pulled his meerschaum from his pocket and tapped in tobacco. I did the same, although I would have preferred more of Mr. Godwin's Scotch courage.

"I would say the occasion was a great success," Dupin offered.

"Unfortunately, I would disagree with your assessment." Dupin prepared to speak but I raised my hand to halt any words of solace. "Pity does not comfort and the overly generous critic is not a friend."

Dupin raised his brows slightly. "You are disappointed that Mr. Dickens did not attend."

"Or perhaps did not desire to."

"That, I am quite certain, is not the case, but we must wonder at this stage if Mr. Dickens was truly the one to organize the reading."

"But Mr. Godwin met with Mr. Dickens, who professed to admire my work."

"Mr. Godwin did of course meet someone who *claimed* to be Mr. Dickens when he organized the reading, but that person may have been an impostor. We must not forget that Mr. Godwin is ill-acquainted with literary figures."

I immediately remembered how our host had presumed Dupin to be me, and Dupin smiled, guessing my thoughts.

"The impostor may have been Mr. Mackie or the dark-haired man I pursued. We have no proof, in fact, that Mr. Dickens has been in correspondence with you at all," Dupin said with an irritating note of triumph in his voice.

"Nothing but a hoax," I muttered. Dupin's suppositions left me feeling all the more dissatisfied with the evening. Not only was my performance of questionable merit, but my hopes of meeting Mr. Dickens might have been—and might still be— utterly in vain.

Dupin offered no words of comfort but merely lit his meer-schaum and exhaled smoke out of the coach window.

"And there is an apparent coincidence we must consider," he eventually said.

"Pray tell?"

"The date selected for your reading."

"The eighth of July? Mr. Dickens—or his impostor—suggested it."

"Exactly," Dupin said. "It is a date of significance to our investigation." I had no idea what Dupin was referring to and he reacted with impatience at my bafflement. "The eighth of July 1790—the date of quite another performance: Rhynwick Williams's first trial."

It was as if Dupin had delivered a blow to my chest. I felt completely hollow and could not speak. Dupin did not bother to. We were soon back at Brown's and my mood was as dark as the night sky.

"Do not torture yourself," Dupin finally said when we entered the foyer. "We will discover your aggressor and vanquish him. Have no doubt." He gave me a slight bow. "Goodnight, Poe. I wish you a night full of sleep and free of dreams." And he was gone.

I looked to the desk clerk for any messages, but he simply shook his head. Exhausted, I climbed the stairs to my room, and when I entered, discovered that the Argand lamp was lit. Sitting in a pool of amber light was a bottle of cognac. I stared at the delectable apparition before me, waiting for some spirit or genie to emerge from it, but it simply shimmered in the supernatural glow of the lamp.

I approached the bottle and there tucked underneath it was a folded piece of paper. My quivering fingers reached for the note, my mind racing.

1 Devonshire Terrace, London
8 July 1840

Dear Mr. Poe,

Heartfelt apologies for being unable to attend your reading tonight, but I am left completely indisposed by the bad wine served at my publisher's house last night. I would appreciate the irony of the situation much more if my health were less compromised. I am certain your reading will be a great success and hope you will forgive me for missing your London debut.

Your Humble Servant,
Charles Dickens

How I wished to believe that the note was truly from the great man himself! But Dupin had poisoned my mind with suspicion, and I could not help but wonder if it was a forgery. I sat for a time, staring at the glowing bottle as if hypnotized, the strangeness of the mystery in which I found myself filling me with its darkness, and when I tried to stifle those unpleasant thoughts, my failure as a performer weighed heavily upon me.

Forgery or not, it will do no harm to sample the gift, said a small voice within me.

I poured a generous measure of cognac into the glass that was stationed by the bottle and cupped it in my hands to warm the contents. The cognac's scent drifted up—it was like a summer's day back home, full of clover with a hint of honey. I was transported to the banks of the Schuylkill, back to the gentle companionship of Sissy and Muddy. Bees glided through a river of pink and white clover blossom, the sun catching flashes of pollen on their busy legs. Soon the glass was empty and I took another and yet another, enchanted with the elixir's ability to bring my memories to life and to blanket my disappointments—indeed to alter the past!

I was back in the theater, no need for a lectern or papers as I moved freely across the stage, reciting my lines without faltering, face and voice conveying each character, my stride, my arms, my hands articulating every sentiment. My audience was gripped, intoxicated with my words, each face written with the emotion of my choosing. First tension—a tightening of the lips and eyes—then hands twisting anxiously and a stiffening of the upper body as fear trickled down the spine. A false calm set the eyes blinking with relief and the shoulders relaxed, but then, in a cunning final twist, the eyes widened and the mouth gasped in absolute horror. The audience was an orchestra, and I was their conductor. They were compelled to respond!

A sharp sound shattered this illusory world, and I found myself in the middle of the room, my now empty glass clutched in my fingertips. I spun to look around me, and my heart galloped at the sight of a man staring back at me.

"Who are you?" I staggered to confront him, and as his face came closer, I realized with shame that he was but a reflection of me—my own William Wilson. I sank to the floor, my humiliation transforming to laughter at the absurdity of my situation. I noticed then that a heavy tome was lying on the carpet with papers scattered around it. After scrabbling about, collecting the papers into a tidy heap, I was left with a terrible thirst and so made my way back to the cognac bottle. Had the stuff evaporated? I poured a generous dollop and returned to the heap of papers, which I lifted to my desk. But something was not right. Disarray—all was in disarray. I eventually fathomed that the mahogany box I had been using as a makeshift bookend had been moved. I grabbed for the box and pulled at the lid—securely locked—then collapsed into the chair and savored some cognac with relief. It was then that I saw the folded piece of paper lying on my writing desk. Very peculiar, very peculiar. My throat dried up with fear; I quenched its aridness with cognac and opened the note. Inside was a jumble of letters:

.tissɔɒl ǝnuqmi ǝm omǝ𝑁

The writing was very neat and familiar. Could it be? I opened my writing desk and removed the lament. I am not a master of autography like Dupin, but it was more than plain that the person who had written the note had also transcribed the lament.

I looked at the paper again and my feverish brain immediately knew how to decipher the jumbled letters. I staggered to the mirror, held the paper up to it and stared at the reflection. There in the glass was my double, in the very agonies of dissolution, holding up a letter that warned: *Nemo me impune lacessit*. The man with my countenance leaned toward me and whispered in my own voice, "No one insults me with impunity." There was a crash and all light was extinguished.

93 Jermyn Street, London
5 May 1790

Dearest Accomplice,
  Three ladies in three days,
  Felt the sharp edge of my blade,
  Three ladies in three days,
  Were terrorised and made afraid,
  Three ladies in three days,
  The Monster's reputation will never fade!
    With deepest affection from,
    the Extraordinary Fellow Himself

93 Jermyn Street, London
16 May 1790

Dear Elizabeth,
  There are impostors! Rogues who sally through London, pretending to be the Monster, trying to usurp his glory. Mrs. Smyth, the lady your Monster attacked more than a year ago, claims to have been assaulted by him again. But did the impostor slice her bottom with a blade? No! She was punched in the face while looking in a shop window. Ridiculous! The Monster would never stoop to such an ungallant action. The second lady to fall victim to an impostor was described by that Angerstein fellow as a middle-sized, very plain and poor woman turned of forty, who was meanly

dressed and carrying a basket of eggs late at night in Charing Cross. The false Monster cut her face! Any person who knows the Monster's deeds is aware that he would not attack such a woman. A plain market woman, a peddler? No, most certainly not. The Monster would not stoop to that.

Yours,
Henry

93 Jermyn Street, London
12 June 1790

Henry,

I have not seen you for two days and pray you will come home and read this letter. It is important—nay, urgent—that you heed my words: the Monster must retire from the stage. He must as you promised me he would! If he resumes his attacks, our fate will be to hang at the end of a rope at Newgate. Groups of men now patrol the street to protect ladies from the Monster. My heart is still pounding as I write this, I am so full of fear.

When we parted from each other at the Duke of Cambridge, you dressed as a rakish gentleman, and I as a dapper rogue in clothing borrowed from the theatre—oh, how I have come to regret that violet frock coat and breeches, the patterned silk stockings and red embroidered waistcoat! It had seemed such a jolly costume to wear for my final performance. But again, I get ahead of myself. Suffice to say, I did as you bade me, knowing that my actions were foolish,

but I truly thought you might finally be persuaded to
let the Monster die if I fulfilled your request for a
closing performance. While you went off to find
your final victim, I made my way along Grafton
Street in search of mine, and there I spied a flower
seller and thought to add a boutonnière to my
disguise. Imagine my surprise when I discovered that
this flower seller was the Welsh ballet dancer from
the flower factory. Such was my fear of recognition
that I put everything into my performance as I chose
and purchased an artificial flower for a boutonnière.
Even so, his eyes remained utterly fixed upon my
face, a frown of deep contemplation furrowing his
brow. "Have we met before?" he finally asked. I
denied the fact, bought several of his artificial posies
to hide my consternation and quickly made my way
down the street.

Not long after this, I spied a woman walking alone
and approached her, nerves still jangling from my
encounter. I held out my nosegay to her and, unac-
countably, she approached me to smell it, thinking it
real, until she spied the hatpin and shrieked. Her cry
unnerved me and I took to my heels. That was when
I saw the tenacious Welshman watching me from the
other side of the street.

All of London is now enjoying the tale of how the
Monster threatened "a terrified beauty" with a
nosegay, and I have been more than a little terrified
myself that the Welshman might tell what he saw to
the magistrate in hopes of pocketing Angerstein's
damnable reward. But then it occurred to me that a
seller of artificial posies may be viewed with
considerable suspicion by those eager to corner our

Monster. Indeed, as I write, a plan is forming in my mind that may be the saving of us. Dear Henry, I wish this letter could deliver itself of its own accord and bring you home.

Yours,

Elizabeth

I heard a crackling sound, like feet breaking through a crust of snow; when I tried to lift my head, a fiery brand pierced through it. A shadow loomed over me, a presence.

"Poe, can you hear me? Poe?" A damp coolness soothed my brow. I tried to open my eyes again. A blurred face was above mine. "Can you hear my voice?"

Yes, but very far away. Or that is what I thought, but could not say. My throat was a desert and my body ached. Again, I tried to lift my eyelids, but light flared into them, glinting like the summer sun on water. I could not place where I was.

"Let me help you up."

I tried to push myself into a sitting position and felt a flash of pain through my palm. Someone tugged under my arms and I was heaved up. At first my legs refused to follow my commands, but at last I scrabbled upward with assistance and staggered to an armchair, where I collapsed again.

When eventually I opened my eyes, Dupin was seated next to me and a pool of shattered glass was upon the floor.

"Here." Dupin handed me a damp towel and glass of water. As I placed the cloth against my brow, I saw Dupin's eyes slide to the near empty bottle of cognac upon the table, but he said nothing. We sat in silence as I sipped at the water and waited for the room to stop moving like a ship upon rough waves.

"Perhaps you should retreat to your bed now. Shall I have them fetch a doctor?" He nodded toward my hand, which was inexplicably bound in a handkerchief, its white stained with fresh blood.

I shook my head and pointed at the letter, which lay on the floor amidst the shattered mirror. Dupin picked it up and brought it to me. I pointed at the shards upon the floor. "The mirror," I rasped, rattling the sheet of paper. "The mirror."

Dupin seemed to understand. He retrieved the largest shard and, with shaking hands, I held the note up to the fragment of mirror so he could read its contents.

"*Nemo me impune lacessit,*" he muttered. Dupin looked up at me, his face very serious.

"Your nemesis has been in this room."

I nodded and my head felt as if a metal spike had been driven into it.

"I must urge you again to avoid that farcical séance. If you go, no good will come of it. He means to harm you—here is the proof." Dupin shook the note to emphasize his words.

"I must go, don't you see." I could not raise my voice above a whisper. "There is a message for me. I am certain of it."

Dupin's brow furrowed; his lips tightened. "You must sleep, Poe. You are still delirious with the cognac."

Dupin helped me get to my feet and guided me to the bed. He poured another glass of water from the jug, took a small apothecary bottle from his jacket pocket and held it over the glass until three luminous droplets fell into the vessel. I watched as the iridescent liquid roiled—alive and dangerous—then blended chameleon-like into the water around it.

"Drink," he said.

And when the glass pressed against my mouth, I could not resist. The world receded as did the metronomic pounding in my head and all went black like spilled ink upon paper.

* * *

Moments or perhaps hours later, I heard a voice. "My darlings, my time with you is almost done." My mother's face emerged from the darkness. It was the color of bed linen, spectrally pale, the bones pressed up against the skin, revealing the shape of her skull. Her parched lips were translucent as a housefly's wings and taut against her ghoulishly exposed teeth. When she coughed, roses flowered on her handkerchief.

"Don't leave us," I whispered.

"I will watch you from Heaven—remember me from this, for it will be yours." Her eyes guided mine to the miniature portrait of her on the bedside table. I clasped my mother's skeletal hands in mine, and her breath rattled like an infernal locust as she gripped my fingers with preternatural strength, pulling me into the abyss with her.

"Poe!"

My eyes opened to the shadowy interior of a coach and Dupin's urgent hand upon my shoulder.

"Exhaustion has overcome you. It is not too late to turn back."

"I was dreaming of my mother." I put my hand to the place where my locket was concealed under my shirt. "Surely a sign that I must proceed, that my grandmother needs to communicate a message to me through Mrs. Fontaine."

"She is a charlatan, I assure you." The coach stopped before Dupin could say more and the coachman rapped to signal that we had reached our destination. I opened the door and stepped out.

"I will go alone if you wish."

"I wish only that you would see the truth." But Dupin exited the coach and followed me toward the unexpectedly insalubrious house that was sixteen Bayham Street. It was not difficult to fathom why the coach driver had demanded payment before ferrying us to Camden Town, which he declared was inhabited by beggars, thieves, prostitutes and murderers.

A serving girl with a pockmarked face and a dour manner ushered us into the drawing room, which proved to be a plain room decorated with cobweb skeins and dimly lit by a few tapers set in wall sconces. The wavering light sent shadows scrabbling along the walls and up across the smoke-stained ceiling. The floorboards were bare, and heavy curtains framed tall windows that glinted with moonlight. A round table stood at the room's center and seven chairs encircled it.

Three matrons of advanced years were in a huddle. They were all dressed unappealingly in purple and bedecked with necklaces and brooches featuring silver skulls, coffins, weeping women, willow trees—the memento mori jewelry so fashionable with ladies of a highly sentimental temperament. An elderly gentleman with white whiskers and hair, wearing very thick spectacles, stood quietly to one side, pipe in mouth. The tobacco was pungent and smelled oddly of overripe cherries, which added to the oppressiveness of the surroundings. Moments later, the delightful Mrs. Fontaine joined us. She was dressed ethereally in a cream-colored gown with large sleeves, a wide collar and a flowing lace shawl, which gave her the appearance of an angel in the flickering light.

"Mr. Poe, I am so glad that you have joined us." Her voice was warm, her expression pleased.

"You have met my friend Chevalier Dupin. He is interested in your work and insisted upon attending."

"Indeed," Mrs. Fontaine said. "I do hope we won't disappoint you, Chevalier." She dipped into the hint of a curtsy; Dupin inclined his head toward her, his skepticism plain. Mrs. Fontaine did not seem to notice Dupin's rudeness for she tilted her head gently, one ear directed toward the heavens, then nodded. "The spirits wish us to begin," she announced. "Ladies and gentlemen, will you join me around the table." She pointed at the chairs. Dupin arched his eyebrow with this pronouncement, but he refrained from comment. Mrs. Fontaine approached the table and rested her hands on the back of a chair. "Ladies, please. Take these seats if you will." She indicated three chairs at the other side of the table. The three elderly women, who appeared to be sisters, ceased their chattering and sat down where Mrs. Fontaine indicated. "Mr. Poe, here. Professor, perhaps here."

My seat was to be between the professor and Mrs. Fontaine, which left Dupin situated next to the serving girl and one of the garrulous sisters, who asked in a loud whisper, "Have the spirit guides descended?"

"Yes, I believe so," Mrs. Fontaine said solemnly. "Can you feel their presence?"

The shortest and plumpest of the sisters contemplated this thought for a moment and declared, "Yes. I feel a presence."

Dupin cleared his throat and arched his brows again, but I shifted my eyes away from him as his supercilious attitude was beginning to irk me.

"Sarah, would you, please?" Mrs. Fontaine nodded at the wall sconces and the serving girl took a candle-snuffer from her apron pocket and extinguished the tapers, until all that illumined the room was the moonlight. When the girl rejoined the table, Mrs. Fontaine said, "Let us join hands." Her soft hand enclosed mine, as did the professor's, whose grip was surprisingly strong. Mrs. Fontaine closed her eyes and tipped back her head, her brow furrowed in concentration. I felt her hand grasp mine more tightly. "What did you say?" she asked suddenly. "Are you here, spirit? Have you something to say?" She appeared to listen intently, her head tilted to one side, her eyes closed tightly. And then, Mrs. Fontaine began to sing a hymn in a clear pleasant voice. Her maid and the three ladies joined in to less agreeable effect. The hymn was unfamiliar to me, and I presumed the same of Dupin. I stole a glance at the professor and found his eyes upon me, or so it seemed as the moonlight danced most oddly upon the glass of his spectacles.

"Would you all please hum along if you do not know the hymn. We must produce enough energy for the spirits to use." Mrs. Fontaine began to sing more loudly, as did the ladies and girl. The professor commenced a tuneless droning, and I joined in, more mellifluously, I hoped, than the tone-deaf professor. Only Dupin remained silent. As the volume of the living increased, the temperature of the room seemed to descend until it felt as if it were the middle of winter rather than a warm July night.

"Do you feel them?" Mrs. Fontaine whispered. "They have arrived, most surely. Sing!"

The ladies near shouted out the rollicking hymn and without instruction we began to undulate our clasped hands. There was a loud tapping upon the table, followed by a muffled shriek from one of the ladies.

"Do not break the circle," Mrs. Fontaine cried out. "Our energy must be unified. Do not break the circle until the spirit has gained strength!" Her hand clasped mine more firmly, as did the professor's. "Do you hear me, spirit? Rap twice for yes."

Two loud taps followed her words. Despite the dim light, I could see that all hands were held firmly clasped above the table and a chill ran through me.

"Have you come with a message? Rap twice for yes and once for no."

Again, two loud taps.

"For whom is the message intended, spirit?"

I wondered how the spirit would manage this with a simple

"yes" or "no" and then the most uncanny thing happened. An object fell from the gloom and landed upon the table. The three ladies shrieked and broke the circle, pressing their hands up to their astonished mouths.

"Thank you, spirit. Thank you." Mrs. Fontaine reached across the table and picked up the object. "A rose. A *white* rose. It symbolizes purity of spirit, eternal faithful love, and Heaven. It is for you, Miss Castleton. It is from a young man."

The three ladies began to murmur like bees.

"Is it Charlie?" Miss Castleton asked with quavering voice.

"Yes," Mrs. Fontaine said firmly. "He has something to say to you." She touched the rose to her forehead. "Wait, it is coming. I almost have it. Yes, thank you, spirit. Charlie says that if he may be so bold as to tell you, he has always loved you."

A cry of distress mixed with joy escaped Miss Castleton.

"He is waiting for you. True love does not fade with time. He brings this white rose because—thank you, spirit—he wanted to give you a bouquet of white roses on your wedding day. Yes, I understand," Mrs. Fontaine said, face turned toward the invisible. "Death may have stopped your union on Earth, but you will be joined in holy matrimony in Heaven."

Miss Castleton emitted a sob. Her sister extracted a handkerchief from her bosom and handed it to her. "Thank you, thank you," she murmured, weeping into its lacy folds.

"Tell him what is in your heart before he leaves us," Mrs. Fontaine instructed. "You must tell him now. His strength is fading."

"Dear Charlie, I have never forgotten you! I count the days until we are together," Miss Castleton cried out.

"He is leaving us," Mrs. Fontaine said. "He says, farewell, my darling Lucy, farewell."

Miss Castleton broke into fresh sobs, and tears glittered on the cheeks of her sisters.

"Take this rose, my dear. Take this rose as a keepsake and dry your tears. Few of us are lucky enough to find one who loves us so dearly." Mrs. Fontaine handed the rose to Miss Castleton, who took it with trembling hands. I felt quite moved by the exchange, but Dupin and the professor remained inscrutable.

"Let us join hands again. There are more messages from the other side. I can feel it."

We reformed our circle, and Mrs. Fontaine began to sing another obscure hymn that preached of everlasting life and the joys of Heaven, but she abruptly terminated the chorus.

"The energy is weak. I can feel the spirits but I cannot discern their words." She dropped my hand and the serving girl's and stood up. Mrs. Fontaine pulled back her lace shawl, and I caught sight of that eye—that *human* eye—pinned to her breast. It stared at me most evilly, rendering me incapable of movement or speech until a clanging jarred me back into the world of the living. Mrs. Fontaine was ringing a hand bell, which was attached by a ribbon to her waist. She began to circle the table, ringing the bell continuously. "Please clasp hands," she said. "I can feel . . . a woman."

My heart leapt at this pronouncement.

"Yes, a woman. A very talented woman—most learned." The hand bell clanged and clanged. "Speak to me, spirit!" Mrs. Fontaine stopped near the window and allowed the bell to fall back to her side. The moonlight seemed to gild her with a phosphorescent ice, transforming her into a creature from a fairytale. Again, she tilted her face to the heavens. "Yes, I hear you. He must stop. He is in danger. Yes, I hear. She says that the time has passed to take revenge upon the man who betrayed us. His task now is to redeem our name."

A chill settled upon me, and for a moment the darkness

seemed to deepen into a velvety black, with only Mrs. Fontaine illumined by the spectral light. Was this the warning from my grandmother? If so, I was baffled by her message.

Mrs. Fontaine stood up very straight, her eyes directed toward us and as she began to speak, her voice took on a new inflection. Her accent seemed almost *French*.

"We who are falsely accused by the duplicitous—by those who are enemies to the truth and to the highest principles of man—we go to our deaths safe in the knowledge that we and we alone are upholding the very spirit of France: liberty, reason and equality. Our innocence will be confirmed in time and our enemies will finally be vanquished. I accept my murder with love for my homeland and all that she truly stands for, and I condemn those who seek to defeat her through treachery and dishonor." A terrible gasp escaped Mrs. Fontaine and her hands fluttered to her throat before she sank to her knees and collapsed into a faint.

"Miss Rowena!" The serving girl jumped up and rushed to her mistress. She began to pat her cheeks gently. I arose from my chair to assist and noticed that Dupin was frozen, his face a mask of astonishment, and then he stormed from the room. I was torn between following him and going to Mrs. Fontaine's aid. The three ladies clucked like over-fed hens, but remained glued to their chairs, as did the professor, who seemed unmoved by Mrs. Fontaine's collapse—I was compelled to go to the stricken lady's assistance.

"Mrs. Fontaine, can you hear me?" She was scarcley breathing. I looked to the serving girl. "Fetch her some water and a damp cloth."

The girl gave me an unexpectedly poisonous look and leaned closer to her mistress.

"Miss Rowena," she whispered. "Please wake up."

Mrs. Fontaine's eyelids fluttered and then opened. "Oh, I feel most . . . depleted. She was powerful. Terribly powerful. Please, help me up."

"Would you like some water? A compress?"

"No, no. I am fine. But they are pressing upon me. I must . . . I must comply or they will torment me all night. Help me up. Please."

The serving girl and I helped Mrs. Fontaine to her feet.

"Dear, you gave us quite a fright," one of the sisters stuttered.

"Please sit," said the other.

"Yes, please do," added Miss Castleton.

"No, I cannot. We must . . . we must adjourn to the cellar. The spirits command it. They will torment me until we do as they ask. Please, help me down the stairs." She grasped onto my arm and led me toward the opposite wall, where there was an open door I had not noticed before. Mrs. Fontaine clung to my arm to steady herself and the serving girl carried a candle, which did little to dispel the deep shadows below us as we descended into the musty cellar. The girl placed the taper into a candleholder that stood on a table and its beam jittered in the blackness, shivering with fear. A pile of stones was arranged on the table top, but I could see nothing else.

"Please, would everyone take several stones," Mrs. Fontaine instructed. "We must raise the energy again. I can feel a presence, a *strong* presence, but I cannot discern what he or she is saying to me. Let us sing." She launched into another hymn and the ladies immediately accompanied her, their countenances flaccid with fear. The professor began to hum, occasionally breaking into words: "I am but a sinner. Dear Lord, forgive me my sins."

Mrs. Fontaine threw a pebble into the darkness that shrouded the other end of the cellar. The ladies followed suit, as did the professor and I. Still singing and humming, we all threw another stone. Mrs. Fontaine sang more loudly and threw yet another. The room reverberated with song made unpalatable by the fear that tinged each note.

"Ouch!" Miss Castleton broke off from singing with a sharp cry. "My word, I have been hit!" A second pebble came flying back at us.

"They are here!" Mrs. Fontaine's voice contained joy whereas the chill of fear infected the rest of us. "Do you have a message for us?" Another stone flew through the air and hit my arm. "For Mr. Poe?" Again, another stone pattered against me and my heart sped up. "Speak through me, spirit, speak through me." Mrs. Fontaine tilted her face upward. "Yes, I hear you." Mrs. Fontaine's voice seemed to alter as she spoke, dropping in tone, taking on a peculiar accent. "I looked to those who were to protect my innocence, with confidence in impartiality. I believed that truth and innocence would triumph over false-hood, but I suffered from prejudice and truth did not prevail. I have tried to forgive, but is there justice when a lie convicts a man and sets the true perpetrator free? Is there justice when a child is condemned to prison before his birth? Surely, when there is no justice, we must make it ourselves?"

There was a loud crack against the cellar wall. And another. One of the ladies yelped as a pebble hit her, far more fiercely than before. And then another until it was clear that the hail of pebbles that flew at us far exceeded the number we had thrown.

"We have summoned a being from the lowest order!" Mrs. Fontaine cried out. "One who died after a life of vice upon this plane. Its intentions are evil. Run! Run upstairs, now!"

The sisters scurried upstairs and the serving girl scuttled after them, with the professor at her heels. Then the candle was extinguished, leaving utter darkness. It was then that my arms were grabbed by preternaturally strong hands, and I was dragged further into the cellar.

"Help!" I called out. "Someone help me!"

There was the sound of a door slamming shut, and I struggled against the malicious spirits that were determined to drag me to Hell. I thrashed and wriggled like a strung up fish, until I felt a heavy crack upon my head and succumbed to nothingness.

* * *

Later, much later, an eerie jeweled light appeared in the sable darkness. I struggled to bring myself back to sentience, to breathe in the airless room. My body ached and as I tried to arise from my bed, the floor rushed away from my feet. Window—I needed to open a window—but I could not ascertain its location. Fear caught hold of me as I discerned movement—there! Near the dark velvet curtains! The jeweled light grew brighter and brighter, then transformed into a woman's eyes that glared like a cat's when they capture the light. As I watched, morbidly transfixed, a second pair of eyes appeared and then another and another! Until hundreds of eyes glowed from the shadows—unnatural and unblinking. A chill slowed my heart and moved through my body—death itself creeping through me, its slow, icy poison finishing me inch by inch. It came to me in a blinding flash of horror that I had swooned—how long ago I did not remember— and now I was trapped, utterly trapped, within my familial tomb, the spirits of my decaying ancestors drawing the life from me so they might rise again. And as these treacherous phantoms waited for sleep to reclaim me, I knew that if my eyes fell closed I would never come back from the darkness.

But my head throbbed and my body ached. I was lying on damp earth, my chin resting upon the floor of my prison, and when I put out my arm, discovered I was at the very brink of a pit, with only empty space in front of me. There was a smell, which increased as my senses cleared; it was the smell of rotting eggs—or the sulfurous fumes of Hell! I could hear noises, faint but somehow disturbing, *creeping* noises moving toward me. As fear gripped me ever tighter, my senses became inhumanely acute. The sound of feet pattered ever closer, and eyes gleamed like a demon's in the blackness. And then, with a rushing, something scuttled past me— soft fur, sharp claws, and somewhere . . . teeth. I jerked back my body, arms thrashing. A soft body thudded against my hand and squealed as it connected with a harder surface. And another! As my panic increased, so did my memory. Pebbles . . . flying pebbles thrown by malicious spirits . . . and now, much more horribly, live things sneaking round me, hoping to taste warm flesh, their preter-natural eyes accustomed to the darkness, unlike my own. I scrabbled to my feet like a tormented madman and flung myself toward the walls of my cell. They were of dank, musty soil, easily scraped and furrowed by my fingernails, yet most assuredly a prison. I felt my way along the unyielding walls, seeking the prison door, until my foot met with emptiness. A shriek escaped my lips as I grappled to steady myself and sank to my heels, determined not to plunge into the bowels of the earth.

How long I crouched on the floor I do not know. The inten-sity of the gloom was oppressive and stifling, and it was a struggle to breathe. I itched at the dusty ground around me, seeking a stone, a clod of dirt, anything to test the depth of the pit before me. At last, I found a pebble and threw it—down, down, down, it went, but there was no thud or splash, no sound of it connecting with the bottom. Most surely the house was situated atop the gateway of Hell itself! Horror conquered me, and then the darkness.

How much later did I awake? The darkness remained, but the terror had softened to fear. I had no sense of the size of the pit so moved forward cautiously, arms outstretched, my eyes straining from their sockets, searching for a faint ray of light.

"Mrs. Fontaine! Are you there? Mrs. Fontaine!"

But all I could hear was the breathing of the rats that lived in my cellar with me, the famished rats waiting to catch me unawares. The noise from their impatient feet and urgent teeth echoed diabolically. How long before they formed a mob and threw themselves upon me, teeth and claws burrowing deep into my still-living flesh?

"Mrs. Fontaine!"

I do not know how many times I called out from my crypt. Had she been hurt? Was she also a prisoner? At last, I found a rectangle of wood lodged in the earthen wall that seemed to be my prison's door, but there was no latch to open it. I pounded heartily upon it.

"Help me, someone!" I repeated my pleas over and over until I collapsed into unconsciousness again.

* * *

It may have been hours or possibly days later that I heard a steady rapping. I could not tell if it came from within my prison or outside it. Then there was a sound of splintering wood and a loud crack! Daylight flared through broken planks.

"Poe! Are you there?"

My stuttering heart calmed. It was Dupin at last. "The pit! Heed the pit!" I croaked with the remnants of my voice.

"Poe, I am here. You are safe." The gleam of a lantern showed him my location. "The devils," he muttered, as he made his way toward me. "Grasp my arm. You must be weak. I am sorry it took me so long to find you."

"The lantern. Shine the lantern. I must see it."

Dupin held the lantern aloft and its feeble beams illuminated the damp walls.

"No, the pit. Show me the pit."

Dupin held the lantern over it. "There is a hole, framed with wooden beams. I think perhaps it was once a trapdoor."

"But what can you *see*? I dropped a stone into it and there was no sound. It seemed to fall into *infinity*."

Dupin held the lantern over the pit, leaned to look into its depths and quickly recoiled. "Let us leave this place," he muttered, trying to usher me toward the broken door, but I clung to his arm, dragging him back.

"You must tell me! What did you see?"

"Here, drink." Dupin handed me a flask. The water was like nectar upon my tongue and throat as I gulped its coolness.

"What was down there, Dupin? Was it the mouth to Hell itself?"

"One might say that," he said softly.

"I must look!" I wrenched the lantern from his grasp with an energy that seemed superhuman and leaned over the pit. As the lantern's feeble light trickled into the gaping darkness, a terrible tableau was revealed. There below were the bones of a man, his clothes still intact, his flesh long gone. It was as if he had been on his knees with head bowed when he expired and had toppled onto his side, hands still clenched fiercely in prayer. His last hours came to me with horrible clarity—the ragged breathing, his collapse into the dust, his final muttered prayers.

"But God did not listen," I said softly.

"Poe, please. Let us leave this desperate place." Dupin leaned over Hell's mouth and took the lantern from my hand, gently pushing me from the edge with his other. I staggered back just as he gasped. Then suddenly, inexplicably, he leapt in.

"Dupin! My God!"

Moments later he scrabbled up from Hell itself and as I went to grab his earth-stained hands with my own, I saw that he was clutching something.

"It is a letter."

And there in the lamplight, I saw the familiar green seal upon it.

I entered a peculiar state after my incarceration. My vision had a terrible acuity, but my other senses were dulled and everything seemed to move more slowly. It was as if I were submerged in crystalline water, my terror diluted to doomed resignation. Perhaps this was what it was like to drown.

The feeling did not leave me when we were returned to Brown's Genteel Inn. Dupin ushered me to my room and prepared a steaming basin of water laced with a pungent elixir.

"Wash with this. It will help restore you after your ordeal."

"Dupin, I need sleep. I am quite overcome."

"That cellar was inhabited by rats and a recently dead man. The soil was most certainly as noxious as the air. This should counter some deleterious consequences of your imprisonment. I have also summoned a French doctor I know—not a charlatan like those who profess to have studied medicine here. He will examine you."

"There is no need. I am simply tired."

"Please." He handed me a wash towel, pushed me toward the steaming basin and adjourned to the sitting room.

It was only as I removed my clothes that I noticed the terrible state of them. What had the desk clerk thought upon my entrance through the door? He had been as courteous as ever, despite my appearance as a slovenly beggar. My trousers were covered in mud and stained green at the knees with what must be slime. My frock coat was equally filthy, and my shirt! The stench that came from it would never be removed. I discarded all my clothing into a malodorous heap, determined that they should be burned rather than laundered.

I leaned over the basin Dupin had prepared for me and sniffed at the water. It smelled of vinegar and garlic, freshened up with rosemary, lavender, peppermint, and finished with a spicy hint of nutmeg, cinnamon and cloves. It was not entirely unpleasant, so I washed myself from head to foot, then put on a clean nightshirt and crept into my bed. The sheets were deliciously cool and smelled of lavender.

Just as my eyelids fluttered shut, voices woke me again. Niceties were exchanged in French, and I heard Dupin describe in brief the hell-hole where I had been imprisoned. Dupin and a gentleman resembling a giant stork entered my bed chamber. He was dressed somberly in a black frock coat and trousers with thin white stripes that exaggerated the length of his legs. A large alligator bag was clutched in his hand.

"May I introduce Dr. Froissart, a most revered friend of the Dupin family and doctor to French Ambassador Guizot. And this, my dear doctor, is Mr. Edgar Poe, esteemed author, literary editor and friend."

"It is a great pleasure, Mr. Poe, although I regret that we meet in the aftermath of such disagreeable circumstances. Chevalier Dupin has told me something of your ordeal," he said in a slow, sonorous voice. Dr. Froissart approached my bedside. "The criminal element in this city is vicious and at times quite ingenious. There are many ways to disguise the murder of a man as an accident. We must ensure that your health is not compromised."

"I had him bathe in *vinaigre des quatre voleurs*," Dupin said. "His clothes were fouled by the rat-infested soil and the air was infected with vapors of decomposed flesh. I am concerned that he was bitten."

"No, not bitten. I batted them away."

"Or he might have been scratched. The foul beasts spread pestilence with claw or tooth," Dupin continued, as if I were unable to hear what he was saying. The sense of being locked inside a dome of water increased.

"Please, Mr. Poe. I must examine you. I apologize for the indignity, but any scratch or bite must be cauterized or you risk an unpleasant death."

Wearily, I eased my legs from under the coverlet and sat up.

"I will send for coffee," Dupin said.

"Tea," the doctor instructed. "It is better in the circumstances."

Dupin nodded and left the room. Dr. Froissart promptly threw open the curtains, then picked up the small table next to my bedside and repositioned it near the window. He extracted an amber-colored glass bottle from his bag and cotton wadding, then unfurled a leather roll that contained sharp metal instruments that glistered in the sunlight.

"If you would," the doctor said, indicating my nightshirt. When I removed it, he gestured that I should stand. "Please, here," he said, indicating a pool of sunlight.

The doctor extracted from his bag a peculiar instrument that resembled a magnifying glass suspended from a metal halo and fitted it onto his head so the magnifying glass was directly in front of his left eye. I watched with the objectivity of a fellow doctor as he clasped a small hammer-like implement and tapped it gently upon my back, then my arms, while inspecting my skin for scratches or bite marks.

"Very good. I see nothing on your skin. Now I must only check your scalp." He tilted my head slightly and such was his height that he had the perfect view of my entire cranium. The doctor removed a metal comb from his tool kit and checked every inch of my still damp head. "Very fine," he said at last. "You may dress again and return to bed if you wish."

There was a perfunctory rap on the door. Dupin entered, carrying a tray of tea things and warm scones. My stomach growled at my mind's dismissal of the offering.

"I could find no punctures of the skin or scalp, which is most fortunate. Now we must hope that no pestilence entered the body through the sinuses or mouth. I will give you a prophylactic you must take daily."

The doctor rummaged in his capacious bag and removed a wooden box. When he opened it, a selection of vials were revealed, all neatly labeled in Latin. He carefully mixed the contents of several vials into a small glass bottle. Dupin watched intently.

"Wormwood?" he asked, eyebrows raised.

"*Artemisia absinthium* is a vermifuge. It also deters fleas, lice and tics and protects against the plague and similar fatal fevers. Most helpful when a subject has been exposed to rats. It also quells anxiety, which is useful given the circumstances."

Dupin nodded. Dr. Froissart closed the bottle and shook it vigorously. He then opened it again and carefully dripped the elixir into a glass of water. "Ten drops morning and night," he instructed before he handed the glass to me. "It has little taste if you drink it quickly."

I sipped the elixir down, relishing its bitterness. The unpleasant feeling it left in my mouth helped to better connect me with the world around me.

"Tea?" Dupin asked Dr. Froissart.

"Yes. No milk."

"Of course not. Most terrible habit of the English. Poe?" Dupin held the pot's spout over the third teacup. I nodded and he delivered the cup to my bedside table. Dupin and Dr. Froissart settled into two chairs and murmured softly about symptoms of pestilent afflictions, while I sipped at the hot beverage. I had thought the tea might revive me, but twilight began to envelop me, and I wondered if a sleeping draft had been put into my cup. When my companions began to speak in French, I felt a conspiring tone seep into their discourse and drew on all my strength to hear their words.

"I have an article from the scene of the attack I would like you to analyze. I suspect it is not what it seems."

I could hear a rustling as Dupin passed something to Dr. Froissart, but could not lift my weighted lids to see what the object was.

"Better to examine the entire thing," Dr. Froissart eventually said. "I believe I will immediately be able to identify what it is in situ. There should be no need to transport it unless required as evidence."

"Unfortunately, it is evidence of malediction rather than any crime punishable by imprisonment. My investigation is for Poe's peace of mind."

Resentment welled up in me to hear Dupin discuss my state of mind with the doctor.

There was the clack of teacups placed into saucers and the sound of Dr. Froissart gathering his things, then Dupin said: "Valdemar is in London—or was four days ago. Have you heard anything of him?"

"No, but I have been distracted. The situation here is difficult and the Ambassador may be called away at any time."

"There are some things perhaps you might check for me. I am convinced he is still in London and planning something. It will offer me my chance if I learn what that is."

They stepped outside my bedroom and I overheard nothing further except my chamber door close. I had an idea to follow them back to Bayham Street, but my legs would barely support me as I made my way slowly into the sitting room. And then I saw the letter on the marble table.

93 Jermyn Street, London
Sunday 14 June 1790

Dear Henry,

The Monster has been captured! I write this news with much relief tempered with caution as the accused is none other than that unlucky Welshman, Rhynwick Williams—the very man who spied the true Monster in the act.

It seems our former ballet dancer is known for pressing his attentions upon the ladies too forcibly (and therefore unsuccessfully), so when the news spread that he was hauled to Bow Street after Miss Anne Porter's accusations yesterday, it was astonishing how many ladies suddenly remembered him as their attacker. Truth conquered by the desire to blame!

Mr. Williams's misfortune unfurled in this manner on Saturday evening. Miss Anne Porter was walking in St. James's Park with another lady and her betrothed, Mr. Coleman, when she became highly agitated, claiming she had just seen the monster who attacked her after the Queen's birthday ball. The gallant Mr. Coleman pursued Rhynwick Williams, but the incredible dolt lost his prey and took to knocking on doors in hopes of finding him again. I would not dare to put such a scene in our play as no sensible audience would believe it! Later that evening, Mr. Coleman came across Mr. Williams by chance at St. James's Place, and he insisted that Williams accompany him to the Porter residence. Williams did not refuse (quite why, I do not understand) and the two proceeded to the Porter's door. When the sisters caught sight of Mr. Williams, they shrieked: "That is the wretch!" And so Mr. Williams was apprehended and taken to Bow Street. Anne Porter went there this morning and selected the ill-fated flower maker from a crowd of people. The false Monster will now go to trial and of course the true Monster must cease to exist. Promise that you will never again assume the guise of the Monster unless onstage in the title role!

Yours,
Elizabeth

The address was sixteen Bayham Street, but it did not much resemble the house I had been to. Decayed trees stood sentry either side of the door and the gray stone façade was overspread with peculiar, faintly luminous fungi, which seemed to draw sustenance from the stone itself. As I approached the house, a violent wind arose and the door opened, drawing me inside, and there before me was the séance table and a chair, the room devoid of all other furnishings. I was compelled to sit in the chair and there I waited, for what I did not know—all I could hear was the howling of the wind and a strange thump, *thump*, thump. And yet I sat and waited, as if bound to the chair with ghostly cords. The wind grew ever louder and stronger until it hammered at the window glass as if something were demanding admission, but all I could see there was a blood-red moon in its fullest phase, glaring in like a god of war.

And then I heard a scraping and the drag of something heavy on the floorboards, closer, ever closer behind me. I turned in my chair and froze in terror at what I saw. There, emerged from the door that led to the cellar, was the man—or what was left of him—who had been interred in the pit, risen to his feet and dragging himself toward me with torturous gait.

I cowered at the séance table, unable to flee. There was a terrible rumbling and the window glass shattered—as the glittering fragments flew around me in the cyclonic air, my gaze was drawn to the ceiling, where a fissure was zigzagging across the plasterwork. This was mirrored by a fissure in the floor, which rapidly widened like an ominous crack in thawing ice. And still the glowing remains of the dead man shuffled toward me, feet scraping along, the wind blowing through the holes that were once his eyes, a solitary sheet of paper flapping wildly in his extended hand. Hypnotized, I reached out to take the letter from him, but the building split asunder and we plunged into the endless depths of the cellar as the fragments of the house rained down upon us.

* * *

I jolted as if I had fallen from a great height. My bedclothes were twisted from battling with them and my skin damp with the dew of fear. I had slept through a full day, or had tried to, but the same nightmare had visited me again and again, leaving me ever more exhausted and unable to leave the safety of my room.

The honest smell of a cooked breakfast sailed through the air and my belly persuaded me to enter the sitting room. Dupin was seated at the table and immediately poured coffee.

"You must eat. And if you feel ready, perhaps we might venture out."

"I am not an invalid, Dupin. Indeed, I am voracious. Sleep was what I needed."

"Certainly your character seems quite recovered if not improved." He smiled slightly to indicate a jest.

I had not forgotten his exchange with Dr. Froissart. I began my breakfast, wondering the best way to find out the truth of what they had been discussing and decided a direct approach was best.

"You have something to tell me, I believe? Something regarding the house on Bayham Street?"

A look of surprise passed over Dupin's face and he took his time eating before dabbing at his mouth with his napkin. "Given your ordeal, it would be wise to step back from the investigation for another day."

"I disagree. To cower in my room will lead my nemesis to believe he has intimidated me and this might embolden him when he advances his next attack."

"Ah, so you agree that Mrs. Fontaine is in league with your enemy?"

"I did not say that, precisely. It is possible she was his victim also." Despite the evidence, I could not quite believe in her guilt. I picked up my cup of coffee, but the tremor in my hand caught Dupin's notice. I wondered if the twitch in my eyelid was also visible to him. He did not comment on either, just shook his head imperceptibly.

"It is possible to make Venus herself vanish from the firmament by a scrutiny too sustained or a mind too clouded by fear. Let us divert our minds today. When our intellects are refreshed we shall see much more. I suggest we play the tourist. Shall we visit the Regent's Park? The design is said to be attractive as are the Zoological and Botanic Gardens. The Colosseum is also regarded as noteworthy."

The idea of Dupin as a tourist was so improbable it immediately persuaded me. He embarked on activities with purpose rather than pleasure, by his own admission. Dupin might visit an exhibition of paintings, but it was to study the technique of an artist, not to enjoy the beauty of the works. He spent considerable time in libraries and museums, but his objective was to broaden the mind rather than satisfy the imagination.

Even his appreciation of wine was overshadowed by his comprehensive knowledge of the wine-making process and the best vintages.

"A novel idea, Dupin. Most interesting. I think I shall enjoy being a tourist with you."

But I was doubly determined to get an answer to my question before we finished our excursion.

* * *

We entered the Regent's Park through Macclesfield Gate, which was very pleasant as the north side of the park looked out over open countryside, the verdant areas of Primrose Hill and Hampstead. Despite the beauty of the place, each creeping shadow and unexpected noise provoked my overly sharpened senses and made my heart race. The park was merry with perambulators enjoying the fine weather and slowly, ever so slowly, the acute memory of the Bayham Street cellar and its venomous spirits began to recede. Dupin had purchased a small guidebook and proceeded to illuminate me with its contents. The Regent's Park had been open to the public for just two years as the Prince Regent had intended to build a residence in the northeast of the park, but he changed his mind and London society gained another handsome space in which to scrutinize their contemporaries and be scrutinized in turn. As we made our way toward the Zoological Gardens, Dupin described the size of the park and the intent of the architect. Whenever I tried to steer him toward the discovery at Bayham Street, he deftly batted away my questions.

"There it is just there. This should be a most lively entertainment. Listen—the roar of a lion. We might be in the jungles of Africa," Dupin said with mock gravity, indicating the manicured gardens around us. I could not help but smile and he delved back into the guidebook. "'The menageries from the Tower of London and Windsor were brought to the Zoological Gardens at Regent's Park. There are over one thousand living animals, including mammalia, birds and reptiles.'"

"Quite the collection." We paid the entrance fee and followed the terrace walk to the gardens, which were admirably arranged. The buildings that housed the exotic creatures were attractive and well-adapted for the animals' needs. Each spacious cage held a surprise, be it a panting polar bear, a sleeping leopard or a grazing rhinoceros. All of these creatures were new to me in the flesh, and I was as entranced as my fellow spectators. Several ostriches grazed on open ground, their flightless wings ensuring that they remained captive without the need for an overhead enclosure. Four giraffes stood together, long necks swaying this way and that as they surveyed a horizon not visible to those of lesser stature.

"The giraffes were herded along like sheep or cattle from Blackwall, their landing place, to Regent's Park," Dupin said.

"Quite the spectacle that would have been. Imagine awaking to see these creatures pass by your window."

"Indeed. Although I believe they were driven through unpopulated areas." Dupin led us onward. "Ah, llamas. Interesting creatures. From Peru." The llama pair grazed side by side, oblivious to our gaze.

"Surely the giraffes are rather more unusual or does the guidebook reveal something extraordinary about the llamas?"

Dupin shrugged slightly. "Perhaps it is the country of their origin more than the animal itself that appeals to me."

"Peru? I was not aware that you had any special interest in the place."

"It is a country I traveled to in my youth—a most extraordinary place. The flora and fauna are unparalleled, particularly the bird-life which is highly sought after by collectors."

"You traveled to Peru?" My astonishment was acute.

"Yes," Dupin said with a studied casual air. "Does that surprise you?"

My laugh of incredulity could not be suppressed. The notion of the urbane Dupin traveling through the wilds of South America stretched my imagination beyond its considerable limits.

"Ah, look here. The simians."

In a series of enclosures before us were a variety of primates. Dupin strode past the exuberant monkeys and a sullen chimpanzee before stopping before a large cage. I quickly followed.

"*Pongo pygmaeus*," Dupin said. "The animal nearest to the human in intelligence. Indeed, the average ourang-outang may surpass the human of limited intelligence."

"Indeed?" I joined Dupin at the enclosure and examined the creature before us.

"Ourang-outangs sometimes live over thirty years, whether in captivity or in the wild." He paused for a moment and examined the beast. "They look almost human, do they not?" Dupin awaited a response.

"Yes, quite. But the legs are rather shorter and the arms are far longer. I would imagine the skull is a different shape, judging by his aspect in the flesh."

Dupin nodded. "Most correct. But if one were to see a deceased *Pongo pygmaeus* dressed in human clothing, posed in an attitude of prayer in a darkened chamber, one might presume that the creature were human."

"Possibly." And then I understood Dupin's suggestion. "Bayham Street."

"Yes. When I collected the letter from the skeleton's hand, I had my suspicions. The clothing, lack of light and posture disguised the obvious elements, so I broke off a finger bone to show Dr. Froissart, who has a superb understanding of anatomy. He confirmed my suspicions when he saw the skeleton intact at Bayham Street. Dr. Froissart estimated that the ourang-outang was dead for more than a decade, given the condition of its skeleton."

I could think of no reply, it was so obvious. How had I succumbed to such a farce?

"Do not torture yourself, Poe. It was a clever fabrication designed to terrorize. The environment contributed to the veracity. You should be relieved that it was a contrivance rather than murder."

No doubt Dupin was correct, but I felt quite numb as I followed him away from the simian enclosures. Dupin took his time, admiring the various mammals on show, saying little more than the Latin names of each creature we saw. Eventually we reached the reptile house.

"Shall we? The collection is meant to be impressive, but perhaps you would prefer to remain outdoors?"

"I think we can be certain that any venomous creatures are securely locked up." I led the way inside, feeling that he had issued me with a challenge. I was determined to prove to Dupin and myself that I was recovered from my ordeal—especially as it was based entirely on a hoax—and fit to continue our investigation. But as soon as the cool, dimly lit chamber enveloped me, I was forced to suppress the bile that rose up in me, as toxic as any reptile's venom. The presence of ladies in the company helped me quell the urge to retch, and I presented a calm façade as we studied the specimens within their glass prisons. These ranged from the innocuous but colorful snake to deadlier varieties, including pythons and a cobra that closely resembled the creature that decorated Dupin's walking stick. When he raised the stick to compare it with the live cobra, the cold-blooded, living thing slithered from its lair at the back of the enclosure and reared up directly in front of us. It stared into the ruby eyes of the golden counterfeit, apparently transfixed, and then suddenly lunged at its twin, fangs exposed, and hit the glass with such force a mere window would have shattered. A lady standing close to us cried out and fainted dead away as if bitten. The reptile, not content with its unsuccessful attack, reared up again.

"I will crush you under my heel like a snake," Dupin said softly in Latin, his eyes staring into the cobra's, utterly unblinking, utterly without fear, until the ghastly thing slithered back to the ground and coiled in upon itself.

"Oh, my word," someone behind us whispered.

"Come, Dupin. I think we have seen enough."

He woke as if from a trance, his face hard, his eyes hooded, and followed me from the reptile house, walking stick tap-tapping on the ground behind me. Once back out in the open air, I confronted him.

"What possessed you to torment the creature?" I asked with an anger I did not fully comprehend myself.

"It was unintentional. I had not expected such a response from the snake."

"And yet you were goading it to strike again, playing the snake charmer!"

Dupin frowned. "No, I attempted to make it submit to my will, and it seems that I succeeded."

"It could have killed us—and the other observers."

"The glass was very strong. That was obvious. We were all quite safe."

Of course he was correct, but I was aggravated by his game, and we walked along in silence until the ornamental plantations succeeded in quieting my temper.

"I am sorry for my outburst. I fear my nerves are strained after my containment."

Dupin nodded. "I should have taken that into account and avoided the reptile house. It was completely my error. Shall we explore the Botanic Gardens? They are sure to refresh our minds—an example of man's artistry combined with nature's, and it is highly unlikely any deadly creatures will be lurking there."

"Let us hope you are correct." I smiled.

As we strolled through the delightful gardens, I thought how much Sissy and Muddy would enjoy them. The atmosphere was certainly a tonic for my nerves and presently my soul grew stronger. I had been duped, yes, but it would not happen so easily again. I was all the more determined to defeat my aggressors.

"You were a reluctant participant in the séance, believing it a hoax from the beginning, and yet you stormed away when your grandmother spoke to you. Why, Dupin?"

Dupin grimaced at my words. "When Mrs. Fontaine spoke to me. The lady is adept at gathering information. It is how she makes her living—duping naïve and lonely ladies from their money."

"That does not answer my question."

He grimaced again. "It was quite a masterly hoax, and I confess that I was caught up in the moment. I cannot adequately explain my reaction."

"The atmosphere was persuasive."

"To most, perhaps. But it is clear how the effect was contrived. The singing of hymns promoted an atmosphere of truth, and the white rose was an impressive theatrical start. Mrs. Fontaine knew her subject's history very well. Either the good lady had confessed it to her at an earlier sitting or Mrs. Fontaine had done some excellent research before commencing her iniquitous charade."

"Was it so iniquitous? She made the lady happy."

"She told her what she wanted to hear. There was no truth in it."

"How do you know, Dupin? Can you be certain that the lady's long-dead lover is not waiting for her in the afterlife?"

"I am a man of science, Poe, not a dreamer of fiction."

"If Mrs. Fontaine is a charlatan, why did she provoke such a reaction from you when she allowed the French lady to speak through her? The lady who, it seems, made a speech before her execution? If Mrs. Fontaine is a fraud, how did she know about your grandmother?" I watched Dupin's face, waiting for incredulity to cross his countenance, as it had during the séance, but I was disappointed.

"As I believe I suggested previously, I am not the ghost you believe me to be. One might easily discover what happened to my grandparents, and this performance was made unconvincing by the simple fact that my grandmother, if she contacted me from beyond the grave, would have spoken to me in *French* as she did not speak a word of English."

I could not resist prodding Dupin. "Perhaps English is the language of the afterlife?"

"Then that is a very good reason to deny the existence of it," he retorted. "Admittedly, Mrs. Fontaine took me by surprise at the séance, but it became all too clear later that her show was but a clever way of undermining my critical faculties. This was part of her larger plan—and the professor's—to imprison you."

My face must have expressed the shock I had hoped to rouse in Dupin. "The professor?"

"Who of course was the scrivener at the hanging and also the man I chased at your reading. Quite the master of disguise, it would seem."

I reflected upon each man, not convinced by Dupin's accusation. "They were of various heights, I am quite certain."

"It was the shoes. Heels of different sizes," Dupin said. "You would do well to remember the abilities of your own grandparents," he added.

As reluctant as I was to cast Mrs. Fontaine as the villainess, I could without difficulty imagine the snake-eyed man as a scoundrel.

"If you are in doubt, still, about the relationship between Mrs. Fontaine and the alleged professor, consider the brooches they wear." Dupin smiled at my confusion. "I trust you noticed the unusual jewel Mrs. Fontaine had on her dress—painted most accurately to resemble a human eye."

I nodded, remembering the brown eye fixed in a piercing glare. "It was life-like and terribly unpleasant."

"That should not surprise us when we consider the eye from which it was painted."

"No, no, Dupin. Mrs. Fontaine's eyes are an attractive violet-gray. They are not brown at all."

"You are missing the point. She does not wear a brooch that depicts her own eye, but rather that of her lover. It is a peculiar tradition. Lovers who cannot be together, whether star-crossed or inconveniently married, are known to wear such brooches as a discreet declaration of their love. The glaring brown eye belongs to Mrs. Fontaine's lover and he, in turn, wears a brooch with a violet-gray eye."

If I had not witnessed myself the brooch pinned to Mrs. Fontaine, I would not believe such a fantastic story.

"The professor—or scrivener or man of literature, whichever is his true nature—wears his brooch pinned to his waistcoat. I noticed it for a moment when we were made to hold hands during the séance, but did not put the pieces together until after your abduction."

"I find it difficult to believe that a woman of Mrs. Fontaine's standing would take such a low-bred ruffian for a lover, that she would be in collusion with a man who would *murder* me."

"It is an admirable trait to be protective of the weaker sex, Poe, but one must not deify womankind. An attractive visage does not guarantee moral principles."

"I am quite aware of that, but surely the false professor is manipulating her in some nefarious way. She is a married woman and it would seem from her attire, if not her address, that her husband is comfortably off."

"Of course that is not her address. It is either the home of her lover or she rents the building for her activities as a medium. It would be unseemly for her to hold a séance at her own abode, particularly if her husband is unaware that she claims to commune with spirits."

There was a disturbing ring of truth about Dupin's statements. How had I missed the obvious earlier?

"I did some research on Mrs. Fontaine during your convalescence, and I doubt it will surprise you to hear that she was once an actress. Mr. James Fontaine saw her upon the stage and was beguiled. After a brief courtship, they were married. It seems clear that Mrs. Fontaine—or Miss Rowena Greene of Chatham as she was back then—knew the scrivener before her marriage, but did the practical thing and married the rich rather than the poor man."

"You make her sound very calculating."

"Calculating? Most assuredly. She was a moderately successful actress of humble means who was given the opportunity to advance herself. She married well, but continues an illicit affair with the impoverished scrivener who posed as an elderly professor at the séance. Hence, the lovers wear the eye brooches as a love token. But the real question is, why did her lover wish to imprison you in that cellar and why was she in support of that foul desire?"

"And why the ourang-outang skeleton disguised as a dead man clutching a letter written by my grandmother?"

"Indeed. Your nemesis does not seem to wish you dead at this point in time. You were meant to read the letter after being terrorized by your imprisonment, and we might also presume that I was meant to rescue you before you expired. Of course I knew the address where the séance was held and went there as soon as I discovered that you had not returned to the hotel. If you were held captive at that address, it had to be in the attic or the cellar."

"And so I was imprisoned by my nemesis just as Rhynwick Williams was imprisoned on the thirteenth of June 1790."

Dupin nodded. "Yes, there is a symmetry there. But we still have not solved the mystery of the scrivener's rhyme—what was Elizabeth Arnold's treachery? Of course she concealed her own guilt of the Monster's crimes, but I believe there is more."

I shivered at his words, imagining the snake-eyed man creeping into my chamber, looking through my things, putting the bottle of cognac there. The threatening note: *Nemo me impune lacessit.* The dank cellar. Cold settled into me like a hard frost.

"At this point in time, you said. My nemesis does not wish me dead *at this point in time.* But you believe that will change in future."

Dupin gave a gentle shrug. "We must consider that possibility."

"Then we must catch the murderous scrivener before he kills one or both of us."

"That is very true indeed. Now let us put aside such thoughts for a while and walk. Our goal today is to refresh our minds."

Dupin led us toward the southeast corner of the park. There was a welcome sense of levity as children played with hoops, raced around with each other or tagged after men with water-carts. We exited the park at York Gate, crossed New Road and came to a walled garden which fronted a house set back from the street. Dupin gazed at me expectantly.

I looked at the house, which was very handsome with a portico of brick and stone and two tall semi-circular bow windows. Dupin was also examining the house with interest, but seemed to have no intention of telling me why we were at that address.

"Do we have an assignation here?" I finally asked.

"No pre-arrangement. I thought we might make an impromptu visit to One Devonshire Terrace as we are in the area."

"I am afraid that yet again I am not following you." And then I remembered the letter that accompanied the bottle of brandy. "Mr. Dickens's house?"

Dupin nodded. "It seems that your schedules rarely coincide. Now that we are here, you shall meet face to face and exchange pleasantries. We might offer to take him to dine nearby to thank him for his interest in your work."

I could feel my face flush with the impropriety of it. "Arrive unannounced at an acquaintance's doorstep? Mr. Dickens may be offended. And given recent events, I am not at all certain of his interest in my writing."

"Nonsense. You corresponded before your arrival, and Mr. Dickens made clear his appreciation of your work. He has offered to help you find a publisher here—this is not promised lightly. He inserted an announcement in the newspaper of your arrival in London and intent to give a public reading. It now seems doubtful that he organized the reading at the Institute, but I intend to discover the truth of that matter. Clearly Mr. Dickens is a busy man, but you will not remain in London indefinitely. You have the opportunity now to make his acquaintance in the flesh and thank him for his help. Few are offended by genuine expressions of gratitude—indeed it is lack of gratitude that offends."

I stared at Dupin, overwhelmed by anxiety. Normally he was a champion of propriety, and yet he was goading me into what might only be described as rude behavior in polite society. This was Dickens's home—a place for retreat—not an office or a gentleman's club.

Dupin observed my anxiety and impatience settled upon his features. "Are you confident that you will have the opportunity to meet Mr. Dickens? Is a friendly letter sufficient to thank him for taking an interest?"

Clearly it was not, but I still had the lingering sense that Mr. Dickens had printed the announcement of my London visit solely because I was a magazine editor who admired his work, but that truly he had no real interest in meeting *me*, a fellow writer. Dupin's patience finally expired. He gripped the brass door knocker and let it fall three times. A weighty silence followed, and I presumed that the house was empty, but then the sound of footsteps came closer and the door swung open. A handsome woman in capable clothing stood before us, a quizzical expression upon her face. Dupin bowed his head in greeting.

"Good afternoon. We are here to see Mr. Dickens. This is Mr. Edgar Poe and I am Chevalier Auguste Dupin. We would like to thank him personally for organizing Mr. Poe's reading on the eighth of July."

"We are sorry to intrude," I began.

"Mr. Dickens could not attend the reading due to illness," Dupin interjected. "We hope he is now recovered." He stared intently at the woman, scrutinizing her reaction to his words. "I suppose you are aware of the kind gesture of your husband?"

She seemed to ponder for a moment and then her features eased into the hint of a smile. "Ah, yes, Mr. Poe. My husband has indeed mentioned you. He admires your work." She looked from me to Dupin and back again. "Unfortunately, he is not in."

"So he is recovered," Dupin said pointedly.

Mrs. Dickens frowned at what must have seemed an odd comment. "He is quite well, thank you," she answered.

"Halloa old girl," a hoarse voice croaked from inside the house. "Halloa."

Dupin and I could not help but stare into the vestibule, but saw no one.

Unease crossed Mrs. Dickens's face. "I am sorry to disappoint you," she said. There was an odd shuffling sound inside the house, and she looked anxiously over her shoulder.

An ancient voice rasped, "Polly, put the kettle on, and we'll all have tea!"

Mrs. Dickens turned her back to us and flapped her skirts. "Shoo! Get back!"

"Put the kettle on! Hurrah! All have tea!"

Mrs. Dickens flapped her skirts again then squealed and skipped to one side. "Get away, you horrid thing!"

Dupin and I were instantly over the threshold, poised to defend Mrs. Dickens, but what we saw next threw us into a state of confusion. A large black raven was hopping across the vestibule floor, attempting to peck at Mrs. Dickens's ankles. "Halloa, old girl," the devilish creature squawked.

Mrs. Dickens flapped her skirts again and skipped backward, trying to preserve her feet from the bird's snapping beak. "Close the door, please," she gasped. "He must not fly away— as much as that would please me. Charles will be most upset if the horrid creature disappears." She flapped her skirts again.

"Does it have a name?" Dupin watched the bird hopping toward Mrs. Dickens. Its wings were half-raised, which seemed to double its size.

"Grip—my husband calls him Grip the Clever, Grip the Wicked, Grip the Knowing, depending upon the temper the creature is in."

"I'm a devil!" rejoined the raven promptly.

"That he is indeed!" She eyed the bird warily.

"Never say die. *Bow wow wow!*"

Mrs. Dickens closed her eyes and shook her head. "My husband teaches him some terrible nonsense."

"Very clever birds. Ravens are capable of accumulating quite a vocabulary," Dupin said.

"Clever, perhaps. Certainly greedy. He won't stop until I feed him something," Mrs. Dickens said. "Would you care for some tea while I am attending to the creature?"

"Put the kettle on! Hurrah! All have tea!" the raven jabbered.

Mrs. Dickens swished her skirts at him again. "Charles is meant to be home for dinner. You may wait for him if you wish."

I was about decline the good lady's offer, but Dupin waded in. "Tea would be most pleasant, Mrs. Dickens."

The bird scampered toward the lady's feet, but Dupin deftly put his walking stick in its path and the creature stepped upon it like a roost, then tilted his head to examine Dupin.

"Tea?" Dupin asked it.

The bird bobbed up and down on his walking stick in an excited manner, watching Dupin all the while with what seemed to be genuine interest.

Mrs. Dickens eyed the bird and Dupin nervously. "Follow me," she said and led us from the large vestibule into a spacious square hall. The raven remained perched upon Dupin's walking stick and he carried it along with him. "I think the library would be best," she said, leading us into a chamber on the right. It was a crowded room, pleasingly filled with books, Dickens's desk and several chairs. It had a view of the garden, with stairs that led out to it. The raven leapt into flight, startling us all, and soared to the top of a bookcase, where he watched us like a god from the heavens. Mrs. Dickens glared at the bird then made her way to the door. "I will just speak with cook. Make yourselves comfortable."

Dupin and I settled ourselves into chairs. "An impressive library," I observed.

"And an unusual pet," Dupin said.

The bird eyed us insolently, head tilted. Then, *pop!* The sound of a cork emerging from a bottle. I looked for the noise's source and discovered that once again it was the uncanny bird. It imitated the sound of a popping cork several times and danced with delight at our reactions. "Keep up your spirits," it said, with a snap of its wings.

Dupin raised his eyebrows. "Acutely observant too."

"I wonder if the creature torments Mr. Dickens as it does his wife."

"Hardly," she said as she briskly re-entered the room. "Charles spoils the creature. It torments all but its master."

"I'm a devil, I'm a devil, *bow wow wow*." Its eyes gleamed with malice.

I had to agree with the tiresome creature. His nonsensical chatter had worn my patience already. "How did Mr. Dickens come by the bird?"

"A purported friend gave it to him."

"The actions of friends can at times make them seem the enemy," I said, inadvertently catching Dupin's eye.

"Indeed," Mrs. Dickens said, nodding.

"Most often when those actions are in your best interest," Dupin said waspishly.

The cook entered the library carrying a large tea tray. She set it upon a small table, curtsied and left. Mrs. Dickens poured tea for the three of us and offered us buttered bread from a covered silver dish, but before we had the chance to partake, the bold creature soared down from the bookshelf and made a grab for the bread. Mrs. Dickens deftly slammed down the lid and the bird landed on the top of a high-backed chair. It eyed the silver dish greedily.

"Would you place this on the floor over there? Then we might have some peace." Mrs. Dickens handed Dupin another covered dish. He did as she requested and lifted the lid to reveal a small plate of raw meat. The raven jumped from his makeshift perch and strode over to the dish like a soldier. It ate the meat greedily and the sight was infinitely disturbing. One could imagine carrion crows on the battlefield, chewing through the flesh of the fallen. Dupin coolly observed the creature.

"*Covus corax*, a highly intelligent bird and quite human in a number of ways, though dare I say their human qualities are not what makes them clever." Dupin's thin smile indicated this was a jest, but in truth this probably was his opinion. "They inhabit most parts of the world and adapt to almost any environment—certainly they will eat almost anything."

The ebony bird listened intently, turning his head from one speaker to another as if drinking in each word.

"True, indeed," Mrs. Dickens agreed. "The bird will consume anything, including my letters, pieces of the staircase and any jewels I forget to lock up in my jewel box."

"It has probably buried or hidden the jewels," Dupin said. "*Corvus corax* do have a propensity for stealing and then hiding their spoils."

"Not unlike some humans," I said.

"It has stolen any number of teaspoons from the dining table and buried them in the garden," Mrs. Dickens told us. "I am sure we haven't found half of them. And he chews away at the garden wall, digging out all the mortar, and scrapes the putty from the windows so the glass falls out. He is a bothersome devil."

"I'm a devil," croaked Grip, before dipping his beak back into the raw meat.

Dupin smiled at this exchange. "Highly intelligent," he said again. "And loyal. Ravens mate for life and live up to forty years."

"Forty years?" Mrs. Dickens muttered with despair.

"Surely the creatures are better known for their scavenging than their loyalty," I said.

"They are indeed scavengers, but Nature needs such creatures. And they are not just opportunists. Ravens are said to lead hunters to deer and caribou so they can enjoy the remains—both hunter and scavenger benefit."

I looked at the raven and found that he was staring at me, head tilted to one side, his gimlet eye fixed on mine, as if daring me to contradict Dupin. The bird gulped down the rest of its meat and launched itself into the air, skimming past my head, before resuming its station on top of the bookcase.

"He is indeed a devil," I muttered.

"Some do believe so," Dupin said. "Or similar. It is said that ravens are the ghosts of murdered people or the souls of the damned. Some native peoples from your country believe ravens can transform themselves into human beings. And of course the kings of this country allow ravens to consume—"

"Never say die! Keep your spirits up," croaked the imp from the bookcase. It was balanced on tiptoe and moved its body up and down in a bobbing dance.

"I think we might discuss more pleasant topics," I said pointedly, noting Mrs. Dickens's blanched face.

"No doubt Mrs. Dickens has heard much more about the history of the raven from her husband," Dupin said.

"In truth, sir, my husband prefers to dwell on the creature's intelligence and canny ways. I have not heard him speak of such dark tales," she said, giving Dupin a suspicious look.

"Forgive us, please, Mrs. Dickens. We men of letters spend too much time with our books and quickly forget good manners and how to converse with a lady. I hope my friend did not upset you when you have been so hospitable."

"It is quite all right," the lady said with a taut manner, which indicated most clearly that it was not. My impatience with Dupin grew—first he showed us to be louts without manners arriving unannounced at the Dickens's home, and then he frightened the poor woman with talk of the Devil. My worries were cut short when we heard the front door opening. I leapt

to my feet, ready to meet Mr. Dickens at last, but the temporary silence was quickly broken by the sound of pattering feet.
Mrs. Dickens stood and said, "Nanny has brought the children
home."

Dupin rose to his feet also, just as the sound of a childish
voice floated into the library. Moments later a small boy ran
into the room. He was a cheerful-looking child of perhaps
three or four years old.

"This is Mr. Poe and Chevalier Dupin. They are acquaintances of your father. Say hello to them."

"Hello," the boy said, retreating behind his mother's skirts.
"And?"

"My name is Charley Dickens. Pleased to make your
acquaintance," the boy recited.

"Very pleased to meet you, Charley," I said.

Dupin nodded his head in concurrence, but said nothing. He
seemed more at ease dealing with a talking bird than a child.
Moments later a tiny girl peeped into the room.

"This is Mamie," Mrs. Dickens said. "Say hello, dear."

"Hello," the girl said in a tiny voice before putting all her
fingers into her mouth.

Our conversation, such as it was, was terminated by a baby's
squalling. The raven squawked once, leapt from the bookcase
and soared overhead. The children screamed and ran from the
room, the raven swooping after them, calling out: "Halloa,
halloa, halloa! What's the matter here!" The baby's crying
increased in volume.

Mrs. Dickens reddened and said, "My other daughter. Katey
is troubled with colic."

I stood up promptly and said, "It was so kind of you to entertain us, Mrs. Dickens. Please give our warmest regards to Mr.
Dickens and tell him we are sorely disappointed to miss him
again."

Dupin stood also. "Indeed, we are grateful for your hospitality. Please extend our regards to your husband."

We followed our hostess down the hall to the vestibule, where her two children, the maid and wailing baby were cornered by the raven.

"I'm a devil," he croaked. "Hurrah!" And then the infernal creature began to whistle, pirouetting on top of something, as if guarding it from all present.

Mrs. Dickens flapped her skirts at the raven again. "Shoo, you devil, shoo!"

But Grip the Clever, Grip the Wicked, Grip the Knowing did not budge. Dupin stepped toward the creature and held out his walking stick again.

"Up!" he commanded. The noisy imp immediately jumped onto the makeshift perch, and Dupin raised it up away from the small packet on the floor. Mrs. Dickens quickly retrieved it and reacted with surprise when she glanced at the packet. "It is addressed to you, Mr. Poe."

The bird stared at me, his eyes shining like the Devil's own, as I reached for the packet with trembling hand. "Most unusual. Thank you, Mrs. Dickens," I stuttered with embarrassment before bowing quickly and rushing out of the house.

"Hurrah! Hurrah! Hurrah! Keep up your spirits!" The raven's words flew out the door after me.

93 Jermyn Street, London.

Thursday, 8 July 1790

Dear Henry,

What a disgraceful theatrical you missed today! A crowd of the Monster's victims were assembled in the court, all baying with the delusion that Rhynwick Williams was the monster who attacked them. Miss Anne Porter led the fray, adamant that she recognised Williams as her attacker, and nothing in heaven or hell would dissuade her of this. Surely it is no coincidence that her fiancé, Mr. Coleman, collected the Angerstein reward after claiming to witness Rhynwick Williams accost her in the manner of the Monster.

Mr. Pigott presented the extraordinary case to judge and jury in grandiose fashion. The prisoner at the bar had made a wanton, wilful, cruel and inhuman attack upon the most beautiful, the most innocent, the most lovely, the best work of nature! Oh, indeed. It was obvious to all in the courtroom that Miss Porter does not merit superlatives. It should have been equally obvious that Mr. Pigott was engaged in blatant rabble-rousing, but this mattered not a whit because the audience was gripped. They listened with wonderment as he described in much dull detail the journey of Miss Anne Porter, her sister Sarah Porter and their chaperone from the ballroom at St. James's to the Porter residence. Mr. Pigott then claimed that Rhynwick was spied by the ladies, who ran in terror for the safety of their home. Miss Anne, who was bringing up the rear of the charge (so to speak), was slashed across the fundament. The crowd hissed and booed at Rhynwick, who cowered in his chair. I felt a sharp stab of pity for him—as if the Monster himself had pricked me—such a ferocious beast was the mob before us. When the crowd quieted down, Mr. Pigott continued Miss Porter's dull tale in infinite detail. I could not help but wonder at the crowd's gullibility. Who could ever mistake Rhynwick Williams for our daring Monster? He is such an insipid, whining little man—a crime, perhaps, in good society—but his actions were on trial, not his character. No real evidence was presented that proved Williams guilty of the crimes in question. I had the strangest desire to stand up and declare, "The worm is innocent—I am the London Monster!" What a sensation that would have provoked! But it was vanity combined with a guilty conscience that provoked such thoughts, and good common sense rescued me from my desire to speak the truth, as I do not wish to dance upon the end of a rope at Newgate.

Mr. Pigott finally concluded Miss Porter's dull tale with the words: "And that is proof that this man before you is the perpetrator." The crowd exploded into an amalgam of cheers, whistles and boos. I could not help but wonder how the Porter spinsters' ability to recognise Rhynwick a day after seeing him on their doorstep in Mr. Coleman's hopeful grip proved anything at all. It was a most terrible travesty. Mr. Pigott completed his assassination by relaying to the court that Rhynwick Williams lodged at a public house in Bury Street, St. James, in a room with three beds in which six men slept—Rhynwick being one of them. Mr. Pigott proclaimed that only a man of unsavoury character would stay in such despicable lodgings and could the word of such a villain be trusted? He asserted that the victims were ladies of unquestionable morals and would never perjure themselves by giving false testimony in court. Oh, indeed!

Miss Anne Porter took the stand first—a dowdy girl of not yet twenty—and the audience erupted into applause and cheers. She flushed, but seemed most taken with her leading lady status. Mr. Shepherd of the prosecution proceeded to ask her uninspired questions, and incredibly we had to sit through the entire story once again! But the audience enjoyed the repeat performance as much as the first. When Miss Anne claimed that Rhynwick had previously insulted her and her sisters with "very gross and indelicate language" and on the night in question had walked behind her and <u>muttered</u>, the crowd roared its objection to such atrocious behaviour. She then displayed to the audience the clothing she had worn on the Queen's birthday— the carnation-pink silk gown, a shift, three petticoats (one of silk and two of linen) and a pair of stays. There was a rent across the back of the dress, which Miss Anne declared impossible to mend. (Clearly she has little affinity for the art of the needle and thread.) She testified that her petticoats were torn, and her flesh had also been cut. Only her stays had saved her from further ruin. All in the court roared at this declaration. (They might have roared with laughter had any been privy to the unappealing sight of the Porter posterior.) Miss Anne concluded with the oath that she'd had a full and complete view of her attacker's face. Rhynwick was the guilty party, and it was impossible that she was mistaken. Obviously the lady's sight is deficient, but no one thought to test this in the court.

Mr. Shepherd then made enquiries about her attacker's clothing. Miss Porter stated that he wore a light coat, which fell across his shoulders, and she believed he wore another coat under that. This of course is true enough, but it is impossible that such coats as described could have been found at the despicable room Rhynwick shared with five other men, because those garments, to the best of my knowledge, are safely in your wardrobe where they belong.

The remainder of the trial did not improve for Rhynwick. Amabel Mitchell, his employer at the decorative flower factory, and the French women who worked with him were hissed and booed when they attested to his good character. Lady Egalatine Wallace— that renowned playwright whose work *The Ton* had its actors booed off the stage—gave her own performance on the stand. She had accused the Monster of attacking her in late May, but declared that the accusation has been one of her little jokes and therefore Rhynwick Williams was certainly not guilty of attacking her.

The accused was at last permitted to present his defence, which was much more eloquent than that of the prosecution, but it was clear that he was presumed guilty unless he could prove otherwise. And as Rhynwick faced the crowd, the last words of his testimony dying on his lips, he looked nervously from face to face until his eyes somehow found mine and his brow furrowed as if trying to remember who I was and where we had met. While locked in this uncomfortable *tête-à-tête*, time stilled and each second felt like an eternity as fear dampened my palms and my heart fluttered like a bird's wings within my chest. Would he accuse me of poking that woman with the nosegay? Would he <u>condemn</u> me?

When he opened his mouth to speak, dizziness truly enveloped me and with a cry I tipped over in an artificial swoon. I lay upon the floor, eyes closed, hoping that my diversion might be enough to distract Rhynwick and our audience. When finally I was helped onto my chair and was sipping at the water given to me, I surreptitiously glanced at Rhynwick. His eyes were still upon me, his face full of recognition—of that I am certain. There was but one thing I could do. "That man," I whispered. "That man!" With shaking finger, I pointed at Rhynwick Williams and said, "That is the man who attacked me when I was leaving the theatre last month!" Horror distorted Rhynwick's features while the crowd roared its disapproval and would not quiet down until the verdict was at last delivered: *guilty.*

I fear that the pronouncement filled me with both guilt and relief. But what choice did I have? It is undeniable that if I had not staged my performance, Rhynwick would have made his own accusation and our destiny would be Newgate and the end of a noose. If only he had minded his own affairs that fateful evening back in mid-June! Angerstein's wretched reward made Rhynwick Williams the most reviled man in London and he forced me to cast the final stone.

How glad I am that this is now over. I will join you in Margate on Sunday and hope with all my heart that the town and its theatre will provide us with a new beginning. We have the chance now to leave our ill luck behind us if Rhynwick Williams is remembered as the Monster who terrorised London.

Your wife,
Elizabeth

"Dickens's infernal bird had flown in through the window and landed upon my writing desk, a folded paper grasped in its beak. The missive contained a vital clue, but the devil would not relinquish it, and when I reached out to steal it, the creature flitted from one corner of the room to the other, eluding my grasp. I recited its repertoire to it, hoping it would respond and drop the paper, but Grip the Clever maintained his silence and kept his prize."

"A most revealing dream. You fear you will never solve your mystery, despite the clues delivered to you," Dupin observed.

"That is certainly true. And it seems that the raven was indeed a harbinger of death as you suggested." I picked up the obituary from the *Kentish Gazette* that had been included in the packet discovered by the raven. Learning of my grandfather's demise had filled me with regret—of course it was highly unlikely that he was still alive at eighty years of age, but I had nursed a fantasy that I might discover Henry Arnold performing the role of revered patriarch in some London theater. Instead he had died in peculiar circumstances, leaving my grandmother at the mercy of her odious father and stepmother. This knowledge made me all the more determined to solve my mystery.

"Obviously the raven was not truly a harbinger of death, but rather a serendipitous embellishment to the supernatural effect your aggressor was striving for," Dupin remarked.

"If only Grip the Wise could tell us who delivered the packet rather than reciting such nonsense! The bird is a devil with his endless patter of nonsense and irksome ways. It is surprising that Mr. Dickens keeps the creature indoors with such young children and a wife who clearly dislikes it."

"Perhaps he uses the creature to escape from his family and work on his books."

At first I presumed Dupin was jesting, then realized he was perfectly serious. "Escape his family? The children seem well-mannered and his wife was very pleasant, particularly when one considers the goading raven and our unannounced arrival."

"The responsibilities of a family keep a man from accomplishing great things."

"Absurd! History is full of examples of exemplary, accomplished men with families."

"But how much more would they have accomplished without their time—and their thoughts—consumed by a wife and progeny?"

"Surely the affection a man receives from his wife and children more than compensates for the time not spent pursuing intellectual and creative endeavors. Indeed, such affection inspires a man."

"Ah, the myth of the muse. If inspiration and genius does not rain upon us from God himself, then it springs from one's muse, who may conveniently be one's wife." Dupin shook his head. "I believe that inspiration and genius are born from assiduous work—wide reading, deep study, contemplation and toiling at one's chosen discipline as if exercising the muscles. The true scholar is not a lazy man, nor a man with a mind divided by the duties of providing for a family. The true scholar sacrifices all in the pursuit of knowledge and truth. My talent is ratiocination, and truly I believe that affections of the heart fog the mind."

Dupin's expression showed his commitment to this philosophy, and I realized that I had no idea if he had ever ardently admired a woman or had experienced all the emotions of love, and yet I could not bring myself to ask him about his experiences of the heart. I suspected that such emotions were foreign to Dupin.

"It is clear we will not agree on the merits of love and family. In all honesty, if it is true that I will achieve less as a writer because I have a wife and children, then it is a sacrifice I am more than happy to make."

"'Tis a pity," Dupin said softly.

His words brought a rush of emotion into me, and I could not stop the flurry that came from my mouth. "Without my wife and her mother, I would be nothing at all. My own dear mother was lost to me, but fate showed kindness when I was taken in by my adoptive mother and father. Fate turned on me again when my adoptive mother died, and I was replaced in my adoptive father's affections by his bastard child and new wife. The imp of the perverse would have conquered me if it were not for Sissy and Muddy—they undoubtedly saved me from myself. I could not write without my wife's steadying influence and dare say she is indeed my muse."

Dupin shrugged his shoulders and sighed lightly. "I understand your grief at the behavior of your adoptive father. It is not how a father should act toward his son, whether natural or adopted. He made a pledge to you and was without honor when he broke that pledge. We must remember, however, that when a man is treated dishonorably, whether by family, friend or stranger, he has a choice: allow grief to overcome him or resolve to find justice."

"Justice? I will never have the life I was promised. My adoptive father is dead and my inheritance is gone forever. All that remains is my talent—such that it is—and I must rely upon it and those I love. Never shall I commit the pernicious actions of my father and my adoptive father. I will cherish my offspring no matter what errors they may make for they are my future and through them my name will live on, if only in their hearts."

Dupin considered my words, then said quietly: "It is true that my parents and my grandparents are immortal within my heart, and I will not rest until I restore their reputations. But I have no ties that interfere with my life's purpose. Your family is your Achilles heel, Poe. You have described how losing them would affect you. What if the reverse were true?"

Dupin's words hit me forcibly as he intended. "They would be left to beg for charity like my grandmother and my mother after her. That is what you are thinking, is it not?"

"Of course," he said coolly. "Just as my father was forced to rely on charity. It is our duty to protect those we love from the same fate, is it not, Poe?"

My pride was quelled by truth. "It is our first duty, of course."

"Our investigation is in support of that duty and each clue we uncover brings us closer to defeating your aggressor," Dupin said. "The new letters reveal much. Now we know the precise details of your aggressor's accusation."

My heart sank as I recalled the letter my grandmother had written to my grandfather on the eighth of July 1790, describing Rhynwick Williams's first trial. "Elizabeth Arnold's treachery," I muttered.

"Indeed," Dupin said. "And it is clear from her letter that she was not the only person who acted treacherously. Miss Anne Porter accused Rhynwick Williams on the thirteenth of June and he was arrested. The Porter sisters then swore in court that

Williams was their attacker, which is undoubtedly a lie. While
Elizabeth Arnold twisted the truth to save her husband and
herself from Newgate, the Porter sisters committed perjury to
secure Mr. Angerstein's reward."

"It is surprising my aggressor did not take revenge upon the
Porter sisters, given that they were directly responsible for
Rhynwick Williams's arrest and testified against him."

"We do not know that Williams did not take revenge upon
them," Dupin pointed out.

This thought filled me with an odd sense of hope. "Quite
right, Dupin. We might discover important information if we are
able to find the Porter sisters. They were not yet twenty years old
in 1790, so there is a good chance that one or both is living."

"True, but surely it will be difficult to locate them."

"I think it is worth the effort. We might begin with the
family home and business—Pero's Bagnio. If the Porters no
longer run the establishment, someone at the address may
know what became of them."

"It is possible," he said reluctantly.

"Shall we try? Surely it is better to speak with the living
about what happened during the Monster's reign than to rely
on such material that might be found in the British Museum
library. Gossip and lies oft reveal as much as purported factual
records."

Dupin glanced at his time-piece. "I wish you good luck in
finding the Porter sisters, but I must decline your invitation for
I have arranged to meet Madame Tussaud."

"The clandestine event she so dramatically referred to?"

"Indeed." The idea seemed to imbue him with a peculiar
energy. "Until later, Poe. Let us discuss the other letters then."
And he was gone.

* * *

"Mackerel! Fresh mackerel!"

"Hot peascods!"

"Oranges. Lovely oranges." A pretty girl held an apron full of the fruit toward me.

"Sheep's feet!" a matron shouted.

Covent Garden was raucous with life. The streets were crowded with people laden with produce as they exited the grand market, and the voices of food sellers rose up around me.

A mere girl with a fragrant basket at her feet entreated me to buy: "Rosemary, for a good memory, sir. Or mint, for your constitution."

The music of the streets continued as I exited the market itself: street vendors hawking their wares, an ancient ballad-singer rasping old favorites, the ring of the dustman's bell. Men wandered up and down the streets wearing boards printed with notices recommending the purchase of household products, patent medicines and other purported constitutionals. The joyous life of the market compensated somewhat for the soot-burnished buildings and noisome effluvia accumulating in the streets. I skirted around brawling customers who had spilled from a public house and quieter ones in the gutter who substantiated the drinking establishment's promise: "Drunk for a penny, dead drunk for a tuppence."

My perambulation through Covent Garden had a purpose. My opinion of my grandparents had been shaped by my aggressor; it was time I tried to learn more about them without that malign influence guiding me. I decided to visit the theater where my grandmother had reached her apogee as a performer in England and then to make my way to St. James's Street in hopes of locating one or both of the Porter sisters.

The entrance to the Covent Garden theater was on Bow Street and very handsome with a symmetrical Greek Doric tetrastyle portico on a podium of three steps. The columns were a good thirty feet high, giving a grand air to the entire structure. I paid a man who was perhaps the theater manager an exorbitant amount so that I might watch the actors in rehearsal, a wish that seemed to cause him quiet amusement.

The auditorium was grand enough to take one's breath away and built to seat a very large crowd. The drapery was scarlet and enriched with golden wreaths, the moldings were gilt and there was a marvelous gold and crystal chandelier. Over the arch of the proscenium was the stage's motto spelled out in golden letters: *Veluti a Speculum*. What a wonderful place to face an audience!

I took a seat and watched as the players assembled. It was not the actual stage that my grandmother had graced, as that had burned to the ground over thirty years ago, but perhaps I would get a sense of the world she inhabited even so. When the musicians began to play, I was hopeful of an operetta of the type she often performed, but instead was presented with a ballet-pantomime of dubious quality. As I watched the dancers perform a piece that would please only the most witless audience, I could not help but imagine the dancers my grandmother had mocked—Gallini's dancers, with whom Rhynwick Williams had performed on that awful day at the King's Theatre when they were driven from the stage by an audience threatening murder. These dancers did not seem much better than Gallini's—far more rehearsal was needed if they were to avoid the hiss of the mob.

I tried my best to feel the presence of my grandmother in that most beautiful of theaters, but she simply was not there, so I left the place of my grandmother's greatest theatrical triumph, the ghostly admonishments of an exasperated ballet-master ringing in my ears.

* * *

"Pero's Bagnio" at number sixty-three St. James's Street had for many years been a cold-bath establishment, and the Porter sisters had lived there in their youth. It had been renamed Fenton's Hotel, and I hoped that one of the ladies had married a Mr. Fenton, who had taken over the management of what appeared to be a successful enterprise. It was an attractive building of four floors with arched windows and doors on the ground floor and window boxes filled with flowers at the upper windows. I knocked on the door, strangely nervous as to what I might discover. The door was opened by a woman I judged to be but a few years younger than myself, much too young to be either of the Porter sisters. I wondered if perhaps she was the granddaughter of one of the sisters.

"I'm afraid we have no rooms, sir," she said.

"I am here on other business, in fact. My name is Edgar Poe, and I am a journalist in Philadelphia, visiting London to conduct research for an article I am writing," I improvised. "I am interested in the Porter family who lived here in 1790 and was hoping to interview Miss Anne or Sarah Porter or a member of their family."

The young woman looked me over and it seems that I passed inspection, for she said, "Sadly Mrs. Coleman—formerly Miss Anne Porter—passed away several years ago. A kind lady, she was. She would come to the hotel to visit with my mother-in-law—the first Mrs. Fenton," she said, gesturing up at the name of the hotel. "Mrs. Coleman did tell amusing tales of the peculiar things that happened here when she was a girl."

"What a pity. To interview her would have been highly illuminating," I said with unfeigned disappointment. "Thank you for your assistance, Mrs Fenton."

"Miss Sarah is still with us," the lady continued. "In Margate, not this hotel," she added when she saw the hope on my face.

"The Colemans bought a lodging house in Margate and she was given a room there."

"Would you happen to know the address?" I asked. "I would very much like to speak with Miss Porter. It is an important historical matter."

This piqued her interest. "Miss Sarah is very interested in history," she said with a wry smile. She beckoned me inside. "Let me search for the card she sent us, Mr. Poe. I did have it, I am certain."

I stepped through the door into a reception area that doubled as a sitting room. Mrs. Fenton retreated behind the hotel desk and pulled out a leather-bound book in which a quantity of trade and visiting cards were filed.

"My husband and I have not been to the premises, but Miss Sarah posts a letter at Christmas. Her nephew included several trade cards, hoping we would send them custom." She flicked through the book until she found the card she was looking for. "Four Neptune Place," she said as she wrote down the address. "Should you travel to Margate, it is said to be a fine establishment." She handed me the piece of paper with the address written upon it.

"Thank you most sincerely, Mrs. Fenton. I believe I will take an excursion to Margate and will certainly tell Mr. Coleman that you highly recommended his establishment."

"That would be very kind of you, Mr. Poe. And do stay with us when you return to London."

"I shall of course. You have been exceedingly helpful." And I took my leave of the site of the Monster's most notorious attack.

* * *

I did not consult with Dupin. I went directly to the desk clerk and asked him to book the two of us passage to Margate and accommodation in the city for two or three nights.

"Of course, Mr. Poe. Most happy to oblige you. I will book passage on the mail coach to Margate on the fifteenth of July, returning on the eighteenth of July. We recommend the White Hart Hotel in Margate, and I will do my best to book two rooms for you there. If it happens that they have no accommodation, they will arrange a good alternative hotel and inform us."

"Thank you, sir. I am appreciative."

"Brown's Genteel Inn endeavors to satisfy its patrons," he said.

"And you have succeeded admirably."

The desk clerk smiled warmly at my compliment.

* * *

The meat stew was infinitely better this time or perhaps my palette had adjusted to English cooking. Dupin seemed far less repelled by the dish in front of him and consumed most of the Smyrna Coffee House's culinary offering before I told him what I had gleaned from Mrs. Fenton.

"We have seats on the mail coach to Margate this Wednesday and should have rooms booked at the White Hart Hotel." I slid the hotel handbill across the table to Dupin. The hotel description was pleasing:

White Hart Hotel
Marine Parade, Margate.
Located directly on the seafront and in close proximity to
Margate Pier, the Theatre Royal Margate,
shops on Queen Street, Margate Sands
and the renowned bathing machines.

"The hotel sounds perfectly acceptable and very near to the location of Henry Arnold's demise. It may not be difficult to locate his grave if he is buried in Margate," Dupin offered.

"Yes, I would like to search the graveyard there. And I very much wish to examine the bathing machines now we know the peculiar circumstances of my grandfather's untimely death." I turned over the handbill and tapped on the map drawn on the verso. "You are aware that I am a keen swimmer. I feel certain I will understand more about his death once I visit Margate Sands."

"There is nothing to be lost," Dupin said.

"Indeed. And was your assignation with Madame Tussaud useful?" I asked.

"Extremely." His eyes took on an acute intensity as he retrieved a folded piece of stationery from his pocket and passed it to me.

The stationery was of excellent quality and its large red wax seal was broken. I noticed that the image pressed into the seal was a caduceus with two fierce serpents that resembled dragons facing each other, jaws agape. Inside was a neatly penned invitation that read:

Chevalier C. Auguste Dupin
Monsieur Victor Delamar cordially invites you to attend
Le Bal des Victimes
at the Baker Street Bazaar,
Nine o'clock on the Fourteenth day of July 1840.
Mask and Appropriate Attire required.

"Who is Victor Delamar?"

"I am not acquainted with Delamar—Madame Tussaud secured me the invitation. Such an event presents the perfect opportunity to ensnare Valdemar."

"I confess that I am unfamiliar with that particular type of ball."

"It is meant to be an homage to those who suffered during the Terror, but it makes a mockery of the pain my family endured."

"I am sorry, but I am not following you."

Dupin folded up the invitation and got to his feet. "No matter, Poe. No matter, for you shall *see*." His eyes fixed on mine, making me shrink back into my chair. "I will arrange our credentials. Your ordinary clothes will do. I will find the masks in the morning." A wolfish grin contorted his face. "You, my brother, shall attend the ball with me and then everything will be clear to you."

I gazed at my friend as he stood before me, his face lit up with horrendous hope, and prayed that he would vanquish his enemy, for if he did not, I feared his formidable intellect would poison itself and he would descend into madness born of grief and failure.

The Kentish Gazette

We regret to announce the sudden and melancholy death of Mr. Henry Arnold of London on the twenty-fifth of July 1790. Mr. Arnold was until recently employed as the pianist at the Theatre Royal Margate and performed as an actor and pianist in London. He was found inside a bathing machine by Mr. John Clarke, who is employed as a dipper and had arrived at dawn to prepare the machine for the morning bathers. Mr. Arnold's clothes were fully ruined by seawater and he could not be roused. Mr. Clarke immediately went in search of a surgeon and brought Dr. Shaw to the scene of Mr. Arnold's incapacitation. Dr. Shaw had Mr. Arnold conveyed to the infirmary where an empty bottle of belladonna elixir was discovered upon his person. Dr. Shaw was unable to save the patient and believes that a surfeit of the elixir, occasionally prescribed for a nervous stomach, contributed to Mr. Arnold's demise, rendering him unable to withstand an ill-advised night swim. A letter on his person alerted the surgeon to his wife's identity, but he passed into the arms of God before she could reach his side. Mr. Henry Arnold is survived by Mrs. Elizabeth Arnold, actress and singer currently performing at the Theatre Royal, and their daughter, Miss Eliza Arnold.

20 Upper Brook Street, Mayfair

5 August 1790

Dear Elizabeth,

My husband, being a kind and charitable gentleman, is prepared to meet the expense of Mr. Arnold's burial. He will do this for the sake of Eliza as the sins of the father should not be visited upon an innocent child.

Further to this, my husband is prepared to provide you with a most generous stipend to cover the costs of your subsistence and modest lodgings for the remainder of your days. The one condition he imposes upon your receipt of this stipend is that you sign a contract that will make him Eliza's legal guardian. He wishes her to be raised as a lady within the bounds of good society. You must forfeit the title of "mother" and any conditions of that role just as you have forfeited the role of "daughter". You will have my husband's word as a man of honour and a guarantee by contract that Eliza will be provided with all that a young girl of her lineage deserves.

If I may take the liberty of advising you, it would be imprudent for you to deny your daughter everything that you have sacrificed through your impetuosity and ingratitude. You must give Eliza the opportunity to be raised in advantageous circumstances. Clearly you are no Mrs. Siddons and Eliza's very existence is reliant upon your luck in securing work in a precarious profession. Will you make Eliza beg for her supper on the street should you fail to earn your crust upon the stage? No mother should make such a selfish choice.

I am enclosing your previous missives so that you may review your situation in full and come to the correct decision. Should you agree to my husband's generous offer, please bring Eliza to our home on the twentieth of August. Arrangements will then be made for your accommodation and stipend. But if you continue on the foolish path you have made for yourself, be advised that my husband's offer will be irrevocably withdrawn, and all ties with our family severed. Any future correspondence from you will be returned unopened.

I trust that you will, this time, choose wisely.

Yours faithfully,

Mrs. William Smith

The malevolent night air infected my dreams, and I awoke infernally early. Determined to put my nightmares to good use, I spent a productive morning working on a tale about a murder perpetrated by a sailor's ourang-outang. It mattered not if the idea came to nothing; the act of exorcising the dark specters that plagued me helped soothe my jangling nerves. I wrote my daily letter to Sissy, conjuring up a false sense of jollity that was the reverse of how I felt after re-reading the letters my nemesis had recently delivered.

To help alleviate the dark feelings that had crept over me, I decided to spend the day visiting the shops of London town until I found the perfect gifts for my wife and her mother. I managed to lose myself for hours in the magnificent Pantheon Bazaar on Oxford Street, which was truly an Aladdin's Cave with its art gallery, knick-knackatory of gimcracks for children, glass-roofed conservatory with exotic plants, aviary full of raucous parrots, cockatoos and macaws, and the endless array of merchandise for sale. I finally settled on some lace, a paisley shawl and a very pretty scent bottle for Sissy, and a good pair of gloves for my mother-in-law.

I arrived back at Brown's Genteel Inn just as Dupin did. He had gone in search of the items required for the peculiar ball we would be attending that evening and was clutching several packets. His eyes were strangely glassy; his face had a veneer of moisture.

"Poe! How fortunate. Shall we adjourn to my rooms? I have secured all we will need."

"Certainly."

Dupin leapt up each stair, and my attempts to keep pace with him half-winded me. He tore open a packet as soon as we were in his sitting room and held up two black masks that resembled blindfolds with holes for the eyes.

"They are very plain. Surely a more elaborate mask is required for a ball?"

"These are perfect. You shall see." Dupin's eyes remained fixed upon me to a disturbing degree.

"I look forward to it. Have you secured costumes as well?"

Dupin took a step back and examined my customary attire: black trousers, waistcoat, stock and coat. White shirt. "A few minor adjustments, and we shall be properly dressed." Dupin unknotted the black silk stock he wore and removed it from his neck with a flourish, then unbuttoned his shirt, leaving it open at the throat. "Please remove your stock and unbutton your shirt as I have, then turn down the collar of your coat at the back like this," he commanded.

I tentatively followed Dupin's lead, concerned that madness had overtaken him, so peculiar were his actions.

"I believe the length of our hair shall suffice. The neck is adequately exposed," he muttered, then handed me one of the black silk masks. "Please put this on so I might examine the overall effect." When I had donned it, Dupin drew a circle in the air, indicating that I should turn. "Very good. There is no need for the top hat or gloves." He reached into his waistcoat pocket. "You would do me a great honor if you would borrow this for tonight." He held out a gold ring set with a lapis lazuli intaglio engraving of the Dupin coat of arms: a serpent with its fangs buried in the heel of a bare foot. It was identical to the *chevalière* Dupin habitually wore on the ring finger of his left hand. I slid on the ring. It fit perfectly. "Now we are indeed brothers and here is the paperwork to prove your right to attend *le Bal des Victimes* with me."

I examined the documents Dupin placed on the table: a certificate confirming the executions of Madame Sophie Dupin and Chevalier Charles Dupin and identity papers for C. Auguste Dupin and François Dupin, his twin.

"The right to attend?"

"Only those who descend from the victims of Madame Guillotine and some aristocrats who escaped her bite may attend. Proof is required and must be produced at the door. These papers are the customary proof."

"I was not aware you had this talent." I nodded at the forged documents.

Dupin shrugged. "It is a minor talent, rarely worthy of discussion, but on this occasion, it will be useful."

"If I am to play your twin, surely we must agree all the details of my identity. There hardly seems time."

"Do not expect to be interrogated, brother. The purpose of the evening for most is senseless celebration. You will be required to do little but eat, drink and dance."

"Are you not forgetting one important fact? Surely Madame Tussaud will be in attendance if the Ball is held on her premises."

"Madame will not divulge your true identity, of that you may be certain. Shall we?"

"As you wish."

I followed my twin into the night.

* * *

Our coach left us about two hundred yards from our destination as Dupin instructed. As it vanished into the darkness, we
made our way toward the bazaar. I had expected the street to
be filled with coaches and the building to be blazing with light,
but there was not a glimmer.

"Do you suppose the invitation was a hoax? It is quite
deserted here."

"Fear not, you shall see otherwise."

I was not persuaded by Dupin's confidence, but followed
him even so. Better together than alone if we were to be
attacked by the mysterious thief. When we reached the door
that led into the bazaar's courtyard, Dupin rapped upon it in a
peculiar manner. Madame Tussaud's son opened it moments
later, wearing a white mask that obscured the upper part of his
long face but not his identity. He looked uncomfortable in
his elaborate attire: a powder blue coat cut longer in the back
than the front, pale trousers that buttoned above his calves, silk
stockings striped with blue, an ornately embroidered waistcoat
and a large white cravat. His hair was powdered, his skin made
up to match the white mask and his lips stained crimson.

"Your papers?" he asked.

Dupin presented his documents and Monsieur Tussaud
nodded his head in acknowledgement, but did not divulge that
he had met us before. He handed us each a printed number.
"Weapons must be left here with your cloaks."

A veritable armory of weaponry had been deposited with
Monsieur Tussaud: pistols, daggers and swords. Dupin did not
relinquish his walking stick with its concealed rapier. Indeed,
he affected a limp as we made our way toward the stairway that
would lead us to Madame Tussaud's grand exhibition
chambers.

When we reached the top of the stairs, we were transported to another world. Ethereal music floated down from

the orchestra concealed up in the balconies, and we were immersed in heavenly blue light. The splendid chandelier had been fitted with globes of sapphire glass, which tinted the light that fell from it, and the walls were hung with azure draperies. This smaller salon was partitioned off from the grand chamber by a cobalt blue curtain appliquéd with a magnificent dragon soaring across it. The plate glass, Louis XIV gilded ornaments and some blue ottomans remained, but the wax figures had been removed. In their place were revelers whose faces were concealed by masks; many were beautifully crafted from exotic feathers or spangled materials, some were elegant but plain, and others endowed the wearer with demonic features. But the masks were far less bizarre than the costumes. Most of the ladies wore simple white gowns with red shawls and a ribbon of scarlet silk or velvet knotted at their throats. Oddly, their hair was cut very short at the nape of the neck, which made the red ribbon all the more visible. Some women wore red ribbons in a *ceinture croisée*, across the back of the bodice.

Dupin noticed my gaze. "They have assumed *la toilette du condamné*. Women who were executed had the hair cut so it would not interfere with the efficiency of the blade."

"The red ribbons make reference to the guillotine's action upon the neck?"

Dupin nodded. "As we previously discussed, *le Bal des Victimes* is for victims of the Terror, but also aristocrats who escaped execution. Many of the latter cannot be considered victims at all for they were as vicious as our persecutors and should wear blood on their hands rather than their necks. See those with the dog ears." He indicated a group of men aged sixty years or more with hair cut very short at the back but worn long on either side of the face like the flopping ears of certain canines. Their clothes were elaborate and expensive:

knee breeches, long-tailed coats with large lapels, silk waist-coats and lacy cravats. "Muscadins. In their youth they formed mobs to terrorize suspected Jacobins, many of whom they executed without trial or bludgeoned to death in the street."

Dupin led the way to an elegantly arranged refreshment table. He helped us each to a goblet of wine. "Very fine," he muttered after tasting his. "From the best French cellars." It was not clear if his words were colored with nostalgia or anger, but it seemed better to divert him from a surfeit of either emotion.

"Shall we explore further?" I pointed to a gap in the curtains.

When we stepped into the next salon, we found ourselves in a sunlit room, or so it appeared. Here the walls were swathed in lemon-colored fabric as were the food-laden tables. Huge Chinese lanterns of yellow silk were suspended from the ceiling and glowed like artificial suns; they were reproduced ad infinitum by golden mirrors hanging on the walls. I noted that a number of men were dressed in an antique fashion and wore long curling locks rather than closely cropped hair or the dog-eared styling.

"And what is their allegiance?" I asked Dupin.

"They were—or descend from—assassins who killed Jacobins for money. While we might describe the Muscadins as hotheads, these were the cool-headed plotters. Their desire for revenge is understandable, but I have little sympathy for their tactics." Dupin looked carefully around the room.

"Do you know the face of the man you are searching for? Valdemar the thief?"

"I was shown a portrait of him in his youth. His looks were most particular. I am certain I will recognize him."

"And Delamar, our host?"

"I know nothing of him beyond this." He indicated the room with a wave of his hand.

"Shall we view the next chamber?" I was curious to see the entire design. Monsieur Delamar was certainly a connoisseur of the elaborate spectacle.

We made our way into the next room and found that it was all in green. Jugglers in suits that matched the leaf-colored draperies entertained a group of revelers. Magnificent ferns inside large glass cases formed a luxuriant perimeter. A tapestry cleverly constructed all in shades of green depicted a large apple tree with a serpent woven around it, a verdant fruit clutched in its jaws. A colossal chandelier with crystals shaped like oak leaves hung from the ceiling, its gas jets housed in globes of emerald glass.

"Do you suppose there is a meaning behind this design or it is purely for effect?"

"An attraction to gaudy embellishments and the grossly theatrical tends to indicate a diseased mind," Dupin stated.

"But this is a masked ball. One expects theatrical diversions. Perhaps the designer wishes to see the effect of the diverse-colored atmospheres upon his guests."

Dupin scanned the furnishings. "Green is the color of life, but also of putrefaction."

"One is said to be green with envy." I indicated a white mask tinted that very color by the light cast upon it. "And yet the tapestry—the tree of knowledge, the Garden of Eden."

Dupin considered this. "Interesting. Most interesting. Perhaps there is a message." He moved quickly toward the next room and again I followed.

The fourth salon was hung with orange draperies and had a joyous atmosphere. A huge golden brazier shaped like a dragon's head stood at the room's center, naked flames flaring from its mouth. An invisible orchestra played a lively tune and revelers danced energetically on one side of the room. Opposite them were tables swathed in topaz fabric and heaped with food, drink, and glimmering candles. A crowd of elderly men gathered there eating heartily as if consuming their last meal.

"Energy and gluttony," I observed.

"Indeed," Dupin said. "Let us get closer."

"They are the correct age?" I nodded at the elderly men.

"It would appear so." Dupin made his way to the table and helped himself to wine and sweetmeats. I did the same. As we ate, he studied the men before us intently. One wore a full mask, and I noticed that Dupin carefully examined the man's *chevalière* and shoes, but moments later he indicated the passage-way ahead of us. "Shall we?"

"Wrong man?"

"I cannot see the design upon the *chevalière*, but the stone appears to be carnelian rather than onyx. More importantly, he is too tall and his shoes were not designed to give him extra height. The thief is not a man of the crowd—he believes himself superior. It is unlikely we would find him in modest conversation with others."

We left Apollo's room and, passing through the curtained archway, entered an arctic world. The chandelier was of frosted glass and glowed like ice. Ballet dancers buoyed up by sequined tulle floated through a birch tree forest on a winter's night. The guests sat upon white velvet sofas or large snowy cushions.

"Winter, frost, ice . . ." But I could discern no pattern. The ladies with their white dresses were almost invisible against the walls, but for the blood red shawls and ribbons.

"Chevalier Dupin! *Je suis ravi de vous voir.*" A bent figure shuffled toward us. She wore a full mask, a peculiar doll's face that contrasted oddly with her cropped iron-gray hair. Her snowy white dress was decorated with red ribbons in a *ceinture croisée.*

Dupin leaned to kiss her hand. "Madame, we were wondering when we would find you. You remember my brother François? My twin?"

Madame Tussaud extended her hand to me. "Of course. I am happy to see you again."

"The pleasure is mine, Madame." I kissed her chilly hand.

"What do you think of the ball, my dears? Have I done well?"

"Most spectacular. I was not aware that you had an affinity for such events," Dupin said.

"Neither hostess nor reveler at any such ball previously, although I believe my stay in prison, awaiting the jaws of the guillotine with Joséphine de Beauharnais gives me the pedigree for attendance." She touched her bent fingers to her gray coiffure. "My hair was cut off, but my head spared due to my facility with wax. It is very fine to have a talent that saves one's life." The ancient eyes beneath the doll's mask scrutinized Dupin and then me.

"Your talent would not have saved you, Madame, if you did not have the presence of mind to suggest that it might be useful to your adversaries." Dupin smiled.

"You are quite correct, Chevalier." Again, the glint of dark eyes under the perfect doll's face, like a strange insect struggling within a chrysalis.

"Why are you mistress of this particular victims' ball?" I asked. "Has my brother's presence in London inspired you?" Dupin shifted quickly to stare at me. Perhaps he thought my question impolite, but it was pointless to avoid the obvious.

The doll's face tilted to one side, quizzical and innocent. "As I believe I made clear, the thought of hosting le Bal des Victimes has never occurred to me, François. It was conceived of by Monsieur Delamar. He paid for all costs and recompensed me generously for my time and efforts. At my advanced age, such generosity cannot be disdained." The doll's face did not alter expression, but the ancient crone beneath seemed to be smiling. "You will surely find the answer to all your questions if you progress to the next salon and the final chamber after that."

"Seven rooms," Dupin muttered. "Seven."

"Thank you, Madame Tussaud. You are delightful and astute company, and the ball is clearly a spectacular success," I said.

"*Merci*, Chevaliers. Go now and find the answer to your mystery."

Dupin and I bowed and left the peculiar vision of youth and decrepitude behind us.

"Seven rooms. What are your thoughts?" Dupin asked as we approached the door molded in the white curtains.

"Seven days of the week. Seven deadly sins. Seven colors of the rainbow. Shakespeare's seven ages of man."

Dupin nodded. "But what analogy is the creator of this spectacle reaching for?"

"As Madame suggests, we must examine each room before we find our answer," I said, stepping through the arch into the next world.

We found ourselves in a violet-colored salon. A table was placed at the room's center. It was filled with a hundred or more large candles, beautifully arranged and encased by four panes of amethyst glass. Dainty violets made from velvet covered the table and cascaded to the floor. Wreaths of the pretty flower were hung from the purple draperies. The dancing violet light was charming until one noted its bruising effect upon those wearing white masks.

We moved deeper into the room, led by sonorous music—clarinets, oboes, the sigh of violins. Narrow tables draped in purple damask were situated against one wall and were artfully arranged. Twisting silver snakes entwined to hold platters that were piled high with clusters of grapes. Goblets of wines completed this ode to Dionysus. Revelers whirled past us, dancing gracefully to the music as plum-colored shadows glided across their figures like dusk deepening to nightfall.

"A color of contradictions," I murmured. "Purple with rage or purple prose. Royalty or spirituality—the color of kings and bishops, the shade most prized by Cleopatra." I waited for Dupin's interpretation, but he seemed immersed in the decor, his face frozen, eyes glaring, so I continued. "Flowers in this shade enchant us: violets, irises, delphiniums, lilacs, wisteria, tulips and pansies—and yet it is the shade of bruises, dark circles under the eyes, lividity—a step closer to death, perhaps. Yet another extraordinary design."

Dupin awoke from his trance. "Most *hideous*," he growled. "And truly this chamber is an intentional affront to my family."

"How so?"

Dupin breathed in deeply then spoke, his voice hard and staccato. "Valdemar murdered my mother with violets. Or more precisely, the scent of them. He delivered expensive candles perfumed with violet to the house as a gift. The maid-servant, knowing no better, put the elegant tapers in my mother's bedchamber as she habitually read by candlelight before retiring. My father found her asphyxiated in the morning—the violet perfume had masked the smell of poison."

"I am sorry, Dupin."

He raised his hand to halt my apologies. "My father had pledged revenge upon Valdemar for the murder of his own parents, but this broke him. He could not produce adequate proof that his nemesis had orchestrated the deed and my mother did not receive justice. One would think that this would cause a man to turn from God, but instead my father committed himself utterly to him and withdrew from the world. I was abandoned to my mother's relatives while my father made a spiritual pilgrimage to the Holy Land, but expired somewhere along the way."

"Valdemar has stolen much from you," I said quietly.

Dupin returned his gaze to mine. "Yes. That is why my father was so fond of saying, 'Unlike property, knowledge cannot be stolen.' I try to live by his words."

"Wise words indeed."

"And I will avenge my family. Valdemar may murder me also, but if so, my last breath will mingle with his own. Shall we?" He indicated the next chamber.

We stepped over the threshold into the final room and both froze—it was the most dramatic and peculiar of all. The chamber was utterly shrouded in black velvet and there were no furnishings but for an immense ebony clock that stood in one corner of the room, its pendulum counting out the seconds. A monstrous chandelier was suspended above the center of the room. One would presume from the previous chambers that the chandelier would cast a shadowy light, but this was not the case. Each crystal was of scarlet and the globes that encased the tapers were crimson. The light that spilled from this chandelier seemed to bathe the room in blood. Directly underneath the gruesome fixture was a rectangular frame covered in a black sheet. It was the size, perhaps, of a bear's cage, but no sound came from within it—indeed the room was silent but for the portentous ticking. And then, a terrible clang arose from the ebony clock, and I saw that midnight had arrived. As the disharmonious bells chimed, more and more guests hurried into the chamber, as if compelled by the ominous sound. When at last the bells of midnight ceased to echo in the shadowy hall, Madame Tussaud made her way to the veiled cage before us. The room was now completely full and through our precipitous timing, Dupin and I stood at the very front of the crowd.

"Fellow guests—brothers and sisters," she said in French. "Thank you for attending *le Bal des Victimes*—it is your birthright and our honorable host, Monsieur Victor Delamar, specifically invited each one of you. I hope the decorations and the atmosphere have met your expectations." Madame paused momentarily, anticipating the thunderous applause she duly received. "Thank you. I am honored. It is as our host wished. And now it is time to unveil the *pièce de résistance*."

She lifted her arm into the air and as she did so, the wires attached to the black shroud pulled it away from the large rectangular frame to reveal a regal man seated in a magnificent oriental chair shaped like a golden dragon, its wings outspread, ruby eyes glinting monstrously, fearsome head reared up in protection of its master who was dressed as if in the court of Louis XVI: a velvet coat, extravagant cravat pinned with an immense jewel, elegant breeches, silk stockings, a waistcoat embroidered with violets and diamond-buckled shoes. The livid flickering light stained his ensemble and the white mask that concealed his face. Behind the throne-like chair stood, most ominously, the guillotine normally present in Madame Tussaud's chamber of horrors.

"Ladies, gentlemen, may I present our host, Monsieur Victor Delamar."

Applause rang out again. Monsieur Delamar sat silently, calmly, absorbing the aculation.

"We will have a few words from our gracious host, but first I must attend to his final instructions. Joseph!" Madame's son appeared from the crowd and joined her. "Please prepare." Joseph nodded to his mother and moved to Monsieur Delamar's side. Madame Tussaud unrolled the scroll she held in her hand and began to read. "'Brothers and sisters. It was my greatest wish to bring you together in celebration of our heritage—our families and our country. The life of the émigré is not easy, even if blessed with material riches, for when one loses his family and dearest friends, suffering is eternal. I have long worn a mask, presenting a façade of contentment—all here have shared my burden. Now is the time to remove our masks and bring *le Bal des Victimes* to its conclusion!'"

Madame removed her mask with a flourish, as did her son. The guests did the same, with spontaneous cries of joy. Caught up in the moment, I removed my own black mask before noticing that Dupin's remained in place. My attention was quickly returned to Monsieur Delamar as Joseph Tussaud reached up and lifted our host's mask, slowly, ever so slowly, until finally the flickering crimson light revealed his countenance. It was a gaunt face, thin-lipped and unsmiling with a high-bridged nose and deep-set piercing eyes. It was a face that emanated evil.

A hush fell over the unmasked guests, but the silence was pierced by an unearthly cry as Dupin, in one fluid movement, unsheathed the rapier from his cobra-headed walking stick and leapt at the man seated before us. Like a dark avenging angel, he plunged his glittering sword deep into the heart of Monsieur Victor Delamar. A gasp erupted from the mob as they took in the blood-red scene, but Delamar remained silent and very still. I watched as Dupin's face contorted with absolute horror. Then he collapsed, as if dead, at Delamar's feet.

The maroon and black mail coach—*Meteor* was its name—had red painted wheels, brightly polished brass work and four handsome jet-colored horses. It created a dashing picture as it sped through verdant countryside on the road from London to Margate.

Comfort and conversation were utterly absent from the first part of our journey. Six of us were crowded into the coach and ten more people were perched on its roof, but the number of passengers did not diminish the driver's ambition to travel at breakneck speed. This had a negative effect on the constitution of a young man who sat across from us, hemmed in by two burly fellows. His complaints of seasickness were met with boisterous ridicule until the contents of his stomach were nearly deposited onto the coach floor. The unfortunate fellow was forced by his companions to take a seat on the roof, which was unlikely to improve how he was feeling, but alleviated the necessity of making any more emergency stops.

Dupin seemed not to notice any of this, and my efforts to break his brooding silence were rebuffed. It was not until he had drunk liberally from a second flask of brandy that he said a word.

"I was certain it was *him*. Certain of it. Madame exceeded herself."

"It is undoubtedly a good thing that your victim was made of wax or you would be in Newgate, as would I as your accomplice."

Dupin tensed and lowered the flask. "I *knew* the repercussions of taking action," he said, jabbing at his head. "But I reacted from *here*." He pulled at the fabric above his heart. "I should have seen the truth."

"The theater of the event was irresistible. It seduced all who were there."

Dupin sighed and took another swallow of brandy. "You cannot comprehend what I would sacrifice to turn the heart I impaled with my rapier from wax to beating flesh."

"I do not know what quarrel you have with Victor Delamar, but it is not worth losing your liberty or your life for him."

"You do not understand," he snapped.

"Then illuminate me." My recalcitrant companion had sorely thinned my patience.

Dupin blinked his eyes disdainfully like a cat. They were full of the coldest anger when he turned to face me fully. "It was not Victor Delamar that I ran through with my blade, nor was it his wax effigy. It was *Ernest Valdemar*, the monster that betrayed my grandparents and then took everything they had of value for his own. The devilish figure Madame Tussaud was paid so well to create is the man who did his utmost to destroy the Dupin family."

"He and Delamar are working together?"

"So it would appear."

"And what will you do?"

Dupin turned his gaze to the window and the world outside. "For now I will do nothing. We will solve your mystery, then I will find a way to force Delamar to lead me to his master."

Any hopes I had of Dupin telling me more about Victor Delamar or the treacherous Ernest Valdemar were dashed as Dupin managed to sleep, or perhaps feigned it, until we stopped at a coaching inn for food, where he ate sparingly and drank liberally, which facilitated his slumbers when we resumed our journey. I was left to answer my fellow passengers' questions about America, which I did as thoroughly as I was able, despite the aggravating persistence of a fellow whose impression of my homeland was formed solely from *The Leatherstocking Tales*. He thought me an English impostor who had never been to that great frontier across the Atlantic as I was not dressed in buckskin leggings and beaded moccasins like Natty Bumppo. Eventually I too retreated into feigned sleep until true slumber possessed me.

When the coach bounced through a large hole in the road and jolted me awake, I wondered if Dupin's theories about the importance of dreams to unlock one's memories were correct, for the grand balloon we had seen above Hyde Park had sailed persistently through my slumbering mind. Once awake the image continued to haunt me—the golden sea-serpent swimming through the cobalt waves, poised to devour the sun with the face of Louis XVI, and the words in golden letters: *Le Grand Serpent de la Mer*. Then an image from the victim's ball came back to me—the dragon on the tapestry in the blue chamber. It was so like the creature adorning the balloon! Le Grand Serpent *de la Mer* . . . so similar to *Delamar*, indeed to *Valdemar*. And then it came to me.

"Dupin." I shook his shoulder. "It was hidden in plain sight."

"What was?" he snapped.

"*Victor Delamar* is a partial anagram of *Ernest Valdemar*."

Dupin frowned, his humor still very dark.

"*Le Grand Serpent de la Mer*—the words on the balloon with the golden sea-serpent. There were seven chambers at the victim's ball, each in a different color. We pondered the meanings of each color, but what we failed to consider was that each chamber featured a dragon or a serpent."

Dupin's brow furrowed in concentration as he summoned back the night of the ball and his eyes flicked back and forth as he looked inwardly, mentally dissecting each of the seven chambers.

"There was indeed a dragon on the blue tapestry," he said slowly. "And there was a serpent with the green apple in its mouth, and the brazier shaped from a golden dragon spewing orange flames."

"The yellow Chinese lanterns had dragon decorations, the glass bowl in the winter chamber had a frosted dragon etched upon it, silver serpents held platters full of grapes in the Dionysian room and the final room had the magnificent dragon chair. A most purposeful motif. Indeed, the invitation had the peculiar caduceus seal imprinted on it."

"Yes," Dupin nodded. "The serpent that I would crush beneath my heel considers himself a dragon. How like Valdemar."

And suddenly it was very clear. "Valdemar wanted you to attend *le Bal des Victimes*. He knew that Madame Tussaud as your dear friend would secure you an invitation."

"And Valdemar was there somewhere, watching me humiliate myself by thrusting a sword through a waxen heart." Dupin glowered with a darker fury, which made me sorry that I had solved the little puzzle.

For the rest of the journey I feigned sleep so I would not have to contend with his foul humor, but his self-pitying behavior had a surprising effect on me. I felt galvanized. It was not a demon or malevolent ghost terrorizing me: it was but a man, and the villain needed to be apprehended. If I let my emotions conquer me as Dupin's had him, my aggressor would never be brought to justice. I was determined to forget what I had suffered and continue my own investigation with a calm heart and clear head.

When we arrived at last in Margate, darkness had fallen, but perambulators were enjoying the night air, which was much fresher than that of London. We rolled along the seafront, where a number of shops faced the road, their windows covered with highly polished and pleasingly decorated shutters; although it was nearly ten o'clock, some of the premises were just closing. Minutes later, we arrived at the White Hart Hotel, which had a rather grand exterior and was situated on the Parade facing the sea.

"Shall we take a walk along the promenade and refresh ourselves?"

Dupin winced as he picked up his bag. "I am afraid I would prefer to retire for the night. Let us meet again at breakfast."

"Very well, Dupin. I hope a good night's sleep awaits you."

"Unlikely," he said as he strode into the hotel.

* * *

My chamber was not so fine as my rooms at Brown's Genteel Inn, but was perfectly pleasant. I opened the window to breathe in the air and discovered a panoramic view of the sea. The moon was a day past full and silvered the breakers as they roamed to and fro. My limbs ached from their lengthy imprisonment in that uncomfortable coach, which had the perverse effect of banishing sleep, so I retrieved the mahogany box from my suitcase and re-read the letters that referred to the attack on the Porter sisters after the Queen's birthday ball. It was Anne Porter who accused Rhynwick Williams on that fateful thirteenth of June and both she and her sister Sarah Porter swore in court that Rhynwick Williams was the Monster. Mr. Coleman collected Angerstein's reward and, purportedly, used it toward the purchase of the lodging house in Neptune Square, so Miss Anne Porter had benefitted from the reward indirectly if she had not received a share of the money. Meeting with Miss Porter was bound to reveal some vital information, I was certain of it. If she had knowingly committed perjury in court I could not fully condemn her, for Rhynwick Williams's incarceration surely saved my grandparents from hanging or, at the least, from being transported. Would I have existed at all if the Porter sisters had recognized Elizabeth Arnold as the Monster?

I looked at the address Mrs. Fenton had written down and then at the handsome map that was drawn on the verso of the White Hart Hotel handbill. I could not see Neptune Square on the map, but Margate was of a modest size compared to London, and I was confident we would manage to find Miss Porter. Whether she would speak to us was quite another thing.

Margate, 20 July 1790

Dear Accomplice,

While you were at the theatre, singing songs written for anyone at all to perform, I was on the promenade, blade in hand, ready to improvise an original performance. It was very dark and the promenade was empty but for those of dubious character—persons who might benefit from a taste of the Monster's blade. I proceeded cautiously, as you have advised so often, and soon spied a woman walking quite alone. She seemed in no fear of her surroundings or circumstances—she was decidedly wishful of companionship and so I moved forward to join her, wielding a sharp surprise for the lady! I crept along cautiously, ever so cautiously, but stumbled on something in the shadows and she was alerted to my presence. As she turned to greet me, I shouted "Ho! Have a taste of my famous blade!" And it cut through her skirts so sweetly. But then, as her face looked into mine, I saw that I knew her. From the theatre chorus— not so pretty as she herself thinks and risen up from the streets. She did not quake nor quail at the sight of the Monster, no indeed. She shouted, "You!" And the Monster ran off into the darkness, his reputation established.

Your Obedient Servant,
the Monster of Margate

The air was scented by the plants that grew along the beach—
wild carrot, toadflax, catmint, burdock, rocket—and bees
darted amongst large hedges of wild fennel topped with yellow
flowers that flavored the breeze with licorice. Dupin followed
me across the sands, reluctance seeping from his every footstep.
Coffee had not relieved his pallor and the morning sunlight
made him wince.

"I give you my word. The seawater will clear your head."
The knowledge that Dupin did not favor the water filled me
with ungentlemanly delight, for I had grown decidedly weary
of his self-pitying demeanor.

"My head is perfectly clear," he snapped. "Persist in taunting
me, and I will change my mind about this ridiculous enterprise."

"Then let us concentrate on what we know from the letters.
Henry Arnold came to Margate some time between the fourteenth of June and the seventh of July 1790, and Elizabeth
Arnold followed him to Margate after Rhynwick Williams's trial
on the eighth of July. She secured a role with the Theatre Royal
Margate whereas he did not. Henry Arnold died on the twenty-
fifth of July 1790 and his body was discovered in a bathing
machine," I said, indicating the painted wagons before us.

"Or he was murdered and his body hidden inside a bathing machine," Dupin interjected.

"Murdered? There was no suggestion in the obituary that Henry Arnold was murdered."

"The obituary notes that a bottle of belladonna was found in Henry Arnold's pocket when his body was discovered and the doctor's opinion was that belladonna caused his demise. We also know that Elizabeth Arnold was desperate for her husband to relinquish the role of the Monster, particularly after Rhynwick Williams was found guilty at trial, but according to the letters exchanged between Elizabeth Arnold and Mrs. Smith, Henry Arnold was accused of attacking a woman on Margate promenade. He died very soon after that."

"And why is this relevant?" I asked.

"Surely it is overly convenient that Henry Arnold poisoned himself with belladonna before he was interrogated for accosting a woman in the same manner as the Monster," Dupin said in a tone that made it clear he thought I was being especially slow. "And why was he discovered inside a bathing machine? Did Henry Arnold have a penchant for night swimming in the sea? Or was someone trying to hide his body? I would presume the latter."

"You do not truly believe Elizabeth Arnold would murder her own husband, a man she clearly loved and for whom she abandoned the comforts of a privileged life?"

"Remember what was at risk when Henry Arnold played the Monster at night. If he were caught, he was unstable enough to blame his wife as the originator of the Monster's crimes, and if he and she died at the end of a noose, what would become of their daughter? At best she would be taken into the care of Elizabeth's father and stepmother; at worst she would be treated as an orphan." Dupin's gaze was of cool detachment rather than empathy, which raised my ire, but I kept my counsel.

We had reached the bathing machines, which were lined up near the sea's edge like a cavalcade of gaily-painted covered wagons. The bathing attendants or "dippers" stood near their vehicles, burly sun-burnt men in rolled up trousers and cotton shirts, some with straw hats and others with handkerchiefs knotted over their heads. The female dippers were equally burly and sun-burnt and were gathered near the ladies' machines a respectable distance away.

One of the great pleasures of life in Philadelphia is the Schuylkill River, and being a keen swimmer, I would have traveled to Margate to experience the novelty of the bathing machines. My enthusiasm was tainted by the idea that my grandfather might have been murdered and his body disposed of in one of the handsomely painted vehicles before us.

I moved closer to a bathing machine of buttery yellow with red trim where an attendant was securing a horse to the front of the machine. The vehicle was cleverly designed: the length and width of the base was about six feet and the wooden walls were without windows; the height was roughly eight feet with a peaked roof—ample room for any man to stand inside it. Large wheels suspended the body of the machine four feet above the ground and there was a door to enter the machine from the sands and a second door at the front from which the bather exited into the sea.

"If Henry Arnold's mind was compromised by a surfeit of belladonna, it could be that he nearly drowned and sought refuge inside a bathing machine for the night," I said.

"It would be difficult for a person in pain or compromised mobility to climb inside such a machine," Dupin replied, indicating the ladder that led to the back door.

"Truly it is not difficult," the attendant protested as he approached us. "Would you care to dip? I have two machines available."

"Where are the bathing machines stationed overnight?" I asked him.

"On the sands near the bathing house, sir." He indicated a rather makeshift structure.

"Do you lock the bathing machines when your work is finished?" Dupin asked.

"There is nothing inside likely to tempt a thief. We keep the bathing costumes in the bathing room at night." The attendant looked from Dupin to me and back again, his gaze filled with suspicion.

"Thank you. Most informative. And yes, we will certainly dip."

"We might simply observe the machines," Dupin suggested.

"I insist. We must experience the sea and the bathing machines to understand what is possible and what is not."

Dupin narrowed his eyes, but shook his head once.

"Very good, sirs. This way." The attendant indicated that I should enter the yellow and red bathing machine and led Dupin to a sky-blue one. His face was grim as he climbed up the wooden stepladder that led to the back door, and I clambered into mine, feeling satisfied with Dupin's discomfort.

The inside of the bathing machine was very practical: a bench, a raised compartment for storing clothing, two towels and a flannel gown for female bathers. Light trickled in through an opening in the roof. I was thrown unceremoniously onto the bench as the bathing machine began to move forward, and it occurred to me that the bench was far too narrow to recline on. My grandfather would have spent his final hours lying on the floor of that bathing machine.

When my carriage came to a rest, I heard the attendant making soothing noises to the horse as he released him from the front of the machine and led him to the back, where he would be yoked for the journey inland. I quickly changed into the bathing costume I had brought with me and folded all my clothing into the compartment. When I opened the door at the front of the carriage, the sea was just below floor level and my dipper was waiting to assist. A number of other bathers were in the sea, but the door to Dupin's machine remained closed. My dipper reached out to help me down the ladder into the water, but I dove in. When I resurfaced a good ten yards further out, it was clear that my actions were not typical. Fellow bathers who stood chest deep in the water stared at me as I swam back toward the bathing machines.

"Sir, I feared that I lost you," the dipper said, his face the picture of dread.

"Fear not. I dearly enjoy the water."

The dipper was not convinced by this declaration and hovered in the sea near me as if worried that I might plunge beneath it again.

I noticed with some surprise that I was the only bather wearing a costume. While it is not uncommon practice in my homeland for men—particularly amongst the lower classes—to swim as God made them, this is never tolerated if females are present. I glanced over to the ladies' bathing machines and saw that the nearest had an awning that stretched out from the machine to the water, completely covering the bather therein. Thus, the ladies remained obscured from male sight and vice versa, preserving modesty for all.

It was then that the door to Dupin's bathing machine finally opened. He emerged and stood at the top of the stepladder, staring out at the water all around him. Silence fell on the bathers as they stared up at Dupin, for he was dressed, most improbably, in a long flannel gown. His complexion had a green hue, extreme biliousness or perhaps merely the reflection of seawater upon his skin. He took two steps down the ladder and gripped its sides. His dipper approached, clutching a length of rope that was securely fastened to the bathing machine.

"Allow me, sir," he said, tying the rope around Dupin's waist, which gave him the look of a penitent monk. The dipper offered his hand, but too late—a large wave surged forward and, without any regard for Dupin's dignity, dislodged him from his perch. He disappeared beneath the water while his skirts billowed up like an inverted parachute. Truly Dupin's element as a Frenchman was air and not water. I swam toward him, but the canny dipper used the rope to yank him up. Dupin spluttered and gasped

"Are you all right?"

"Quite fine," Dupin said, glaring. He staggered on the sandy bottom and paddled wildly with his arms to steady himself. His composure lapsed again when he noticed the other bathers' state of undress and his complexion instantly shifted from green to pink.

I nodded at the flannel gown. "Does it fit?" I could not resist asking.

Dupin narrowed his eyes, but did not respond.

"Would sir care to dip?" his attendant asked. "Very good for the constitution."

"Yes, of course he must dip." The malicious words came forth before I could stop them.

The dipper grasped Dupin by arm and with the other hand, pushed his head underwater. He hauled him up again and dipped him twice more, as if baptizing him. Dupin spluttered and flailed like a cat in water, but was no match for his assailant. When at last the ritual was finished, Dupin's eyes were ablaze and, without a word, he climbed into the bathing machine and shut the door.

"A few more minutes, sir," I said to my dipper before striking out away from the shore. With each stroke, I wondered if Henry Arnold had tried to swim through these waters one dark July night, only to succumb to the waves. Had he managed to struggle to the shore and seek refuge in the bathing machine, a place that was a comfort to him as he lay dying? Or had he been placed there by someone who failed to save his life and abandoned his corpse in that makeshift tomb? Or, worse still, had he been murdered and his body hidden inside the vehicle, the villain knowing that he would not be discovered until morning? And *how* had he been murdered? The obituary revealed nothing concrete about my grandfather's cause of death and none of the letters clarified the circumstances of his demise. When I climbed into the bathing machine, I was no closer to a solution.

* * *

My dipper had instructed us to follow the footpath that hugged the shoreline, and we found four Neptune Square without difficulty. The lodging house was very charming and Mrs. Coleman, the wife of Miss Porter's nephew, was a cheerful pink-faced woman of middle years. I introduced us as journalists who were writing an essay concerning the affects of violent crime on innocent victims and said we wished to interview Miss Porter about the London Monster. Mrs. Coleman seemed oddly unsurprised; she merely requested that we take a walk along the promenade and if Miss Porter were happy to speak with us, she would be prepared by our return. We followed Mrs. Coleman's instructions, and when we arrived back at the lodging house, Mrs. Coleman ushered us in.

"Miss Sarah will see you in her sitting room." She led us up a flight of stairs to a gloomy room and indicated that we should sit facing a gilded armchair I feared was decorated to resemble a throne. "She won't be long." And she closed the door.

Velvet draperies like theater curtains concealed two windows and repelled the light. The room was oppressive with stale air and extraneous furnishings. A crowd of porcelain figurines—all courting couples dressed in garish costumes—was gathered on the mantelpiece, as if at a ball. Framed prints covered the walls.

Dupin noticed where my gaze was directed and said, "Each is concerned with the London Monster. It is quite a collection."

Upon closer inspection, Dupin proved to be correct. There were colorful illustrations of ferocious knife-wielding demons chasing their victims, young ladies donning copper pots to protect themselves and lively courtroom scenes along with newspaper stories and pamphlets about the Monster.

"It seems Miss Porter is accustomed to giving presentations about the Monster and for being recompensed for her time." Dupin drew my attention to a faded, handwritten card that said *Gratuities,* which was placed next to a brass bowl on the occasional table adjacent to the throne-like chair. "Perhaps she is waiting for the sound of coins before she makes her entrance," Dupin said sardonically, as he placed several coins in the bowl. "Let us hope my offering meets her expectations."

"And let us hope the performance has value." I smiled.

Almost immediately the door to Miss Porter's other chamber opened and a Skye terrier with fur as yellowed as antique lace stalked into the room and emitted a low growl. I wondered if Mrs. Coleman had engineered a malicious prank and "Miss Sarah" was a performing dog, but there was a swish of silk and a very thin, stern woman with regal posture that belied her seventy years entered the room. She was swathed in an ill-fitting yellow silk ball gown from an earlier era, its low décolletage somewhat alleviated by the strategic placement of some lace.

"Chevalier Dupin, Mr. Poe," she said, nodding at us. "I am Miss Sarah Porter, victim of the Monster and sister-in-law of the man who captured him. I understand you wish to hear all the details of my terrible tale for your essay."

Dupin's eyebrows inched up.

"Indeed we would," I said.

Miss Porter eased into her ornate chair and the dog settled onto the footstool next to her. She indicated that we should take our seats. "Then let us begin." She cleared her throat and straightened her back. "My sister Anne and I both had new gowns for the Queen's birthday ball." Miss Porter indicated the dress she was wearing. "It was quite an occasion and an honor to be invited, but little did we know that the notorious Monster was waiting in the darkness, determined to make us his victims." Miss Porter projected her voice as if in a large theater and emphasized her words with peculiar stilted gestures, moving as if she were a very large marionette. She described the night of the Queen's birthday ball in great detail; it was only when she related the specifics of the attack itself that her story diverged from my grandmother's account.

"The bells were about to chime midnight and we were making our way down St. James's Street. Suddenly came a voice." Miss Porter stood and cupped a hand to her ear. "'What ho, is it you?' It was then that I turned and saw . . . the Monster!"

Miss Porter yanked open the window curtains to reveal a monster of a man with bulging eyes, snarling mouth, a nimbus of flame-colored hair, knife held aloft. I emitted a yelp and Dupin a gasp. Miss Porter smiled in triumph. It quickly became apparent that the figure before us was merely wax and had suffered badly from time and the elements, the hands malformed as if from some disease and the face made hideous.

"I will not be humiliated again," Dupin muttered. I pressed a hand to his shoulder to discourage him from leaping up.

"The wax figure is extraordinary," I said. "How did you come by such a terrifying creature?"

"The Monster was a popular attraction at Mrs. Salmon's wax works in Fleet Street and when the lady died, it was purchased for me, a gift I did not appreciate at the time. In the end, I suppose it has earned its considerable cost. Shall I continue with my oration?"

"Please," I said quickly before Dupin could offer a response.

Miss Porter struck another wooden pose. "I ran to the doorstep as quickly as I was able, urging my sister to follow, and as I knocked upon the door and called out for help, I hoped we might be saved. But to no avail. I felt a terrible pain across my flank." She showed us the back of her dress, which was torn, and her feisty little dog growled at the indignity his mistress had suffered. Miss Porter turned to face us again and said sotto voce, "He had cut right through my gown and into my flesh."

Dupin wore a façade of calm but there was acid in his voice. "The Monster cut both your gown and your sister's?"

"Indeed. Two silk gowns, one pale pink and one yellow, and all that lay beneath them were ruined by his terrible blade."

"How interesting. The transcripts of Rhynwick Williams's trial state that your sister Anne Porter had her skirts cut by the Monster and that you were hit about the head," Dupin continued.

"All occurred as I am telling it," she said in an offended tone. "I was there after all."

"Obviously you were," I said, hoping to placate her.

"Your attacker's face was visible, despite the late hour? It was, without doubt, Rhynwick Williams?" Dupin pressed.

"I saw him perfectly clearly. I have no need of spectacles, young man. Rhynwick Williams accosted me several times previously and was no stranger to me."

"And would you know if Rhynwick Williams is still alive? I believe he would be seventy-three or seventy-four years of age," I asked.

"I really could not tell you that. Of course his victims feared that he might resume his crimes upon his release, that he might seek revenge against those who testified against him."

"And did he?"

"Mysterious things happened that he might have caused, but there was no proof," she said enigmatically. "Of course he should never have been released. His crimes were a hanging offense—the lenient sentence was an affront to all the ladies of good breeding he injured and whose clothing he ruined. Such depravity and he received but six years in Newgate, where he was permitted to entertain visitors with music and dancing and flagons of wine? It was a holiday for him! You must put that in your essay."

"Rhynwick Williams was permitted to entertain visitors in Newgate prison? Did you witness these events?" Dupin asked.

"The wretch mocked me by sending an invitation to a 'ball', but of course I did not go."

"What a pity." Dupin's expression made it clear that he thought the story a fabrication.

"I have taken the stand at two trials, Chevalier Dupin, and have been interrogated by the reprehensible Theophilus Swift. I care not if you believe what I tell you, but you would be wise to scrutinize the evidence before forming an opinion, sir." Miss Porter pointed at a framed notice on the wall.

I quickly made my way to it and Dupin followed. Inside the frame was a handwritten invitation.

Rhynwick Williams requests the pleasure of your company at
The Monster's Ball
to be held at Four o'clock, 13 August 1790, Newgate Gaol.
Entertainment, refreshments and supper to be provided.
Répondez s'il vous plaît.

A framed newspaper article from *The Oracle*, dated the twentieth of August 1790 was displayed next to it.

"Perhaps you would do me the honor of reading the newspaper account aloud, Chevalier Dupin?" Miss Porter asked. It was obvious that she had taken great offense, but this did not worry Dupin, who read the article in a clear, neutral voice.

"'The depravity of the times was manifested last week, in an eminent degree, in Newgate. The Monster sent cards of invitation to about twenty couples, amongst whom were some of his alibi friends, his brothers, sisters, several of the prisoners and others, whom we shall take a future opportunity to notice. At four o'clock, the party sat to tea; this being over, two violins struck up, accompanied by a flute, and the company proceeded to exercise their limbs. In the merry dance, the cuts and *entrechats* of the Monster were much admired, and his adroitness in that amusement must be interesting, from the school in which he acquired this branch of his accomplishments.'" Dupin paused, grimacing slightly at *The Oracle's* little joke about the former ballet-dancer turned frock-cutting villain, and continued. "'About eight o'clock, the company partook of a cold supper and a variety of wines, such as would not discredit the most sumptuous gala, and about nine o'clock departed, that being the usual hour for locking the doors of the prison.'"

Dupin turned to face Miss Porter and gave her a slight bow. "And did any of your acquaintances attend this purported ball?" he asked. "Your sister and Mr. Coleman must also have been invited if Rhynwick Williams was mocking you?"

"Of course they did not go," she snapped. "But if you do not trust the evidence before you, I am acquainted with someone who did attend the ball, and he will not be difficult to find."

"A friend of Rhynwick Williams's?"

"I suppose he may be that, although he claims to be my dearest friend when he is in need of assistance," she complained.

"What is this person's name and where are we likely to find him?" I asked gently.

"His name is Mr. Robert Nicholson and he is in Newgate

prison. Or he was last week when he wrote to ask for another loan with which to satisfy his creditors."

"Mr. Nicholson's crime is penury?" Dupin asked.

"Penury is a misfortune, not a crime," I protested.

"Mr. Nicholson's very words, spoken on many occasions, but it should not take a man fifty years to learn abstinence from gaming tables when he never wins at them."

"Persistent debtors make unreliable friends," I offered.

"And the most awful husbands," Miss Porter said bitterly. "He took as much from me as the Monster and now I must exist on my historical orations and the charity of my nephew and his wife. If I had not secured a divorce from Mr. Nicholson, I would have joined him and the Monster in Newgate. What justice would there be in that?"

"None, I am sure. Thank you for your marvelous oration. We are most obliged for your time." I added some coins to the brass bowl, and dragged Dupin away before he could insult the lady again.

"Edgar. Dear Edgar."

It was a woman's low, sweet voice that came from far away, but I could hear each word distinctly. A shadow loomed over me, a presence.

"Edgar. Open your eyes."

I struggled to do so for they were sewn shut with the thread of my lashes.

"Edgar, I am here."

Dust glittered in the air and a face appeared in a nimbus of light. Her countenance was blurred by the radiance, but familiar—my grandmother.

"I have a message for you. Listen closely."

I tried to focus on the face before me, but my eyes seemed swathed in a veil of gauze.

"The mahogany box. Examine it carefully for it holds further secrets—secrets that may save you from my enemies and yours."

As I struggled to sit up, her features faded slowly into the glare that surrounded her, until all that was left was a beam of sunlight flickering through the gently swaying curtains and a shadow of angelic aspect dancing along the wall.

Had I truly been dreaming? I climbed from my bed and tried to clear my head of fog and echoes. I would be spending the day alone as Dupin had received an urgent message from Dr. Froissart and was meeting him in Herne Bay. I had decided to visit all the places my grandparents might have frequented in Margate to look for unexpected clues and perhaps to get a better sense of them.

A serving girl arrived with a pot of tea, poached eggs with toast and sausages. While I broke my fast, I re-read the letters written while my grandparents were residing in Margate, but I could not erase from my mind the words I had dreamed or heard or imagined. *The mahogany box. Examine it carefully. It holds further secrets.* I picked up the box and scrutinized every aspect of it, convinced that there was something to discover that I had failed to see before. I rapped upon the top, the bottom and each side, then shook the thing vigorously. I tried the brass handles, the escutcheon, unlocked it, removed the letters, tested the weight. It did not feel overly light or overly heavy for a box of its size with a solid mahogany base. And then it came to me—a solid base of almost three inches? I prodded and prized each panel, then felt something shift. The right panel, loose. As I worked upon it, a crack developed where the side panel met the bottom. Slowly it slid upward, but no cavity was revealed. Perhaps the bottom was false after all. I pushed at the newly revealed edge of the base and it slid back revealing a gap, a chamber with papers within it. *Hidden in plain sight.* My fingers tugged and pushed until a small cache of letters fell out, three in total. I searched through them—the same handwriting, that of my grandmother, my grandfather . . . but *why*? Why hidden here when the other incriminating letters were not?

Secrets that may save you from my enemies and yours. A portent from the dead. To ignore it would be folly. With hands that fluttered like insect wings, I unfolded the letters and discovered two threats and one plea for forgiveness. And I understood. If one is under dire attack, unsavory actions may be justified if in defense of one's child and one's own self. Had my nemesis found the compartment and read the letters? Surely not, for he would have removed and destroyed any evidence of his vengeful and violent nature. Now my exploration of Margate would have a clearer focus—I would search for an overlooked clue or detail that would answer the question of Henry Arnold's demise: misfortune or murder?

I gulped down the remaining tea and placed the map of Margate in front of me so I might mark the locations referred to in my grandparents' letters. The Theatre Royal, promenade, pier, lighthouse, bathing machines and, of course, the White Hart Hotel were all noted on the map as were the main thoroughfares. But then I noticed something odd. There was an "x" drawn on the spot that I now knew to be the location of 4 Neptune Square. Looking more closely, I saw a "1" marked on Marine Parade, which the map key labeled as the White Hart Hotel. There was a "2" written at Cecil Square—it was not noted on the key, but I knew from the letters that my grandparents had rented rooms there. A "3" was written on Queen Street, but not defined, and "4" was identified as the Theatre Royal, on the corner of Hawley Square and Addington Street. Most peculiar.

Thinking back, I remembered that I had not chosen The White Hart Hotel: it had been booked for me. My nemesis had discovered where I would be staying and had put his skills as a scrivener to use, drawing up the map on the verso of the hotel handbill and delivering it to me at Brown's Genteel Inn. Surely it was a thinly veiled message and there was nothing to do but visit each place noted on the map.

I left the White Hart Hotel determined to unravel the enigma of the map, but as I walked along Marine Parade, a wave of biliousness came over me, and I stopped to gulp down the sea breeze like medicine. I could not shake off a strange lightheadedness when I continued on my way. The sun glittered on the sea and splinters of light pierced my eyes. I sought shade as I walked, but it continually eluded me, and I moved as if in the aftermath of a terrible spree while words from the letters infected my mind.

Eliza and I have not seen you for days and you have left us in desperate straits. I fear ending up on the streets of Margate.

What was true and what was false? I had thought the sea air would improve how I felt, but instead my thoughts began to jumble, my head to throb gently, words from the letters mixing together, a distillation of the emotions between my grandparents just before Henry Arnold's death. I tried to clear my mind, but as I turned into New Street, I saw a flash of kingfisher blue skirts and a woman walking quickly, then a glimpse of the woman's face as she looked back at me—my grandmother, I was certain. Oddly, this did not surprise me. I followed her ghost-like presence into Cecil Square, where I saw her entering a neat brick house: number thirteen.

The rent money is missing—spent on gin from the empty bottle you left next to the box where my wages are kept. I cannot tell you how my heart sank when I found the compartment empty.

The letter you wrote has left me in a foul humour. Interminable accusations! Do you think me so witless to spend our rent money on gin?

As I stared at the boarding house where my grandparents had lived, the sunlight nipped at my eyes, and I experienced the most peculiar sensation, the hideous dropping off of the veil that separates everyday life and that other world we are not meant to witness. It was as if I were inside a reveler's opium dream and the past was visible before me.

* * *

Elizabeth stood before the threshold, peering through the door of their rooms, surreptitiously watching Henry. He put something in his pocket, closed the mahogany box and hid its key in her jar of hairpins on the dressing table. When Elizabeth entered the room, he pretended to check on Eliza in her cot. She placed bread, cheese and a bottle of gin on the table. Henry immediately opened the bottle and poured himself a large glass.

I have grown weary of your insistence that I sit at home like a tiresome spinster while you sing at the very theatre that deprived me of employment—you add insult to injury.

Henry's eyes darted toward the door like a cornered animal and his anger was palpable. He poured himself another glass of gin and finished it in a long gulp, kissed Elizabeth's cheek brusquely and made his way out the door. As soon as he was gone, Elizabeth opened the mahogany box and searched through folded letters, her face tense with worry. When she closed the lid, it was as if a door closed upon my vision of the past.

* * *

I directed my gaze to the map and found "3" on Queen Street. I made my way there and discovered an apothecary shop with a large window in which two sizeable carboys were proudly displayed, one filled with a violet-colored liquid, the other with citrine. When I peered through the window I saw a dimly lit shop with large wooden counters and cabinets on the walls that held a multitude of drawers neatly labeled in Latin. Several large glass jars on a shelf housed coiled serpents with jaws agape. A small stuffed crocodile was displayed on another shelf, teeth exposed.

A man with thin gray hair and piercing light blue eyes stood at the counter serving my grandmother. She slid a piece of paper to the pharmacist. His eyes narrowed slightly when he read it, but he turned to the apothecary jars and bottles: *Artemisia absinthium, Chininum hydrobromicum, oxymel scillae, oleum pini pumilionis, opio en polvo, calomel, syrupus sennae, papav* and *tolu*—medicines or poisons, I did not know. He located an apothecary jar labeled *Atropa belladonna* and placed it on the counter, then proceeded to mix a tincture, which he decanted into a small, cobalt blue bottle. The pharmacist's unblinking eyes captured Elizabeth's as he pushed the bottle toward her.

"*Atropa belladonna*. Atropos was one of the three Fates. She held the shears that cut the thread of life. Use it carefully, madam."

Elizabeth paid for her purchase and turned her gaze to mine. The carboys in the window glowed as if they contained a hellish brew. *Atropa belladonna* . . . And she was gone.

* * *

I found myself walking again, making my way from Queen Street back to Cecil Street and on to Hawley Square. There was no proof that my grandmother had bought the belladonna that was found on my grandfather's person, the drug that might have caused his death. And yet I felt that it was true. Had Dupin tainted my thoughts? Or had my uneasy belief come from the letters I had read? I soon arrived at the corner of Hawley Square and Addington Street, where the Theatre Royal was located, a place that brought my grandmother success and my grandfather ruination.

Who would blame a man for keeping the gin bottle to hand when forced to play the same tune again and again when the singers cannot remember the lyric?

Let us finish the play and move forward. I am certain we will secure you another position at the theatre.

I knew that my grandmother had a coveted role in *The Waterman* and *The Beaux Stratagem*, whereas my grandfather had lost his position as a pianist. If Henry Arnold had pursued his role as the Monster, putting both their lives in jeopardy, might his wife have poisoned him as Dupin suggested?

With that ominous thought reverberating through my mind, I crossed the threshold and found myself in another world. The space was in use as a chapel rather than a theater, but it had no affinity with the air of Heaven or a place of worship. Candles illuminated the interior with fickle light and a briny scent permeated the air—old seawater, stagnant and dank, creeping along the heavy old stage curtains, settling in like poison. A mystic vapor hovered around me—the theater's hungry ghosts. They urged me to climb onto the makeshift altar that had been their stage, and look down at the theater seats, which fanned out endlessly. I could almost hear the players' voices, the music from the piano. The candlelight glowed like a swarm of fireflies, my head was whirling, the whispers grew louder.

I am a more accomplished pianist than that usurper!

My grandfather, undone by drink, made excuses for his culpability and envied the success of his wife. A shadowy movement drew me to the back of the stage, where I found old props and abandoned theater accouterments, and then a door. When I opened it, the courtyard outside blazed with light, and I stepped back in pain as a man shuffled through the door, mumbling.

An honourable gentleman acquaintance, Mr. Charles Tubbs, found Henry in the gutter quite unable to stand up, his clothes fully ruined, his mind disrupted, his speech incoherent.

I watched with horror as Henry Arnold staggered and rubbed at his eyes. He was drenched through with perspiration, his mind thoroughly confused—his very life spirit seemed to be slipping away. Was he undone by gin or poison?

Elizabeth . . . the Monster, I am the Monster . . .

She stood next to me, her face full of fear, as the new piano player, Mr. Charles Tubbs, ushered her husband out of the theater. Elizabeth picked up a flask of water and went into the courtyard, where Henry was stumbling aimlessly. She took the cobalt blue bottle from her pocket and tipped its contents into the water.

I wonder what all would think of the talented Mrs. Arnold if it were known that her greatest performances were on the streets rather than the theatre boards?

When she told him that the flask contained gin, he grabbed for it, and she guided it to his lips. Elizabeth promised Mr. Tubbs that she would take her husband home and refused his offers of assistance.

* * *

When I stepped from the cool darkness of the theater into the courtyard, the sun bleached the color from the sky, blurred the edge of things, and I lost sight of my grandparents. I looked at the map and saw that number "5" was the location of the bathing machines, number "6" the pier and number "7" the lighthouse. I was feeling terribly ill, my head pounding and throat parched, but I was determined to find a message within the map, for surely there was one.

Remember that when one has nothing at all, there is nothing to be lost by telling the truth. Do not vex me lest you wish to incur the Margate Monster's wrath.

With an unsteady gait, I made my way to Marine Parade, where other perambulators seemed to shy away from me. When I reached the sands, I caught a flash of kingfisher blue and saw Elizabeth leading Henry to a blue and yellow bathing machine, and somehow it was dark and the sands were deserted but for my grandparents. I crept toward them, but they took no notice of me. Henry's countenance was swollen and red, his tongue protruded as if trying to gather moisture from his parched lips, while his eyes glittered strangely and were black and empty as death. Elizabeth tucked the cobalt blue bottle and a letter into Henry's frock coat pocket, then climbed up to open the bathing machine door. She pulled him up inside and settled him on the floor. His eyelids were closed and his breath ragged.

Please come home. Your wife and daughter miss you deeply, despite our predicament.

Words from the letter found on Henry's person when he was discovered in the bathing machine. Constructed to suggest innocence?

Elizabeth closed the bathing machine door and made her way back across Margate sands. Tears shimmered on her cheeks.

He passed into the arms of God before I could reach his side.

A low moaning cry from the bathing machine, but she did not look back.

* * *

I was startled into fuller cognizance by someone shaking my arm.

"Are you all right, sir?" asked a bathing machine attendant.

"Yes, yes, quite fine Too much sun." And I made my way across the sands, to the pathway that led to the pier and the lighthouse. As I walked, I tried to breathe in the sea breeze, hoping it would un-jumble my thoughts and banish the specters of the past.

Had I witnessed my grandfather's true demise? Or had those letters made me conjure up that terrible scenario?

I walked the full length of the pier, looking around me for a flash of kingfisher blue, for another glimpse of the past. But I saw nothing. When I reached the lighthouse, I stared out over the harbor to where the bathing machines stood. And still I witnessed nothing. The specters were gone.

"Look at the sea—how dark it is."

They were with me again!

I felt a hand tug at my coat pocket. Before I could cry out, someone shoved me hard, and I was tumbling from the pier toward the dark water below and into its chill embrace.

A lapping sound, rhythmic. Cold. Wind in my ears and the sound of gulls laughing. My cheek buried in sand, eyes burning with salt. Water rolled over me and away again. My eyes slowly opened to an expanse of stygian green beneath clouds the color of over-ripe plums. Thunder growled softly and a wild light sizzled through the purple. Water swept over me again, and I saw one hand clawing at sand and the other gripping the rim of a wheel.

"There he is."

Rough hands pulled at me until I was sitting, but still clinging to the wheel of a bathing machine. My clothes were drenched in seawater, my skin itching with brine. I ached and was infinitely weary.

"Poe, it is Dupin. How did you get here?"

"I know not . . ." The sands seemed to shift underneath me and a blade of sunlight pierced my eye, making me howl.

"Let me help you up."

Dupin pulled me to my feet, but the morning brightness threatened to fizzle into black, so I hunkered back down and dropped my head between my knees. "Deeply, breathe deeply," I muttered to myself.

"Let us get you to the hotel. Are you able to walk?" Dupin put my arm over his shoulder and somehow we trudged back to the White Hart Hotel.

"A vision," I muttered. "It was all a dream within a dream."

* * *

We left Margate at two o'clock on a steam packet named the *Eclipse,* despite Dupin's protests that I should rest at the hotel a further day. He had found me at dawn, and I had submerged into a dreamless sleep until one o'clock, which reinvigorated me enough to get on board the vessel to London. I did not wish to tarry another day in Margate—I had eluded Death once and had no desire to grapple with him again.

"Are you feeling at all recovered, Poe?"

"Somewhat. My mind was in a terrible confusion yesterday, as if both asleep and awake."

"Indeed. You might have drowned. What possessed you to go to those damnable bathing machines in the night?"

I shook my head. "No, that is not what happened. I saw things from the past, terrible things. Someone pushed me into the water and then all was darkness until I came back to myself on the sands, next to the bathing machine."

"Had you been to a tippling den in my absence?"

I confess that I should not have been surprised by Dupin's question, but I was. "No spreeing—I had nothing to drink at all. My mind was terribly disturbed as if by opium, but truly it was not I who made it so. Perhaps I am becoming ill."

Dupin held up a cobalt blue apothecary bottle. "Are you tell-ing me that you did not drink its contents?"

"Absolutely not. It is Henry Arnold's—or more precisely, Elizabeth's. She put it in his pocket."

Dupin stared at me. "This was found on your person. In *your* coat pocket."

Was I going mad? The visitations or visions—I remembered everything and what I had seen made sense in the most awful way. Perhaps my overly vivid fancy had conjured it all from the letters, but surely not from an unraveling mind? I thought back to those moments on the pier.

"I felt someone tug at my coat," I said slowly, "then he pushed me into the water. I remember falling toward the sea as if I were in a dream."

I did not tell Dupin how a strange calm came over me when I floated up to see yellow, lavender and pink-stained clouds exploding from the sea like fireworks. When the water sluiced over me again and pulled me under, I felt no fear, did not flail but simply let myself sink, ready to give myself to the darkness around me, until I heard a voice, faintly at first, *Sissy's* voice, calling out to me, repeating my name over and over again until I kicked and clawed through the water, fought against the greedy fingers of the sea and felt my knees upon the sand. When I next opened my eyes, my arm was linked through the bathing machine wheel, and I was holding on for my very life.

Dupin sniffed at the cobalt blue bottle and his frown deepened. "When did you begin to feel peculiar?"

"Directly after breakfast."

"Where did you have breakfast—at the hotel?"

"Yes. The girl brought a tray. A pot of tea and a cooked breakfast."

Dupin examined the blue bottle again. "Belladonna is a poison that can kill or cause a trance and hallucinations. Did your heart pound, your mouth feel dry and was your vision compromised? Specifically, did strong sunlight injure your eyes?"

"Yes. I felt as if I were caught in a dream and as I followed the map, I saw Elizabeth and Henry Arnold—I saw her poison him with belladonna and leave him in the bathing machine."

"Hallucinations. I believe your aggressor put tincture of belladonna into the tea. It seems he followed you to Margate."

A wave of nausea passed over me. I felt as if I were back on the *Ariel* in the aftermath of my spree and leaned over the side of the *Eclipse*, but thankfully did not disgrace myself.

"I presume you did not see the person who pushed you."

I shook my head. And then I remembered the mahogany box. "But there is new evidence that might reveal my agressor's identity. Indeed it suggests Rhynwick Williams is the culprit."

Dupin frowned. "Would you care to explain?"

"Showing you would be best." I opened my suitcase and removed the mahogany box.

"I remember the contents of the letters," Dupin said, impatience sharpening his words.

"But you have not read the three letters that were hidden in the concealed compartment."

Dupin was instantly like a wolf on the hunt. "Show me."

I slid the panel and revealed the cavity in the bottom of the box and the three letters secreted within it.

"Extraordinary," he muttered. "How did I not see it? May I?" He took the box and closed the panels, examined the box's edges, then opened the compartment again. "Simple design, but extremely well-crafted. It is almost impossible to see the join." He looked back to me. "And the letters?"

"I believe Elizabeth Arnold hid them there as a form of protection. One is a threatening letter from her husband and the other a threat from Rhynwick Williams, dated the twelfth of November 1795, not long before his release from Newgate. He swears he will find her in America and exact his revenge."

Dupin nodded. "And the third letter?"

"My grandmother wrote it to my mother on the sixteenth of March 1798, the date of her eleventh birthday. It is clear that she feared for her life and wanted her daughter to know that she loved her. You may read them."

Dupin extracted the letters from the compartment. As he read, I focused on all that was around me and tried to steady myself. Our captain wore a gold-braided uniform and a top hat—the former gave him a military bearing and the latter made him resemble an undertaker. A notice was posted on the paddle steamer that instructed: *Do not speak to the man at the wheel*, which did little to deter our fellow passengers. I wished that I could feel some of the gaiety that surrounded me.

"Most interesting," Dupin said. "Rhynwick Williams certainly wished to take revenge upon your grandmother and if he succeeded, perhaps it gave him access to your grandparents' letters."

Dupin's words made sense. "Although I suspect Williams did not read the hidden letters, for surely he would have destroyed the threat he made to my grandmother."

"That is indeed likely," Dupin agreed.

"And if Rhynwick Williams is determined to take revenge for my grandmother's treachery 'on her whole line, beyond her death'—as the letter states—then we might presume that he has tried to keep his identity a secret, to prevent me from having him arrested."

Dupin considered this for a moment. "That is a logical conclusion if Rhynwick Williams is your aggressor, or is behind the attacks made upon you," he eventually said. "We cannot, however, forget Mrs. Fontaine and her *inamorato*, a man of many disguises. As it seems likely that you were surreptitiously poisoned with belladonna yesterday, we must also consider whether your compromised condition on board the *Ariel* was in fact inflicted upon you rather than self-inflicted."

I had blamed myself for succumbing to the imp of the perverse and breaking my promise to Sissy, but if Dupin were correct, my conscience would be salved, despite the damage to my reputation.

"Given that Mrs. Fontaine and the professor colluded to imprison you in that cellar, we must wonder if they also drugged you on the *Ariel*. While it is clear that Mr. Mackie was antagonistic toward you, from what you have told me, there were other passengers who had access to your quarters."

I felt as if I had been pummeled in the stomach. "Impossible, Dupin, absolutely impossible. Mrs. Wallis nursed me when I was ill and her husband the doctor examined me. It cannot be them."

"It would not have been difficult for Dr. Wallis and his wife to feed you wine mixed with laudanum and then persuade you in the aftermath of the concoction's deleterious effects that you had overindulged in drink. One would only need to add the elixir to your wine at dinner or to your drinking water and, once the effects had taken hold, place empty bottles of drink in your stateroom. Posing as a doctor and his nurse would allow them both complete access to you. It is quite simple to keep a person in a compromised state if one pretends to be caring for him. Of course I have not seen Dr. and Mrs. Wallis—is it at all possible that they might be Mrs. Fontaine and the professor in disguise, remembering her virtuosity as an actress and the many roles the scrivener has capably performed?"

The vision of Mrs. Wallis appearing in the door of my stateroom in a halo of light came back to me. "But Mrs. Wallis was fair-haired—like an angel—and Mrs. Fontaine is dark-haired," I said.

"Let us not forget the many disguises your grandmother and grandfather wore when playing the Monster. Surely Mrs. Fontaine is capable of donning a fair wig to deceive you."

Dupin's theory filled me with horror, but I could not find a flaw in his scenario. Had I been confined to my bed, delirious and vulnerable, in complete disarray mentally and physically through their actions? How they must have laughed at my deplorable condition! And they would have been free to go through my most personal possessions, all my thoughts put to paper, all my emotions turned to words. And while I was lost in the endless darkness of my nightmares, they could have murdered me at any time of their choosing. I had been utterly at their mercy and yet I lived.

"They enjoyed tormenting me upon the *Ariel* and by delivering the letters in uncanny ways so that I might suffer more as the full story of my grandparents was disclosed to me. Presumably I am only alive as my aggressor wishes to communicate something else to me."

"Yes," Dupin agreed.

"Therefore, I must fathom my aggressor's identity for if he reveals himself with the final piece of his story, he will murder me."

"I believe that is correct," Dupin said. "But we will discover him first, have no fear."

As much as I valued Dupin's friendship and intellect, I was not confident these assets would fully protect me from a villain who seemed capable of walking through walls and vanishing into thin air.

There was a brilliance to the morning, as if all around me had been repainted with colors a shade or two richer. Street sweepers scurried with their brooms, hoping to earn a coin by clearing the path for a lady's skirts or a gentleman's good boots. A young girl decorated in spangles performed a lively dance upon a square of cloth for pennies thrown at her feet. Nearby, an ancient man who could scarcely move his rag-stuffed shoes shuffled slowly and sang in a voice so broken the words were indiscernible. The sunlight had drawn out other street entertainers like summer butterflies: an Oriental juggler, an acrobat who could twist his body into shapes that defied natural human form, and a conjuror who plucked coins and colored scarves from the pockets, hats and ears of his spectators.

This atmosphere of life and color died away when I reached Newgate Prison. It was as imposing by daylight as it had been at night surrounded by the mob, for it had been designed to instill fear in those who gazed upon it. The ponderous building was dark and squat like an ancient toad crouched in some dank place; the carved chains over the entrance and the dearth of windows instilled a sense of unease as the architect had intended. I had made my way to Newgate alone, as Dupin had advocated spending the day at the British Museum, combing through news-papers for information about Rhynwick Williams. He had little faith that Miss Porter's former husband would yield up any illu-minating information but I disagreed, for surely there was knowledge to be gleaned from someone who had been impris-oned with Rhynwick Williams.

The man who stood before me was the prison's turnkey. Mr. Turley was perhaps five and thirty years of age, very short, and appeared to greatly relish his food, as the black suit he wore fit him so tightly his breathing was inhibited. His broad-brimmed hat imbued him with a comical air rather than the gust of dignity he was aiming for, but he seemed kind and was eager to please. I had claimed I was writing a scholarly article about the prison for a learned Philadelphian journal and had offered to pay a gratuity for a tour and interview with Mr. Nicholson, who was indeed residing in Newgate as Miss Porter had claimed. Mr. Turley was under the misplaced notion that he would gain great renown in Philadelphia if he assisted me.

"We'll go to the men's yard first," he informed me as he led the way from the keeper's house at a nimble pace, absent-mindedly jangling the large set of keys he carried. "That is where the more respectable class of men is confined—debtors and the like."

"Is that where we will find Mr. Nicholson?"

"Indeed it is," Mr. Turley said, shaking his head. "If he were able to gamble away his very soul, he would do so."

"So I have heard."

We passed the turnkey's lodges and bedrooms, walked through a heavy oaken gate, then down a long, narrow maze of a stone passageway. As we walked, Mr. Turley regaled me with factual information about the prison until we reached the men's quarters, which was a large whitewashed room without decoration that housed two dozen inmates, who stared sullenly at us.

"This is where they take their meals," Mr. Turley said, indicating the table, "and where they sleep." He pointed at the floor and the row of mats that dangled on large hooks above it. "And that is where the prisoners normally meet with visitors." I peered through the iron grating he showed me and spied another grating about one yard away. "Nothing can be passed between the prisoner and his visitor—no tools for escape and no forbidden items."

"I assure you, I have no such implements upon my person," I told him with a smile.

"I wouldn't presume so, sir," he said solemnly. "But it has happened, indeed it has." He shook his head, remembering some dark event, then turned to gesture at the men before us. "And these are the prisoners."

"Thinking of moving in, sir?" an insolent-looking boy of about fourteen years piped up. "Me—I'd prefer Botany Bay to here. Or where you're from if they was still having us."

"Quiet, you. Stop your impertinence," Mr. Turley said without much feeling or authority.

There were three men who looked to be over the age of seventy, and I wondered which had been the friend of Rhynwick Williams. "May I interview Mr. Nicholson?" I reminded my guide.

"Nicholson—come here, please," Mr. Turley called out. "Mr. Poe here would like to speak with you. He is visiting from Philadelphia."

"Philadelphia, the Quaker city? That is quite a journey." A wizened man emerged from the group and tottered toward me. He had one good eye and one that was pearled white. His clothes had been very fashionable many years previously and gave him the air of a specter emerged from the past. "Robert Nicholson," he said, extending his hand. I shook it gently as the flesh was withered to the bone, the skin as papery as dried corn husks.

"You have the privilege of meeting Mr. Poe, a scholar who is writing an article for a learned journal," Mr. Turley informed the old man. "Mr. Nicholson is from Scotland, but Newgate has frequently been his home. He has left us many times, but never fails to return."

"Born in Inverness, made impecunious in London," Mr. Nicholson explained with a smile that revealed a paucity of teeth.

"Habitual debtor. Many have come to Mr. Nicholson's assistance, but he is unable to avoid the gaming table, despite losing much more often than he wins."

I found I could not judge the man an utter reprobate, for certainly my mother was saved from the poorhouse by kind friends, and I had accumulated considerable debt through gambling in my youth.

"I was told that you knew Rhynwick Williams, the man convicted as the Monster." I expected Nicholson to hem and haw, but he responded immediately.

"Of course, yes. Rhynwick Williams, sent to Newgate as the Monster. I attended the ball he held here. I remember it very well," the ancient man said. "Indeed I remember many things from my distant past more completely than what occurred just yesterday. Quite a night it was," he added.

"A ball, Mr. Nicholson? Where?" The turnkey frowned.

"In the yard," he said. "August 1790 and the weather was good. I had not been here long, nor had Rhynwick Williams."

"Please tell me more about this ball, Mr. Nicholson. Surely Newgate is not the usual location for such an event," I said.

Mr. Nicholson nodded. "To call it a *ball* is perhaps an exaggeration. It was a gathering of perhaps fifty people. Williams sent invitations to his relatives, friends from the flower factory— some lovely French ladies as I recall—other acquaintances who supported him during his trial. Some fellow prisoners such as myself attended also as we were, of course, already here. We had tea and light refreshments to begin and there was music for dancing—violins and a flute. Our host was quite an accomplished dancer. I believe he was once on the stage."

Such details made it difficult to doubt Mr. Nicholson's story. I nodded to encourage him.

"Later we had a cold supper and a goodly amount of wine. The other guests departed at nine o'clock as that was when the prison doors were locked."

I looked to Mr. Turley, who eventually grasped my silent question. "No visitors are allowed to speak with prisoners after nine, it is true, but a prisoner may not host a ball. Truly you must be misremembering, sir." Mr. Turley was discomfited by the notion and continued to shake his head gently in denial.

"Perhaps it was possible in 1790? Do you think it might have been possible then, Mr. Turley?"

"Well," he said. "I would not know for I was not there. Fifty years ago the rules may have been different. But certainly not now."

"It was quite an event," Mr. Nicholson said wistfully. "I do not think I have participated in as lively an occasion since."

"And you will not again," the turnkey said firmly, determined to nip any rebellious thoughts in the bud.

"What about me, sir?" the young rascal piped up. "My mother oft calls me a monster. Might I have a ball like that one did?"

"Certainly not," Mr. Turley said.

"It is my understanding that Rhynwick Williams persisted in claiming his innocence and petitioned for a retrial, which was granted in December 1790. He was found guilty again, but for the reduced charge of misdemeanor. Given your knowledge of the man, Mr. Nicholson, do you believe he was guilty or innocent?"

The old man laughed. "Rhynwick Williams certainly admired the ladies, but in truth he was rather afraid of the fairer sex. It is difficult to believe that he would have had the bravado to slash a woman's skirts, much less attack a host of women. Certainly he was frightened of his wife."

I felt a scurrying like a column of ants along my spine. "Wife? Rhynwick Williams had a wife?"

"Indeed, sir. He met her at the Monster's Ball as it was called. She was a prisoner also, although I do not know her crime— penury perhaps, but she had an unpleasant temper, so her crime might have had a more violent aspect to it."

"I was not aware that male and female prisoners might fraternize." My words were spoken in part to myself, but Mr. Turley took it upon himself to answer.

"It happens," he said, offended piety constricting his words. "With unfortunate consequences that add misery to misfortune."

Mr. Nicholson chuckled. "Certainly that was the situation for Rhynwick Williams. Destitute, imprisoned, with a newborn infant and a woman determined that he would support her and the child."

"A son born in Newgate?" The tingle along my spine grew stronger.

Mr. Nicholson nodded. "His brother the apothecary was most displeased—additional mouths for him to feed."

I immediately began to calculate what age Rhynwick Williams's son might now be. Rhynwick Williams was imprisoned from July 1790 to late 1796. If the child were born when he was incarcerated, his son would now be somewhere between forty-five and forty-nine years of age. But I needed proof of the son's existence, not simply an old man's memories.

"Do you remember the year of the child's birth?"

Old Mr. Nicholson thought for a moment, his good eye closed, his cloudy eye directed toward me. "I cannot remember

when he was born," he said, his words sinking my hopes. "But
he was christened in May 1795—when I was not long out of
Newgate and living with my sister. I recollect this as I was invited
to the christening."

"Where was he christened?" I demanded, excitement getting
the better of my manners.

The old man shrugged as if the answer were obvious. "St.
Sepulchre's Church."

"The infants of prisoners are all christened there, given the
church is just across the street," Mr. Turley added.

Of course it made sense, and I was anxious to visit the place
and try to find out more about Rhynwick Williams's mysterious son.

"Thank you, Mr. Nicholson. You have been exceedingly
helpful."

"I am glad of it. And dare I say I would be more glad if you
found it in your heart to advance me a small loan that might
assist me from my current situation." The old man gave me a
gap-toothed smile that flooded me with guilt, but as my hand
approached my pocket, Mr. Turley shook his head.

"Be happy that you have assisted a scholar, Mr. Nicholson.
Let that be your reward. It is the duty of your friends and
family to remedy your debts, not Mr. Poe." And Mr. Turley
whisked me away before I or the old man could say another
word. He led me down another dark corridor at a lively pace
until we came to an open quadrangle.

"This is where the condemned men may take exercise," he
informed me. "And where Mr. Nicholson claims the ball was
held." He shook his head again, clearly upset with the notion.

"Extraordinary," I said.

I was desperate to run to St. Sepulchre's to see if I could find
proof that Williams had a son, but I had no choice but to finish
the tour. We proceeded at pace through the yard and eventually

came to the press-room, a long murky chamber with but two small windows in the stone wall. A pair of men were slumped upon the floor in a posture of absolute dejection.

"Dead men," Mr. Turley said. "The condemned are brought here on the morning of their execution."

The prisoners must have heard this pronouncement, but neither acknowledged it. I remembered poor Mr. Courvoisier, how his spirit must have suffered sitting in this place before he dangled from the rope. My grandmother must also have feared such a fate, hence her treachery.

Mr. Turley led me through a maze of winding corridors, and I asked questions about the construction of the prison, its history and its most notorious inmates out of courtesy, but absorbed little of what he told me. My excitement regarding what I might discover at St. Sepulchre's Church made the blood tingle in my veins and my thoughts jitter as if influenced by a quantity of mint juleps. At last we reached the entrance to the prison, where I mumbled some promises about sending Mr. Turley a copy of my scholarly article and made a less than gracious exit.

* * *

The harsh sounds of Snow Hill dissipated as I stepped inside St. Sepulchre's Church. I paused to absorb the grandeur of its interior—two rows of Tuscan columns divided the space into three aisles and the edges of the groined ceilings were orna-mented with doves. An elaborate carved and gilded altar stood majestically beneath three windows and there was a magnificent organ. Gentle light filtered through small windows and the air dozed with quietude.

And yet, death connected St. Sepulchre's and Newgate. Before every execution, the bellman traversed the tunnel that led from the church to the prison and when he reached his destination, would toll his hand bell twelve times, exhorting the prisoners waiting for the noose to repent. But what of the babe, the child of a criminal imprisoned in Newgate, awaiting baptism?

I made my way through the church, doing my best not to disturb the prayerful huddled upon the pews as I searched for someone who might help me. There must have been something suspicious in my actions for as I turned to shift my attentions to another part of the church, I found myself face to face with a very tall, stern-faced elderly man with white hair and piercing blue eyes who wore the simple black cassock of a clergyman.

"Are you lost, sir?" he asked in a deep, hard voice. If it were he who recited the verse exhorting repentance to the condemned, they would go to the gallows with true fear in their hearts.

"I was searching for someone to assist me in finding a record of baptism. I was informed by Mr. Turley that it would be here."

He stared at me as if he had intuited my slight exaggeration regarding what Mr. Turley had said. "Why do you seek this record? Do you believe that the person has not truly been baptized or is a pretender to some other's identity?"

My excitement at having discovered that Rhynwick Williams might have a son had made me overlook the possibility that I might meet with resistance in gaining access to that vital piece of information: his son's name. How should I respond? If I hid the truth would he fathom my deception with his gimlet eye, and if I told the truth would he deny me if he happened to know the history of Rhynwick Williams and the Monster?

"I am looking for the record of an infant baptized in May of the year 1795. I am afraid I do not know the precise date. His father was Rhynwick Williams. He and the child's mother were both imprisoned in Newgate at the time of the child's birth. I am a relation of Miss Sarah Porter of Margate, who was attacked most fearfully by Rhynwick Williams. She is now being terrorized by some other demon she suspects to be the Monster's son. I am here to help Miss Porter by verifying whether Williams had a son and if so, what his name is."

The clergyman examined me as a taxidermist might study a dead bird. He grunted once, opened the door before me and stepped inside. The room held a desk and shelves filled with books. He advanced to the shelves and quickly found a large, leather-bound volume and sat down at the desk with it. I hovered in the doorway and without a glance or a word, he beckoned me in with a brusque wave. I sat in the chair in front of the desk and waited while he ran his finger down the pages as he read them.

"Christened in May 1795. Father, Rhynwick Williams?" he asked.

"Yes."

"Mother, Elizabeth Robins?"

"I believe so," I lied.

"Their son George Rhynwick Williams was christened here on the thirty-first of May 1795." He turned the volume round and indicated the entry.

"But Rhynwick Williams was still a prisoner then. He was not released until December 1795. Surely the date is incorrect."

"The date is correct," the clergyman said firmly. "Such situations occur more often than we like amongst the criminal classes imprisoned in Newgate."

"The child was named George Rhynwick Williams?"

"That is what I said." He closed the leather-bound volume.

"Many thanks, sir."

"I hope the information will aid Miss Porter."

"It will, I am certain."

He simply raised his heavy brows and said, "Good day, sir."

* * *

My mood was jubilant as the coach jounced through the narrow streets that led back to Brown's Genteel Inn. Rhynwick Williams had a son of five and forty years, an age that coincided with the man who posed as the scrivener, professor and the glowering man at my reading. Given Dupin's relentless pursuit of Valdemar, the man who had destroyed his family, I could not deny that George Williams might wish to harm me, even if I had nothing to do with my grandmother's false accusation of his father Rhynwick Williams. I also could not deny it was conceivable that Dr. Wallis was George Williams in disguise, but the horror of that possibility was leavened by the knowledge of my aggressor's true identity. It would be more difficult for George Williams to remain a ghost with uncanny powers.

When I entered Brown's Genteel Inn, I was looking forward to discussing what I had discovered with Dupin, but all disappeared from my mind when the desk clerk delivered over a small packet addressed to me in Muddy's hand. At last! News from home; words from those I loved. I was overjoyed at this unexpected treasure and returned to my chambers in haste, where I immediately tore open the packet. Eight letters spilled onto the onyx table, and I settled into the armchair to read of every small thing my darling wife had spent her time on. After a deeply pleasant interlude, I read the letter from Muddy and all my joy turned to ash.

Philadelphia, 10 June 1840

My dearest Eddy,

Virginia has not been well. When she took to her bed the evening after you left, I presumed her heartsick with your absence, but she was unable to keep down anything but broth for three days and remains poorly. She has begged me to tell you nothing of her illness, but I would not like to deceive you. If you return to us sooner rather than later, it is bound to have a restorative effect upon our girl.

  With greatest affection,

  Muddy

More than a month for news to cross the Atlantic! How helpless I felt, which was further compounded by the fact that it would take six weeks to sail to Philadelphia. What would I discover when I arrived there in the closing days of August?

I immediately set about organizing my return and enlisted the aid of the dour night desk clerk, who showed surprising sympathy for my predicament. He promised to arrange the earliest passage he could and was true to his word. Several hours later I had a ticket to sail on the *Grampus* from London to New York on the evening of July the twenty-first. An anxious heart drove me to bed early, where I re-read Sissy's letters, hoping they would sweeten my dreams. When I extinguished the light and settled into the darkness, it occurred to me how much the letter sent but never received might alter a person's life.

Broad Street Theatre, Charleston
16 March 1798

My dearest Daughter,

I am writing this on the eleventh anniversary of your birth, a day that has always been so dear to me. Enclosed here is a lock of my hair to help you remember me, for I fear our time together might not be as long as I would wish. If you were not of such tender years, I would endeavour to explain what I must leave to you in written form.

First, know that you are truly gifted as an actress—such an ability to charm an audience! I have found some success upon the stage, but you will surpass me if you pursue the same calling. If so, I hope your talent will serve you well and the theatrical life will continue to be to your liking, for it is not an easy one.

And now I must broach less pleasant subjects. The enclosed key is for a box that will be released to you along with this letter upon your sixteenth birthday should I die before that happy occasion. Letters are concealed inside the box that were written during a terrible time in our lives in England and explain the demise of your father. Should I too die unexpectedly, they will surely reveal who is responsible.

This Pandora's box has held other letters I should have committed to the fire in England, but until now I could not do it as they were all that remained of my life with your father. Nostalgia is a dangerous emotion and too often I have read those letters to remind myself what a strange and unexpected journey my life has been. If fate intervenes and the letters—one might call them love letters—are still within the box, I beg you to destroy them unopened. It pains me to imagine that anything might make you lose your affection for me. Being the good daughter that you are, I know you will respect this wish.

Never doubt my love for you, dear Eliza. If I unwillingly leave you, your stepfather will provide for you—as will your talent—but if tragedy befalls your stepfather, Mr. Usher and Mrs. Snowden have given me their word that they will take you under their wing.

Let me end this missive on a more cheerful note. I hope every birthday you celebrate will be as delightful as today. I am certain, my dear daughter, that you will more than equal my successes and will avoid my many mistakes. Always know that I cherish you and that every hard choice I have been forced to make was always with a view to best serving the two of us so that we might remain together.

I remain affectionately,

Your Mother

The coach swerved and jostled along at great speed, bouncing through every hole and catapulting off each rise, which had us both clinging grimly to the seat and warding off the ceiling. We had set off infernally early to a location Dupin would not reveal, and while I had been cross about leaving Brown's without coffee, I was now truly awake without it.

After Dupin banged on the coach ceiling for the third time, the vehicle's pace slowed enough for me to finish telling him what I had learned during my trip to Newgate Prison.

"His name is George Rhynwick Williams and he is forty-five years of age—surely he must be my tormentor."

Dupin took a moment to compose himself, such was his astonishment. "I am surprised that I did not discover anything of the son's existence in the newspapers, given the Monster's notoriety." He shook his head in disbelief.

"But now that we know the identity of my aggressor, I am at a loss as to what I should do."

"*Nemo me impune lacessit*—let us not forget Williams's warning: 'No one insults me with impunity.' If that is the motto of one's adversary, then it is prudent to assume he also subscribes to the dictum: 'If you insult my family, you insult me.'"

Dupin's presupposition filled me with revulsion, but it seemed likely that he was correct.

"Knowledge always gives some advantage, Poe. George Williams can no longer play the malevolent ghost. He has made you suffer and, as we discussed before, he will take his final revenge when he chooses to reveal himself, for surely he wishes you to beg for mercy."

"And you know this because it is what you would wish from Valdemar?"

"Not at all. I did not wish to make him a supplicant. I want the justice of his death."

Dupin's cold words hit me hard. "But I am innocent! I am not responsible for my grandparents' crimes."

"Williams sees things differently, I assure you. Your grandmother gave a performance at Rhynwick Williams's trial that ensured he was sent to prison in her stead. No son would forgive that. There is bad blood between your families and that presents you with two choices. Now that you know who your aggressor is, you could take all that we have fathomed to the police and hope that they believe you. Perhaps they will arrest George Williams and Mrs. Fontaine for locking you in the cellar, poisoning you with belladonna and pushing you into the sea. Of course we do not have conclusive proof of any of these events, beyond my corroboration of your claims. And if the police do believe your accusations, the story of your grandparents' crimes will be revealed to the world."

My joy at discovering the identity of my aggressor was now fully tarnished as I felt the truth of Dupin's words. "And what is my other choice?"

"Kill George Williams before he destroys you," Dupin replied.

"Murder? You are advocating that I murder the son of the man whose life my grandmother helped ruin?"

Dupin shrugged with a nonchalance that horrified me. "It is

clear that Williams will not rest until you are in your grave. One cannot truly consider it murder when you are defending your own life. Think about your wife and her mother, for they will not be safe so long as Williams pursues you." Dupin paused to let me absorb his words, then added, "Of course your situation is not unlike that of your grandmother."

I could not deny that, but equally I could not easily take a man's life.

"*Amicis semper fidelis*, Poe. The faithful friend stands at your back, hand on the hilt of his sword. George Williams is your enemy and therefore mine—I will not hesitate to destroy him, fear not."

Perhaps I should have felt more gratified at Dupin's pledge, but his talk of calculated murder was too cold, too near to madness. "Thank you," I said carefully. "Let us hope that neither of us need face a confrontation with Williams, for I am sailing to Philadelphia tomorrow."

"Truly?" Dupin asked with surprise.

"I received a letter from my mother-in-law informing me that Sissy has been ill. I arranged passage as soon as I found out. I should have told you last night."

Dupin waved away my apology. "I only wish that I might have been of assistance. As your wife was in good health when you left Philadelphia, it is likely that she has fully recovered, but of course it is your duty to return immediately."

"It is more than duty, there is simply no other fathomable course of action, and I can only pray that her health has indeed improved. I could not forgive myself if that proves not to be the case."

"It is important that you put all thoughts of your wife's health to one side until you are by her side or you will undermine your own constitution," Dupin advised.

"I will do my best. It is horribly difficult, but I am aware of the truth in your words."

We sat in contemplative silence until the coach slowed and drew to a halt on Fleet Street.

"I failed to find anything useful about Rhynwick Williams at the British Museum yesterday," Dupin said. "But I did discover something I believe you will find of interest." He opened the coach door and got out. I followed and found that we were outside a neo-Gothic church. "St. Dunstan-in-the-West," Dupin announced. "It was rebuilt in 1831, but there has been a church on this site for eight hundred years. You will find this information relevant," he added. Rather than leading us into the church itself, Dupin made his way to the churchyard. He walked methodically and without hesitation through the burial ground until we reached the northeast corner of the cemetery, where the stones were most disfigured by time and nature. He stopped in front of a small, plain gravestone, and I was dumbstruck by its inscription.

HENRY ARNOLD
MUSICIAN, BELOVED HUSBAND AND FATHER.
BORN 15 AUGUST 1760.
LEFT THIS WORLD 25 JULY 1790.

"Proof that Elizabeth Arnold used the funds provided by her father to give her husband a decent burial—if she did indeed receive the funds promised in the letter dated fifth of August 1790 from Mrs. William Smith."

I managed a nod, but my words stuttered into dry air—truly I had not expected to feel grief cutting into me so harshly. Dupin quietly moved several paces away and left me alone in contemplation. I read the simple words again and again, a life summed up with terrible brevity. It was true that my grandmother had done the honorable thing and given her husband a decent burial, but was he not worthy of a longer epitaph?

Perhaps a verse and a cherub or two? I tried to think of a prayer
or appropriate poem, but my mind was dulled by sadness. His
death had been wretched and here he was alone without family
or friends to visit his grave. No one deserved to be remembered—or perhaps forgotten—in such a way. As I stood above
the bones of my grandfather, I wept as though I had known
him, for whatever he had done and however he had died, it was
certain that my mother had dearly loved him.

The shrieks of a magpie broke my solitary contemplation. I
watched as it pattered along a seraph's shoulder and hopped
onto the heavenly creature's flared white wing. The bird rasped
again. *One for sorrow.*

"Most appropriate," Dupin said softly, voicing my thoughts.
He turned his gaze from the bird back to me. "Your grandmother was quite a remarkable woman. She managed to leave
her husband with a memorial, despite her precarious financial
position and opposition from her father and his wife. Indeed,
it is clear from her letters if not her final actions that she cared
deeply for him. Her affection may have been embroidered
with the darkest of emotions, but it cannot be denied that she
loved him."

I looked to Dupin with surprise, but his eyes were focused
on the cavalier magpie as it preened its own feathers while
roosted upon the mighty marble wing.

"Do not forget that Truth," Dupin said, waving his hand at
the glistening angel before us, "can be manipulated through
context. Your nemesis—George Rhynwick Williams—has
delivered the letters he has wished you to see. The tale he has
constructed for you is designed to cause you pain. Do not give
him that satisfaction," he said.

"Thank you, Dupin. Most truly."

* * *

The coach ride back to Brown's Genteel Inn was subdued, with each of us lost in contemplation. Neither Dupin nor I had truly concluded our personal missions satisfactorily, but it was not possible to remedy that on this journey. It was noon when we entered Brown's.

"I am going to organize my things for the journey tomorrow, but would you care to join me somewhere for an early supper?"

"Perhaps we might try Rules in Covent Garden for supper at six o'clock?" Dupin suggested.

"Very good."

As we made our way toward the stairs, the desk clerk called out, "A message for you, Mr. Poe."

My heart near stopped with fear that dreadful news had crossed the Atlantic. I rushed over to the desk and he handed me a letter sealed with black wax. I snatched it from his hands and collapsed into a chair in the foyer, where I immediately ripped the letter open. My fear was slightly dulled when I recognized the elegant hand of the scrivener—of George Rhynwick Williams. Dupin hovered nearby as I read the note.

The Assignation
Five o'clock, 20 July 1840,
The catacombs beneath the Anglican Chapel,
All Souls Cemetery, Kensal Green.

There was no signature, but who else could it be but my nemesis? I handed the note to Dupin.

"Williams is aware you are leaving," Dupin said. "You would be wise to ignore his invitation."

"You know I cannot do that."

"Make a counter-offer then. Suggest a meeting place that is less isolated and, frankly, less macabre."

"How? Williams knows where to find me, but the reverse is not true and I set sail tomorrow."

"Not if you are murdered."

"You confuse me, Dupin. Earlier you urged me to take action against Williams as you declared he would not rest until I was in my grave. Now you wish me to flee from him."

Dupin frowned. "If you meet with Williams in the catacombs, he will have all the advantage, for surely he has well-acquainted himself with the location."

"If we stand together, Williams will find it difficult to murder me. And I would hope to reason with him, to apologize for the actions of my grandparents. I will make it clear that I do not condone what they did and that until the letters arrived, I was completely unaware of what had occurred. Surely that will be enough reparation for him—we are not Montagues and Capulets."

"I believe Philadelphia's William Penn said, 'Knowledge is the treasure of a wise man.' If you will not be dissuaded from this folly, then we must go fully prepared. I will hasten to the British Museum and search for a plan of the catacombs. I suggest that you purchase supplies: two lanterns, candles and, if possible, a weapon for yourself. We should set off by three o'clock so we might arrive at the catacombs before your nemesis and gain some advantage."

"Let us prove ourselves to be wise men," I agreed. "And let us vanquish George Williams's enmity with reason if we are able."

Dupin raised up his walking stick and gazed into the ruby eyes of the golden cobra. "We might try," he said.

* * *

At three o'clock, we were in a coach traveling west to Kensal Green as planned. Dupin unfurled a scroll of paper, which revealed an intricate plan of the catacombs.

"Very meticulous work, as always."

"Accuracy is important when one's survival might depend upon navigating a strange location. This shows the relationship of the chapel and colonnades to the catacombs beneath them, which cover nearly an acre of ground. As you can see, Williams will have numerous places to conceal himself," Dupin said. "There are two entrances—a flight of stairs from the west of this terrace and a staircase here that descends from the interior of the chapel into the catacombs." He indicated each with his index finger. "And see here—from the central area a main passageway runs north to south and another runs east to west. The vaults radiate out in four directions from these. There is said to be space for a thousand coffins, which are to be laid on stone racks in numbered loculi. The numbering is not noted on the plan, but might prove useful when we are inside. Ventilation shafts were to be constructed to allow light into the catacombs, but we must be prepared for full darkness." He nodded at the lanterns I had bought.

"Presumably Williams will have his own copy of the plans and has explored the catacombs previously."

"Indeed," Dupin said. "And that gives him strong advantage."

"But we are two, which must be in our favor."

"We should not presume that Williams will come alone. While it is unlikely Mrs. Fontaine will participate in this meeting, they certainly had another accomplice at the Bayham Street house—in addition to the serving girl, of course."

I recalled the pebbles thrown at us—purportedly by the spirits—when Mrs. Fontaine, the professor and serving girl were all standing next to me. Dupin was correct. Williams had another accomplice, perhaps two. This knowledge should have made me anxious, but instead a strange exhilaration swept over me. Soon the final piece of the puzzle would be revealed by George Rhynwick Williams, and I hoped the confrontation between us

might result in a kind of truce. But if Williams were determined to murder me, Dupin and I would put an end to his
mission. And soon, very soon, I would be on my way home,
the past truly put behind me, for it would most certainly never
be visited upon my wife.

The coach left us just near the gate to All Soul's Cemetery
an hour before our assignation. I was immediately struck by
the deceptive allure of the place. A pleasant gloaming was
created by the avenues of silver firs, flowering shrubs and
herbaceous plants—it would be an enchanting location for a
picnic or afternoon perambulation if one did not know it was
a refuge for the Dead. As we made our way toward the catacombs, we moved deeper into a netherworld inhabited by hosts
of angels mingling with phoenixes and butterflies, all carved
from marble, and imposing mausoleums decorated with
symbols borrowed from ancient cultures: pyramids, lotus-
flower reliefs, Egyptianizing heads, obelisks. Vaults were
adorned with friezes of wreaths or garlands, eternal flames and
curling snakes that held their own tails in their mouths—promises of immortality, eternity, Death vanquished. We moved in
silence along the pathway between elegant and overwrought
tombs. I knew that the location was chosen to unsettle me, but
that did not ease the sense of creeping doom. From his expression, Dupin felt it too. When an imposing building came into
view, he murmured: "The Anglican Chapel."

It was a stately construction that gleamed white against the
backdrop of green vegetation. Four colossal Doric pillars
composed the chapel's portico, which faced the Central Avenue.
Double covered colonnades stretched on either side of it and it
was paved with stone flags and granite setts. The overall effect
was one of grandeur and judgment.

"The entrance to the necropolis," Dupin said, scanning the
area around us carefully. "The chapel doors remain open, but

there is no attendant in sight. It is likely that Williams paid him to go home for the evening. I had hoped we would enter the catacombs before him, but we cannot rely on that hope."

"Surely if he has made himself well-acquainted with the catacombs before today, there is little need for him to arrive much before the time he appointed."

"Perhaps," Dupin said. "But caution must rule us. Let us find an advantageous place to position ourselves." He gazed intently at me. "It is not too late to abandon this madness."

"It is," I said firmly. And it was. I felt like a soldier marching into battle when the enemy had the upper hand, but duty and belief denied retreat.

We mounted the stairs and entered the chapel, which had a beautifully painted ceiling and a stained glass window that lifted the spirit while the bier in the center of the room had the opposite effect. Dupin walked to a door on the left side of the chapel, opened it and peered in. "The catacombs' entrance," he said in a low voice. "Do you recall from the map the general layout below?"

"I believe so."

"Let us wait to light the lanterns until we are away from the staircase. That way if Williams is now inside, he cannot know if it is us or some other come to visit the dead. And descend carefully as the stairs are narrow and winding."

I nodded. We stepped inside, and I pulled the door closed behind me. This left the stairway very dark, concealing us but also anyone who might lurk below in shadow. The temperature dropped as we descended cautiously and the smell of damp earth with a hint of decay made me feel faint with revulsion. It was as if I were back in the cellar, with the rats and the bones of the creature lying in the pit. Perhaps there was more to Dupin's suggestion of portents than I had cared to realize. When we reached the bottom, Dupin moved forward and I quickly followed lest I lose him. I could see nothing in the inky blackness and heard little but the faint rustle of Dupin's clothing. I felt my way along the damp walls until I came to a gap and then another and yet another—entrances to vaults, I presumed. At the fourth entrance, I heard a scratching sound and saw a very faint light.

"In here." Dupin's voice. I turned inside. "There should be light coming from the portals, but nothing. It was an error not to check them from outside."

"Should we return to the surface?"

"Too late," Dupin said. "We would forfeit any advantage we might have gained. We need to explore the catacombs undetected by Williams so I may situate myself in a place to easily come to your aid when you meet him—if, of course, he shows himself."

It had not occurred to me that Williams might not meet me face to face, but Dupin was correct—my presumption was naive. What criminal would forfeit the upper hand in such a situation?

"And check the loculi numbers should you need to orient yourself." He lifted his lantern and spilled light onto an arched vault, which was fronted with a cast-iron grill. Coffins rested on the shelves inside and I reeled at the sight of them. Behind me was another arched vault with twelve loculi, some sealed with individual iron grills and some left open without regard for the potential looters that plagued other burial grounds. They were numbered as Dupin had said. A flash of red in the lamplight made my heart still—someone crouching in the darkness! Then I saw it was but a scarlet cloth atop a coffin.

"Let us advance north," Dupin said. "Avoid the main passageway so it is more difficult to track us. Light your lantern only if necessary. That way Williams may mistake me for you." The light from Dupin's lantern glimmered on the catacomb walls, but had little effect on the murky black that surrounded us, which made it difficult to see the shape of the interior. We wove our way through narrow vault passageways, but halted as a staccato rush of noise assaulted us. Creeping forward we were met with a furious shadow flickering in the light that spilled through the bars of the western gate.

"A bird," Dupin whispered and my captured breath hissed out from my throat. "Let us make our way forward and then head east and circle back to the stairwell," he instructed.

He crept on but I was mesmerized by the terrified creature that fluttered against the bars again and again. To release it would put me in plain view; I hoped it would not succumb to its own fear before the gates were opened in the morning.

"Poe." Dupin's voice trickled back to me, and I followed the soft glow of his lantern. We zigzagged from vault to vault to obscure our trail and crossed the northern passageway into the northeast quadrant of the catacombs. As I followed Dupin, the light from his lantern bobbing like a ghostly creature, the content of the loculi, were illumined in short bursts. Some coffins were decorated with brass stud-work patterns; others were covered with gold-embroidered cloths that glinted in the candlelight or wreaths of immortelles that resembled fresh blooms in the shadow. Some coffins were very plain, and some were tiny and on the highest shelf, the final resting place of a child or infant—the air was thick with melancholy there. Some loculi were sealed up with mortar to prevent unwanted entry to the tomb or perhaps exit from it. Dupin searched for any sign that Williams had preceded us, illuminating first the left and then the right—a number of the vaults were quite empty and could provide ample space for a person to conceal himself.

Just as we began to cross the eastern pathway near the far edge of the catacombs, an unearthly wind blew through them and Dupin's lamp was extinguished. Instinctively I crouched to the ground, hoping to avoid a blow to the head that might incapacitate me.

"Quickly," Dupin whispered.

We scuttled like subterranean creatures along the floor. The rustle of clothing and scratch of shoe leather on stone reverberated through the dank air. I tried to quell the noise of my breathing until dizziness threatened to conquer. We entered another vault where Dupin paused. The harsh scratch of a Lucifer match, the stench of sulfur, then a glimmer of light. Dupin cautiously held his lantern aloft as we pressed our backs against the wall and surveyed the vault. Nothing. And then there was a faint sound: a careful footfall upon the catacomb floor or perhaps some other creature—rat or mouse or injured bird—pattering along the ground, but the location was difficult to ascertain. Moments later, there was another sound, the clang of metal upon metal, and a deep voice with a French inflection echoed through the gloom.

"You believe that your forebears were innocents sent to the guillotine, Chevalier Dupin? That they were deceived by me?"

The reverberating question took me by surprise and increased my sense of wariness. I had of course expected to hear the voice of George Williams, but instead we were issued with a challenge from someone masquerading as Dupin's nemesis. The deception was utterly plain—why speak in English when both Valdemar and Dupin were French? The note had been sent to me rather than Dupin and it was preposterous to think that Valdemar was in league with George Williams.

"It is time to face their misdeeds—to learn what the Dupin family did to earn the eternal enmity of the Valdemar family."

Before I could say a word, Dupin ran back from whence we had come, lantern in hand, abandoning me to the treacherous darkness.

With shaking hands I tried to strike a Lucifer match, but could not conquer the darkness. Fear accelerated my thoughts. Surely this was a ploy concocted by Williams to separate us and, astonishingly, he had succeeded—Dupin's obsession had endangered both our lives. At last a match caught and I touched it to the candle wick. The flame took hold and wavered in the hostile air. I did not know whether to follow Dupin or wait where I was and hope that I might find a way to rescue both of us.

It was then that I heard footsteps on the wooden stairs, or so it seemed. I crept along the corridor, making my way toward the center of the catacombs, looking for a shadow that might indicate Williams's presence or that of an accomplice. Every sound was amplified ten-fold and seemed to be coming from several directions at once. I could not fathom if this was because of the structure of the catacombs or my quivering nerves. When I reached the end of a vault that provided a view of the staircase, I peered out, searching for Williams's lamplight, but there were only shadows before me. I listened for any sound that might reveal his location—or that of Dupin and the man who played at being Valdemar. As I waited, each muffled noise set me on edge until the tension became unbearable, and before I could stop myself, my thoughts became words.

"Williams, are you there? Williams?"

There was a scrabbling sound behind me, and I whirled to face it. Candlelight shimmered across the walls, but I saw no one, heard no one. I moved east, away from the catacomb door, a peculiar desperation arising within me. "Or perhaps it is Monsieur Valdemar?"

A voice somewhere to my left, in another vault, stilled my feet. "You were correct the first time, Mr. Poe. Well done. It took you some time, but you arrived at the truth. Monsieur Valdemar is not here. Your friend Dupin should take caution. It is often what we cannot see that poses the greatest threat to us."

That thought was indeed foremost in my mind, for I still could not fathom where my nemesis was situated.

"Show yourself, Williams. Why play the coward?"

His poisonous laugh echoed in the darkness, circled me, taunted me. "I am not the player, Mr. Poe—although it has been said that all men and women are merely that. Truly it was the Arnolds who played many parts."

"As have you during our brief acquaintance—a scrivener and ballad seller, a professor at the séance, a literary critic at my reading and now Valdemar. Why the disguises, why the riddles? What is it you want, Mr. Williams? An apology for the actions of my forebears? If so, I gladly grant you that, but surely you cannot blame me for your father's troubles."

The air went thick and dead with silence. Ghostly fingers slid over my skin—I could *feel* my enemy's presence but could neither see nor hear him. I inched my way to the next vault, but found only caskets and empty loculi.

"I was not yet born when he was incarcerated," I said to the darkness, my voice quivering like a candle flame.

A serpent-tongued breeze licked the back of my neck as Williams's voice slithered into my ear: "Fine words from a man whose grandmother relied on disguise and whose lies sent an innocent man to Newgate in her stead."

I whirled to grab onto him, but he was not there. I must have gasped my frustration as his laugh—or the Devil's—echoed from another vault.

"If what you say is true, I am certain she regretted her action."

"I fear I know much more of that than you do, Mr. Poe, and your presumption has no basis in truth."

"How can you know that? Surely you never met my grandmother and cannot know what she thought," I said desperately.

"Charleston. The twentieth of July 1798. Precisely forty-two years ago—quite uncanny, one might say. Or fated."

My heart stilled. Charleston—where my grandmother last performed. Where she was last seen and where she purportedly died. "Explain yourself, Williams."

"The guilty die nightly in their beds, wringing the hands of ghostly confessors, on account of sins they dare not reveal." Williams's voice came from behind me and I whirled, flinging lantern light in a circle around me, but there was no one there. I turned again, backing my way down the vault's corridor, swaying my lantern left and right, its weak beam barely disturbing the shadows that pressed in upon me. Despite the cool air, perspiration trickled down my back. Williams seemed everywhere and nowhere at once.

"I am sorry for how your father and your family suffered, but tormenting me will not erase the past. I—"

But his voice cut through mine. "You must ask yourself, Mr. Poe, how might we escape the phantom that seeks retribution when four walls cannot confine it and time does not defeat it?"

The horror of Williams's curse was eclipsed when the lantern-light revealed something so hideous and peculiar my heart stilled—an eye glinted back at me from the catacomb floor. A human eye! I could not resist its hypnotic gaze. It drew me nearer, ever nearer, and just as I crouched down to stretch out my fingers to grasp that terrible orb, there came a rushing and a mighty clang as metal crashed into stone just above my head. I scrabbled along the clammy floor, hoping to escape a second thrash of blade, but like a winged fury it followed me with a terrible hiss. I rolled as the blade touched my back and ripped through my jacket, piercing my flesh with ice and then fire. A yowl reverberated against the stone walls as a wave of darkness rushed in, drowning me with eternal night.

* * *

Fetid vapors crept over me and a thick dampness rose up from the stone floor. When I eased my eyes open, a pale light glowed before my eyes and I smelled blood.

"Poe?" A voice, faint. The touch of fingers upon my shoulder. I struggled to sit up.

"Williams . . ."

"It is Dupin."

My mind was fogged and my right hand was clenched. When I opened it, that eye so gruesomely cut from its socket stared back at me. I gasped in terror and then saw that it was the eye that had decorated Williams's waistcoat at the séance, the replica of Mrs. Fontaine's enchanting violet eyes—and somehow it seemed appropriate that it had rescued me from certain death. I slipped it into my own waistcoat pocket.

"Williams had a blade—a sword or knife. He tried to murder me, but I believe it is a minor wound."

"Let me see," Dupin said in a low voice as he raised his lantern. I turned, revealing where Williams had tried to cut me. "You were fortunate," he said. "The blade cut through your coat, but merely scratched the flesh." I turned back around. Dupin's voice was as grim as his countenance. "I am sorry. So terribly sorry. I gave chase to Valdemar, but he seemed to be everywhere at once. When I heard your shout, I ran this way and saw Williams near your prone body. I drew my sword, but Williams knocked the lantern from my grip. I could hear his breath and struck, but while my blade found flesh, I could not know if the wound were mortal. He retaliated, swinging wildly with his fists so that I lost my footing and hit my head on the edge of a loculus. And then I lost him." He lifted the lantern and peered into the shadows.

"Do you fear he is waiting to attack again?" I whispered.

"He may have taken the opportunity to escape, but we cannot discount the possibility that he is still here."

"Then we must leave this place quickly." I relit my lantern from Dupin's candle and struggled up to my feet. We made our way cautiously toward the staircase—throwing lamplight into all the shadows. I preceded Dupin up the stairs and when we reached the top, I pushed the door, but it would not open. I tried again, rattling at the handle, but it was tightly shut.

"Let us push together," Dupin said. A moan of pain escaped him as we heaved against the door, which remained stubbornly closed. "He has sealed it shut. We must try the west gate and hope that it is not locked."

We made our way down the stairway, Dupin in obvious pain, his step faltering. Every sound that met my ears filled me with dread, knowing that Williams might be lurking in the shadows, waiting for his opportunity to vanquish me. But we made it to the gate safely, and when I saw daylight falling through the bars, my spirits were lifted until I noticed the bird upon the ground—dead. This filled me with unspeakable horror. I shook the gate, knowing before I touched the iron bars that it was securely locked.

"We should wait until darkness to light the second tapers," Dupin said, "and find a way to conceal ourselves in the loculi should he return."

Nausea swept over me: lie amongst bones and corpses, the unquiet ghosts and mournful specters? "I cannot do that. I would rather sit here and risk Williams's blade again. I cannot hide amongst the Dead for truly it will drive me mad." As if prompted by my words, my candle sputtered into a heap of wax.

Dupin nodded and closed his eyes in pain or perhaps contemplation. Eventually he spoke again. "I have a thought." He made his way back toward the stairway, with me trailing directly behind him, wary of every hint of movement. He stopped in front of two metal poles that connected floor to ceiling, placed his lantern on the floor and began to wind a handle attached to one of the poles, but why was a mystery to me. "This is a catafalque, although I cannot be certain it is operational."

"I do not understand."

Dupin paused to press his fingers to his head, then breathed in deeply and worked at winding the lever again. "Look up, Poe."

In the lamplight I saw a dark shape emerging from the ceiling—a shape the size of a coffin. "The bier from above?"

"Yes." The catafalque descended slowly, and Dupin paused again, his breathing labored.

"Will we be able to climb the pole up through the floor?"

"No," Dupin said. He held up his lantern. "I believe iron plates close to conceal the bier's descent into the catacomb."

"Then why? What have we to gain?"

"Observe the catafalque." Dupin turned the handle in the other direction and when I held the lantern aloft, I saw that the bier was rising up toward the ceiling again.

"We will escape on top of it?"

"We can hope."

I took over the labor of winding the handle and the mechanism creaked like some ancient machine until at last it rested at the bottom. The bier was wide enough to hold a casket and a single person.

"Clearly we may only ascend one at a time, with one operating the catafalque," Dupin said.

"You must ascend first," I said. "You are wounded." But as the words left my lips, I felt subterranea closing in—the damp walls and earth, the darkness, creatures that fed on flesh, Death itself. Panic seized me as Dupin climbed onto the bier—how like a corpse he looked! I filled my lungs with air and puffed it out, then did so again, and again, until I heard nothing but the whistling of my own breath. I took the catafalque handle in my palms and began to turn it, using the rhythm of my breathing to winch the bier up bit by bit. And as I did, I could hear my pocket watch—*tick, tick, tick*—each second percussing more loudly than the previous one until its beating was as nervous as the uneven patter of my heart. My hands were slick with moisture born from fear and as the bier stuttered its way upward, each inch hard won, I was increasingly anxious that the catafalque would plunge back down to the catacomb floor. Beads of sweat slithered down my back; each rustle and scratch behind me made my skin prickle and heart stutter, anticipating the whistle of blade through air. My arms began to ache with the effort and my palms to hurt as blisters formed upon them. The catafalque creaked as metal scratched against metal, setting my teeth on edge, and each passing second was agony. I tried to turn the handle faster to speed the bier to the catacomb ceiling and my left hand slipped. For a terrible moment, I feared all was lost, that the catafalque would come crashing down and Dupin would be flung to the unforgiving stone floor, but I secured it with my elbow and re-gripped the handle. Fear gave me strength, and I turned that handle like a madman, putting all my weight into it, each painful gasp echoing in the catacombs until at last the catafalque reached the top. I prayed that the mechanical doors to the chapel would open.

The bier vanished, as if by magic, and I felt a moment of relief. And then an unearthly squealing noise cut me to the core. My fears coalesced into chiaroscuro visions of Williams piercing Dupin's chest with a blade, of Dupin falling to the chapel floor, bleeding, dying. But a glimmer pierced the black— the door was opening!

"Poe, quickly!"

I ran toward Dupin's voice as if the Devil himself were after me and leapt through the puddles of light on the stairs until I reached the upper floor. When I emerged into the chapel, which glowed with the last of evening's glorious pink and golden light, my relief curdled. There on the floor, in a cloud of blood, was the genial desk clerk, the man I had exchanged pleasantries with most every day since I had arrived in London. There he was, eyes wide open, face contorted with shock and pain.

"George Rhynwick Williams," Dupin said softly. "It is over, Poe. Your nemesis is dead."

* * *

The mysterious scent of Dupin's special unguent brought me round from my stupor. He applied some under his own nose and breathed in deeply, after which he looked considerably revived.

"How? How can it be him? And . . . and this?" I gestured at the blood.

"It is surprising. I pierced him with my blade, but as I was in full darkness, I did not presume to wound him mortally."

I could not take my eyes away from the desk clerk, from *George Williams*. I should have felt relieved that my nemesis, that man who wished to kill me, was dead himself, but oddly I felt cheated. I had wanted to reason with him, to make him understand that his desire to murder me was unmerited, and now I was denied that.

"Poe, it is better this way. You are wrong to think words would have stopped him from seeking his revenge. I *know.*" He gripped my arms and shook me gently. "You must believe me. Now come, let us make our way back to Dover Street."

I nodded, but the sight of Williams on the ground brought another wave of nausea upon me. "Will we simply leave him here?"

Dupin shrugged. "What other option do you see?"

Truly there was none, but it seemed callous—*wrong*. I wondered if I would feel the same if Williams's face had a more hardened, vicious aspect. "We might inform the gatekeeper," I finally said.

"Perhaps, but the gatekeeper would be obliged to summon the police, who are unlikely to let you set sail until they fully investigate the matter," Dupin reasoned. "You must remember that the man attempted to murder you. Do not feel you are obliged to do the honorable thing. In this instance, it would be foolish."

I rose to my feet and followed Dupin out of the chapel. The last of the day's light was seeping away, rendering the sky cerulean and the figures that guarded the memorials luminous. As we crept past them, I felt that every angel, every cherub, glared at us with righteous fury for leaving a dead man awash in blood on the chapel floor and telling no one of his murder.

LONDON, TUESDAY, 21 JULY 1840

The relentless thrumming of rain continued all night and the sea was turbulent. Thunder cracked and the mast was hit by a jagged sword of fire that sent blue flames up and down its length. With an intolerable bang, the mast was split in two and the top half fell slowly toward the sea, sails flapping like gigantic wings around it. A huge wave leapt up in response and flooded across the deck where I stood, frozen with terror, and then, I know not how, I was tangled up in the sails and roiling sea water, and I felt hands—dead hands—upon me, pulling me through dark water, the ghost of a sailor abandoned to the waves somewhere far away from the sight of land. I thrashed and fought, but the breath oozed from my lungs as the water filled them and darkness took hold of me.

I awoke in my bed full of relief, only to discover the furniture a-glow with phosphorescence from the sea and water lapping all around me, rising ever higher with great speed, my bed a sinking boat. The sound of splashing footsteps circled around me, but I saw no one.

"Help!" I cried out. "Help me!"

"No one will help you," a voice whispered, "for no one will

believe you." And with those words, the ghostly sailor pushed my head under the water and held it there, his decaying light fizzing around me like a trapped bluebottle.

* * *

How many hours later?

I resurfaced to light trickling over my face and something scrabbling at the door. More asleep than awake, I leapt from my bed and, wearing my nightshirt like an avenging angel's tunic, flung open the door. Dupin recoiled—as did I—for it seemed that my double was before me, the horror in my own eyes reflected in his. We stood in absolute silence for I know not how long until a girl delivering breakfast arrived and stared at us both with unease.

"We agreed to meet at eight o'clock," Dupin said hesitantly.

"Yes. Of course. I fear I have overslept. Please, come in. I shan't be long."

A short time later I returned to Dupin and greedily drank down the coffee he poured for me.

"You must be gratified that you were able to conclude your mystery before returning home," he said.

"Indeed. Without your assistance, that would not have been possible. I am most grateful, Dupin, and apologize if I seem distracted. I am still bewildered by the identity of my nemesis."

Dupin nodded. "When a person exhibits positive qualities and has a genial countenance, it is difficult to imagine that they might engage in nefarious activities. Of course it is highly accomplished criminals who are able to do this, to hide their true selves behind a contradictory façade."

"A most convincing façade. And Williams's position here gave him access to our comings and goings."

"And our rooms," Dupin added. "It was not difficult for him to contrive the illusion of a ghost tormenting you."

"Yes, I can see that now. But I do not understand how Williams came to have my grandparents' letters, and now I will never know."

Dupin frowned. "I must confess, I presumed Williams would tell you everything before he attempted to murder you. It is the way of such criminals who engineer a complex crime—they wish you to know how clever they are."

"Certainly that seems true, although I could fathom little of what Williams said to me in the catacombs."

"What precisely did he say?" Dupin asked.

"'How might we escape the phantom that seeks retribution when time does not defeat it?'" I said softly. "Williams asked me that—or words to that effect."

"Endless retribution, the persecutor but a ghost. How fitting. Was there more?"

I did not need to rack my memory, for the words came to me unbidden. "'The guilty die nightly in their beds, wringing the hands of ghostly confessors, on account of sins they dare not reveal.'"

Dupin slapped his hand upon the table in anger. "Of course. Hidden within plain sight, and yet I failed to see it."

"I am afraid that I still do not."

"While we fathomed that it was not your adoptive father's widow who sent your curious legacy to you and eventually concluded that the sender was somehow connected to Rhynwick Williams, we failed to adequately question how your nemesis originally obtained the letters. It seems likely that Rhynwick Williams bequeathed the mahogany box and its letters to his own son, George."

"But how did Rhynwick Williams obtain them? Certainly no one would presume such letters existed and my grandmother would not tell anyone of their existence. Indeed, I am surprised she did not destroy them as she suggests was her intent in the letter written to my mother."

Dupin nodded. "The letters concealed in the hidden compartment tell us that Elizabeth Arnold feared for her life. More precisely, she feared that Rhynwick Williams might try to murder her. If Rhynwick Williams was in Charleston in March 1798 as her letter to your mother suggests, we might dare presume that Elizabeth Arnold's death is connected to Williams's arrival in America."

My breakfast soured in my stomach. "You are suggesting that Rhynwick Williams murdered her? But we were told she died of yellow fever."

"That may be the cause of her death, but what if Williams watched her succumb to the disease and then made off with the mahogany box and its contents? And if Rhynwick Williams recently expired, his possessions would pass to his son. And so began the repercussions of your legacy."

Then I remembered what Williams had said to me and was filled with horror. "The twentieth of July 1798," I muttered.

"Pardon?"

"Williams recited that date when in the catacombs, but did not explain himself."

Dupin nodded. "One might presume that it is the date your grandmother died, the date that Rhynwick Williams found the evidence that would have incriminated her if she had survived. We do not know when George Williams discovered that your grandparents were the true culprits— did his father complain of the injustice to his family? Did he reveal the letters to his wife when he stole them from your grandmother? Or did George Williams only become aware of the letters upon the death of his own father? These are the questions that you are unlikely ever to

answer now that Williams is dead, but it must be somewhat comforting to know that you and your family are
now safe from his wrath."

I nodded. "Again, I thank you. Truly, Dupin, this journey has
been more than bewildering and in many ways frightening, but
I do not doubt that had you not come to my aid and joined me
in this investigation, my family and I might have suffered a
mysterious demise in Philadelphia."

"I have said it many times, but that is because the words are
true: *Amicis semper fidelis.*"

And then a sense of shame came over me. "You did not tell
me what occurred during your meeting with Dr. Froissart, and
I was too preoccupied to ask. Did the doctor discover anything
of value?"

"Only that Valdemar has returned to Paris. He had some
information that might prove useful in future, but nothing of
immediate worth. I was heartened to learn that my reputation
was not ruined when I made myself ridiculous. Madame—ever
the true friend—convinced all that it was part of the show.
Only Valdemar knows otherwise. I do not doubt that I will
destroy him, but unfortunately that was not my destiny here in
London." He looked at his timepiece. "I must allow you to
finish your preparations for your journey. I hope you will not
mind if I do not accompany you to the ship."

"Not at all."

He stood up, as did I, and Dupin solemnly shook my hand.
"Perhaps you will return to Paris and conduct a reading of your
works. Please know that my home is yours."

"What a pleasure that would be. Or perhaps you will venture
to our shores. There are certain to be crimes in Philadelphia
that would benefit from your skills."

"Perhaps." Dupin opened the door and stepped into the hall-
way. "Farewell, Poe. Safe journey."

And as the door closed softly between us, I wondered if I would ever see my friend again. I hoped that I would.

* * *

It was oddly strange to be leaving Brown's Genteel Inn, the place that had been my home for several weeks. When I entered reception, I found the dour desk clerk waiting for me with my final account, which I settled up.

"We are sorry you have curtailed your stay with us, Mr. Poe, but time will not wait for you—if your wife is ill, of course you must return to her side. Our family is all that matters. We at Brown's Genteel Inn wish you a very safe journey home. Thank you for staying with us."

Soon I was in a coach on the way to the East India docks, where I would board the *Grampus*. I tried to lift my spirits with the thought that soon I would be on my way to Philadelphia and those I loved. My journey to London had begun with the aim of proving that my grandparents had been defamed by a slanderous hoax, but had concluded with the discovery that I was indeed descended from criminals, both of whom had died ignobly. And I had learned a much more disconcerting truth— that like my grandmother, I would kill a man if he threatened the safety of those I love.

EPILOGUE

PHILADELPHIA, NOVEMBER 1840

Home. I closed my eyes and took in the sounds and smells of Philadelphia as the *Grampus* sailed into port. Sleep had not been my friend during the six weeks it took to traverse the Atlantic. By day I worried about my wife's health, while darkness took me back to the catacombs and my final encounter with George Williams that had so nearly culminated in my demise rather than his. But when at last I arrived at our faithful brick house on the first day of September and crossed the threshold to embrace my wife and her dear mother, all that had happened in London that summer seemed to evaporate like shadow exposed to sunlight. I was home and with those I loved; surely the past did not matter if I left it locked up with those infernal letters?

Sissy's health had improved since Muddy had written of her decline. To set her further to rights and to improve my own compromised state, we returned to our routine of walking along the river. The Delaware Indians named it the Ganshohawanee, which means *roaring waters*; the Dutch called it the Schuylkill— *hidden creek*. It was a river of contradictions, full of bold energy

and secret dark pools that drowned the unwary. It was a contra-
diction that reminded me of myself, the side I showed to my
family and the dark twin I concealed from them.

We enjoyed an Indian summer that lasted until the middle of
October. Sissy would sit and do needlework or read while I
swam to rebuild my strength, and Muddy collected wild greens
for our supper. For my wife's sake, I tried to shake off the
melancholia that had gripped me since that evening in the catacombs when Death had chosen my nemesis over me. Attuned
to my moods, she had invited me to unburden myself on more
than one occasion, but I had retreated into silence. Why worry
her with what might have happened? And, in truth, I could not
help but fear that the actions of my forebears would taint her
view of me. Would she have pledged herself to the grandson
of a common criminal and a murderess? I did not think so.

The late October winds scattered orange and red leaves
through the air like sparks until the trees rattled bony fingers,
and when the river shallows thickened to ice, our idyll along the
Schuylkill came to a close. As darkness increasingly outweighed
daylight, I wrote with a fury to unburden my very soul, transforming the memories that haunted me into tales that I hoped to
sell. With this thought in mind, I accepted the invitation of artist
John Sartain to join him at the Artists' Fund Hall for an exhibition on the eighteenth of November. Sartain had recently been
hired to do some embellishments for the first edition of George
Graham's new magazine, and I had ambitions to place some
tales there.

The exhibition proved a pleasant diversion for Sissy, and Mr.
Sartain did his best to charm. It was an impressive collection
and I thoroughly enjoyed the tour until the very end when I
spied a familiar countenance. My heart stilled. No! It could not
be! Violet eyes stared boldly into mine—*her* violet eyes. I could
not be mistaken for I gazed daily into their counterfeit, the gem

kept hidden in my waistcoat pocket, the talisman that had protected me from Williams's blade down in the catacombs. I stepped forward, her name upon my lips—Mrs. *Fontaine*. And then I shook my head to wake from the half-slumber that had overtaken me and saw that it was but a painting before me, a portrait in a gilded oval frame done in a vignette manner—the arms, the bosom, the hair melted into the shadowy background, which added to the image's veracity, as if the lady were a radiant specter emerging from the gloom. The portrait transfixed me, its features and expression so life-like that it seemed Mrs. Rowena Fontaine was right there before me, as though she had followed me from that wretched house in Camden Town to the Artists' Fund Hall in Philadelphia.

"A most extraordinary subject. It was difficult to do her justice in paint."

I turned to see a dark-haired fellow staring at me. Sartain and my wife were with him.

"Allow me to introduce the artist, Mr. Robert Street," Sartain said.

"Most impressive, sir. A very fine collection of paintings." I shook the hand of Sartain's friend, who studied me intently, *too* intently, which made my nerves jangle all the more. Mr. Street turned back to the painting I had been examining.

"Yes, a fine collection, thank you, although many say that no other painting here is so fine as this one."

"It is wonderful, indeed. Who is the subject?" I hoped against all hope Mrs. Fontaine had a doppelgänger in Philadelphia, and she remained in the country of her birth.

The artist frowned, tilted his head this way and that, and then waved his hand dismissively. "An actress, I believe, from London."

The chill that had enveloped me deepened. "When did you paint the portrait of Mrs. Fontaine?" My words turned to dust

in my mouth when I saw my wife knit her brows, wondering
how I knew the name of the woman in the portrait.

"Mrs. Fontaine?" The eccentric painter frowned and then
smiled broadly. "Ah, yes. You are quite right. I painted the
portrait in early October soon ater she arrived in Philadelphia."

Mrs. Fontaine in Philadelphia, recently arrived. It could not
be coincidence. What business had she in this city other than
revenge for the death of her beloved George Williams?

"But really you must be painted, Mrs. Poe." The artist was
smiling brightly at my wife. "I hope you will not be offended if
I say that your beauty is extraordinary. I would be honored to
paint your portrait."

My wife smiled. "Thank you for your kind offer. Perhaps in
future."

"Oh, but you must allow it now. Beauty fades, time dimin-
ishes us."

She shook her head again, and he turned his attentions to
me. "Then I must paint you, sir. One must never underestimate
the power of posterity." He indicated the portraits that hung
from the walls surrounding us. "These men will never be
forgotten."

"No doubt you are correct, but I am afraid I must decline," I
told the artist. And I knew that some things *should* be forgotten.
How I wished that I could forget Mrs. Fontaine and George
Williams and all that connected us. And yet how could I if Mrs.
Fontaine were now truly in Philadelphia?

Sissy and I made our way home in a haze of unease, my wife
watching me carefully as if for signs of fever and me peppering
the air with words of no consequence to keep the truth from
spilling out. The wind taunted us as we walked and there was
a smell of snow in the air—I said as much as I pushed my quaking hands deep into the pockets of my coat. When the fingers
of my left hand met with a folded square of paper, a gasp of

pure fear escaped me. I knew that the pocket had been empty before we attended the exhibition, I was more than certain. How? How had she done it? I wanted to shout the words but swallowed them back as Sissy's hand touched my arm.

"What is it, Eddie? Are you hurt?"

What could I tell her? That the woman whose portrait she had admired had been there, at the Artist's Fund Hall, watching me—watching *us*. Somehow she had slipped the paper into my pocket as if she were a phantom or a demon from Hell itself. How could I tell my beloved wife that the woman who wished harm to me and to all those I loved had traveled to Philadelphia to watch and wait for her moment?

"I am quite all right," I lied. "Truly I am." A flickering light appeared in the darkness like an apparition—candlelight dancing behind window glass. "Look, we are almost home. Come, let us get into the warm." I took my wife's arm and led her to our house, my fingers still clutching that venomous square of paper.

I did not take it from my pocket until later that night. We ate the meal Muddy cooked for us. We discussed the paintings and the peculiar Mr. Street. I talked about my plans for a new magazine. And when Sissy and Muddy retired to bed, I at last removed the letter and unfolded it.

Philadelphia, 18 November 1840

Dear Mr. Poe,

Our few meetings in London did not culminate as I had planned, but we will meet again, you have my word. *Nemo me impune lacessit.* My arrival will be unexpected. You will think it is nothing—the wind in the chimney, a mouse crossing the floor, a cricket which has made a single chirp. But you will comfort yourself with these delusions in vain. When the time comes for our final meeting, you will know the terror felt by my father when he stood trial, the anguish he suffered in Newgate, the sorrow of his family when he was taken from them. Your only solace will be a swift retribution and when I have taken that, my father's business will, at last, be finished.

Make sure you leave your mark, Mr. Poe. Time will not wait for you.

I remain respectfully yours,

George Rhynwick Williams

Williams! How could it be? It was not possible, but the note was most assuredly in Williams's handwriting. In my mind's eye, I could clearly see the man sprawled across the chapel floor, blood pooling around him. It was he—Williams—the desk clerk from Brown's Genteel Inn, the man who had smiled to my face when delivering my messages, but had spied upon me and plotted my murder. But how? He had been *dead,* no heart beat, no breath, Dupin's rapier had cut through him as if he were a wax effigy, but this time his victim truly had been flesh.

And then, suddenly, it came to me. *Autography suggests that Courvoisier's lament was penned by a left-handed person, as was the case with the handbill for Brown's Genteel Inn.* Dupin's words, the science of autography. And yet we both had forgotten that crucial clue. I recalled when the desk clerk—the taciturn, dark-haired, dark-eyed man—had drawn me an impromptu map to Southampton Way and how his left hand had curved in such an awkward fashion so it would not smear the ink as he wrote. That desk clerk normally worked at night, and we saw him less frequently, but I was certain he was of a similar height and build as the scrivener, the professor, Dr. Wallis—all in disguise, all one and the same. My nemesis. The dead man was his colleague, who worked during the mornings. Whether he had been paid to help Williams in his plan or had been duped into assisting him, he had died for his complicity. I thought back to the morning of my departure from London, when the night desk clerk had bade me a kind farewell. *Our family is all that matters.* I shivered to think how a seemingly innocent platitude might truly be a threat.

I did not sleep well that night. Every creak, every rustle sent me bolt upright in bed. And it was the same the next night and the next after that. I tried to put Williams's threatening letter from my mind, but it haunted me. And the more I tried to hide my unease from Sissy, the more afflicted I was. Daily my mood grew blacker. *Nemo me impune lacessit*—the threat tormented me. And yet I went back to those accursed letters day after day until I knew I had to rid myself of them. But could I burn them? Throw them into the Schuylkill? Bury them in the forest? I could not.

So I left the letters interred in their casket and put the violet eye in with them. I took up three planks from the flooring of our bed chamber and deposited all between the scantlings, then replaced the boards so cleverly, so cunningly, that my accursed inheritance would remain safe from prying eyes and safe from me.

* * *

As I have said before, I am lucid, I am calm. There is a certain over-acuteness of my senses that makes everything too sharp— the glistering of sunlight, the bang and clatter of teacups in saucers, of spoons and knives and forks upon the plate, but truly there is no madness within me. Every night I take great care to protect us from the inevitable. I make certain the shutters are fastened against the thick darkness of night itself and as I lay in bed, I watch for skulking shadows across the walls and listen intently for any sound of evil worming its way into our good, little house.

And when morning comes I mutter "I am safe" and try to forget that which haunts me. There are some secrets which do not permit themselves to be told, and I have sworn to the ghosts of those who precede me that what is written down in these pages will go to my tomb with me. And I am more than certain that this is the wisest decision I have ever made.

FURTHER RESOURCES AND READING:

I thoroughly enjoyed the research required to write this novel, and especially appreciated the enthusiastic expertise of staff at the Edgar Allan Poe National Historic Site in Philadelphia; the catacombs of All Souls Cemetery, Kensal Green; and the Philadelphia Free Library, which holds the Colonel Richard A. Gimbel collection of Edgar Allan Poe materials, including Dickens's pet raven, Grip.

Some non-fiction works and resources on Poe and the Monster that might be of further interest to readers are:

Peter Ackroyd, *Poe: A Life Cut Short* (London: Chatto & Windus, 2008)

John Ashton, *Old Times: A Picture of Social Life at the End of the Eighteenth Century* (London: J. C. Nimmo, 1885)

Jan Bondeson, *The London Monster: A Sanguinary Tale* (London: Free Association Books, 2000)

The Edgar Allan Poe Society of Baltimore, *The Collected Works of Edgar Allan Poe: A Comprehensive Collection of E-texts.* (www.eapoe.org)

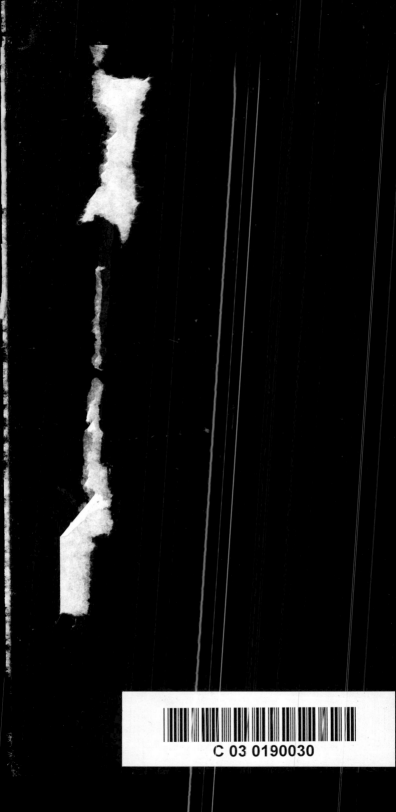